MISSION TO MAHJUNDAR

BY VERONICA SCOTT

To my daughters Valerie and Elizabeth, and in loving memory of Matthew
for all his encouragement and support through the years

Acknowledgments

Joyce L, Julie C and The E-book Formatting Fairies!

CHAPTER ONE

This place feels primed for disaster. Despite their local escort's best efforts to hurry him through the crowded market, Mike noticed many of the stalls were closed, the vendors having left early and shuttered their inventory away. Other sellers seemed to be practically forcing their wares on the passersby, as if there was a deadline they were afraid to miss. Crowds of people thronged the place, some buying supplies, others talking furtively in small clumps. The situation report on the planet had said the political climate was stable, even with a dying emperor.

Sitreps were notoriously incomplete or dead wrong.

Shifting the heavy bag of equipment he was carrying, Mike exchanged a glance with his sergeant before tapping their guide's shoulder. "Always this crowded?"

Without slackening his stride, the gaudily dressed local officer shook his head. "No, tomorrow is the first day of a major festival. People are stocking their larders for feasting. The plaza will be nearly empty by nightfall."

"A pity our briefing didn't mention the festival, or we'd have come in tomorrow. Our mission could have waited one day." Ducking past a man carrying four rolled-up carpets, nearly falling over a pair of small street beggars, Mike shoved a half-drunk youth out of his way. His limited store of patience frayed, Mike felt a dull headache pounding. "After this melee, encountering mountain bandits will be a picnic."

He stepped onto a broad, green-tiled walkway that bordered the flagstone street. From there, the going became somewhat easier. The small party made progress for a couple of encouraging minutes before a new impediment arose. Behind Mike came a fanfare of blaring, slightly out-of-sync trumpets. What traffic there was in the street came to an immediate halt as people started shoving, struggling to get to the sides of the thoroughfare, leaving the center of the road clear.

"It must be the empress and her party, on their way home from their observances at the temple complex." Their guide, who'd introduced himself at the tiny spaceport simply as Captain Rojar, peered into the distance, one hand shading his eyes. "Let's wait and see the fine sight. A treat for you."

Granted, Mike's hypnotraining in the primary Mahjundan languages might not have been all-inclusive, but there'd definitely been a faint tinge of sarcasm in the man's remarks. Mike studied Rojar's bland expression for a moment, but the officer's tanned face and half smile betrayed nothing. Over his shoulder, Mike said in Basic to his cousin Johnny, the Special Forces sergeant accompanying him, "Watch our six. I didn't think this crowd could make me any more nervous, but the tension definitely ramped up in the last two minutes."

Glancing at the nearest citizens, Johnny Danver nodded. "Kinda quiet and sullen compared to what it was, ain't it?"

Deciding to push the issue with their guide, Mike said, "Why don't we move on? We could make some real progress while the crowd waits for the parade to go by."

Hands on his hips, eyes narrowed, Rojar did a nervous survey of their position, as if marking where they stood in relation to some landmark only he knew, before shaking his head once. He made a slicing motion. "No." Belatedly, he attempted to soften the refusal with a bit more explanation. "Much better to wait. No doubt you'll find this glimpse of our royal family highly interesting."

"No doubt," Mike agreed, his own tone sarcastic now. Exchanging a rapid glance with Johnny, he settled in to wait for the promised parade, keeping a close eye on their gear, piled on the walkway at his feet. There was no point in struggling through the crowd independent of their escort. Arriving at the palace without the guy and having to wait for him to catch up would get the job off on the wrong foot for sure. Mike took a swig of water from his canteen, to cool his throat and his temper. One thing the report had been accurate about–Mahjundar was hot, even in midafternoon.

Although she'd never lived in the temperate mountain forests, Princess Shalira imagined she'd prefer them to the hot lowlands. Whenever she visited the tiny temple of her patron goddess Pavmiraia on the outskirts of the city, as she was doing today, she pretended the heat and intrigues of the capital and the court had been left behind. This chapel and her vivid daydreams provided special refuges for most of her life.

The floor was cool beneath her bare feet as she strolled twenty paces from the door to the altar, passing the snoring priestess, sprawled on a bench no doubt, mouth probably wide open. *Not many come here anymore, not many at all. Will anyone worship the goddess when I've gone?* Tears pricked Shalira's eyes as she felt for the padded knee rest, bowed her head, and knelt in front of the altar.

"Do you know this is to be my last visit?" she whispered to the goddess she could no longer see. "Do you care? Will my pleas still reach your ears when I've completed my appointed journey?" Shalira fingered the amulet around her neck, the familiar whorls of the much-worn pattern under her fingers soothing her anxieties. For the thousandth time she reminded herself this impending trip wasn't her choice so much as the least of evils. She took a deep breath. "Maybe my life will improve, away from the empress and her schemes."

Settling more comfortably on the knee rest, she tried to visualize the chapel – graceful murals of forest and mountains on the walls, a small fountain in the courtyard outside, the larger than-life-size statue of the goddess herself, perpetually gazing to the east, a half smile on her face. Though Shalira'd not beheld these sights in well over fifteen years, she felt sure she was remembering them accurately.

A cool breeze smelling of moss and tiny flowers blew her long hair away from her face, and instinctively she lifted her chin to enjoy the stray breath of air.

Footsteps came down the aisle behind her, an unfamiliar, light tread. The newcomer halted a few feet behind the princess, who was already pivoting, unwilling to have her back to a stranger. *For all the good it'll do me if the intruder harbors evil intentions.* She curled her hands into fists.

"No need to fear me, Your Highness. I offer a parting prophecy for your journey." The woman's voice was sweet and low, disarming. "You'll travel farther than you dream, experience many things both good and bad, and even unexpected, but the blessings of Pavmiraia will wrap around you. Never doubt, but follow your heart in all your choices."

"Thank you, priestess." Unclenching her fingers, Shalira tried to calm herself with a deep breath. "Are you recently assigned to this chapel? I didn't know there were any new celebrants."

Gentle laughter like the chiming of bells. The woman touched Shalira's cheek with the tips of her fingers. Annoyed, the princess straightened her spine, disliking anyone touching her, much less someone she didn't know. "Indeed not," said the bold newcomer. "I've been here since before your time. I came to bid you farewell, for I also take my leave of this place."

"Who *are* you? I don't recognize your voice." She tried to keep impatience out of her tone. People who made her guess their identity were another frustrating aspect of her existence on the fringes of the court.

"Yet you know me - you call upon me with great frequency." The cool fingers lifted away from her face. "One of the last of the true believers, you."

Confused and angry someone would take advantage of her blindness, would dare to impersonate the goddess, Shalira hesitated to utter scalding words. *I want this to be real,* whispered a voice deep in her heart. *I want some magic; surely I deserve some magic.*

In the next moment, she felt a whisper-soft kiss on her forehead before the intruder said, "Stay true to your heart in all which faces you. Go with my blessing, hold tight to your dreams, even in great adversity. The things you wish are worthy of being granted, but must be earned."

Love, children, a home of my own—my vision restored. Maybe this arranged marriage I go to will satisfy a few of these.

Blinking hard, she realized the footsteps were receding, a faint pattering as if the woman was dancing to a tune only she could hear. Despite stiff knees from kneeling in prayer, the princess took a few faltering steps, bumping into the railing around the altar, clutching the wood to keep from falling. "Wait, please wait—"

"Who are you speaking to, Your Highness?" It was the gravelly voice of her one loyal guardsman, Saium. His heavy footsteps echoed in the tiny chapel as he crossed the threshold, shoving the door aside with a scrape of warped wood on stone. The smoky scent of the pipe he'd indulged in wafted around her, as he approached with the uneven sound of the limp he tried to conceal when his bones ached.

The elderly nun coughed, stirring on her bench.

How did the other woman leave? There wasn't any sound of the door before Saium entered. Bewildered, Shalira toyed with the end of her long braid, twining the loose tendrils around her fingers. "Did you see her?"

"See who? No one entered or left since your arrival." Saium was next to her now, taking her elbow in one huge hand with a light clasp, overly familiar, but allowed from him. "The empress is impatient to leave the temple complex. She's been waiting—"

"And *she* is extremely annoyed to be delayed by an ungrateful girl!" Empress Maralika's shrill voice echoed in the small chamber like fingernails on a slate, the sound startling the elderly priestess into falling off her bench with a thump and a quickly smothered curse.

Saium dropped to his knees as Maralika's quick steps rapped on the stone floor like a drum tattoo, moving in their direction. Shalira stretched her stiffened joints, turning her head toward the sound of the empress's approach. "My apologies for delaying you, Your Majesty. As I'll never be here again, I had to complete the proper leave-taking of the goddess." *Did Pavmiraia herself speak to me? Bless me?*

"Considering I was kind enough to bring you along today, the least you could do is observe the demands of my schedule." Tapping one toe on the stone floor, Maralika laughed. "Although from the dilapidation of this place, I might have done you a disservice. Surely, no goddess, no power, still dwells in *this* environment. Better you'd worshipped at the temple of the new gods, the ones I give allegiance."

"I prefer the old ways." Shalira kept her voice mild. They'd had this fruitless argument before.

Maralika snapped her fingers. "And much good your loyalty has ever done you. Come along now." The empress wheeled, her robes sweeping across the floor with an angry swish, leaving the temple as rapidly as she'd entered a moment ago.

Not quite sure where she stood, or how many steps it would be to the door, Shalira held out her hand. "Please?"

Saium clasped her fingers in his. "My pleasure, Your Highness."

Together they strolled from the temple, the hot sun striking like a slap on her face as she crossed the threshold under her guardsman's guidance. The princess blinked back tears, wishing for a fleeting second she could run into the temple and find true sanctuary there. *Don't be childish, people are watching.* People were constantly scrutinizing her. She was an object of curiosity, pity, and speculation at her father's court. *Well, I'm leaving all this behind now, aren't I? Maybe change will be a good thing.* Smiling despite the gnawing dread in the pit of her stomach, she walked steadily toward the restless horse the empress insisted she ride. She could hear the stallion's hooves striking sparks from the paving stones as he challenged the grip of his handler. When Saium boosted her into the saddle, Shalira took comfort in the fact there would be only a few more days to struggle through before she left her present troubles behind forever.

If he'd been in charge of the imperial procession, the soldiers would've marched in better formation, with a crisper gait. Mike couldn't remember the last time he'd seen a supposedly crack regiment display such an uncaring, lax attitude in front of the local populace. Heading the column was a contingent of mounted guards, wearing gaudy uniforms, cut from the same iridescent fabric as Rojar's, and sporting helmets with long, curling feather crests. Involuntarily, Mike glanced at his own black and gold uniform.

Busy whittling a stick of wood he'd picked up from somewhere, small yellow pocket knife sending the shavings flying, Johnny laughed out loud. "Makes you glad the Sectors don't go in for much color."

"We'd never be able to do our job." Mike hefted the bag he was carrying, not wanting to set anything else down on the busy street. "The enemy would see us coming a mile away."

His cousin held out the crude carving. "My best attempt at local fauna, that winged lion thing." He tossed the quickly done piece to a nearby boy who'd been watching him open-mouthed, before snapping his knife shut and tucking it in a pocket of his utilities.

Mike nodded at the standard bearers marching behind the guards, holding aloft the banners of the imperial household. "You mean that? The *cherindor?* You need a lot more practice." The mythical, winged feline rampant on the banners resembled pictures he'd seen of Terran lions, but with a barbed tail and three eyes. The image was apparently ubiquitous in the city. He and Johnny had been joking about it in fact, while they'd waited for Rojar.

"Wings are tricky to carve. Just passin' the time."

Rojar elbowed Mike in the ribs, pointing with his free hand. "Her Imperial Highness Maralika. You're privileged today, Major Varone, to have a glimpse of her magnificence."

Definitely sarcasm. Mike stifled a flash of irritation. Getting embroiled in local politics, even accidentally, wasn't on his agenda for this search-and-recovery mission. He might have to request another liaison if this guy was going to cause problems with his hostility toward the ruling family.

The off-key trumpeters strutted by, blaring yet another fanfare. Now the empress appeared, carried in an elaborately painted litter, a muscular soldier at each corner. She was semi-reclining, so Mike couldn't get a good look at her face full on. Elaborately coiffed black hair, sparkling with jewels, framed a rather hard profile, somewhat disguised by cosmetics. *But for all I know, she's the Mahjundan standard of high beauty.* He took a second look. *Not mine.* She waved languidly at the crowd with one pale hand as her litter proceeded along the parade route. Three rings flaunting gems the size of pigeons' eggs caught the sun, throwing rainbows across the crowd as she flicked her hand.

Grim-faced guards walked on all sides, tougher than the gaudy troops who'd marched first in the parade. These men had their weapons at the ready, constantly scanning the mostly silent crowd.

A party of boisterous younger people rode horses behind the empress. Laughing and talking amongst themselves, they made no pretense whatsoever of acknowledging the crowd.

"Ladies-in-waiting, courtiers, some of the favored royal children," Rojar told Mike. "We're close to the end of the procession now. We'll be able to go on our way in a minute or two, after the priests and servants."

A girl riding slightly behind the others caught Mike's eye. She was wearing a pale blue dress, edged in lavender and gold. The lack of riotous, clashing color alone made her stand out to Mike in this crazy kaleidoscope of a city. But then he took a second glance to admire her beauty, masses of glossy black hair framing her lovely oval face. Brows drawn together in a fierce frown of concentration above almond-shaped eyes, she sat straight-backed in the saddle, one hand clenched in a death grip on the pommel, the other clutching the reins. Holding the horse's green-tasseled bridle was a guard in the most subdued uniform Mike had seen yet on the color mad planet - brown-and-emerald with no braid or gaudy ribbons. Having a keen eye for horses, Mike could tell her magnificent stallion was ill at ease, sidestepping nervously, tossing its head, wild-eyed and sweating. He was about to ask Rojar a question about these two when suddenly there was a massive explosion farther to the east, toward the palace, followed by another, smaller blast.

The shock wave knocked Mike to his knees, hands going automatically to his ears, which ached from the concussion.

The crowd went berserk, screaming, pushing, running in all directions.

Instinctively, Mike reached for the blaster customarily at his hip. *Damn, not this trip.*

The neat column of the procession had fallen to chaos on the roadway. The horses bolted, one plowing through the crowd right behind Mike, knocking people over like straws. Caught in a knot of Mahjundans, forced away from his companions by the unruly mob, Mike's attention was riveted on the black stallion, rearing and lashing out. The guard in green was nowhere to be seen.

Mike pushed against the packed, sweating bodies surrounding him, yelling above the din for people to get out of his way. His attention was focused on the beautiful girl who'd seemed such a reluctant horsewoman. The stallion was circling, bucking, gathering itself to bolt while she did her best to control the terrified animal. Lips compressed, eyes unaccountably closed, the woman he'd become fascinated by before the explosion was holding the reins tight. Mike ran across the green tile border and into the street, which offered easier going. Most people were trying to escape from the square altogether, putting as much distance as possible between themselves and the potential danger of another explosion. Sprinting to the horse, Mike made a wild grab at the reins.

Seeing her at closer range, he revised his estimate of her age upward by about ten years—not a girl in the late bloom of youth after all, but a stunning woman. "Hang on, lady, I'll help you dismount. Once you're safe, I can try to get him calmed down for you," Mike said, pitching his voice at a level he hoped would cut through the incredible din in the square. "You're doing fine, just don't let go of the reins, ok?"

She opened her eyes, turning in his direction. "Oh, please—"

The stallion bucked harder, breaking the rider's hold on the saddle. She slid off like a rag doll. Cursing, Mike let go of the horse, which promptly bolted. He managed to break the girl's fall, going to one knee as he caught her. To prevent her from being trampled by the crowd, which surged into the space the distressed horse had kept clear with its lashing hooves, Mike carried her in the direction the panick-stricken people were flowing. "Come on, we've got to get away from this mob!"

It was like swimming in a riptide. Going with the flow initially, Mike angled toward the far curb and got himself and his trembling companion across the roadway.

"I can walk," she said, voice faint. Making no effort to leave the security of his arms, however, she had her eyes closed again.

Rather than waste time arguing, he carried her as he clambered over fallen people and maneuvered around debris until they fetched up in the doorway of a bakery. The sweet smell of fresh breads mingled incongruously with the stench of smoke from the bomb blast. With a muttered apology, Mike set the woman on her feet behind him, so he could defend them both if necessary.

Drawing his belt knife, which was the only weapon he'd been allowed to carry through the city gates, he felt better. Now prepared to deal with whatever might happen next, he crouched in the doorway, trying to keep the woman out of sight behind him as much as possible. Mike surveyed the plaza, identifying no immediate threats. *No one paying us any attention right now, too much confusion and panic.* He had no way of knowing if the empress had just been the target of an assassination attempt or whether the bombers had hoped some members of the royal household would be unlucky enough to be caught in the blast so close to the parade. If it was the latter case, his job was to keep the terrorists from stumbling over his companion. *Time to reassure the woman I rescued.*

Half-turning to check how she was doing, he said, "Sorry for the rough handling, miss. Someone apparently has it in for the royal family today."

One hand was clenched around a small red purse tied to her belt. She was staring slightly over his shoulder with beautiful caramel-brown eyes, golden highlights sparkling in their depths. Reaching to touch his shoulder with her free hand, she let her manicured nails drift ever so slowly to his face.

She's blind? He allowed her to run her hand over his features for a moment.

Finishing her rudimentary scan, the woman patted her hair and cleared her throat. "Your voice is unknown to me, sir, but thank you for your help. What of my guardsman? I'm anxious about his safety."

You should be worrying about your own skin, lady. "I didn't see him after the explosion. He probably got dragged away by the crowd. There were a lot of people in the market, and they became a mob with one thing on their minds—escape. I had a hard time working my way to you and the horse." Mike took a deep breath of her perfume, floral with a woodsy undertone, while he reconnoitered the square again with practiced efficiency. "The excitement will subside in a few minutes, after which I'd be honored to escort you to the palace."

"Most kind." She stood patiently, one hand at her throat, toying with the turquoise and green necklace she wore. "I wish we knew what had become of my guard."

He checked conditions in the plaza. The crowd had thinned out now, leaving behind a colossal mess of broken pottery, crushed food, torn awnings, and everywhere, the injured. Mike guessed most of the casualties had been knocked down and trampled in the panic, since the lethal effect of the bomb itself had been localized. *Is this the explanation behind Rojar not wanting to walk any farther? He was on edge, anticipating something from the moment we met him.*

The woman leaned back until she was propped up by the bakery wall. "Could—could you tell me what's wrong with my arm? I think it's bleeding."

Returning his knife to the sheath first, he took her slender, tanned arm and pushed several jeweled bracelets and the blood-stained fabric of her sleeve out of the way. A jagged metal shard was embedded in her upper arm, blood dripping onto the sheer silk dress. Examining the wound carefully, Mike was relieved to find it messy but superficial. The blood was already clotting. "Not too serious, just a big metal splinter. Hold still and I'll pull it out. Have you got something we can use for a bandage, until you can see a doctor?"

With her free hand, she tugged a wispy lavender scarf from her ebony black hair. "Will this do?" she asked, holding it slightly off to his right.

Mike reached over to take the scrap of fabric. "Fine. Now try not to move." Getting a firm grip on the twisted fragment, he drew it out, doing his best not to enlarge the wound. Then he wrapped the puncture firmly with the scarf. "You probably won't even need stitches," he said cheerfully. The woman stood quietly during the whole procedure, closing her eyes and breathing too fast, her chest rising and falling. She nodded at his remark but didn't answer.

Mike surveyed his handiwork, then peered at her face. "Only a small piece of shrapnel, but pretty jagged. You're pale. Are you sure you're up to walking?"

Stepping away from the wall, she straightened her shoulders resolutely. "I'll be fine. We must get to the palace. They'll be searching for me, and if there's trouble on the streets, I shouldn't be out."

"Let me help you, then." He laid his hand on her uninjured arm, to guide her down the bakery's three shallow steps.

She pulled away from him abruptly, eyebrows drawn together in a frown. "I can manage."

Mike didn't relinquish his grip on her wrist. "I don't care if you know every inch of this plaza on an ordinary day—there's too much debris at the moment. You won't get ten steps without tripping over something. Now, do I guide you or do I carry you?"

Wordlessly, but with the hint of a curve to her lips, she extended her other hand. Closing her fingers over his with a strong grasp, she allowed him to lead her from their sheltering doorway. Mike decided against walking in the roadway. *Too conspicuous.* He set a path along the fringes of the plaza, sticking close to the shops. It wouldn't be as direct a route to the palace, but they'd attract less attention, a goal high on his priority list at the moment.

"Are there many injured?" she asked, brow wrinkled, voice soft with concern.

"Afraid so. Must have been quite a bomb. There are people attending to the wounded now, though." Steering her around a spilled cart of melons, past a decapitated sheep, he was glad she couldn't see the carnage. Collateral damage and human casualties were increasing as they got closer to the smoking bomb crater.

Empress Maralika's empty litter was tipped sideways, the solid wooden undercarriage facing the side of the street where the bomb had gone off. *Gave the empress some protection.* The litter appeared undamaged in the middle of the roadway, about fifty feet short of the worst of the blast zone. Lying in the street, one of the four guards who'd been carrying the litter was moaning and clutching at his chest.

Mortally wounded, nothing I can do to help. "Detonated too soon, apparently," he said to himself, mentally measuring the distance from the crater to the litter as he guided the girl past the dying soldier.

A voice hailed him in Basic from the side of the road behind them. "Mike!"

He spun around, breaking into a relieved grin. "Am I glad to see you. Where's Rojar?"

The sergeant gestured as he took in the woman standing hand in hand with Mike. "Right behind me. Been rescuing damsels in distress, have you?"

"She's blind," Mike said in Basic.

Rojar sprinted to join them but stopped abruptly when he focused on Mike's companion, making a sharp salute in her direction, which of course the woman couldn't see. "Your Highness, Captain Rojar of the emperor's guard, at your service." Waving his drawn gun, he glared at Mike. "And this person with his hands on you is Major Varone of the Sectors, newly arrived on Mahjundar. Outworlder, she can order your death for touching her—she's a princess of the blood direct."

"Nonsense," said the woman in a sharp tone. "Such drastic measures would hardly be an appropriate way to reward his kindness after I requested his guidance across the plaza." Then, and only then, did she disengage her hand from Mike's. "I'm somewhat disoriented. Are we close to the family gate?"

Taking a second to double-check, Rojar answered in the affirmative. "Indeed, Your Highness. We have only to cross the last hundred yards of the plaza. Allow me to procure a litter for you. All this blood on your dress—are you—"

"A scratch only, but I'm lightheaded. These gentlemen will stand watch over me while you go for the litter." The princess nodded her agreement with the captain's suggestion. She swayed a little as Rojar rushed off in search of suitable transportation.

Putting an arm around her waist, Mike kept her on her feet. Quickly, he steered her to a nearby cart and had her sit on the open tailgate, kneeling solicitously beside her. "Are you sure you don't have any other injuries?"

She shook her head. "I'm fine. I think it's the shock of the whole event. Only military men such as yourself remain calm in the face of bombs and assassins, right, Major?"

"Oh, the explosion left me searching for cover, I promise." Mike laughed with her. "We weren't expecting such a rousing welcome to your planet."

"I thought your accent rather unusual." She nodded.

"And we studied so hard to get it right," Mike said, in mock despair. *She's getting paler by the second. Better keep her talking and alert.* "Where's our gear?" he asked Johnny.

"I've wrangled it into a heap, over there, out of the way, and set two of Rojar's men to guarding it while I located you."

A moment later Rojar returned, accompanied by a small troop of guardsmen and a litter. After making sure the princess had no objection, Mike placed her gently on the pillows lining the conveyance. The guards whisked her through the ornate gilded gates of the palace. Mike watched her go, before turning his attention to his companions.

"Quite a welcome you prepared for us, Captain Rojar." He stared more closely at his sergeant, doing a double take as he realized Johnny's shirt was blood soaked under the arm. "Why didn't you tell me you were hurt?"

"Nothing but a scratch. Don't blame you a bit for not noticing sooner, not with the princess to distract you." Johnny punched him in the arm and laughed good-naturedly. "Better get the stars out of your eyes now though and get on with our own program. Don't recall any orders in the briefing about rescuing royalty."

"I agree with the sergeant wholeheartedly, Major." Rojar chivvied them to another, unadorned iron gate a short distance away. "Let's get to your assigned quarters so we can have the wound attended to."

Once inside the compound's walls, Rojar led them through a large courtyard, shaded by trees with fern-like foliage. The place was bustling with servants and courtiers. Mike was relieved to get out of the crowd and into the dim, cool hallways of the palace itself, even if there were confusing corridors to be navigated. A servant waiting outside one door, apparently for their arrival, sat cross-legged on the black marble floor, idly fanning himself with a riotously colored feather fan. Scrambling to his feet as they came down the corridor, the man opened the panel and was bowing by the time Mike reached him. Following them into the room, the servant crowded Rojar, nearly tripping.

"This is your suite while we're in the city, Major." Rojar indicated the servant with a careless wave. "We should dispatch him to fetch a healer for your sergeant's injury before the wound festers."

"Won't be necessary, thank you," Mike said. "We brought our own medkit with us. I can take care of Johnny's arm myself."

The servant bowed nearly to the green tiled floor. "Captain Rojar, the chamberlain sent twice to remind you the feast begins at the sixth hour. You and the outworld officer are expected before the wines are brought in."

"We won't be late." Rojar frowned. "Go tell the kitchen to serve dinner for the sergeant, here in the suite."

Closing the door behind the retainer as he left, Rojar let his control slip for a minute, revealing a tired and worried face. Mike wasn't sure he'd actually seen the fleeting play of expressions, because when the captain turned fully back to him, his countenance was as composed as ever.

"Pretty fancy quarters for a couple of Special Forces operators. Why do they think we need all this space?" Mike asked.

"And perfumed pillows to sleep on?" Johnny grimaced and tossed a few to the floor before he sat on the couch to examine the wound on his arm. He dug two more pillows out from under him, adding them to the pile on the floor. "I hope it won't hurt anyone's feelings if we rearrange a bit."

Rojar didn't appear to care what they did, now that he'd delivered them safely to the palace as ordered. "You're the honored guests, after all. Do as you please, enjoy yourselves. The mountains will be quite another story, I promise you. The clans there will serve your heads on a spit at *their* welcoming banquet."

"How events play out in the mountains remains to be seen," Mike answered, choosing to maintain a good natured tone. "Are you going to be okay, cousin?"

"I've taken worse knocks than this." Opening the medkit, the sergeant sorted through his supplies one-handed. "Besides, at least all those medinjects we took will get some local bugs to battle. Hell, the injects sting more than this scrape. You go and enjoy the food."

"Your dinner will be brought to you, Sergeant," Rojar assured him. "Major, I must go change into a dress uniform for the banquet. I'll be back for you in half an hour." He saluted and let himself out the door.

Bemused by the idea of an even more elaborate costume being required merely to dine, Mike raised an eyebrow at Johnny. "I can't wait to see the dress uniform, can you?"

Gritting his teeth as he sprayed medication on the wound, Johnny shook his head. "Gaudier than a Terran peacock, no doubt. No one'll see you for the glare of his buttons."

"Just the way I prefer it on this planet." Mike picked up the medkit and moved closer to help. "Now, let's get this wound sealed. I'm not doing this mission by myself while you loll around on sick call."

With the practice born of long years, Shalira came awake instantly when a slight shift in the air alerted her to the presence of someone in her bedroom. Sliding her hand under the pillow to clench the hilt of the dagger she kept there, she sat up, back firmly to the headboard. "Who goes there?"

"It's only me, Your Highness." Saium's familiar, raspy voice was welcome.

Releasing the knife, she frowned. "What brings you to my room in the middle of the night?"

She heard a match flare and smelled the acrid smoke as he lit candles. "The emperor summons you."

"Now?" Fear sent spikes of adrenaline through her nerves, bringing a surge of nausea in its wake. "Is Maralika going to be there?"

"No, the summons is for you alone. Kajastahn sent his body servant to waken me. I'm to bring you to his chamber through the old secret passages." Saium was at the closet now, searching through her garments, judging by the sounds of rustling silk and clattering wooden hangers.

Shalira swung her legs off the bed, sliding her feet into the slippers she insisted the maids must line up properly, ready for her. Holding out her hand, she accepted the dress Saium handed her, recognizing her favorite by the embroidery on the sleeves. Lavender and cream, she'd been told. Her favorite colors, when she'd been able to see.

Saium's footsteps thudded on the carpet as he moved to the door. "I'll wait outside so you can change. Don't be long."

When the door had closed, she took off her nightgown, retrieved her underthings from the proper bureau drawer, and shrugged into the dress. Her hair was impossibly tousled, so she brushed it once or twice before catching the curls back in a hasty braid. Counting the steps, she reached the door.

Saium had her elbow before she could even step from her room. "We must hurry. Never a good idea to keep the emperor waiting, even in the dead of night."

She'd no idea where they were in the palace after the first few twists and turns. Trying to count her steps or identify any of her customary landmarks made her dizzy. She surrendered to Saium's lead, knowing he'd never allow her to come to harm. They walked for a long time through a dank hall or tunnel, apparently unlit, since Saium had stopped for a moment to grab a torch and light the flame. Brushing one hand against the wall as they proceeded, she found rough, unfinished stone under her fingertips.

"Stay away from the wall, you'll get your dress dirty," Saium warned in a whisper.

She yanked her hand back, feeling like a child who'd been scolded. "Where are we?"

"In the hidden passageway leading to Kajastahn's private chambers. When he was younger, he liked to spy on his courtiers."

Not surprised, because she knew her father to be a devious, untrusting man, she said, "Did my mother use this corridor to visit him?"

"She refused to venture in here alone, so I was brought into the secret arrangements, trusted to escort her to his rooms."

Shalira pondered the information for a moment as they kept walking. "But why use the tunnel at all? All Mahjundar knew she was his Favorite."

"How can you be so ignorant of the politics, living in this court your entire life?" Saium sounded annoyed. "Yes, your mother was his Favorite, but he didn't want anyone to know *how* besotted he was with her, how much time he spent in her arms. Such knowledge would have made her even more of a target. Kajastahn trusted I'd never betray their secret. Hush now, we're nearly there."

They stopped for a moment as Saium set the torch into a holder on the wall before guiding Shalira up a set of steep stairs. At the top, her escort knocked twice and a door swooshed open. Leading her through the entrance, he said, "I've brought the princess, Your Majesty."

"Took you long enough." The supercilious voice belonged to the emperor's body servant, not Kajastahn himself. Sniffing, the man said, "He's gone back to sleep. Let me wake him. She can sit there while you wait in the tunnel."

Saium guided her to a chair and Shalira sat, ankles neatly crossed, nervously adjusting her skirt. She could hear her father's labored breathing close by. Pressing her hand, Saium whispered into her ear, "I'll be right outside if you need me."

Swallowing hard, she nodded. The guardsman had to yank his hand away from her clinging grip, but then Shalira straightened, determined not to give in to fear. *After all, this is my father. He can't have sent for me without good reason.* She pushed away the nagging fact he hadn't wanted to see her privately for over ten years. The room smelled of illness—decaying flesh and infection overlaid with medicinal herbs and cloying perfumes.

"All right, he's awake and I've given him an elixir to ensure wakefulness and lucidity," said the servant, standing right in front of her. "The medicine works for a short while."

Startled, Shalira was unable to quell her instinctive recoil at the man's proximity. "He's so ill, then? The rumors are true?"

"I'm dying, girl," rumbled the emperor's voice from a short distance away, followed by a massive coughing spell.

The servant bustled noisily about, giving the ailing ruler something to drink and rearranging the bed pillows, Shalira decided, before asking his master, "Shall I stay, sir?"

"No. I need to be alone with my daughter, and there's so little time left."

"Very good." Shalira heard the glasses and bottles clinking on a tray as the obviously disapproving servant left, the door closing softly behind him.

"Damn it, come closer, into the light." The emperor's admonition was harsh, although his voice quavered a bit. "I want to see you."

Shalira stood. "I can't see the light."

"Follow my voice then. They tell me you've become quite clever, developed many tricks to minimize your disability." Kajastahn sounded querulous. He caught his breath as she left the chair and walked a few steps nearer to the bed. "By the Ten Gods, you've become her twin!"

"No, sir, only her daughter." Shalira paused, hands fisted at her sides.

"And mine." His voice rang strong on the declaration, yet didn't sound especially proud. "I never believed those claims your mother played me false with her damn guardsman." Kajastahn was racked by coughing.

"I don't understand—"

"I didn't summon you here in the middle of the night to rehash old gossip. I know my Favorite didn't cuckold me, not with Saium, not with any man. No one would have dared," the emperor said. He fell silent, breathing heavily and shifting against his headboard as if no position gave him comfort.

Mother and Saium? Thoughts whirled in Shalira's mind. Pointed remarks and hints made by impudent courtiers over the last few years gained new meaning in light of what the emperor had just said. *But why bring this up now?* "Why am I here, sir?"

"Heard you were caught in a terrorist explosion this morning."

"I was on the edge of the blast, yes. I took no harm, other than a superficial wound in the arm. The military officer from the Sectors rescued me." Touching the fresh bandage on her upper arm, Shalira felt her cheeks grow warm as she remembered how commanding and strong Major Varone had been, how gallant. *I wish I knew what he looked like.* She pushed the stray desire to the back of her mind. Important to concentrate in this rare audience with her father.

"Not the first sign of unrest and rebellion. Maralika thinks she and her son will rule after I die, but she may have miscalculated how much the people will swallow. New taxes, new gods, she's imposing too much change, moving too fast. Make no mistake, though, she'll hold power for some span of time after I'm gone, which is why I wanted you well away from here."

Shalira was startled again. "I thought my marriage was arranged to ensure peace along the western border? To seal a treaty?"

"Come closer." Kajastahn patted the edge of his bed and Shalira obediently moved toward the sound, sitting once she had bumped into the mattress. A heavy, beringed hand closed around hers. Stroking her hand with his thumb, the emperor said, "I've not been much of a father, not since your mother died and your brother was killed. Too painful to behold you." Unspoken was, *Why them? Why not you?*

Pain clenched around her heart to hear him admit what she'd always suspected. Shalira fought not to cry. Time for self-indulgence later. "What's changed now?"

"I don't have much time left. Trying to settle old debts, fix some problems I allowed to fester. Now look, Bandarlok is reputed to be a strong man, holds what's his. I think he'll keep you safe, even if you aren't to be his chief wife. Give him an heir with royal blood and your position will be secure, even after I'm dead. Maralika can't touch you there."

Icy shock poured through her, and Shalira's heart skipped a beat. "I don't understand. Are you telling me he's already married?"

"Customary among the hill people, just as it is here in the city. By the Ten Gods, girl, surely you didn't think a powerful man like him was going to take a blind woman past her prime as his chief wife? Not even with the dowry I sent." Kajastahn's laugh was like acid on top of his harsh words.

Shalira fought not to faint, drawing in deep breaths and digging the fingernails of her free hand into her palm. Never once had it entered her mind she'd be one among many wives. *He makes it sound as if Bandarlok had to be paid to take me off his hands.* She wanted desperately to be anywhere but in this room, listening to Kajastahn's revelations. She'd been so proud to have the marriage arranged for her, to be serving a critical diplomatic purpose for her father. How little she'd understood. Forcing herself to remain seated, Shalira waited for the next blow to fall.

Perhaps sensing his daughter wasn't finding this explanation palatable, the emperor released her hand. Shalira heard him noisily drinking some liquid. Burping twice, he continued the justification of his actions on her behalf. "Well, if I'd done nothing, Maralika was proposing to send you to the Abbey of Obedient Sisters to the south, where I'm sure she'd have had you murdered as soon as I'm gone. Give me some credit. It's not as if worrying over the fate of one girl is at the top of my duties. I got you a husband despite all the odds. You do the rest. Get yourself pregnant by him is my advice."

"Yes, Father. I'm grateful you're taking an interest in my fate." Shalira forced the words from her lips. *Well, he's right, life for me will undoubtedly be better out there in the western forests, even as a secondary wife, than here in this poisonous court. Or at the abbey!* Recalling horror stories of the abuses suffered by unprotected novitiates at an institution little better than a prison, Shalira derived some comfort in her father's arrangements for her future. *I'll make it work, just as I've done ever since I went blind. He has no idea how resourceful I am. No one does.* Sagging confidence restored, she had a clever new idea.

The emperor endured a long coughing fit, unable to catch his breath. Shalira sat, not knowing what she should do for him, if anything. He hadn't given her permission to leave or to touch him. Eventually, Kajastahn fell back against his pillows, shaking the bed frame.

She decided to press her luck. "Thank you, Your Majesty, for…everything. May I ask for one more boon tonight?"

"As long as you aren't petitioning for anything costly. I've paid enough to get you married." His voice sounded wary.

"I'd like the two Sectors soldiers to travel with my wedding caravan as an additional escort."

"Don't trust the men Maralika assigned to the job, eh?" The realization amused the old man, judging by his raspy chuckle. "Maybe you've inherited something of my cunning along with your mother's beauty. Even Maralika's cutthroats will think twice about harming you in front of offworlders. Get you to Bandarlok safely. Good girl. All right, I'll give the order." He caught her hand again, rubbing his bony fingers across her palm. "So like your mother—amazing. Well, she'll be pleased I've taken care of your future."

He expects to meet her in the afterlife soon and doesn't want any reproaches about his treatment of me in this life—cold comfort. Shalira stood. "May I go now?"

"Said all I have to say. No need to linger. Fetch my servant."

Helplessly she raised one hand. "I…can't. I'm not familiar with your rooms." She heard the sound of a small gong close by.

"Useless girl," the emperor said as the door to the room opened, followed a heartbeat later by the creaking of the door to the secret tunnel. "I hope Bandarlok is taken by your beauty and ignores the rest."

"The Sectors soldiers?" she reminded him, resisting for a moment as Saium took her elbow.

"Said I'd order it and I will, in the morning." Kajastahn chuckled. "I'm sure they'll be upset. Sectors citizens don't like anything interfering with their high-and-mighty mission. Well, they can't do anything on Mahjundar without my permission, so they'll damn well escort you to the high lands and like it."

Satisfied, Shalira yielded to Saium's gentle tug. *Surely there's something else to be said? Some word of affection?* "Thank you, I'll miss—"

"You won't miss me. We've not even spoken for ten years, so don't try to play the dutiful daughter. We don't need any farce. I've done what I needed to do tonight. Now leave me in peace."

Angry and hurt at the same time, Shalira allowed Saium to draw her away to the tunnel entrance.

"Shalira!"

She homed in on the sound of her father's voice. "Yes?"

"Go with the blessings of the Ten and cherish the knowledge of how much your mother meant to me."

How much she meant to you, not a word about me. "I will, Father." She stepped over the threshold, and the door closed behind her.

CHAPTER TWO

Incessant knocking woke him early the morning after the banquet. Rubbing his temples, Mike rolled over and groaned. *The local wine is potent stuff. Whoever's hammering at the door isn't helping my headache any.* "Okay, I'm coming," he shouted, working his way out of bed and heading for the entrance, throwing a pillow at Johnny along the way. "Get me some headclear, would you?"

"Sure thing. Did you want me to give Rojar some, too?"

Pausing in his tracks, Mike scratched his head, yawning. "Rojar?"

Rubbing his eyes, Johnny said, "You dragged him back here with you last night, drunker than any man I've ever seen. Don't you remember?"

Mike frowned. "Vaguely. Let me get rid of whoever is battering the damn door, then we'll deal with Rojar." He yanked the portal open. "Do you know what time it is?"

Blinking, hand raised to knock again, the servant standing in the hallway retreated a step or two. "You're summoned to the prime minister's office for a ceremonial breakfast in half an hour, sir. It would be best not to be late."

Mike shut his eyes in disbelief for a moment. *They go in for pomp and ceremony at breakfast on this planet?* "How do I find this office?"

"Captain Rojar will escort you." The servant darted glances both ways to be sure the hall was empty before leaning closer. "Have you seen Rojar since last night? He missed his duty watch, and if he doesn't attend this ceremony with you, they're going to arrest him for dereliction of duty. The empress has a vendetta against him."

Conscious of the headache ravaging his nerve endings, Mike shook his head gingerly. "Haven't seen him, but I'm sure he'll show up. Thanks for the warning."

"I'm his cousin. Clans have to stick together to survive in this place." The servant bowed and walked briskly away.

Mike shut the door and grabbed the headclear inject Johnny was holding out to him. "Did you hear the discussion?"

"Yeah, cousins have to stick together." Johnny shot him a sardonic look. "Not a news flash."

Mike rolled his shoulders as the drug took effect. "Best invention ever."

"No argument there. Good thing they provide an unlimited supply to operators in the field." Johnny winked. "I'm glad you're handling the high level protocol requirements. This place has too much politics for my taste. We'd better get Rojar sober and presentable, fast." Another inject in his hand, Johnny walked toward the adjoining room of their suite, from which Rojar's loud snores could be heard.

In between the first course and the second, the visibly bored prime minister presented Mike with a jeweled, totally useless dagger in appreciation of his having saved Princess Shalira from the bombing in the plaza.

"Thank you, sir, I was happy to be in the right place at the right time." Mike accepted the gift, examining the workmanship. Mahjundan enameling was admired even in the Sectors. A nice souvenir, but hardly a serious weapon.

"Good," said the prime minister, absorbed in spreading a second layer of jam onto a roll. "Then you will be highly pleased to know the emperor has such faith in your abilities after yesterday, he commands your presence in Princess Shalira's caravan, escorting her to be married to a powerful tribal chieftain in the forested highlands at the edge of the mountains."

Mike paused, cup halfway to his lips. "I'm not sure I understand, sir. My own mission is urgent. Surely the princess has a sufficient escort with her father's troops?"

The prime minister shoved the dripping roll into his mouth and cleaned his fingers on a snowy napkin. After a bout of vigorous chewing, he swallowed hard, choked, and shook his head. "Perhaps you mistake my meaning, outworlder. If you don't choose to travel with the princess, the emperor won't issue a permit for you to leave the capital at all." Tilting his head, he regarded Mike with his eyes half-closed. "Do you wish to reconsider your decision?"

Beyond angry, Mike kept a rein on his temper. *Can't cause trouble with the local officials. Command would be upset. All kinds of diplomatic complications.* "Permit me to consult with my liaison, Captain Rojar, to get a better understanding of the caravan's route."

"Shalira leaves tomorrow and greatly desires the honor of an outworlder escort. I was told you were impatient to leave, so the emperor has arrived at a solution for both of you." The prime minister picked up his next breakfast pastry. "Unless you have more to discuss, we're done here." Ostentatiously turning his back on Mike, he addressed some pleasantry to the woman seated on the other side of him.

Rojar tapped Mike on the arm. "The caravan goes north first to make a pilgrimage to the tomb of Shalira's mother." He sketched out the route on the tablecloth.

"Do you see how many days of riding this detour adds to my schedule?" Mike demanded, keeping his voice under control. "How can anyone expect me to agree to this?"

Rojar sipped his juice. "As the prime minister said, if you don't agree, you have no mission."

"Unacceptable." Mike shoved his plate away, causing the people near him to stop talking and stare. He nodded to the prime minister. "With your permission, sir, I'm going to excuse myself and go survey my gear, talk to my sergeant about this proposed change."

The official waved his hand and resumed his flirtation with the woman.

Rising, Mike left the dining room with rapid strides, trying to regain his calm. Wisely, Rojar didn't see fit to follow.

A voice hailed him from behind. "Major Varone!"

Pausing, Mike waited for the hurrying guardsman to reach him, pushing through the ever present crowd in the hallway. Recognizing the man who'd held Shalira's horse, he noted a large, nasty, purple bruise, half-hidden by wavy white hair. "I see you were injured at the plaza?" Mike asked. The older man had a truly impressive head of hair, confined to a thick braid. "The princess was so concerned about you right after the blast, she asked about nothing else. How is she today?"

Touching his bruised temple gingerly, the guard nodded. "The blast knocked me off my feet, and the damn horse kicked me. I was out for hours. Lucky not to have been trampled. The princess is well, thanks to you."

"A rider at her level can't handle a horse so spirited and poorly trained," was Mike's critical assessment. He spoke more sharply than he'd intended, but his family raised horses on Azrigone.

This assessment apparently infuriated the guard, who drew himself up and glared at Mike. Green eyes narrowed, face flushed, he demanded, "Don't I know it? Doesn't she know it? Terrified of the brute she is, but the empress insists—and what Maralika wants must be so. If only the emperor—" Evidently about to commit some major breach of Mahjundan manners, he shut his lips tight for a second and then added, "Thank you for saving my lady yesterday."

"I was there. I was lucky. Anyone would have stepped in." Local politics weren't his problem.

"Maybe. Maybe not. I think the princess was fortunate for once." The last was muttered under the man's breath. Mike wasn't sure he even heard the comment correctly. "Princess Shalira requests your presence this morning, to discuss the matter of travel."

"Now?" Mike wasn't sure he was in the mood for any more conversation about the change in his plans, even with her.

Nodding, the princess's guard said, "She regrets not having the chance to ask you to join her caravan before the emperor issued his decree."

"All right, I'm not doing anything else at the moment. Lead on—?" Mike gestured toward the bustling corridor.

"Saium." Making a quick bow, he took off at a rapid pace, taking Mike into a hallway he'd not been in before.

"Was she born blind?" Mike asked, curious about her disability.

"Not a good idea to ask too many questions in this cursed city." As if invoking a good luck charm, his companion rubbed at the tattoo on his upper arm—a fierce bird of prey, outlined in green and black.

"I merely want to avoid causing her distress. Your loyalty to the lady does you great credit, but I don't like riding into a situation unprepared. I want to understand the background. I'd rather not have to ask her these questions, but I have my own orders, which take precedence over anything your emperor wants." Mike tried to alleviate the confrontational tone they'd taken. "I have a niece who was born blind on my home planet," he went on more softly.

"I've heard such things can be mended in the Sectors," the guard said speculatively over his shoulder, as they progressed through the halls.

"Not always. In my niece's case, the nerves were undeveloped at birth. Nothing organic can be done, and first her parents, then she herself refused cyber-enhancement. But she's a successful musician on several instruments. Can play anything she's heard once, gives concerts all over our Sector."

"My lady wasn't born blind. She lost the use of her eyes at age ten," the man told him. "In our world, it's a disgrace not to be whole in body and in senses. Life has been hard for her. Of course, the empress was pleased to watch the daughter of her greatest rival left without a husband."

Tired of mystery and doublespeak, Mike swung Saium to face him. "Wouldn't it be better for the princess if I had the full picture of what's going on? I want to know what kind of trouble I'm supposed to be expecting, for her sake. It's not my planet—I'm not on anyone's side. My priorities are to get my job done and go home."

Saium stared into Mike's eyes for a long moment, before checking both ways to make sure the hall was relatively deserted. He leaned close to Mike's ear. "Fifteen years ago, Shalira and her brother went for a morning ride along the river alone, as was their custom. Apparently they were set upon by assassins in a well-planned ambush. The crown prince died on the spot. My lady—a mere child of ten at the time—was found unconscious nearby, with few visible wounds. Yet when she awakened days later, she'd lost her sight."

Before the soldier could say anything more, Mike heard the sounds of women laughing. A group of people approached from the other end of the long corridor.

"The Empress Maralika," Saium whispered. Backing up to the wall, he went to one knee, head bowed subserviently.

Mike scrutinized the women mincing in a colorful parade toward him. As he shifted into parade rest, strong perfume enveloped him in a nausea-inducing wave, several scents mixing in an unpleasant effect.

"Ah, the outworlder!" Maralika came to a stop directly in front of him, standing so close her orange and red skirts swirled against his legs like a silken net. He met her gaze. Appraising him from head to toe in an insultingly frank manner, she didn't speak for a moment. "What a pity," she sighed to the nearest lady-in-waiting. "So handsome, in an alien fashion. To be wasted when the mountain clans kill him, which they will." Tilting her head, she smiled, gazing flirtatiously upward through spiky black lashes. Tapping him on the chest with her fan, she said, "Tell me, why weren't you there to rescue me in the square yesterday? Surely the life of the empress is worth more than the continued existence of some useless, pitiful girl? After all, who would miss our little Princess of Shadows?" Using the fan, she forced him to raise his chin. "Plainly, I was the assassins' target, and your gallantry would have been properly appreciated, I assure you."

Taking the fan in his fist, he removed it from her grasp, lowering his chin to stare at her. "Your Majesty appeared to be well guarded and well served yesterday." Polite on the surface, Mike's voice had a hard edge. "I observed that more than one of your faithful soldiers died to save your life." With a slight bow, he returned the fan to her.

His tone and his answer apparently displeasing her, she spun on her heel and swept down the corridor without another word, her companions following, whispering and giggling. One, more daring than the rest, peeked over her shoulder at Mike, dissolving into laughter as she skipped around the corner.

Sliding one hand up the wall to steady himself on his apparently bad knees, Saium got to his feet. "Not wise to insult the empress."

"I might have missed something there, but I'd say she insulted me first." Mike straightened his tunic and shrugged.

Saium studied him for a moment, then puffed his cheeks out and nodded. "Whatever my lady doesn't tell you, outworlder, I give my word I will." He walked in the opposite direction from the way the empress had gone and Mike hastened to catch up.

He had to be satisfied with the guardsman's pledge because a minute later, Saium opened a hidden door and led Mike through a short corridor painted in a soothing pale green color. The ever-present Mahjundan cherindors were there, he noted with amusement, but here the predators were hidden among the pastel leaves of a fantasy jungle. Saium let Mike precede him through a door covered in a carved seashell motif, walking into an antechamber embellished with ocean scenes in pale, cool colors on the walls.

"Her Highness will be with you in a moment, Major. She asks that you be seated and wait." Saium indicated a grouping of furniture that included a couch and two matching chairs.

Realizing he was relaxing under the influence of the soft, simple colors of the room, Mike sat as suggested. *Who chose this restful color scheme? Couldn't have been Shalira. Maybe her late mother?* The garish, clashing colors and tapestries of battle scenes and monsters that crowded every available flat wall in the rest of the palace were absent here. Nor was there any heavy incense burning. The breeze brought the refreshing, light scent of flowering plants from the garden beyond a half-open door.

A faint whiff of the perfume from yesterday came to him, deliciously floral. Shalira came through the draperies across the room, dressed today in a simple lavender robe, edged in lapis with a thin ribbon of white lace at the hem. Her glorious black hair floated free, curling slightly, held from her face by a lapis-and-white ribbon edged in gold. Her only jewelry was the oval green and turquoise pendant. Pausing for a moment on the threshold to set a basket of cut flowers on a low table, she walked across the floor to him.

Startled, Mike rose, admiring her skill at creating the impression she could see her visitor. His niece at home employed the same techniques, keeping everything in fixed locations and knowing exactly the number of steps it took to move from one thing to the next, seemingly effortlessly. *Wonder what the polite greeting is for a Mahjundan princess? Briefing didn't cover the contingency.* Deciding to go for polite if insipid, he said, "Your Highness appears well today."

She extended her hands to him and he reached out to close his much larger, rougher hands over her soft ones. "Thank you for coming, Major," she murmured in her low, musical voice as she drew him towards the pale green sofa by the window. Indicating he was to sit at one end, she curled up at the other. Kicking off a pair of high heeled sandals, she tucked her bare toes under the edge of her dress. "Would you care for a beverage? Iced rubyfruit drink, perhaps?"

He glanced at the silver tray carefully positioned on the low table beside her. Crackers and cheese were artfully arranged next to the juice pitcher and matching glasses. "Sounds refreshing, but whatever you'd like, your highness."

She served them both, holding the glass with one finger tipped slightly over the edge to alert her when the proper level of liquid was poured. Despite having seen his niece manage the same task in a similar fashion, Mike was impressed. *I bet Shalira had to learn these things the hard way, unlike Cheryl, who had the best therapists and teachers in Sector Ten.*

Having gotten Mike to meet with her, the princess seemed unaccountably at a loss for how to begin. She sipped at her fruit drink and toyed with the hem of her gown and then her jewelry, rubbing her fingers over the whorls of the pendant in a slow circle. Mike tried to put her at ease. "I'm admiring your necklace, exquisite enamel work."

Shalira nodded. "This was my mother's before she died. I never take the necklace off, not even for a moment. I'll wear it till *I* die."

"Of course the sentimental value must be—"

"This is the symbol of Pavmiraia, my patron goddess," Shalira said, holding the ornament away from her neck as far as the golden chain would allow. "And it's a locket." Fumbling for a moment, the princess depressed one portion of the decorative pattern and the case flicked open.

Mike leaned closer, expecting to see a portrait, perhaps of her mother, but the interior was empty, nothing but shiny polished gold reflecting the light.

Shalira laughed, the sound flat. "It's the custom for women to hide their most cherished dream inside the locket of Pavmiraia, but I've had no hopes worthy of submitting to her, not since my brother died and I became blind." She snapped the locket closed with decisive finality. "Symbolic, of course, but a nice idea."

"The prime minister gave me a fine dagger this morning on behalf of your father, for the small service I was privileged to offer you yesterday. There's similar enameling on the hilt."

"It was the least he could do—the least—" Her voice trailed off. Taking another sip from the frosted glass, she held it to her temple for a moment, rolling the cool glass from side to side as if her head ached.

"Are you doing okay?" Mike asked, watching how she frowned. "Any after effects from yesterday?"

"I'm fine," she said, sitting up straighter. "I didn't sleep well last night."

A little silence fell between them. Mike had the distinct impression the princess's thoughts were elsewhere. Finally, she sighed. "At the presentation ceremony, did the minister ask if you'd be willing to ride in my caravan?"

"Ask? More of a threat." Mike knew his frustration was showing. He sipped at the sweet drink. "Ride with you or have my own mission cancelled."

"And you don't sound pleased. I wish I could have made the request myself." She nibbled on a cracker, brushing crumbs from her lap.

"Forgive me, Your Highness, but why do you want us to go with you?" He leaned forward. "I'm on an urgent mission. Your route causes me quite a delay, which I can't afford without good reason."

"You're searching in the mountains for a lost military ship, aren't you? To give those who died the proper burial, set their spirits free?"

"Well, yes." Mike was aware Command had used those terms to explain the request for access to this closed world. The Mahjundans, with their various beliefs about spirits, death, and proper conveyance to the afterlife, understood and had consented to a burial detail. *Of course there's another, more important strategic reason for me to delay my hard-earned retirement and accept this last mission.* He wasn't about to explain the classified background to anyone, not even this beautiful, solemn woman whose proximity was definitely having an effect on him.

"But the dead have infinite patience, Major. Surely you can spare a few days for the living?" Leaning forward, she set her glass on the table, perilously close to the edge.

He shifted the glass to a safer location. "Your Highness—"

"You may call me Shalira, if you like." Scooting slightly toward him, smiling, she raised her elegantly curved eyebrows. "One who has saved the life of a princess is entitled to the use of her name."

"Thank you, I'm honored, Shalira, but—"

"Would you let the life you saved be lost so soon?" Tears shimmered in the depths of her unseeing brown eyes as she turned her face directly to him. Mike couldn't look away, even though he knew she wasn't actually seeing him, or his reactions. He put his glass on the table too hard, cracking the base.

"There are those who don't want me to reach my wedding. The palace rustles with rumors of plots, schemes in motion to take advantage of this final opportunity to kill me. Once I'm safe with my bridegroom-to-be, I'll be beyond the schemers' reach, but I have to *get* to him." Shalira rubbed her elegant fingers across the pendant as if it were an amulet giving her strength. "I hope that if you ride with me, those who plan my murder will be afraid to proceed under the attention of outworlders."

What do I say to this? He hadn't anticipated an appeal along these dramatic lines. "Do you think the bomb yesterday was an attempt to assassinate you?"

"No, assuredly Maralika was the target." Shalira shook her head. "The empress is pursuing a host of unpopular actions—forbidding the older forms of worship, tearing down temples, forcing the people to pay taxes to her new gods, consolidating power for herself and her son. My father is not a well man, Major. Everyone knows he doesn't have long to live, and she plans to rule when he's gone."

"But there's opposition to her?" Mike was aware there was. Planetary politics had been a prominent part of his briefing, but he was curious how much Shalira might add.

"Her son is the heir since my brother was murdered, but the throne of Mahjundar has often been claimed by bloodshed rather than by rule of law. I *have* to get away from here, before the emperor dies." She laughed, the sound bitter. "Playing the Princess of Shadows won't protect me after his death."

"Princess of Shadows?" *Nothing about that in our briefing.* He remembered the empress had also used the term to refer to Shalira.

"It's an old folktale about a girl of royal blood who hid from her enemies in the shadows of the palace walls, disguised as a beggar, until her true love rescued her." Gesturing to her eyes, Shalira said, "It's meant as an insult to me, since I can't see, not even shadows, and I've lived the past fifteen years on the fringes of the court, out of the 'sun.' I'm tolerated, protected only because my mother was the emperor's Favorite till she died. If I reach the safety of my bridegroom's people, then I'll be safe, free of the empress's plotting and hate. My mother's clan is among his subjects." Shalira blinked hard, and then her face crumpled as she wept.

Used to comforting younger sisters in distress, Mike didn't hesitate. Moving closer, he gathered her against his shoulder and let her sob without interruption for several minutes. Patting her back, he realized she was overwrought and genuinely fearful. Her apparently genuine distress pulled at his sympathies. When the wrenching sobs became small hiccups and sniffs, he reached for the lacy napkin beside the juice pitcher.

As he pushed the soft cloth into her hand, he said, "I don't know the rights and wrongs of the situation with your complicated family, but if you attach so much importance to having Johnny and me ride along for a few days, I guess I can stretch my mission schedule." *And what Johnny will say when I change our orders, I'm not going to think about. Dancing attendance—playing bodyguard—for a minor Mahjundan princess is not the way Command deploys first-tier military resources.*

Wiping her eyes, she sat up, long lashes starred together from the tears. "You'll ensure I get to my wedding alive?"

I've never seen such a beautiful woman before, nor one less aware of her own effect on me. Probably a good thing. He took her right hand in his. "Among my people, a bargain is sealed with a handshake. My word as an officer, I'll do my best to protect you while we ride together. Fair enough?"

She wrapped her fingers around his, clinging to his hand, bringing it to her soft cheek. "More than I'd dared to hope, Major."

"The name is Mike." He released the trembling fingers. "Is there anything else we should discuss? Anything you think I need to know?"

She reached for her glass, and Mike surreptitiously nudged it closer to her searching hand. "It's hard for me to talk about this." Shalira took tiny sips of the rubyfruit juice, as if playing for time.

"If you'd rather not, I can ask Saium. Don't distress yourself." Mike hated to see her so uncomfortable.

"Empress Maralika is sending me to my wedding with a handpicked escort of men loyal to her. The officer she put in command, Captain Vreely, is the man I've always believed was involved in my brother's murder and the attack which left me blind. I've no actual memories of the events, only feelings and forebodings. Nightmares." Shalira lowered her head for a minute, touching her eyelids with a delicate hand. "Any imperfection is abhorred in our society, you know. The failure of my eyes kept suitors from seeking my hand once I was of age."

Mahjundan men are idiots—her eyes are the most beautiful I've ever seen. She's one of the most gorgeous women I've ever met. Mike forced his thoughts away from the princess's beauty, concentrating on the matter under discussion. "But this chieftain you're going to marry knows you can't see?"

Shalira seemed troubled, wrinkling her brow and lowering her sightless eyes as she started worrying the fringe on the closest pillow, but all she said was, "A large dowry has been paid. He'll keep me safe, and I'll be happy living freely in the open forests, away from this hot, hateful city."

Mike pondered the ramifications of what she'd shared, added to the quick overview Saium had given him in the hall. "So you've never actually met this guy?"

Bristling as if she heard unwarranted criticism in his tone, she said, "No. Why does it matter? Arranged marriages are the custom for the high-born on Mahjundar. It is how things are done." She tilted her head, sculpted eyebrows drawn together in a frown.

"I see." *If it's fine with her, it's hardly my place to question the arrangement. Why do I care, anyway?* But his mind had moved on to the topic of how well a palace-bred princess would fare in the wilderness with forest nomads. *What is it with me and this woman? I just met her yesterday. She's none of my concern.*

Fortunately unaware of his consternation, she was providing her misgivings about the trip in calm detail. "I don't know how Maralika plans to have me killed. Many things can happen on a journey, safely out of sight of the city. Maybe the horse she insists I ride will throw me and save her henchmen the trouble of committing a crime." The princess rubbed her arms as if suddenly chilled. "I think she's been hoping for such a fate, ever since she gave me the cursed animal."

Mike took her hand to prevent her from worrying at the knotted fringe of a pillow between them. "We'll settle the easiest problem first and switch horses, all right? I'll have Saium show me the stables. We'll pick a nice calm mare or gelding for you."

"Already, you chip away at my biggest worries." Impulsively, she hugged him.

Patting her back in his best imitation of an avuncular acquaintance, Mike discreetly pulled away, disturbed by how his body responded to the softness of her curves, the enticing perfume. This was no time to start thinking of Shalira as a potential bedmate. If any woman ever had to be strictly off-limits, it was her. *Unfortunately.* He cleared his throat. "It's all settled, then. Johnny and I'll dance at your wedding in the highlands before we continue on our way to accomplish our own mission."

"I ask no more."

She might not ask, Mike thought, as he made his way through the mazelike corridors to his own suite and the waiting Sgt. Danver, but he had a suspicion something more would end up being required of him by events on this ad hoc excursion he'd just agreed to. *What had the mission briefers said? Nothing was ever simple and straightforward on Mahjundar. Expect the unexpected. Yeah, but who could have foreseen this set of complications? Princesses are the stuff of kids' fairy tales, not an assignment for a first-tier operator like me.*

As the door closed behind Mike, Shalira laid her head on the back of the couch, toying with the pillow fringe again. *Thank Pavmiraia he agreed to accompany me tomorrow. I know my father left him virtually no choice, but Mike doesn't seem to be the kind of man who'd be diverted from his mission without a fight.* Probably a good idea she'd decided to add a personal appeal this morning. Or at least that's what she'd told Saium, hoping he couldn't hear her heart beating faster at the idea of more private time with the outworlder. *I wonder what he looks like?* His voice was deep, his accent charming, with a little lilt she enjoyed. *Especially when he says my name. He's taller than I am, taller than most men at Court—I could tell yesterday when he was leading me through the streets. Strong, no nonsense. He gave his word to protect me on this journey. Hopefully, his escort, plus the other precautions I've already taken, will be enough to foil whatever Maralika is planning.* Swallowing hard, she reviewed the few arrangements she'd put in place for this journey into the unknown. Bone weary after the emotional meeting with Major Varone on top of her encounter with her father in the middle of the night, Shalira allowed herself to drift off into a nap. Saium, faithful as always, would be guarding the door.

CHAPTER THREE

Sighing in contentment, Mike surveyed the road to the east, where not even a wisp of the city could be seen any longer. His horse shifted footing on the ridge. *Good to be on horseback again, after too many years away from my home planet. I can't wait to finish this assignment and get back there. Stake my claim, start my own ranch.* Far below, a couple of miles away on the great road, Mike saw the dust cloud from their caravan. A wave of dissatisfaction passed through him like acid, ruining his peaceful mood. *Maybe I should have fought harder against being drafted into this large group, which is* not *going in a straight line to my mission's location. But when Shalira added her appeal to the emperor's order—*

I'm a fool for allowing myself to be persuaded, even by a blind princess with beautiful eyes. I know better than to delay the job Johnny and I are on. Mike unfastened his canteen and took a deep drink of the lukewarm water. All the tech on this closed planet was old-fashioned, even the canteens. But until they split off on their own, he and Johnny didn't want to bring out too much of their customized gear for fear of arousing Mahjundan suspicions of contraband. Closed planets ruled by despots were invariably paranoid about imported technology reaching the citizens.

Mike shook his head to clear the cobwebs, anchor himself in the present moment, here on the trail. *I'd better get back to the column before dark.* He checked the trio of fat game bird carcasses tethered by the feet to the rear of the saddle. Hunting for the dinner stewpot had been his excuse to take the black stallion for a long run over the broken country, tire the high spirited animal out, settle him down. *Better not leave Johnny, Saium and Rojar to keep tabs on Vreely's thugs for too long without reinforcements.*

As Mike descended the last rise toward the caravan, Johnny split off from the column and galloped to meet him.

"I see you had good hunting," his cousin said, as soon as they were close enough to exchange words. "Vreely is spitting solar flares about where you went and when you'd be back. I learned some fine new Mahjundan swear words when he expressed his opinion of you riding Shalira's horse."

Mike patted the black stallion on the neck. "We got along fine once he understood who was boss. Vreely bothering the princess at all?"

"No. She told him she gave you the horse as a further reward for saving her life in the plaza. He shut up then. Actually, he's pretty much ignoring her. He's setting a hell of a pace though. My butt is *sore* and all my muscles are tied up in knots." Johnny stood in the stirrups for a moment, causing his chestnut horse to flick its ears and sidle across the path a few steps.

"I know what you mean." Mike laughed as they turned their mounts and headed back to the road together. "Last time we rode something without wheels or antigrav was on spring roundup in the high pastures, remember? When we were on leave?" Too late, he remembered the occasion he was recalling was prior to the most disastrous mission they'd ever run, so he changed the subject. "What's Vreely's rush?"

"Dunno. He has a specific campsite he wants to reach tonight. Princess Shalira is holding up all right, so I didn't see any point in complaining. After all, we're *supposed* to be in a hurry ourselves." Chewing on a toothpick, Johnny glanced sideways at Mike. "You're not getting ideas about this girl, are you?"

Mike knew it would be futile to put his cousin off. They'd known each other for too long. "I find her attractive. And I admire her guts."

Tossing the toothpick into the weeds, Johnny raised one eyebrow. "But?"

"But I haven't forgotten we're escorting her to her wedding, okay?"

"Just checking. I've never known you to let personal interests sidetrack an op before. Pretty odd behavior." His cousin looked Mike over from head to toe, as if the answers to the puzzle were written on his uniform. Shaking one finger at Mike, Johnny said, "You can bullshit Command all day long about the emperor giving you no choice, but you and I know damn well we could have taken off on our own assignment the moment we got out of the city. Vreely sure as hell wouldn't have tried to stop us. He *hates* our presence on this trip."

Mopping his forehead, Mike protested. "Hey, I feel a bit responsible for her, after the way she and I met after the bombing. Nothing more, I promise. I've no intention of getting involved with a local bride-to-be." Laughing, Mike spurred his horse into a trot for the last few yards to rejoin the column, which had unaccountably halted.

As he rode closer, Mike could hear raised voices. *Vreely and Shalira.*

"I insist we stop," Shalira was saying as Mike nosed his horse into the group surrounding the princess.

"Your Highness, our task is to get you to the temple, the tombs and your bridegroom, in that order, as rapidly as possible. Not spend days on the road, halting at every tiny shrine or roadside attraction that captures your attention." Vreely's tone wasn't respectful or deferential in the least. He gave Saium a glare that should have set him on fire. "I'd appreciate it if your man here would stop mentioning these opportunities."

"But he tells me this is the glade of Pavmiraia, representing my last opportunity to pay my respects at a shrine dedicated to her alone. I can't just ride by." Shalira wasn't giving an inch.

Taking a swift glance at the small area of greenery and ruins under discussion, Mike didn't see any reason not to let the lady have a few minutes to worship, if doing so meant that much to her. "Look," he said, "The horses could use a break. If visiting this shrine is so important to Her Highness, why not take advantage of the pond and the shade for a few minutes?" He touched her arm. "You weren't planning on a long stop here, were you?"

"No, I suppose not. I only want to offer a quick prayer," she said. "Will you escort me?"

"I'd be honored," he said, ignoring Johnny's smothered curse.

A few moments later he was walking beside her, guiding toward the tumble-down ruin set in the midst of seriously overgrown trees, next to a small pond and a gurgling stream. The rest of the column had remained behind, on the fringe of the oasis, per Shalira's request.

He felt a cool breeze, the first one of the day.

Shalira stumbled over an exposed tree root and he cursed himself for inattention even as he kept her upright. "I'm sorry, I'm not a very good guide. You'd probably have been better off with Saium."

"I wanted you to see this," she said. "No apologies needed."

"Why? Why did you want me to come here in particular?"

"I think you don't really want to be on our planet, nor riding along with me in a slow caravan. I've heard you didn't like the crowded capital or the palace," she said. "I was hoping this place might give you a different idea of Mahjundar, to take with you, when you leave." Her lips curved in a mischievous smile. "And I liked the idea of a few moments alone, out of the saddle. Do you object?"

"Not at all. I apologize if I've been taking my impatient mood out on you. Nothing personal, Your Highness." He helped her climb a few crumbling stairs and they stepped into a pavilion, open to the sky. Lush grass grew up between the cracked flagstones and flowering vines wound around the pillars. "It's quite beautiful. Would you like me to step aside while you worship?"

"Very kind of you. I need to be standing in the exact center, please."

He led her to the round mosaic in the middle of the platform, colors still bright. As they stepped onto the slightly upraised pattern, there was a sudden trill of musical notes and a brightly colored creature fluttered around his head. Automatically he recoiled, free hand going to his gun.

No doubt feeling him tense, Shalira crowded closer. "What is it? What's wrong?"

"Are we likely to be in any danger from a bird-butterfly kind of thing?" Focusing on the tiny, brilliantly-hued creature as it fluttered around him, Mike felt a little silly. But there were deadly predators on other worlds that seemed just as harmless at first glance and it wasn't his nature to take chances.

"I'm sorry, a what?" Her forehead wrinkled as she puzzled over the term he'd used in Basic.

"I don't know what to call it in your language. They weren't mentioned in our briefing. Some kind of flying warbler?" The creature set down on his shoulder for an instant, fuzzy antennae vibrating, and then launched itself into the air with another trill of bell-like notes that seemed too loud to be coming from such a tiny being.

"A myrdima of Pavmiraia! Do you really see such a marvel?" She turned her head left to right. "I thought I heard music."

"It's flown off now, to the trees. It was pink and purple and red, with furry white antenna. About the size of your fist."

"We'd be blessed indeed, to be serenaded by Pavmiraia's songbird. None has been seen in this area of Mahjundar for centuries. They withdraw, as the old gods withdraw, because the people's faith wanes." She shook her hand free of his, not rudely. Arms outstretched, she twirled, dancing, humming under her breath. She made graceful hand movements in time to her tune as she swirled. Pausing for a moment, she said, "I feel so free here, momentary though the sensation may be. I haven't felt so unencumbered since I was ten and my world fell apart."

Not knowing what to say to her personal revelation, but feeling pleased she was happy, Mike leaned on the nearest pillar, scanning the ground for snakes or any other menace. He hoped Vreely would let Shalira enjoy her brief excursion for a bit longer. The man had been impatience personified since they'd left the capital city.

"Uh oh, look out, the whatever-you-called-it is back, with a friend," he said. "Stand still and maybe it'll land on your hand."

She closed her eyes and extended one hand, giggling a moment later as the little creature settled on her outstretched fingertips. "That tickles."

"They have tiny, fuzzy feet," he told her. "Gave me goosebumps."

A green-and-blue companion followed suit, touching down on her other hand. Shalira began to sing in a lovely, high soprano and after a moment the myrdima joined in with their crystalline three notes. Mike thought he'd never heard anything so beautiful, on any world. As Shalira continued to sing, in a language he didn't understand, more of the tiny warblers arrived, in a rainbow of colors, each adding its own three notes to the performance. They placed themselves on the princess's hair like jeweled ornaments, and more hovered around her in a cloud. Entranced, Mike thought there must be several hundred in all. A few even floated over to where he stood, although none landed on him. The colors ornamenting the wings shone in the sunshine, particularly vibrant against the drab, dusty landscape.

If they're waiting for me to sing, they've got nothing but disappointment coming. He bit his lip, not wanting to make a sound that might interfere with Shalira's serenade. He wished there was a way to record the scene, or to somehow share it with the princess, who would never know what a beautiful picture she and the magical creatures made. He locked the vision away in his own memory, as one of the most special moments of his life, an unexpected grace note in the midst of a tense and frustrating mission.

The song ended on a high note and then the myrdima stopped contributing their music a moment later. The entire flock took wing and spiraled around Shalira like a technicolor whirlwind, rising straight up into the brilliant blue sky before streaking south in a fast moving vee formation.

She lowered her arms, hugging herself. "Are they gone?"

"Yes." He pushed himself away from the pillar and walked over to her. "I wish you could have seen how incredibly beautiful they were, like living jewels. You with them—stunning. I'm sorry, I know that's probably not the right thing to say but I'm nothing but a simple soldier. Not good with the fancy words."

"No, it's all right." She held out a hand and he took it. "I'm glad the goddess gifted us both today. I'm glad we alone shared the moment."

"We'd uh, we'd better be getting back," he said, drawing a shaky breath. "Which seems so anticlimactic after an experience like that."

"We won't speak of it to them. Please don't mention it." Her face was set in lines of concern, brow furrowed. "The moment, the blessing was mine, ours, not to be shared, not even with Saium. Much though I love him, he doesn't worship Pavmiraia."

"Neither do I," he felt compelled to point out.

"But you intervened with Vreely to provide me this opportunity, so you surely deserved to be in the moment with me." As they walked from the platform, Shalira gave him a mischievous smile. "Have I succeeded in my goal of providing you a different view of Mahjundar?"

"That was amazing, Your Highness. Yes, I'll never think of the planet in quite the same way again." *Or you.*

Hours later and many miles further in the journey, Vreely called a halt as dusk was gathering. Mike had to admit it was an excellent location, on a slight hill, with a stream and some large trees for shelter. It was the most easily defensible spot he'd seen all afternoon. Vreely established camp in an exemplary fashion, posting guards, organizing things in a way any officer would appreciate. *He might be an assassin and worse, but he knows his business when it comes to military matters.* The man had all the personality of an ice slug, which was neither here nor there.

Mike tethered his horse close by Shalira's, Johnny and Rojar positioning themselves nearby. As they were rubbing their horses down, Saium came with a dinner invitation from the princess.

"Glad to join you," Mike told him. "I had good luck hunting this afternoon, so I can add fresh protein to the menu. Johnny, give him a hand with roasting these birds, would you?" He unhooked the skein of plump quail-like birds and passed it along to his cousin. "I bagged them, you can clean them."

Taking his cousin's agreement for granted, Mike wasted no further time in joining Shalira. Sitting on a small camp chair in front of the tent, face tilted to catch the evening breeze, the princess had her almond-shaped eyes closed. Humming a tune under her breath, she was a picture of contentment.

Mike's heart beat a little faster as he walked toward her. Despite what he'd told Johnny, he wished he'd met Shalira under different circumstances. She affected him the way no other woman ever had, not on his home planet, not on any world. The more they talked on this unexpected journey, got to know each other, the more he enjoyed her intelligence and her humor. *I hope this forest chief is going to appreciate what he's getting in his bride.* He cleared his throat and trod deliberately on a stick, breaking it with a crack as he walked closer, so as not to startle her. "Good evening, Your Highness."

Turning in his direction eagerly, she gave him a wide smile, dimples appearing in her cheeks. "Did we ride fast enough for you today?"

"No complaints." Mike sat on a big exposed root next to her chair. "Are you holding up all right?"

"I'll be glad when we get into the forested steppes, since it should be much cooler there." Lifting her hands to her hair, she released a cloud of soft curls from the chignon holding them in place all day. She combed her fingers through the tresses a few times to remove tangles. Mike found himself consumed with a desire to run his own hands through her silky hair. Rolling his shoulders, he berated himself for his weakening self-control. *What is it with me and this woman?*

"Not much traffic on this road, is there?" he asked, trying to divert the trend his thoughts were taking. Picking up a small twig, he drew idle patterns in the dust.

"It's not a main route to anything but the Valley of Tombs." She frowned, tilting her head. "If I weren't so happy to escape the confines of the city, this journey would be boring. I wish I could see the countryside we're riding through. Saium was describing the landmarks for a while, but he ran out of different ways to talk about hills and dust!" Her delighted laugh was musical.

"You aren't missing much," Mike agreed. "Nothing more of interest to stop for today after the glade of Pavmiraia. The countryside is bare, brown and hot."

"Not like your home world?" Fingers flying, she plaited her hair into a thick braid.

"Not at all. My planet, Azrigone, is lush, with excellent pastures and meadows. We raise Terran beef and sheep and sell to the luxury markets in the surrounding three Sectors. The Varone family brand is well known for its high quality." Mike snapped the twig in two and threw the pieces away. *I sound like a commercial.*

"Did I hear the sergeant say you two grew up together?" Done with the braid, she tied a lavender ribbon around the end and flipped it over her shoulder.

"Yes, we did. We're part of a large extended family on our home world."

"I don't think he likes me very much." She ran her hands slowly over the low table at her side, apparently searching for a cup. "He hasn't said more than two things to me all day. Does he blame me so much for delaying your mission?"

Mike handed her the mug as he answered the question. "Don't take it personally. He's a quiet guy by nature and he's got his own reasons for being anxious to get this job done and go home to Azrigone. A couple of our last assignments were pretty fucked up, I mean ugly. And we're not supposed to be on active duty any more but Command has a way of changing the rules when they want something bad enough."

"Are you always assigned to the same team?"

"Growing up together on a frontier planet made Johnny and me a tight unit, with some unique combat aptitudes the inner planet guys don't have, or don't develop to the same degree. Good thing, or we'd never have survived in some of the hellholes the military dropped us into. Especially the last mission." Mike stopped abruptly.

Sipping her juice, she let the silence go on for a moment. "Bad memories?"

He stretched out his legs, leaned back, trying to force himself to relax. "Not to be shared around a campfire. This jaunt to Mahjundar is a picnic compared to some things we've done."

"Did you ever see these aliens they speak of—what are they called? The Mawreg? Are they as fearsome as rumor tells?"

Controlling his visceral reaction to any mention of the enemy, Mike counted to ten mentally before answering her innocent query. "Count your lucky stars the

Mawreg aren't interested in this Sector and this planet. Empress Maralika would be the least of your concerns then."

She reached over, sliding her hand down his arm until she could pat his hand. "We won't speak of it further. I hear in your voice how much this topic distresses you."

He didn't argue. He and Johnny had gone in ahead of the troops on more than one world, had done cleanup sweeps on outposts where the Mawreg had been defeated, seen things he could never describe to an innocent like Shalira. He'd more than earned the acres of fresh, clean, high mountain pasture and lowland riverfront waiting in his name at home. *All we have to do is get through this one last assignment.*

"You okay?" Johnny was standing beside him, holding a skewer with roasted game birds, fat and dripping. "Man, you were at least twenty sectors away just now."

"Daydreaming about all the prime acreage we're going to claim when we get home." Feeling a little guilty for explaining his cousin's attitude to Shalira, he took the meat and started carving for his companions. Rojar and Saium joined them, bringing bread, fruit and a bottle of the lethally potent Mahjundan black wine.

Mike reached for the dark green bottle. "Rojar, buddy, you're restricted to one shot only. Takes too long to sober you up, otherwise."

The rest of the evening passed pleasantly, with a good meal and easy, companionable conversation. Proving to be a natural raconteur, Saium told stories from his youth in the forests and mountains. Mike and Johnny provided a few heavily edited adventures from their service years. At moonrise, the princess and her maid retired to their tent for the night.

Mike and the others slept in a protective cordon around the small tent, but there were no incidents to break the long night. As each man in Shalira's private, ad hoc guard force stood his watch, Vreely's soldiers kept their own official sentry duty but never ventured anywhere close to Shalira's tent, staying on the perimeter of the camp.

Vreely had his men packing their gear at dawn. Even the princess was given no time for breakfast, but ate dried rice cakes covered with thick jam like everyone else. Mike was grateful Johnny had decided to brew up some coffee from their personal stock as he stood the last watch of the night. Soon, the column was riding at a steady pace westward down the deserted highway as the huge sun climbed over the horizon.

Mike rode side by side with Shalira. "What should we be expecting this afternoon at the tombs?" He was peeling fruit for her as they rode, controlling his horse with the pressure of his knees, all his attention on cutting the red peel off in one long strip with his heavy hunting knife. In reality, he was keeping a close eye on Vreely. Jumpy today, the officer was tense, short with his own men, openly rude to Saium.

"I'm not entirely sure myself," the princess said as she accepted another wedge of the translucent fruit. "Mmm, my thanks. I do so love this delicacy, and I can't peel it for myself. Which I hate to admit, so I rarely ate it at the palace." Wiping a bit of juice from her chin, she laughed at herself. "Back to your question, first we have to make an offering at the temple, then we can open my mother's tomb."

"Open? Dig out from under tons of boulders?" asked Johnny, who was riding on the other side.

She scoffed at the idea, shaking her head. "If my petition in the temple is granted, we'll be given a key by the gods, to open the tomb door."

"If this petition is denied?" Mike said, tossing the fruit core off the trail and reaching into his saddle bag for another.

"Then Vreely would take me back to the city. Since I'm past the customary age of marriage, Empress Maralika has indicated I'd have to enter the Abbey of the Obedient Sisters, who live on a remote southern island. I'd be one of their novices, subject to all manner of torment. I'd rather die cleanly and get it over with." Shalira sounded serious and upset. "I must get the things my fiancé requested. There isn't any other way. He made it clear he wouldn't enter into marriage, no matter how large a dowry my father sent, unless the tribal insignia came too."

"Why were the items buried with your mother, if they're so important?" asked Mike.

"They were significant to her too, in life." Shalira made a little fluttery gesture with her hand. "I don't know why the clan chief wants them so desperately, but undoubtedly the totems are venerated treasures to the hill people, whereas they were a source of amusement to the nobility at court."

The day was another hot, cloudless scorcher. As the sun climbed directly overhead, the road came to an abrupt end in a box canyon. The way was blocked by a temple, built in a style reminiscent of the emperor's palace, but obviously far older. The roof was in poor repair, there were jagged cracks in the masonry, and the steps and walls were overgrown with creepers. In some places, the vegetation completely obscured the building, and stubborn vines were pulling the stones apart. The western flank of the building had collapsed at some point in the past, probably in an earthquake.

Mike surveyed the unpromising façade, exchanging dubious glances with Johnny, and asked Shalira, "How often does anyone come out here, Your Highness?"

"Rarely. Only royalty are buried in the valley beyond. Why? How dilapidated is the temple?" She turned toward him in the saddle, forehead wrinkled in concern.

"Pretty abandoned and desolate, but the main part of the building is standing." Judging from the obvious distress on her face, she needed reassurance and a redirection of her thoughts. "What's the plan?" he asked.

"I enter the temple and present a petition for permission to open the tomb. If I'm successful, I'll be given a key and we can enter the valley, going directly to my mother's tomb." Shalira's hands clenched on the reins until the knuckles were white. "I have to make the ceremony work. There are no other choices. I told you."

Dismounting, Mike handed his reins to Johnny. The black horse had been on good behavior all day, not surprisingly after yesterday's run, but now he was a bit skittish. The clumps of dried rollweed blowing in the hot wind spooked all the horses. Mike helped Shalira from her saddle, discreetly turning her to face Vreely, who'd walked up behind them.

Vreely had his usual scowl as he glanced from Mike to Johnny. "Remain here, outworlders, this ceremony is none of your business. I'll escort the princess into the temple." He reached out a black-gloved hand to take Shalira's arm.

Mike shifted her one step to the side, interposing himself between them.

"Not a chance we're going to miss this. Sergeant Danver and I promise not to get in the way, but we're definitely going in. The Emperor specifically requested that I accompany Her Highness on the entire journey, every step of the way," Mike lied with a big smile. *Vreely can't contradict me. He has no way to know differently.* "I have to obey orders."

Shalira tightened her grip on his hand, trembling slightly. Raising her chin, she said, "It's all right, Major Vreely, we'd better do as my father requested and permit the outworlders to view this ceremony." Clearing her throat, she rushed on, as if to prevent the officer from making further objections. "As I remember from when we were here for my great-uncle's funeral, there's a steep flight of stairs going up to the temple. A stack of torches should be inside the entrance, which of course all of you need, even if I don't." Smiling slightly at her self-deprecating humor, she tugged on Mike's arm and stepped forward.

Repositioning his hand at her elbow, he forestalled Vreely yet again. He and Shalira started up the fifty-two stairs to the forbidding entrance, which was flanked—of course—by the expected cherindors, lovingly carved in pink and gray stone. Johnny and Saium trailed by a few paces, followed by Vreely and two troopers. The rest of the Mahjundans stayed with the horses. Mike glanced down the stairs once or twice. *Interesting how relieved those guys are not to be included in this part of the trip.*

When he reached the narrow platform at the top of the stairs and was standing under the outstretched stone wings of the cherindors, Mike released his hold on Shalira. "Wait a minute, Your Highness. Deserted place like this, probably has snakes and other vermin living in it."

Drawing his old-fashioned Mahjundan projectile gun from its holster, he checked whether the others were ready before asking Shalira, "Now what?"

"We go inside. You can light the torches for yourselves. There will be a long, straight walk to the shrine." She started forward without hesitation.

Mike had to hurry, kicking aside a tangle of rollweeds in her path. Vreely's troopers grabbed torches from the jumbled stack just inside the doorway. When the flames were burning brightly, Mike urged her forward with a gentle hand on her lower back. He could feel how tense she was, like a drawn bow. Moving his free hand to clasp hers as they walked through the corridor, Mike kept a sharp eye out for snakes. He caught glimpses of intricate, faded wall paintings emerging from the shadows as they passed, temporarily illuminated by the flickering torches. Every few feet, small statues were set into niches in the walls. *The entire place has the air of an abandoned museum. How are we supposed to get a key or anything else here?*

"Snake!" yelled Johnny, firing his gun at the same moment.

Screaming, Shalira wrapped herself around Mike, blocking any chance he had at making a shot. A scaly red-and-brown body that had slithered from one of the niches fell lifelessly to the floor by Saium's feet, although the jaws still snapped a few times. The guardsman jumped back and pumped another two bullets into it for good measure. The snake was easily four feet in length.

Shalira clutched at Mike and buried her head on his shoulder. Her words were muffled, her voice shaking. "I hate snakes. Right now, we're living in one of my worst nightmares come true."

"It's all right. I'm not going to let anything hurt you," Mike whispered, giving her shoulders a reassuring hug. He set her gently on her feet in the center of the corridor. "You concentrate on getting the key and let me worry about the wildlife, okay?"

"Each to our own mission." She put a hand to her hair, readjusting one of the emerald-tipped pins, before resuming her progress to their ultimate goal.

Mike could see an open, lighted area ahead. Sure enough, in ten paces the corridor widened into a round room. Skylights in the domed roof allowed the hot sun to provide a level of illumination totally lacking in the corridors, while the thick stone walls kept the temperature reasonable.

To Mike's right, two snakes slithered away through cracks in the wall. He'd been warned about the highly venomous reptiles in the briefing before landing on Mahjundar. Since the briefing he'd received said a bite was invariably fatal in mere minutes, Mike was happy to see the creatures were nonaggressive today. It was anybody's guess how well the generic antivenom shots in Johnny's medkit would work.

Chittering in protest at being disturbed, a flock of gray birds circled the room in a mad whirl of wings right below the ceiling before flying out a central skylight. When the room was still, Mike made a rapid survey. The walls had at one time been painted a bright white, but were now grimed over, with peeling plaster.

Ten mystical symbols had been painted at intervals on each wall, at what would be shoulder height for Mahjundans. The red, green, turquoise and yellow drawings had undoubtedly been blindingly bright at one time, but were now faded into near obscurity from sheer age. Mike found his vision blurred if he tried to stare at any one of the symbols for longer than a moment.

In the center of the room was a raised dais, edged in bright turquoise tile, supporting a waist-high, square block of dull red stone. The same ten symbols had been painstakingly etched into the altar's sides, highlighted at one time with yellow, bits of which could be seen in the deep grooves of the carving.

Shalira stepped forward, going up onto the dais, drawing Mike with her. She was holding his hand so tightly he couldn't have stayed behind without violently pulling free. *But I want to stand here with her, support her.*

Leaning over, Mike realized the top of the red stone was polished enough for him to see his reflection in the surface. "No dust?" *How is that possible?*

The top had two perfectly shaped oval indentations, each about a yard long and half a yard wide at the center. Although several messy nests were in the rotunda directly above, there were no bird droppings anywhere on the stone. Flicking the safety before holstering his gun, Mike reached out to touch the gleaming surface.

"What the hell?" His fingers stopped six inches above the block, as if he'd tried to press his hand through glass. Cursing, he yanked his hand away. His skin, reddened where it had met the invisible obstacle, felt if it had been scorched by open flame.

"Careful," Shalira said. "The Altar of the Ten Gods deals harshly with the uninitiated."

"I'll take your word for it. I meant no disrespect." He blew on his fingers. "How old is this place? Why doesn't your father do something about fixing it up?"

"The temple dates to the earliest beginnings of civilization on Mahjundar. There used to be hundreds of these temples scattered throughout the empire. But the worship of the Ten Gods is fading, except perhaps in the most rural areas." Shalira frowned. "Empress Maralika doesn't believe in their power, preferring new temples, alternate beliefs."

Mike considered the fading paint. "So she doesn't exactly encourage your father to spend money on the old gods?"

Shalira pursed her lips. "I was sure I heard my father approve funds for this work."

Mike remembered what he'd been told in his briefing about the Empress Maralika's accounts in the big, secretive banks on New Switzerland. *I bet I know where the authorized funds ended up.*

Vreely was tapping his booted foot impatiently on the bottom step. "We're wasting time. Get the key, Your Highness, and let us get on with the journey."

"What do you need to do?" asked Mike, pivoting her to face him.

She faltered, closing her eyes and rubbing her forehead. "I—I'm not totally sure. I observed the ceremony performed in reverse at my great-uncle's funeral, when my father commended the key for his tomb to the keeping of the Ten."

Of course, she hadn't been blind then. This whole errand must be stirring up powerful memories for her—better get it over with as fast as possible. Mike glanced at the impatient Mahjundan officer. *Maybe Vreely's right about some things.*

"We must make an offering." The princess freed her hand from Mike's. "Could you open this pouch for me and set the items in my hands?" Fumbling at her belt, she detached a small red leather purse, which she held out.

Unknotting the rawhide strip at the neck of the purse, he removed ten different things loosely packed inside, carefully depositing them in Shalira's cupped hands. There was an iridescent feather from some rare bird, a sachet of rich perfume, an exquisite jade carving of a deer-like creature, ten tiny golden bells strung on a fine chain, and other miniature treasures he'd no time to examine. *One for each god, I suppose.*

"This is the last item." He laid an enameled brooch encrusted with baroque pearls on top of the pile in her hands and tucked the small purse away in a pocket.

Tightening her fingers around the precious hoard, Shalira raised her arms. Bathed in sunlight streaming from the skylights, she chanted in a variation of the Mahjundan language that his hypnotraining hadn't included. Her voice was lyrical, mesmerizing in the way the rhythm rose and fell. Realizing he was dizzy, Mike blinked hard, reaching to steady himself against the red block.

Within the chamber, a humming had begun, like an accompaniment to the chanting, but in a much deeper tonal range. The strange sound vibrated through his spine and behind his ears in an unpleasant way. As if a breeze had sprung up inside the room, the dust and debris on the floor shifted hither and yon, moved into small piles. It was as if he and Shalira were cut off from the others, isolated on the island of the dais by sound and a wall of wind. Now the princess lowered her offering toward the block's surface. Mike reached out, guiding her hands toward the closer of the two oval depressions. Electricity tingled through his nerves, blue fire danced in the air and he couldn't release her fingers. His hands supported hers.

This time there was no invisible shield to prevent him from touching the stone. Contact with the altar hit Mike like ice water. Shivering, he felt Shalira trembling violently next to him, but the princess continued her ritual with no break in the song, although her voice grew wobbly. At last, their hands separated, and he jerked his fingers back. Shalira held one final, lingering note, suddenly opening her cupped hands.

The gifts she offered drifted the last few inches into the stone oval. One by one, as if falling through thick glue, the items touched the rock and disappeared in showers of red, yellow and turquoise sparks.

Shalira fell silent, licking her lips and lowering her head. She took a step backward. Hastily, Mike reached out to steady her and prevent her from toppling off the edge of the dais. Head against his chest, she leaned into him. "Is the offering accepted?" Her whisper was so thready he could barely hear the words. "Is there a key in the other bowl?"

"Lords of Space, there *is* a key." He guided her fingers to the key that had materialized as a result of her entreaty. Carved from the same red rock as the altar, the massive key had three sparkling jewels set in the long shaft. The gemstones glowed red, yellow and turquoise as Shalira clutched it to her chest.

"Are you all right?" Johnny leaped onto the small dais. "The dust kicked up so fierce I couldn't see you. When I tried to climb up to watch your six, I was knocked clean off my feet. Felt like a force field. I'll have the bruises to show for it tomorrow." His focus drifted to the princess, and he whistled. "Proper key for a tomb you've got there."

"Your Highness, if we're finished in here, I think you need to get into the sunshine and relax for a few minutes before we open your mother's tomb," Mike said. "You're shaking like a leaf. I don't know about anyone else, but I could use a shot of black wine."

"I'd like to sit and drink a cup of tea," she agreed in a faint, raspy voice, clearing her throat.

The small party retraced their steps through the dark corridor without incident. Evidently the snakes had decided it was better to be somewhere else for the balance of this afternoon.

Rojar was waiting at the bottom of the stairs. He eyed the key Shalira was carrying, but didn't ask any questions. In one hand he had a mug of steaming tea for the princess. In the other, he held the wineskin. "Here, I brewed spice tea for you, Your Highness. I've attended enough royal funerals to know the chanter needs an energy-reviving drink after the ceremony. I've fixed up a place in the shade for you to sit."

"Thanks," Mike said on Shalira's behalf, taking the wineskin. "Lead the way."

They took a break for at least half an hour while Shalira gradually recuperated. Sitting on a horse blanket Rojar spread out for her, she drank two cups of the spice tea. She kept her eyes closed as if her blindness wasn't enough of a barrier between herself and the world right now. Mike had a long drink from the wineskin, enjoying the inner warmth it provided. Despite the heat of the relentless sun, he felt chilled to the bone. Sitting beside the princess, he wondered what challenge they'd face next on this strange quest. He debated offering Johnny's services with the medkit, but on the whole she seemed physically fine, merely withdrawn.

After she'd downed the second cup and had more color in her cheeks, Mike touched her hand. "How are you doing?"

Opening her eyes, turning to the sound of his voice, she placed the empty mug on the blanket beside her and stretched. "Nothing to complain about. The tea helped steady my nerves. I didn't mean to be rude, but I've been praying and resting, taking in the energy left in this holy place," she said, rising but not moving away from him.

It was hard to concentrate with Shalira standing so close to him, her perfume a gentle accent. As he hastily stood, Mike fought his physical reaction to her proximity, resisted the temptation to sweep her into his arms. Forbidden fruit indeed.

"Do you know," she said, "if I'd been born a thousand years ago, I would have been a high priestess? Even a hundred years ago, the gods were still respected, worshipped. I could have found my home in a temple, made my place happily, because I'm one who can channel the energy of the gods. Blind or not, I would have been cherished." She bit her lip and winced, as if perhaps she'd not meant to reveal so much emotion.

"Is channeling energy what we did in there?" It was as good a description as any of what he'd felt during the ceremony.

She nodded, a wistful expression on her face. "Yes. I've never felt anything but crumbs of the power before. Until today, with you at my side. But now the people venerate other gods or no gods at all, and there's no need for priestesses with my gift. No need for me even here at what used to be an important shrine."

Saium walked up, interrupting the intimate moment. "Are you ready to proceed, Your Highness?"

"We'd better get going if we want to finish our task and leave the valley by dusk." Her voice was husky, probably from the singing, but definitely stronger. "We can ride into the valley. Mother's tomb is the fifteenth one on the left side of the canyon."

"I'll recognize it." Saium stared fixedly at the key.

"Then let's get going," Mike said.

CHAPTER FOUR

As he rode through a narrow defile at the crumbling western side of the temple, Mike realized the canyon opened up beyond. The valley was long, perhaps five miles. He hadn't ridden more than a hundred feet before passing the first of many heavy stone doors, each set flush into the canyon walls. The massive stone portals were well over nine feet tall, carved from single slabs of stone. In the center of each door was an indentation shaped like the key Shalira carried.

"I think my father will be the last to be buried here," Shalira said somewhat sadly as the column picked its way through the valley. "If there are any priests left by the time he passes on. Empress Maralika certainly doesn't intend to be placed here, although I know he's authorized a tomb to be prepared for her. I doubt if her son, the heir, subscribes to any religious views, never having heard a whisper of anything spiritual about him." She laughed.

"No problem with grave robbers, I'm guessing," Johnny said as they rode past another huge, blank door, this one veined in gray and black marble. "I wouldn't want to be here at night. I can see why Vreely is so pushy about us getting the job done and getting out of here."

Saium spoke up. "The next door will be the emperor's tomb, then we arrive at the tomb of Shalira's mother."

Mike rode past a dark, gaping hole in the canyon. One of the big black slabs of rock lay flat on the ground, waiting for the not-too-distant day when it would seal off the mortal remains of Emperor Kajastahn.

A few hundred feet farther was a sealed tomb, and here the party stopped. Shallow steps had been cut into the canyon wall, leading to the door. On the face of the panel, above the key-shaped indentation, a single word in the elaborate cursive form of the Mahjundan written language had been painstakingly chiseled.

"Lindia," Saium barely breathed the name. He crowded his horse against Shalira's and reached for her hand.

Mike glanced at the old guardsman. *What exactly did the relationship between the emperor's Favorite Wife and her faithful guard involve? Man's acting pretty broken-up, even all these years later.* Waiting patiently for Shalira to regain her self-control, he let his horse crop at tufts of grass. The princess was speaking to Saium in a low voice, both appearing to be having trouble maintaining their composure.

Acting like a man with a deadline, Vreely wasn't so restrained. He and his troops were already dismounting and fanning out in the narrow canyon. "Your Highness, you must get on with your duty," Vreely said, gripping her horse's bridle. "We don't want to be caught here after dark."

"Give her a break, man," Mike said. "She doesn't need your prodding to do her duty."

Horse pushing his a bit to the side, Shalira reached out in his direction. "I'm reluctant to disturb my mother's sleep, but Captain Vreely is right. Will you help me dismount, please?"

Sliding off the stallion, Mike came to lift Shalira from her saddle, setting her gently on the first stair, holding her a fraction of a second longer than necessary.

"I've never seen a tomb opened," Shalira told him, fidgeting with the oversize key. "I only hope this will work."

"You've been spectacularly successful so far." Mike tapped one finger on the key. "You got this, right?"

Biting her lip, she nodded.

"Well, then no reason for things to fall apart now. Let me help you up the stairs—there's a lot of loose gravel."

Hand in hand with him, she climbed the five stairs, coming to stand in front of the massive slab of black stone. Shalira positioned the key in front of her face and Mike wrapped his fingers around hers to orient it to the door's indentation. With Mike's help, she pressed the key into the depression, matching all the curves to the lines of the strange locking mechanism.

The jewels in the shaft of the key flashed, and there was an audible click. Howling wind shrieked through the canyon, buffeting them all. Mike's ears were keen enough to hear the grinding of some inner mechanism as the door prepared to open. Grabbing Shalira unceremoniously, he carried her down the stairs, joining their fellow travelers, now scattered about on the far side of the canyon.

When the noise stopped, the wind and miniature dust storm died away. Mike gazed across the canyon to see the door hanging wide open, suspended on invisibly set hinges.

"All right, door's open," he said, jaw clenched. This spooky stuff made him nervous. "Now what?"

"The princess goes into the tomb and retrieves her clan insignia." Vreely slapped his black riding gloves against his thigh. "I suppose you want to accompany her into the tomb, as you did at the temple, outworlder? Be my guest! My men and I'll stay out here while you consort with the dead."

With an air of having lost all interest in the proceedings, the Mahjundan shouted orders to his troopers to light a fire and make him something to eat. Mike stared after him speculatively, then glanced over to meet Johnny's narrowed eyes. His cousin's furrowed brow and thinned lips suggested he felt the same concerns Mike had about what Vreely might be planning.

"Please, come with me," Shalira begged, apparently mistaking his silence for reluctance. "Saium and Sergeant Danver may come also, but I don't want others to intrude on my mother's sleep."

Unconcerned, not offended at his exclusion, Rojar handed Johnny the two torches he'd brought along from the temple. "You'll need these."

"Keep an eye on things, will you?" Mike said in a low tone meant for Rojar's ears alone, before taking the princess's hand to lead her to the steps once more. Together, they climbed the small incline and waited for Johnny and Saium to catch up.

Shalira raised her head, sniffing the air. "Do I smell moss blossoms?"

Reaching inside his tunic, Saium yanked out a slightly crushed, wilting bouquet. Glaring at Mike as if daring him to laugh, the old warrior said, "Lindia loved flowers."

Stretching her hand to brush the blossoms, Shalira smiled. "So she did."

Johnny lit the torches and held one out to Saium, which he took in his free hand. Then the quartet stepped into the entrance of the tomb.

The air inside was cool. Mike remembered having been told once that caves maintained an even temperature in the fifty-degree range. *Tomb like this must be similar to a cave.* The torches only partially alleviated the total darkness, but did reveal murals on the walls of the vestibule. The vertical surfaces had been smoothed and painted with an intricate pattern of bright green leaves and tiny pink flowers, creating a realistic effect in the uncertain, flickering light.

"Wait a minute," Mike said as Shalira tugged at him to keep walking. "Hadn't we better take some precaution to keep the door from closing by accident?"

She shook her head. "The door would resist any force on Mahjundar right now."

Saium nodded to reinforce Shalira's words. "Go outside, try it, if you doubt."

Even though both the princess and her guard were convinced, Mike wasn't taking their safety on faith. "Johnny, go check."

In a silence broken only by the hissing of the burning torches, Mike waited with his companions until Johnny rejoined them, his face a study in bewilderment. "She's right. I couldn't budge the door an inch, even with Rojar pushing too."

Struck by a new problem, Mike touched Shalira's arm to get her attention. "How are we going to shut the portal when you're finished? Surely you don't plan to leave your mother's tomb open for any passerby to trespass?"

"According to the legend, the door will stay open for three hours before closing itself, the key vanishing." Shalira smiled. "Don't worry, we'll complete my errand and be on our way before you know it."

Glad she can sound so calm about it all. Setting foot in the tomb had apparently steadied her nerves while the surroundings had the opposite effect on him. Concerned, he gave his cousin a once over, but Johnny avoided his gaze.

"Any other questions, or can we proceed?" Saium edged toward the dark mouth of the tunnel.

"Hell no, no more conversation," said Johnny, waving him on with an extravagant gesture. "Let's get on with the tomb raiding."

Only one passage led out of the vestibule. After setting the timer on his wrist chrono, Mike took Shalira by the hand to walk down the ramp leading deep into the canyon side. The torchlight illuminated intricate floral paintings on both sides.

Like being in an arbor on a moonless night. "Are all the family tombs decorated this way?" Mike asked.

"I've never seen the tomb," Shalira responded. "But it's been described to me. I was told my father put his finest artists and craftsmen to work on the task as soon as he realized Lindia was dying."

"Not much farther now," Saium warned.

Mike stumbled over an unseen threshold as the passage ended abruptly in a large open room. There were brass sconces set into the wall on either side of the entryway. Johnny and Saium stuck their burning torches into the waiting sockets.

"Incredible." Mike visually quartered the room. "If I hadn't seen this myself, I wouldn't have believed it."

A perfect oval, the chamber resembled the inside of a white lattice gazebo. More of the trompe l'oeil flowering vines had been painted as if twining through the latticework. Here and there, tiny jeweled, birdlike creatures like the myrdima which had serenaded them at the sacred glade were set into the foliage. Even the roof above was painted to mimic a dark blue starred sky, with the planet's two moons rising on the far side of the vault.

Mike stared for a long minute. *Some Mahjundan Michelangelo gave his all to this effort.*

"After Shalira was born, her mother never regained her health. She'd lie by the hour in her gazebo, reading or napping." Saium spun in a tight circle, staring at the walls. "The gazebo was Kajastahn's favorite trysting place. Lindia used to say it was their private world, away from all the troubles of the court and the harem."

Shalira dropped Mike's hand, taking a tentative step toward the sound of Saium's voice. The old man folded her into a bear hug and Mike heard the princess choke back a sob. Unseen by her, the grizzled warrior wiped away a furtive tear with the back of his hand.

Motioning to Johnny, Mike walked out into the center of the "gazebo," where the pure-white marble sepulcher had been placed. A life-size figure of a woman had been carved on the top as if lounging on a couch, waiting for expected company. Delicately colored stone resembled living flesh in the torchlight. Glancing at the effigy's face, Mike retreated an involuntary step.

The lifelike brown eyes were half-open, the coral-colored lips parted as if to speak.

Annoyed at himself for being so jumpy, Mike walked closer, examining the statue. Lindia was an older version of Shalira all right, but to his eyes, the princess was more delicately featured than her mother, with a sweetness of expression lacking in Lindia. The stone face, though undeniably beautiful by any human standard, displayed a hint of something off-putting.

"Probably the sculptor's fault," he muttered, then checked his chrono. "We've used up about half an hour, folks. I think we'd better find the clan insignia. Do we have to move this statue, open the casket itself?"

"Oh, no!" Shalira's horrified exclamation echoed in the small room. "My mother's remains are not to be touched."

"Merely asking," Mike said, without apology. "I don't see anything in here but the bare walls."

"You wouldn't." Shalira shook her head. "Burial possessions are hidden in secret niches to deter grave robbers should any manage to breach the door spells."

"I don't see any sign of niches, either." Frowning, Johnny rested his hands on his hips and kicked at the edge of a flagstone. "Can't anything be simple on this damned planet?" His voice rose.

"Why don't you take a run to the door and assess the situation outside?" Concerned about his cousin's edginess and knowing Johnny was uncomfortable in enclosed spaces nowadays, Mike thought it might be wise to send him back to the exit.

"Good idea." The sergeant contemplated the two torches, but didn't reach for either. "Guess I don't need a light. That passage was the definition of straight and narrow and my enhanced night vision works under these conditions if I just remember to activate the implant." Chuckling, he headed out the single opening, running one hand along the stone wall as a guide.

With Saium's help, Shalira doffed her lightweight riding cloak, laying the garment gently on the floor. The guardsman withdrew a small leather pouch from his broad belt and placed it safely in her cupped hands. Unknotting the cords by touch took her a moment of fierce concentration, but then she withdrew an object swathed in rolls of velvety cloth. While Saium hovered, making small hand motions as if he wanted to take the bundle from her and open it himself, Shalira extracted a small glass vial. An emerald-green stopper flashed in the smoky torchlight. Even in the gloom of the "gazebo," the liquid contents of this unique container shone and glowed golden.

"What do you have there?" Mike stepped to her side.

Shalira tilted her head in the direction of his voice. "My mother's nurse was a wise woman, a healer, an initiate in the goddess Pavmiraia's secrets. After my brother was killed and I was left blind, she worked tirelessly to gather the ingredients for this potion. Some she had to commission from across the Great Sea, which took several years to acquire. When she had the recipe complete, she secretly left the palace to brew this mix. Whether from the sorcery involved, or whether it was a coincidence, she was near death when she returned, dying within a sevenday." Shalira shook the vial in her hand. "All for the liquid in this bottle."

"What's it supposed to do?" Mike had a sneaking suspicion what Shalira was going to say.

"Restore my sight for the space of an hour. She bade me to keep it safe and use it only if my life depended on my eyes."

"Then perhaps you should save it. Tell me and Saium what to do," Mike suggested urgently, not liking the ominous appearance of the bottle, golden glow or not.

"Don't fear for me." Shalira regarded him so warmly he forgot what he'd planned to say next. "My life does depend on this. If I fail to get the clan insignia, Bandarlok won't marry me. Then I'm doomed to return home and enter the Abbey of the Obedient Sisters, which is a virtual death sentence. The empress will have me killed."

"Shalira—" He stopped, shaking his head. *What am I planning to say? Am I going to offer to take her away from all this, go back to my home world with me?* Mike swallowed hard, surprised into silence by a flood of unexpected emotion choking him.

Not waiting to hear more of his opinions, she unstoppered the little flask, sucked in a breath and held it, drinking the contents in one quick swallow.

Gagging, Shalira staggered backward, dropping the bottle, hands rising to her throat. The vial shattered on the stone floor, spraying shards and droplets of moisture everywhere. Mike rushed to her side, catching her one-handed as she swooned toward the cold floor. "Bring me the cloak to wrap her in. She's convulsing."

Avoiding the broken glass, Mike sat on the freezing stone floor, cradling the unconscious princess while she shook. "Damn it, we never should have let her drink that stuff. What if it's poison?"

"Her nurse would never have poisoned Shalira," the older man answered, his face calm, voice low. "Have faith, as Her Highness does, and wait, outworlder."

Skidding on the stone floor, Johnny came running into the chamber, gun in hand. "We got major troubles." He stopped short at the sight of the unconscious Shalira. "Lords of Space, now what?"

Holding the princess tight against the tremors racking her body, Mike frowned. "She drank something she believes will restore her vision and the side effects are pretty bad. What's happening in the valley?"

"We've been double-crossed. Vreely showed his colors all right. Heard shots when I was walking to the door, so I double-timed it out to the steps and found Rojar in a helluva fight with three guards. Next thing I know, they're all shooting at me, so I returned fire and ducked inside."

Not good, not surprising. I should have taken more precautions. Mike shifted to create a more comfortable position for Shalira, whose tremors were decreasing. "What happened to Rojar?"

"Don't know. Last I saw, he was surrounded by guards, yelling for us to get out of the tomb before it was too late." Johnny was keyed up, eyes wide, movements jerky.

"Any other way in or out of here, Saium?" Mike asked.

The guardsman shook his head.

Mike gathered Shalira in his arms and carefully stood. "Here, take the princess. Johnny and I are going to the door to check things out. You stay put, understand?"

Accepting the princess's limp form while she began to murmur indistinguishable words, perhaps beginning to revive, Saium said, "As soon as she wakes, we'll search for the insignia."

"Good plan." Activating his own enhanced night vision with a mental command to the implant, Mike drew his gun. Left a guy with a hell of a headache if he used the vision for very long, but sure came in handy.

The two men worked their way up the corridor cautiously, in case any of Vreely's men had ventured inside, but the tomb remained empty. Evidently, their enemy was willing to let time do its work and seal them in with no further effort required from him or his men. Experimentally, Mike threw a rock across the opening and out the tomb door. He was rewarded with a fusillade of the local bullets. Ricocheting inside the vestibule alarmingly, the gunfire forced the two Sectors Special Forces operators to duck into the protective cover of the tunnel.

"Bastard must have all his guns trained on this entrance," Mike said.

"Yeah. Be suicide to try to rush them. How much time left?" Johnny was breathing hard.

Mike glanced at the readout of his chrono. "Two hours. We've got no reason to think the spell won't work, either. So far, all of Shalira's other predictions about this place have been right on the mark." He pounded his fist against the wall. "I thought Vreely might try something after the temple, but when he didn't, I figured we were home safe."

"You've been kinda distracted by Her Highness." Johnny's remark wasn't accusatory, just factual. He was making a quick search of the small vestibule. "Nothing we can use in here."

"And no cover anywhere close to the mouth of the tomb, either." Mike considered their options, which took a depressingly short amount of time. "You stay here in case Vreely gets tired of waiting and decides to rush us. I'm going to the crypt to let Saium know the situation, see if there's anything in the burial chamber we can use."

"Maybe the princess could whip us up some magic," Johnny said without much humor, settling into a defensive stance with a view out the tomb door.

"I'll be sure to ask her." Mike clapped Johnny on the shoulder and ducked into the long tunnel.

"Yeah, you do that," his cousin called after him.

Mike traced his steps back to the burial chamber as fast as he dared, given the sloping, slippery tunnel. *Wouldn't do anyone any good for me to break a leg.* Nothing presented itself as a feasible course of action. *No use wishing for all the modern gear stashed in our saddle bags. Might as well hope for the battleship Andromeda to come and hover with all guns blazing.*

As Mike slid into the chamber, Shalira was getting to her feet, leaning heavily on Saium's arm. They both regarded him with hopeful expressions but he had to shake his head.

"Vreely's got us nailed down. If we take one step outside, we're going to be blown away."

Releasing her grip on the guardsman's arm, Shalira took a deep breath and walked directly to Mike. Speechless with surprise, he realized she could now see with those great, luminous brown eyes. *How is this possible?*

"I refuse to believe this trip has all been for nothing. You'll think of something, I know it." She focused on his face for a long, aching minute, as if memorizing each detail. Reaching out, she touched his cheek gently. Before he could react, she kissed him lightly on the lips, then walked across the "gazebo."

Stopping at the foot of her mother's sarcophagus, Shalira stared into the carved face, so like her own, and yet so different.

"I don't know if I can do this," she said on an in-drawn sob, rubbing her eyes. "My eyes burn."

Mike holstered his gun and joined her, taking her in his arms. "Irritated by the smoke from the torches," he said. "You don't have to go on with this search for the insignia if you don't want to. There—there could be other options—"

"No." She laid a finger gently on his lips for a second. "I must carry out my father's instructions. It's his dying wish for me to marry Bandarlok, to ally our people more closely again. He's depending on me. I know you'll think of a way to get us past Vreely, so I've no choice but to do my part."

Resolute, she dried her eyes and pushed herself free of his embrace. Walking to the foot of the effigy, she took a deep breath and sang the first measures of a chant, a low-pitched, wordless melody. Standing motionless, she extended her hands, palms up in appeal.

This time there was no shrieking wind to answer her. Only a brilliant spark of fierce red light, dancing above Lindia's carved fingers. The shadowy illumination from the torches made it appear that the hands of the effigy lifted slightly, casting the red spark toward the wall. A deep feminine sigh, like the sound of a name, echoed in the chamber, but Mike was sure the sound didn't come from Shalira's lips. The hair on the back of his neck stood on end when the deep whisper repeated again and he retreated an instinctive step.

Shalira's attention was riveted on the spark, which danced fleetingly above her head before shooting in a direct line across the chamber, striking the wall in an explosion of soundless miniature stars, all of which winked out before touching the floor.

Eyes burning, Mike blinked. The afterimage danced in front of his closed eyelids. When he risked opening his eyes again, Shalira was standing in front of the spot where the red spark had self-destructed.

Mike scrutinized the statue. *Nothing but cold stone.* Rolling his shoulders to break the spell, he walked over to the princess.

Searching the walls for something, running her fingers lightly over the painted surface, she didn't even acknowledge his presence. "Saium, bring the torch."

As the guardsman brought the light closer for her, Mike could see a tiny glint of red fire in one bird's jeweled eyes. Shalira pointed excitedly, shaking her finger at the spot. "The key to the niche must be here."

Leaving them to their task, Mike crossed to the mouth of the corridor, listening for the sound of shots, which would mean Vreely had abandoned caution and was coming in.

"All right," he heard Shalira say with great determination. He swung back to see her standing with her hands on her hips, directly in front of the jeweled bird, which Mike now realized was an actual stuffed creature, with rubies inserted in place of the eyes, not merely one of the skillful wall paintings.

Shalira lifted the tiny bird off its concealed perch, twisting the small branch clockwise with her free hand. A small door to the left shot open with a snap, revealing a square cavity at chest height. She nodded to Saium, who reached inside gingerly and brought a long, gnarled wooden staff into the light. It was topped with a magnificent, lifesized, painted carving of a bird of prey. "Our clan insignia," Saium said in a hushed whisper. Carefully placing this against the painted wall, he then reached into the safe once more, lifting out a necklace gleaming golden in the torchlight, set with a large number of pale, milky gemstones and black pearls as large as grapes. In the torchlight, enhanced by his vision implant, Mike could see an inscription running across the edges of the center panel, stamped into the gold.

Eyes wide, face set in reverent lines, Shalira took the ornamental collar and picked up the staff. Saium rushed to get the leather saddlebag he'd carried into the tomb. The Mahjundans wrapped the clan treasures in a soft cloth brought along for the purpose, collapsing the cleverly-designed staff upon itself and stowed them away before turning to Mike.

"Yes, now what?" he said, in answer to their unspoken but clear question. "Johnny was hoping you could work more magic."

Taking his request more seriously than he'd intended, she frowned. "I'm sorry, I only know a few chants my nurse taught me, nothing to help us in this situation." She rubbed her eyes with the back of one hand, blinking repeatedly. "My vision is fading in and out. The potion must be wearing off. I feel so strange." Brow furrowed, eyes no longer glowing so brightly in the flickering lights, she stared hungrily at Mike.

"The torches are burning lower too, so we've probably used up most of the good air, which doesn't help how you're feeling." He tried to be reassuring since she seemed to be worried about the diminishing effects of the medicine. "The last resort is a suicide rush out the door before it closes, hoping they can't get all of us. Vreely has us outnumbered so the odds aren't good."

"I'll go first, draw their fire, and then you and the sergeant can attempt to reach cover with the princess," Saium volunteered.

"A good plan for the last resort," Mike agreed. "But we'd draw straws for the point position." He stared at their surroundings for a moment. "I can't believe there isn't another way out of here. No offense, but with all the intrigue and deception I've seen on this planet, I'd think secret passages would be just your thing. Isn't Kajastahn's tomb the next one over?"

"Yes, why?" Shalira asked. "I'm not following your logic."

Mike grinned. "Try to tell me he wouldn't have some kind of passage between his tomb and the one his beautiful Favorite Wife occupies for eternity? How did they get back and forth to this gazebo in real life, anyway? Did he walk through the gardens each time?"

Saium stared at Mike, eyes wide in amazement. "How did you know? The emperor had a secret tunnel running from his private wing of the palace to Lindia's gazebo. He was like a child when he got it all prepared; couldn't wait to show her. She deemed his concerns great foolishness at first, but after we got used to the city ways, she appreciated his ability to come to her without anyone knowing."

"Without Empress Maralika knowing, you mean?" Mike said. "All right then, let's assume he's done the same thing with this gazebo for afterlife trysts."

Peering as closely as the torchlight would allow, they searched the walls for any hidden doors or levers of any kind. Mike made three circuits of the place before he admitted defeat. He joined Saium, who was bent over, clutching at his chest and straining to breathe. Leaning on the wall beside her guardsman, Shalira held her hand over her eyes.

"How did the secret entry to the gazebo work?" Mike asked.

"I was never privy to details," Saium gasped out between harsh inhalations. "She'd have me wait outside the private part of the garden before he arrived."

Mike turned to the princess. "Shalira?"

She shook her head. "I didn't even know there was such a passage, let alone the secret of its use. I will have to ask her."

The lack of oxygen must be affecting her. "What do you mean, ask her? Ask who?"

"My mother, as I did when I sought the location of the tribal insignia," Shalira said, frowning. "Channeling the powers and asking her is the only way to find out for sure."

"Too dangerous, my princess," Saium protested, putting his hand on her arm. "Calling the dead twice brings disaster. She could take us into the eternal night with her!"

"We're going to die for sure if I don't petition her spirit." Pushing her hair out of her face, Shalira shook her head emphatically. "My mother wouldn't commit evil against us. If there's a way out, she'll tell us, but you and Michael will have to do the watching."

When she raised her head, Mike could see the difference in her eyes immediately—pupils no longer glowing with inner light, more like painted glass than the expressive eyes of a living woman. She sighed. "Lead me to the foot of the effigy, and I'll chant once more."

"Wait, let me get Johnny first. If there is a door and if we can get it open, I don't want him to miss his chance to go with us," Mike said. "An escape hatch might not take us to Kajastahn's tomb the way we're hoping, you know."

Running up the narrow corridor, he found it took more effort than before, as the available oxygen was about gone. Johnny was sitting patiently right inside the lip of the tunnel, safely out of sight of those waiting for them to die. The sergeant eyed him as Mike came into the dimly lit vestibule.

"Situation?" Mike asked, taking cover next to Johnny. Breathing fresh air was a relief.

"Vreely hasn't tried anything. Every now and then, his soldiers shoot off a few rounds, to let us know they're still waiting. I heard Shalira's poor servant girl screaming for a while."

Mike shook his head, momentary anger flickering in his heart for those who preyed on the helpless. "There wasn't anything you could do. Now listen up, we're going to try a long shot in the crypt. We're thinking Kajastahn may have ordered a secret passage constructed between his tomb and this one. Trouble is, we already searched for a door with no luck. Shalira is going to ask her mother—" He raised his hand to forestall the question Johnny was plainly going to ask. "I know the whole idea sounds crazy, but then everything *on* this damned planet is slightly nuts, right? We've got forty-five minutes or so left before our only option is the grand suicide rush out the front door funnel of death here."

"Okay, I'm game for conducting a séance. It's as good a way as any to spend the last hour of my life." Holstering his gun, Johnny followed Mike.

The sergeant stood quietly at the edge of the chamber while Mike guided Shalira to the foot of the effigy. Annoyed at himself, Mike realized he was averting his eyes from the statue's cold face. "What we want to see will be a spark of red light," he explained over his shoulder to Johnny.

"Right." Thumbs hooked in his belt, leaning on the wall, his cousin made no effort to keep his skepticism from showing.

"Ready, Shalira?" Mike squeezed her hand as she nodded. "Then let's go for it." He stepped away but stayed close enough to catch her if she became light-headed.

"I hear the doubt in your voice, Sergeant Danver, but channeling the powers and spirits is my gift," she said. Not waiting for a response, she began a low-pitched chant. She extended her arms, hands palms up in supplication, as before.

This time her song droned on for three or four minutes, endlessly repeating the same phrases, but there was no answer whatsoever. The effigy remained uncaring, cold stone, no soft sighs disturbing the air. Shalira broke off mid-verse, swallowed hard, began singing again, her concentration obviously slipping under the strain. Choking a bit, she compressed her lips, shaking her head. Hands on the edge of the bier, head down, breathing hard, she said, "Mother, much as I regret disturbing your rest twice, I need your help. Please."

Mike caught a whiff of intoxicating perfume which hadn't been present before, so intense it robbed his lungs of the already scarce oxygen, leaving him dizzy and short of breath. A dim red spark flickering between the fingers of the statue caught his attention. "Keep trying," he whispered. "I think this idea is going to work."

Echoing through the chamber, a loud crack heralded intense shaking as if an earthquake had begun. Thrown forward, Shalira struck her head a glancing blow on a corner of the bier and fell lifelessly to the floor. Mike tottered against the rolling ground and managed to pick her up, checking the pulse at the base of her throat.

"She's alive." Eyes narrowed, he glared into the face of the statue, locking eyes with it. "Come on, don't condemn your daughter to die in here. Don't let the empress win—show us the goddamn way out."

As if spurred by his curse, the ground below his boots heaved. Mike put out a hand to steady himself and his precious burden against the bier. Touching the cold stone, his fingers burned as if doused in acid and he yanked his hand back. Red sparks flew from the edges of the bier, whirling together like a dust devil, higher and higher, drawing his attention to meet the eyes of Lindia.

There was intelligence in those eyes this time.

He could have sworn Lindia's effigy blinked. Her lips struggling to say something, the beautiful face shifted and shimmered, as if someone or something was trying to animate the cold stone into a semblance of life.

"Just—show—us—the way—OUT," he said, hardly able to form intelligible words, horrified by what he was seeing, "and we'll leave you to your peace."

The red sparks flew, crashing against the wall next to a white-faced, open-mouthed Johnny, promptly winking out. After one more paroxysm, the ground was quiet.

Mike stole a glance back at the statue and he felt as if his heart stopped beating for a moment.

Instead of gazing straight ahead so anyone entering the tomb would immediately see the image of Lindia full in the face, the statue's head was now turned in the direction of the western wall, where the sparks had flown to mark a destination only she'd known.

Carrying the princess, Mike retreated, one cautious step at a time, eyes locked on the statue, until he felt the wall at his back and Johnny's hands catching at his arm.

"Lords of Space, what the *hell* happened? Did you see—"

Mike shook his head impatiently. "Not now."

"Yeah, maybe not ever," Johnny agreed, swallowing hard.

Mike issued orders. "Saium, take the princess. Johnny, get the torches."

"There's nothing here," Johnny said a moment later, as they brought the waning light from the torches to bear on the section of wall indicated by the sparks. Even when he focussed with his special night vision, the surface appeared to hold nothing more remarkable than the intricate paintings of leaves and flowers and the latticework of the gazebo. Mike ran his hand over the fresco as high as he could reach, to the low roof, and then bent to examine the floor.

"Don't worry about singeing my hair. I've got to see." Mike motioned for his cousin to bring the torch closer.

"Found it." He pointed at a small, floor-level button in the wall, painted over as if intended to pass for the center of one of the lavender flowers. Without the guidance of the red sparks, he probably never would have found it, as the small disk was set flush with the stone. Glancing at his companions for a moment, Mike gave the button a push.

He stumbled out of the way, his Special Forces reflexes saving him as part of the floor slid back with a snap, revealing an endless flight of stone stairs. He wasted no time in jubilation over the proof of his theory. "Johnny, take point. I'll bring up the rear. Saium, can you manage the princess?"

Nodding, the older man adjusted her slight weight in his arms. "Of course. But we've got to take the saddlebag with the tribal insignia. We must not go without those."

"Right." Mike crossed to the other side of the chamber, keeping as much distance between himself and the statue as possible. Glass crunched under his boot as he retrieved the bag. Glancing down, he saw shards of the vial that had contained Shalira's magic eye potion. With some vague idea of having a scan run on the substance, once he was home in the Sectors, he carefully selected two of the largest pieces and also scooped up the chipped emerald stopper. Tucking them into the saddlebag, he ran to join his impatient companions.

With Johnny in the lead, the group descended the long flight of slippery, damp steps.

Chapter Five

There were fifty-two stairs leading into the stygian gloom. For lack of anything better to occupy his mind, Mike counted them as he descended. Behind him, he heard a quiet click as the trapdoor sealed off their escape.

"These stairs better be taking us somewhere good, folks," he said, "because the door just closed, and we don't know where the switch is on this side."

At the bottom of the staircase, the corridor widened slightly, so at least they weren't going to be grazing their elbows. Apparently conscious his torch wouldn't burn much longer, and not knowing how far they had to travel, Johnny set a fast pace.

Considering he was suffering most from the bad air, and had the unconscious princess to carry, Saium held up well. Mike was at the rear, saddlebag slung over his shoulder, trying not to think about how much longer his torch would burn. He walked for what seemed like an eternity, treading carefully on the uneven tunnel floor. Water dripped from the ceiling, making the surface slick in spots. Once or twice Mike heard slithering sounds behind them and even swung around abruptly with the torch, but if there were snakes in the gloom, the reptiles stayed hidden.

Finally, the tunnel sloped upward.

"Coming to another flight of stairs, folks," Johnny warned them.

"Hold up," Mike ordered. "Saium, can you slide over enough for me to get past?"

The older man squeezed against the stone wall. Being careful to hold his torch well out of the way Mike moved past to join his cousin. "Vreely may have thought of this, too. We'd better be careful in case he's sent someone into the emperor's tomb to wait."

"Any bright ideas about how we're going to open the trapdoor at this end? This is so nuts anyway," Johnny said, shaking his head. "What the hell was the emperor building tunnels for? Ghosts don't need tunnels to travel, do they?"

Mike laughed. "Nothing makes a whole lot of sense on this planet, does it? I can't remember another mission where things were so bizarre. Be glad Kajastahn thinks his ghost needs a tunnel and trap doors. I'll go first, since I have a better idea what I'm scanning for than you do."

"Be my guest." From his tightly compressed lips to the tense set of his shoulders, Johnny plainly wanted the whole episode to be over. The torch in his hand was quivering ever so slightly. His attitude indicated he would do whatever it took to get out of the tunnel, into fresh air again.

Mike climbed another long flight of stairs, hoping he wouldn't find himself in a life-or-death fight immediately upon entering the next tomb.

No secret control devices were needed here since the practical tomb builders had installed a big lever at the top of the stairs for their own convenience. Pulling on the rough wood, Mike encountered resistance. He tugged again with greater force, awkward and one-handed. The door over his head groaned and opened about half way.

Swearing, he gave one last yank, only to stagger back clutching the broken handle in one hand while the trapdoor stayed where it was.

He called over his shoulder to those at the foot of the stairs. "We'd better get out of this tunnel in a hurry. I broke the works. If this door decides to close, we can't stop it, and we can't reopen it."

As his companions started their ascent up the staircase, Mike lifted his torch past the threshold and cautiously peered into the gloom to reconnoiter. A giant stone bier was waiting in the center of the empty space, carved top set off to the side. From Mike's location, it was impossible to make out any features, but he had no doubt a lifelike effigy of emperor Kajastahn waited patiently to entomb its model. Illuminated in flashes as he moved the torch, murals of hunting and battle scenes met his eyes.

I saw enough of those renderings during our stay at the palace to last me a lifetime. He wasted no more time in examining the surroundings. Happy to see Vreely hadn't covered all contingencies, Mike laid the torch aside on the floor for a minute to pull himself into the room. "All clear. Lift Shalira to me."

He managed to get the unconscious princess out of the tunnel with a lot of difficulty, the close quarters making it hard to maneuver. Mike held her while Saium and Johnny crawled thankfully into the bigger chamber. The guardsman retrieved Mike's abandoned torch as he entered the room.

"Apparently a duplicate of Lindia's in design," Saium said, sweeping his torch carefully through the air. He pointed with the flaming tip. "There's the exit corridor."

"Right," Mike agreed. "Head for the entryway. We can plan our next move there, in fresh air and sunlight. I'll take care of Shalira, and you lug the saddlebag."

Johnny took point again, with Mike behind and Saium bringing up the rear, huffing and puffing. Walking into the diffused sunlight of the vestibule, Mike felt his nerves unwind a bit. Johnny took up his station by the open door while Mike made the princess comfortable on her loosely woven gray cloak, the saddlebag serving as a lumpy pillow.

Satisfied he'd done all he could for now, Mike drew his gun and stepped away. "Johnny, take a recon run and see what Vreely is doing. The other tomb door ought to be closing in about fifteen minutes, so they're probably still on station."

"You planning our own ambush?" asked the sergeant.

Checking his ammo, Mike nodded once. "Hell, yes. I'm not giving Vreely a chance to develop some other clever gambit for finishing us off."

"Back in five." Johnny ducked out the gaping entrance and was gone, working his way down the valley toward Lindia's tomb, taking full advantage of every bit of cover.

Mike considered where best to station Saium. "Stay here and guard the princess. If she regains consciousness while we're gone, I don't want her alone, in an unknown place."

Hefting his gun, the guardsman frowned, bushy white eyebrows drawn together. "I owe those thugs a thing or two myself. I want to be in on the kill."

"Someone has to stay with Shalira." Mike wasn't prepared to yield the point.

"Someone has to stay where with me?" Clutching her head with both hands, Shalira sat up. From her expression and reluctance to move, she was expending a tremendous effort to function. Swaying dizzily, she didn't try to stand. "I have the worst headache."

In a heartbeat Mike was at her side, kneeling to place a steadying arm around her shoulders. "Easy now, we're safe, hidden in the vestibule to your father's tomb."

Closing her eyes, she licked her dry lips. "What happened to me?"

"You banged your head on your mother's sarcophagus and you've been out like a light ever since. You may have a concussion, so I want you to lay back and rest easy." He helped her to recline, smoothing the saddlebag under her head into a more comfortable pillow.

"My mother's spirit showed you the secret passage?" she asked.

Mike didn't answer right away, not wanting to relive any part of the last scene in the tomb, nor try to explain what happened, not even to Shalira.

Fortunately, Johnny came sliding back into the entrance. "The vultures are sitting in the valley, apparently counting the minutes till the door slams, trapping us." He peered into the gloom, eyes narrowed as he realized Shalira had regained consciousness. "Glad you're back in the land of the living, Your Highness."

"Thank you, Sergeant Danver. Michael, what are you going to do?" She half-rose on one elbow and clutched at his arm as he made to rise from where he was kneeling at her side.

Gently, he disengaged his sleeve from her grasp. "We're going to deliver some payback, exact a little justice on your behalf and ours. Stay here, out of harm's way until I return."

If he expected any protest, he didn't get it. The idea they might fail and Vreely's men might find her apparently didn't even occur to the princess. Merely nodding her agreement to stay in the vestibule, she closed her eyes. "Be careful, please, all of you."

"Vreely had his chance at me, and he missed it," Johnny said. "He ain't getting another opportunity, my word on it."

Leading the others from the tomb, Mike moved from the cover of one boulder to the next, ducking behind stands of the impenetrable rollweeds as he worked his way down the valley toward Lindia's tomb. Johnny and Mike had been doing this kind of thing ever since they played kids' games on their home planet and then on a life-or-death basis in the last twenty years as Sectors Special Forces operators on countless worlds. Vreely had no idea of the vengeance that was coming his way.

Saium kept up easily, noiselessly, apparently drawing on the skills he'd learned as a boy in forests and mountains of Mahjundar.

After a few minutes, Mike reached a position to the side and behind Vreely and his men, who were in a half circle facing away from them, all guns trained on Lindia's open tomb.

Nudging Mike's arm, Johnny pointed with his chin, to a spot beyond the horses. A small bundle of colored rags lay there in a broken heap. "The maid," he whispered, face drawn in grim lines.

Mike nodded, continuing his assessment of the soldiers. "Waiting for us to make a last break. Not too worried about the outcome, either, judging by the careless way they're handling their weapons and joking around."

"They're in for a surprise." Showing his teeth in a feral grin, Johnny didn't try to disguise his eagerness to engage the enemy.

"Vreely's mine," Mike said, taking careful aim. "On the count of three."

At the last second, the Mahjundan major moved and Mike's bullet only grazed his shoulder. Johnny and Saium were more fortunate, killing their first targets. The remaining six soldiers dove for cover behind rocks and returned fire. Saium picked off the one closest to the tomb when the man overconfidently ducked out to try for a quick shot.

"Going to be a standoff unless we get the drop on them again somehow," Johnny said, picking off a soldier who rashly tried to streak for better cover. "Mike, let's you and me work our way up the valley wall, try to get behind them."

A fusillade from the empress's guardsmen sent rock splinters flying from the top of the boulder sheltering Mike. Immediately, Saium popped up and answered the fire, ducking to safety as another concentrated round of incoming imploded where he'd been seconds before.

Mike holstered his gun. "You're right. This could go on all day if we don't outmaneuver them. Saium, lay down covering fire while we try to outflank them."

Taking the guardsman's agreement for granted, he and Johnny slunk into the tall grass and boulders, going toward the temple, far enough away to get out of Vreely's direct line of sight, before climbing the steep slope unseen by the Mahjundans. Mike found it fairly easy to work his way across the top of the cliffs without being spotted. Settled in behind a big red rock, Saium shot often enough to keep Vreely's troops pinned down. Mike's plan called for the decoy to keep any of the soldiers from making an escape.

Vreely evidently decided Mike had to be out of ammunition or else trying some kind of flanking maneuver. Suddenly, he and his remaining four men made a concerted rush for the tethered horses. Mike and Johnny shot from their new location high on the valley wall. Rising, Saium started blazing away. Only Vreely managed to get to the mounts. He ducked under one, tugged the reins free and, keeping the horse's bulk between him and the attackers, rode at a breakneck speed toward freedom.

Keeping his balance somehow, Mike slid down the steep hill, gun in hand. He half rolled to a stop next to the thoroughly spooked horses, and stood. Yanking the reins off the tether line, he mounted the black stallion and galloped after Vreely.

The assassin had a head start, but the black horse was faster. Mike was gaining ground easily. As soon as he came into the limited range of the local weapons, he shot, but missed. Vreely returned fire as the horses swerved around the next bend of the valley. Stinging along Mike's cheek signaled the enemy had scored a near miss.

As the half-ruined temple came into sight a few hundred yards ahead, Mike urged his horse to greater speed. *Once Vreely's out of the valley, he could go to ground anywhere and I won't be able to spare the time to hunt him down. Can't let him escape to carry tales to the empress.* Trying to accelerate in response to Vreely's furious goading with his spurs, the other horse stumbled on a patch of gravel, collapsing with a frightened whinny. Mike rode at full gallop, leaning on the stallion's neck to obscure his quarry's field of fire. The Mahjundan fought to free himself from the stirrups, rising and getting off one more shot as Mike dismounted in a spray of gravel from his horse's abrupt stop. The bullet whizzed by his head and Mike didn't give the enemy another chance to kill him, firing at point-blank range.

When Mike came walking slowly back through the twisting valley to his companions awhile later, he was leading the black stallion, Vreely's body slung over the saddle. Johnny and Saium were carrying the bodies of the other soldiers into the open tomb directly across from Lindia's. They stopped to watch him cover the last few yards.

"Vreely's luck finally ran out, gentlemen," Mike said as soon as he was in earshot. "He won't be doing any more dirty work for Maralika."

"Stick him in the tomb with the others." Johnny hooked his thumb toward the cave. "Saium and I figure the less evidence we leave for the empress, the less trouble later."

"Not a bad idea, but how are we going to get the door closed? It isn't even placed on its hinges yet." Mike turned and stared at the black door to Lindia's tomb. Sometime during the fighting, the portal had quietly and efficiently closed itself, per the legend. The key was nowhere to be seen. Mike swallowed hard, imagining their fate if Kajastahn had been a less superstitious man.

"The hell with the damn door," Johnny said. "I'm sick of all this mumbo-jumbo stuff. I figure we can start a big enough rock slide on the valley wall to do the trick. The debris will appear natural. We brought a few small explosive charges in the climbing gear, remember?"

"Anyone check on Shalira?" Mike asked, as he dumped the late Captain Vreely from the saddle.

"Twice," Saium assured him. 'She sleeps now. I told her about the poor maid."

"How'd she take the news?"

"Shalira only asked that we not inter the girl with her murderers," Saium said with a shrug. "The serving girl was a spy for the empress. We were aware of her true loyalties, of course, and Her Highness never confided in her unless it was something she wanted Maralika to hear. Still, the poor girl didn't deserve what was done to her today."

"I guess we can honor the request for a separate resting place. There must be another tomb we can give to the maid." Mike contemplated the long valley.

"I'll take care of it," Saium told them. "I know the proper words to be said."

"Fine. Johnny and I'll finish here."

Johnny pointed at Mike's cheek. "You ok?"

"Just a scratch, nothing to worry about." He touched the mark with his fingertip. "I had to put down the other horse. Vreely's mount broke its leg when it fell."

"Just one more innocent casualty of the day," Johnny said.

Mike and his cousin worked in silence after that, piling the bodies inside the empty tomb. The sun was close to the horizon, ominous black clouds rising over the far rim of the valley.

Dusting his hands on the seat of his pants, Johnny asked, "What's the plan now?"

Hands on his hips, eyes narrowed, Mike surveyed the steep hills surrounding them. "We seal off the tomb with your landslide. Then I want to get the hell out of this valley before the storm breaks. I don't want to spend the night here in the open."

"Couldn't pay me enough to bunk down in one of the empty tombs, not after what we saw today," Johnny said.

"No," Mike agreed. "Talk about an idea with no appeal at all. If you can finish up here, I'm going to get Shalira. If she's awake, she's probably nervous being by herself."

Walking to their packs, Johnny rummaged in the contents, pulling out explosives. "Go ahead. I'm going to set off the charge and start the rockslide in a couple of minutes."

His own grim errand completed, Saium said, "What can I do to help? Those clouds are ominous, and this area is famous for sudden downpours and flash floods. We don't have much time."

"We don't need to be caught in a flash flood," Mike said, frowning in dismay. "Thanks for the warning." He wasn't too pleased with himself. There had been a lot of luck involved in their escape from the empress's plot. *Luck has a way of deserting you just when you need it most.*

Leaving his two companions busily at work on their assigned tasks, Mike hiked through the valley and climbed to the emperor's unfinished tomb.

"It's me," he called as he came through the entrance, not wanting to startle the princess if she was awake.

"Is the fighting over? Are we free to go from here?" She was sitting, arms wrapped around her knees, propped against the rough stone wall. "What of Vreely?"

Crossing to her side and laying a hand on her shoulder in reassurance, Mike said, "He's dead. You'll never be troubled by him again."

Mike was glad she sounded a little stronger than when she had first awakened after escaping her mother's tomb. *Maybe the sleep did her some good.* Even in the half-lit vestibule, he could see a tremendous bruise on her temple, where she'd grazed the edge of the sarcophagus. "I'm here to escort you to the horses. We'll be ready to ride out soon. A major storm is brewing and this valley isn't the place to take shelter, for a lot of reasons. Saium says flash floods come right through here when it rains hard enough."

"No argument from me. I want to leave and never come back. This has been the most awful day." She reached out in his direction. "Please—"

As he pulled her to her feet, she came naturally into his arms. Breathing deeply of her floral perfume, accented with a note of entrancing spice, he enjoyed the way her soft curves pressed against him. Weary from the tension and the adrenaline of battle, Mike stopped fighting his attraction to her, tightening his embrace.

Not resisting the intimacy, she leaned into him, putting her arms around his waist, head resting on his chest. "How can I ever thank you for all you've done today?"

"Johnny and I want to go on living too, you know," he said lightly. "How's your head?"

"Pounding." She touched the area around her eye gingerly. "I keep dozing off, as if I hadn't slept a full night."

He examined the bruise as closely as he could in the dim light. "You might've suffered a concussion. Riding a horse isn't the best idea under the circumstances but we've got no choice. I'll have Johnny do a diagnostic once we make camp outside this valley."

"Thank you, as always." She squeezed his hand.

Seeing the sheen of tears in her eyes, he caught her chin, gently raising her face to his. "What's on your mind?"

"My poor maid." Shalira sighed and swiped at her eyes. "She was the empress's spy, but—"

He laid one finger on her lips. "Don't guilt-trip yourself. Her death wasn't your fault, and you can't help her now. I promise you, Vreely and his men paid for their crimes." Bending over, he gave in to the impulse to kiss her, which he'd been fighting all day. At first it was a gentle meeting of their lips, as she responded to him, instinctively moving closer. Then he held her against him and deepened the kiss, his tongue seeking hers. Her arms went around his neck, her breasts pressing against his chest. Tenderness, desire, and a host of other unfamiliar emotions flooded through him as they clung to each other.

A moment later Shalira protested, pushing against him. Immediately he let her go.

Hand to her lips, eyes wide open, cheeks flushed, she said, "We shouldn't have—*I* shouldn't have indulged myself."

He caught her fingers, bringing her hand to his lips and kissing her palm. "We both wanted to, don't deny the truth."

She slid her hand from his, clenched her fingers into a fist and hid it behind her. She half-turned away from him. "It doesn't matter what I wanted."

Mike was torn between duty and desire, buffeted by emotions that had broken loose from where he'd locked them away. Unsure what to do or say, unsure what he'd do with her answer, but driven to ask, he said, "Are you still set on traveling to the highlands? Marrying this guy you've never met?"

"You speak as if I have freedom to make choices." Her immediate response was surprisingly angry in tone. "I must carry out my duty to my father and marry Bandarlok. There's a treaty to be honored and a large dowry was paid, so the chieftain would agree to the union." One hand raised as if to fend him off, Shalira retreated.

Mike caught her in his arms when she stumbled over loose rocks on the tomb's floor. "What if there was an alternative? Would you be willing to consider it?"

Averting her face, Shalira's voice was low and crisp. "You're talking madness now. What alternative, as you call it, do I have? Where else can I go? Back to the capital? I told you, the empress will have me killed. The emperor would do nothing to prevent it, since I'd have sullied his name by breaking the marriage agreement. Are you suggesting I wander alone in the badlands until I perish?"

Wishing he hadn't baldly blurted the question out, Mike tried to fix his mistake without fully committing himself to a future course of action. "Of course not. You could—you could ask for asylum in the Sectors."

He wanted to protect her, keep her safe from all the troubles of her own world. The idea of handing her over to the unknown, probably barbarian, forest chieftain felt wrong. The reality of never seeing her again afterward was like a knife to his heart. She was meant to be *his*, he knew it to the core of his being but she had to make the choice. "I can make it happen, if you choose. I wouldn't mention the possibility otherwise."

She waited in silence for a moment, as if expecting him to add something else to his explanation. When he didn't, she threw out her arms. "What would I, a blind exile from backwater Mahjundar, do in your outworld? Throw myself on the mercy of your politicians? When they desperately want to make a treaty with my father so they can exploit our mineral resources?" Snorting in a most unladylike fashion, Shalira raised her head. "I refuse to be an object of pity, a recipient of charity. At least here I have a place, precarious and unappealing as it may seem to you." Eyes flashing, lips compressed, she brushed tears away. "But even more important, I must carry out the emperor's wishes."

Mike wanted to take her in his arms again. There was so much more to say. He licked his lips, reached out to her but she held herself stiffly away from him as soon as she felt his touch. He kept his gentle hold on one slender wrist. "No, you're mistaking my meaning. I apologize, Your Highness, I'm expressing myself badly. I've started this all wrong." He ran his other hand through his hair and groaned at his ineptitude. Whatever had possessed him to bring the subject up without preamble? Without committing himself? "I didn't mean to distress you, and I apologize. I just thought, I mean, on the trail these last few days, at the temple, in the tomb...it seemed there was something between us, something we both felt, or I'd never have spoken."

Shalira shook her head. "The subject is finished. It has to be."

He let his arms drop and stepped back a little. *I'll try again later, after dinner perhaps, when she's calmer. I know there's something between us, attraction she can't deny. Maybe I should have started a little more slowly on asking her to come with me. Led up to the subject.* "Shall I escort you to the horses now?"

"Yes, Major Varone. I think you'd better." She stood stiffly in front of him, wrapping herself in the cloak he handed her. There was a minute of silence, as neither made any move toward the entrance to the tomb. Finally, Shalira spoke again without looking in Mike's direction. "I don't want you to misunderstand. I never meant to hurt you."

Hoping she was rethinking her plan, he said, "Then let me explore getting you some other options—"

But the princess was shaking her head. "You're an officer. You understand the demands of duty. No less than any soldier, I must carry out the emperor's orders. There's no use, no use at all, in discussing anything else. What I might want, what I might feel as a woman, rather than a princess carrying out the terms of the emperor's treaty, none of that counts. Don't you see? I've been given no choices to make." A single tear rolled down her cheek and she closed her eyes. "The things you spoke of are impossible. Perhaps if we'd met under other circumstances, but as matters stand, I have no choice. Honor demands I walk the road I've agreed to. I have to live with myself, Major."

"We'd better get back to the others." Mike repressed the urge to wipe the tears from her face and kiss her again. *She made her position clear all right, no point in prolonging the pain for either of us.* "Johnny should be setting off an explosion to trigger a landslide any minute now, so don't be dismayed by the sudden noise, your highness."

But Johnny unexpectedly came through the tomb opening. "We've got complications."

Mike contained his exasperation, keeping his voice level despite an overwhelming urge to swear. "Now what?"

The sergeant glanced at Shalira. "I uh, I think the lady's fiancé has come to collect her. Big guy, leading about twenty armed riders, just came galloping into the valley. Saium's palavering with them now in some dialect we weren't trained on."

"Bandarlok came," Shalira exclaimed, "I trusted he would."

Despite the immediate anger rising in his heart, Mike had ice in his veins. "You sent for him? When?"

"I sent word to him of my fears of treachery, told him he might lose all if he waited for Vreely to bring me to the highlands. Saium found a reliable messenger, paid a sizable bribe." She frowned, smoothing her dress with a nervous gesture. "I'd suggested Bandarlok meet my caravan before we reached the temple, but perhaps there were unavoidable delays."

"Was this before or after you had your father draft Johnny and me into escorting you?" Mike tried not to let his anger show through, but Shalira recoiled as if he'd slapped her.

"I—I hadn't met you, had no idea of asking you for help—"

"But then we came along and you thought you'd hedge your bets. Nicely done, Your Highness. I guess I'm a sucker for tears and sad stories." *How could I forget she was raised in the poisonous stew of the palace? I was briefed—it's all games and manipulation with her people, and she's apparently no different.* Still burning, rightly or wrongly, from her refusal to even discuss an attempt to seek asylum in his world, Mike used this new development to stoke the flames of his anger so the pain of losing her wouldn't strike so deep. "Johnny, let's escort the lady to her eager bridegroom. Then we can proceed on our own mission with no further delay."

Without another word he guided her from the tomb and down the stairs, Johnny trailing behind with the saddlebag containing the relics they'd retrieved. A large group of colorfully dressed warriors, some armed with bows, others carrying swords or guns, was waiting at the foot of the stairs. The men inspected Shalira with interest, the boldest making laughing comments behind their hands. Off to the side Saium stood, frowning. He pushed past the newcomers to meet Shalira and her escorts.

"Which one is the man of the hour?" Mike asked, releasing Shalira's hand. He made a quick assessment of the newcomers. *Can't say I like the looks of any of these brigands.*

"Bandarlok waits for the princess a short distance from here," Saium said as he took her elbow to lead her away from the tomb entrance. It was slow-going over the rocky ground and Shalira was unusually unsteady. Over his shoulder, Saium added, "The chief said it wasn't proper for her to begin their relationship by descending from the heights while he stood on the ground."

"Really?" Still angry at how Shalira had maneuvered him, Mike was briefly tempted to mount his horse and leave the vicinity, but he realized he'd never forgive himself if he rode away from her now. *I need to see this through so I can forget her.* He paced after Saium, Johnny trailing them.

The warriors came behind, muttering and laughing, which grated on Mike's nerves. A hundred feet or so away stood a man who had to be Bandarlok. He was as tall as Mike, well over six feet, but built along the lines of a battle cruiser. He had thickly muscled arms and legs, long dark red hair caught back in two messy braids, a beard and a huge gut that bulged unattractively under his black leather shirt. A crudely sewn flag bearing the insignia of the bartuk, a kind of Mahjundan bear Mike recognized from the wildlife briefing, was held aloft by a youth who had to be a son, given his hair color and outsize frame. Two bartuks were tattooed in blue on Bandarlok's upper arms.

Saium took the duty of spokesman. "I present the Princess Shalira, daughter of the Emperor Kajastahn, come to be your bride, mighty Bandarlok, as per the treaty."

As Shalira made a slight curtsey, Bandarlok stared at her with a coldly evaluating eye. "I've heard of your beauty, princess," he said in a booming, gravelly voice. "Your father's emissaries told the truth for once."

"I–I thank you for the kind words, sir." Shalira retreated a step closer to Saium.

Stepping forward, Bandarlok took her by the hand, pushing her guardsman out of the way. He shoved her hair off her forehead, forcing the princess to tilt her chin so he could get the fading sunlight to fall directly on her face. "This bruise results from some mishap along the trail, I assume? It will fade?"

"Yes, my lord. I struck my head, in my mother's tomb today. I'm sure any discoloration will soon disappear." Shalira sounded anxious to alleviate his concern.

"Good. The mark is disfiguring, and I've accepted enough already, blind one."

She shrank from the flat, disapproving tone. Bandarlok had spoken as if he blamed her for acquiring the blemish on purpose to displease him.

The chieftain laughed, crushing her slender body to his for a noisy, slobbering kiss on the lips. "Never mind, having finally seen you, the bargain is sealed." One huge, rough hand roved familiarly down her back, cupping her butt as he continued to hold her close. "I might take you even if you don't have the additional items I requested."

"I brought the Windhunter Clan insignia from the tomb," Shalira said in a strained voice, making futile efforts to gracefully step out of the embrace. "Saium has them in our packs."

"Excellent. I'll take possession of the items later, when we make camp for the night." Bandarlok nuzzled her neck, wrenched the pins from her hair to run his fingers through the long silky locks.

Mike reined in his temper as long as he could, watching her reaction to Bandarlok's wandering hands. *This is her choice, and I've no right to interfere. No right at all.* But as the silver hair pins clattered to the ground, he said, "Not to intrude, sir, but we should let my sergeant check the princess's condition."

"And you are?" Bandarlok's frown was monumental.

Mike had faced more imposing enemies than this barbarian. He kept his voice neutral, businesslike. "Major Varone, Sectors Special Forces. Her Highness sustained a nasty blow to the head earlier. She might have a concussion."

Narrowing his eyes, Bandarlok stared at Mike over Shalira's head. "Ah yes, the outworlders. The palace sent a messenger to inform me you were escorting her, along with the empress's troops." He stared around the valley. "Who I see you've handily disposed of."

"As Her Highness had suspected, the men assigned to be her guards tried to assassinate her earlier today," Mike said. "We took appropriate action."

Laughing, Bandarlok nodded. "I'll safeguard my prize now, eh?" He caressed Shalira's cheek, but his attention was on Mike. "Your task is concluded, Major. You can be on your way with no further concerns. Unless you need guides to the Djeelaba Mountains, perhaps? Such arrangements can be negotiated, for a price."

Mike made an immediate decision. *No way in hell am I taking guides supplied by this character.* "My sergeant and I are well equipped with maps, thanks. But the message must have been garbled—we're to escort the princess all the way to your settlement." He ignored Johnny's quickly muted reaction. Shalira swung her head in his direction for a second. "My orders came directly from the emperor's vizier." He shrugged. "So we'll be riding along. May I suggest we get mounted, leave the valley before the storm breaks?" A crash of thunder overhead added emphasis to his remark.

Bandarlok frowned. The warriors behind Mike's back muttered. He heard the rustling of men palming weapons, prepared for action if their chief gave the order.

"I need to set off the explosion, seal the tomb," Johnny reminded him in a low voice.

"Very well, we'll leave this place of death, establish camp before dark, and we can discuss your orders from the emperor while we eat," Bandarlok said. He glanced over at the string of cavalry horses Saium and Johnny had assembled as they'd cleaned up the valley after the battle. Rubbing his chin, an acquisitive gleam in his eyes, the chief nodded. "I'll take the horses as further payment on her dowry, since dead men have no need of such fine mounts and I do."

"Excluding *my* horses and gear, of course," Mike said, hand on the gun at his hip.

"Of course." Bandarlok's agreement was immediate, his grin toothy. He pulled Shalira to face him again, bending low and speaking slowly, as if she were a child or a halfwit. "You'd have no way of knowing, of course, but women of the clans are not so forward with their appearance as you city folk."

"What do you mean?" Fine wrinkles furrowed her brow as she listened to the admonition.

He waggled a finger in front of her nose, which of course she couldn't see. "Women don't ride as if they are the equals of the men. I've told my warriors not to be offended by your actions today." He made a dismissive hand gesture. "No need to concern yourself, I've brought a wagon for you to ride in, as a high-born female should. Come, let me escort you to the conveyance, and then we can be on our way."

"Kind of you," she answered. "I feel unwell from my fall, so perhaps a wagon is the best solution for tonight."

In the next minute, Shalira stiffened, choking back a gasp of outrage as Bandarlok picked her up like a child, carrying her in his beefy arms to the waiting, enclosed wagon. Ignoring her repeated requests to be set down, he deposited her inside, closing the dark brown leather curtains at the rear. He started shouting orders to his men, who scattered to collect the horses and gear of Vreely's squad.

Brow furrowed, Johnny glanced from the wagon to Mike. Swallowing any comments he might have made about the scene that had just concluded, he said, "I'll finish the demolition work and fetch our mounts."

"Fine. The sooner we're out of here the better." As Johnny was leaving, Mike snagged his sleeve. "Get our blasters out of the locked packs, would you? I'm done walking around with inferior gear on this planet to be politically correct. Fuck the rules of engagement. What the Foreign Service types don't know won't hurt them."

"Now you're talking! Wish we'd done that yesterday." Saluting enthusiastically, Johnny trotted off.

A few minutes later the anticipated explosion came from high on the valley wall, followed by a rumbling, crashing rock slide. As Mike rode out of the valley, the dust was settling under a fine mist of rain. The only evidence available to any searchers from the city would be Vreely's dead horse, which he couldn't conceal. *Let them chew on the mystery and think what they want.* There'd be no definitive answers without moving the tons of boulders covering Vreely's last resting place. *The empress isn't likely to order such a search.*

Johnny reined his horse in to match Mike's speed. "I think I might have used a tad too much explosive there, but it did the job."

"The results are what counts," Mike answered tersely. He spurred the stallion forward, wanting to avoid any further conversation with anyone for a while.

Rethinking the scene in the tomb between himself and Shalira, he pondered what she'd said to him. He certainly understood the demands imposed by duty and he had to admit an appreciation for her two-pronged strategy, obtaining the services of two of the Sectors' most deadly operators to ensure she reached her groom alive and getting word to Bandarlok to arrive early, in the valley. It wasn't her fault he'd managed to fall in love with her on the trip to the tombs. He should have kept his hands to himself and his mouth shut. Never mind she'd seemed to reciprocate his feelings, at least to some extent. Offering asylum without making it clear how much she'd come to mean to him personally had been a bonehead move. *We're never going to have another chance to talk about it now. But how can she seriously plan to marry this guy, no matter what her father paid in dowry? She's the one who has to live with the consequences, day in and day out, not the emperor.* Mike rode in a moody silence, wrapped in his bleak musing. He knew Johnny was watching him, clearly reluctant to break Mike's concentration. *I've got to get my head back in the mission where it belongs. Certainly before I talk to the overbearing chieftain again.*

CHAPTER SIX

The threatened storm failed to break. The dark clouds covered the sky from edge to edge of the horizon, filled with rumblings and ominous flashes. Like a solid weight pressing on Mike's shoulders, the humidity grew oppressive, but very little rain fell.

Striking away from the road, Bandarlok set a fast pace, leading the column for a good hour and a half in a straight line for the highlands. The Djeelaba Mountains towered beyond, improbably lofty, tops hidden by the cloud cover. They were so tall they created their own weather on the highest peaks, which could be an added complication for the mission, although in this season of the Mahjundan year, the likelihood of blizzards was less.

At length, the small party of riders and the accompanying wagon carrying the princess came to a grove of sturdy trees clustered beside a small lake. The rapidly setting sun threw long shadows from the trees across the rippling water.

"We won't find anything better before dark," Bandarlok announced as the group sat in the saddles, allowing their weary horses to drink. "Best make camp here."

Mike cast an eye at the sky and the lengthening shadows. The worst of the storm clouds had stayed centered over the Valley of the Tombs. "We've a tent for Her Highness in the gear, which will provide privacy for Johnny to examine her."

"What makes you think I'm going to allow any man to touch my woman?" Bandarlok said. "Particularly an outworlder?"

"She took a pretty bad fall back there in the tomb. Someone needs to check out her condition." Mike kept a tight rein on his temper. It was imperative Shalira get medical attention; getting into a confrontation with Bandarlok wasn't going to accomplish that. "Maybe my guy can assist your healer?"

"Sure, I'd be more than happy to help," Johnny agreed, taking his medkit out of the saddlebags.

"I didn't bring a healer on such a simple trip," Bandarlok said, rolling his eyes. "My warriors don't require pampering for anything less than grievous wounds suffered in battle."

"Well, the princess needs a healer, so I guess it'll have to be Johnny then." Mike rested his hand on the butt of his blaster, willing to push the issue however hard he had to, to ensure the princess was properly cared for. He forced the next words through gritted teeth. "You want your bride to be fit for the wedding, right?"

Relaxing, Bandarlok nodded. "When you express the situation in such terms, I can agree. She shall have her tent and the medical services."

Shalira had no clear memory of the events after they'd escaped her mother's tomb. She remembered every word she'd exchanged with Michael in the entrance to the unused tomb, however, and the stabbing pain in her heart after she allowed herself one tempting kiss. The intimacy had only made it more excruciating to know she had to follow her path of duty to carry out her father's wishes. *I wanted Michael to hold me, kiss me once, so I'd have the memory to sustain me through the long years ahead as Bandarlok's wife. But oh, now I know what a broken heart means.* And then he'd been so angry when Bandarlok showed up. He'd no right to be upset—she'd sent word to Bandarlok long before the outworlder even set foot on Mahjundar, but Michael had given her no chance to explain. Maybe his reaction said something about the depth of his true feelings for her? Was he jealous of Bandarlok's claim on her?

She'd regained consciousness on her back, lying somewhere unknown, still fully dressed. Mike, Saium and Bandarlok argued somewhere in the distance. She tried to call out to them, to plead for quiet, to beg for water, but her voice was a dismal croak. When she flung her hands out, scrabbling her fingertips over the surfaces on either side of her, there was only a canvas floor around the mattress, as if she was in a tent.

Weeping, she yielded to the maw of the vertigo. Suddenly, Johnny was there in the tent with her, his deep, quiet voice calming as he took off her boots. "Shh, Your Highness, I'm trying to make you a bit more comfortable. Nothing more, I promise. Don't distress yourself. Lie still and let me check this head injury."

"Hurry up, outworlder. It isn't proper for you to be in such close proximity to my woman," said Bandarlok from somewhere off to the left, his voice grating and too loud. "Can she travel tomorrow morning or not?"

"Too soon to say, sir, but she's seriously ill from the blow on the head, so I doubt it. I need to do a proper examination."

Attempting to sit up, Shalira was racked by dry heaves. Johnny supported her, gently rubbing her back. "I'll give you something for nausea in a minute, ma'am."

Easy tears flooded her eyes as she realized how weak she felt. Grateful for his attempt to give comfort, she said, "I'm sorry to be so much trouble."

"Nothing to apologize for. You probably got a concussion when you hit the corner of the sarcophagus. The nausea's all part of it." He was reassuring, helping her lie back as the spasms faded.

"I'll be outside by the fire," Bandarlok said. "Tending a sick woman isn't a proper task for a warrior. Her present condition disgusts me."

Shalira heard the tent flaps fall with a soft whispering sound. "I—I'm sure he didn't mean to be insulting."

"No worries." Johnny laughed. "I've had worse things said to me. Or about me."

"What of Michael?" She reached out, hoping he was in the tent as well.

Johnny took her hand and squeezed gently, leaning close. "He's worried about you, but Bandarlok won't let him come near you. The best we could manage was for me to come in, do a quick exam and report back. Your fiancé didn't bring a healer with him, and I'm a medic."

"Oh." Disappointed but not surprised, she lay back as he drew a warm blanket over her. Perhaps it was for the best if she didn't spend any more time with Michael. "Thank you, sergeant."

"No problem, ma'am."

She heard small rustling noises as he got items out of a pack, laying them on the blanket beside her. Rubbing her temples, despite the fact the motion gave no relief, she said, "Where are we?"

"Camped by a pretty little stream, a couple of hours' ride from the Valley of Tombs. Bandarlok had his men set up the tent for you. The rest of us are gonna sleep in the open, including him."

Grateful for the information, Shalira relaxed a little. The idea of sharing her tent with her husband-to-be was too overwhelming to contemplate tonight, sick as she felt. She was beginning to realize how terrifying it was to be entirely in Bandarlok's power. He demonstrated no respect for her royal blood. As soon as she felt better, she'd have to establish some boundaries, a more balanced relationship with the man. She refused to let herself worry about the possibility Bandarlok would insist on keeping the current demeaning approach to her. "Where's Saium?"

"Outside, standing guard." Matter-of-factly, Johnny did a quick exam, checking her reflexes, among other things. "You can't see, not even silhouettes?" he asked at one point.

"Of course not. The potion I used in the tomb wore off long ago. You know that. Why are you asking?"

"Just medical curiosity on my part, ma'am. Nothing to worry over." After concluding his exam, he said, "Mild concussion, nothing too serious. I'll recommend to Bandarlok we stay put for the next day, maybe two. By then you should be out of any danger, good to travel."

Shalira clutched at his arm. "What about you and Michael?"

"Mike told Bandarlok we're going along to his settlement, said the emperor had ordered us to accompany you there." He laughed. "I go where Mike leads, always have since we were kids."

"I'm grateful. It'll be nice to know you're both still with me."

"Only till we see you safely to your new home." He folded her hand around a cup and obediently she drank, relishing the cool water. "It's not too much of a detour."

His answer was flat and she felt oddly disappointed. But what had she expected? Why would Michael stay? She'd given him her answer, hadn't she? Better for them both if he moved on.

The sergeant touched her hand, interrupting her train of thought. "If you're done with the water, I'm going to give you something for the headache and nausea." Johnny pressed something to her upper arm for a moment, creating a feeling of pressure and localized heat.

Handing him the mug, Shalira felt a warm lassitude spreading through her body from the site. "Thank you."

Rubbing her arm, he laughed. "You probably won't be thanking me when I wake you up at intervals all night, but I gotta follow protocol for a concussion patient."

"I'm sorry to be causing you so much trouble," she said drowsily, on the verge of drifting off.

"Happy to help. Now, the water jug and the cup are about a foot off to the left of your bed, if you want more later. Try to drink as often as you can." She could hear beeps and clicks as Johnny packed up his medical tools. He leaned close to her ear. "Walk carefully with this Bandarlok guy until you know him better, okay? He seems to have a hair trigger."

"I will," she promised in a matching whisper. "Can you ask Michael–"

He squeezed her fingers tightly as the tent flaps snapped open and Bandarlok's voice boomed inside the tent. "Why is this taking so long? I said you could have a few moments to treat my woman, not all night."

"I'm done, sir." Johnny stood and walked away, his steps thudding on the tent floor. "I'll have to check in on her every few hours from now until dawn, make sure she hasn't slipped into a coma."

"We can discuss the need for such measures later." Bandarlok's voice faded as the two men moved out of the tent.

Johnny had awakened her all through the night as promised, but even though they were alone each time— Bandarlok having refused to interrupt his own slumbers to tend to her— Shalira was too disoriented from the concussion and the powerful medications to talk to the sergeant about Michael again. And truth be told, she felt a little frightened of her new situation. She didn't want to know anything else that might confirm her growing suspicion she'd landed in a spot even less desirable than her life in the palace. *I'm sick, not thinking right. Everything will be fine when I'm more myself, on my feet and able to reassure Bandarlok. He's worried about me, like a proper husband-to-be.* But the optimistic words sounded hollow even to herself.

She'd spent the next day drowsing in the tent, the sounds of activity all around outside. Saium brought her meals and escorted her to tend to her private needs, guarding her privacy until she was ready to reenter the tent. He too was unusually silent, even for him. Her mild suggestion late in the afternoon to allow her to sit outside for some fresh air was met with a sigh.

"Bandarlok has forbidden it," Saium said.

Enough was enough. Annoyance made her reply sharp. "I'm a princess of Mahjundar, I can certainly sit outside if I so desire." She gathered herself to rise and stalk out of the tent.

Saium laid one hand on her shoulder, gently pressing her to sit. "Best not. Conditions have changed since your mother and I left the highlands. The women of the clans lead much more restricted lives now, or so they tell me. I don't think it wise to go against Bandarlok's express command. Maybe when you've had a chance to get to know him better, you can negotiate more freedom for yourself."

Unease sent a trickle of hot dread through her nerves. She licked dry lips. "Are you saying I'm his prisoner?"

"No, of course not," he said a bit too rapidly, with too much force. "I merely suggest you—and I—need to conform to the social rules here, find our footing before we start pushing for changes."

On the surface, a sensible suggestion. So why do I feel as if I'm caught in a net? Shalira decided to try another conversational tack, something happier.

"Are any of your old friends from our clan riding with the column? Met any Windhunters?"

There was an odd moment of silence before Saium said, "No, Bandarlok brought only his own clansmen, to honor you, I'm sure. And the men of the Bartuk Clan are known for being short of words and cold to those outside their own tents." He paused. She could hear him fiddling with her dinner dishes. "Your Highness, I might go with the outworlders, to act as their guide to the Djeelaba Mountains, since Rojar was killed at the tombs."

"What?" Panic grabbed her by the throat, choking her. Never in her wildest imaginings had she worried about Saium leaving.

Patting her hand, he said soothingly, "Now, girl, you'll be busy with your husband and babies soon enough, if the gods be generous. Safely ensconced in the heart of Bandarlok's encampment, guarded by all his warriors. You'll have no more need of me, nor time for me."

"I always need you, Saium. You're like a father to me." Terror was rising in her gut, a physical pain causing her to regret the dinner she'd eaten. Saium was her bulwark against the world, her ally. How would she manage this challenging new life without him?

He cleared his throat. "Well, here's the thing, Your Highness. Bandarlok has made it clear he'll allow me to attend you on this journey, in deference to your blindness, but once we reach his camp, we're to have no more contact. You'll be living in his inner court, in the tents of the women, and I'm not allowed there. He said he expects you to manage for yourself, among the other females. I tried to argue but he, well, he has a quick temper."

"Johnny said the same thing," she remembered aloud. *Why doesn't Bandarlok talk to me about these matters? Ask my opinion? Or at least give me a chance to ask him questions about what he wants?* "But it would be a comfort to know you were still there, in the camp, even if we couldn't meet."

"Of course. I haven't decided anything one way or the other," he said, too quickly. "Don't upset yourself."

Waking abruptly from an ominous dream of dark figures who looked like Vreely chasing her while Bandarlok's cruel laugh sounded in the distance, Shalira sat up with a gasp. She clutched at her chest as her heart raced. She was disoriented for a moment but the scent of crushed pine needles from the thin mattress under her brought her back to current events. A sudden lurch sent her reeling into the varnished wooden side of the small wagon. A stark reminder, that Bandarlok decreed she must be transported in seclusion, rather than ride.

The conveyance bumped over ruts and tree roots on this seldom-used track they followed. Shalira was surprised she'd dozed off at all.

The lurching of the wagon was making her nauseated. The leather curtains were closed, keeping her in a stifling-hot environment. What breeze there was had to come in through a few inches of clearance between the ragged edges of leather and the wooden frame of the vehicle. Greedily, Shalira pressed her face to the crack, breathing in some refreshing air. She knew better now, after four days of travel, than to attempt to leave the wagon, or even ask the guards to open the curtains. Bandarlok had been serious about women not riding, and adamant about her having minimal contact with anyone among the tribe but him.

Fingering her locket, she blinked back tears as her thoughts circled again to the few precious moments in the tomb with Michael before Bandarok had arrived. If only the outworlder had spoken more about his feelings when they were alone, instead of just inviting her to run away and evade her duties of state. *If he'd said he loved me, what difference would it have made? I still couldn't have chosen differently. Foolish girl.* "But I wish I knew if his feelings match mine," she said softly. *I hope I can arrange a few moments to speak to him before we part forever, make things right somehow.* A sudden idea sent her into mild panic. *What if he and Johnny were already gone, off to accomplish their own mission?*

Shalira leaned as far out of the wagon as she dared and listened intently. After a moment, she heard Johnny whistling not too far away, which he liked to do as he rode. *Good, they're still with the caravan.* She sat back, punching the scented pillows to make herself more comfortable.

Her head ached, but nothing like the fierce, raging pain she'd been in when Bandarlok first arrived. Then she'd been dizzy and nauseated. It had been harder than usual to walk with dignity, much less conduct a sensible conversation with her fiancé. By the time Bandarlok had swept her off her feet without so much as a by-your-leave, she'd been about to faint. The idea of a private wagon had been a blessing then. *I couldn't have stayed in the saddle, not even on my gentle mare.* Shalira rubbed her forehead and sighed.

She leaned back against the wagon's side. One by one, her few allies were going to leave her, including Saium. Never in her wildest nightmares had she contemplated the absence of Saium. But he *was* going to leave, she was sure. And she didn't blame him much. Her own few brief conversations with Bandarlok over the past four days had been odd, tense. Nothing she did or suggested met with his approval. *All his actions seem to be about keeping me out of sight, away from anyone but him.* Yet she'd no sense he found her particularly attractive or desirable, despite the many fulsome compliments he paid her, and his roving hands. On the contrary, she got the distinct impression he harbored a dislike for her.

Well, maybe this new development will help the situation, if he's uneasy about my blindness. She blinked hard and was rewarded with shooting stars of white light. Before taking her nurse's potion in the tomb and hitting her head, Shalira had never seen anything. Since the age of ten, when she'd been found next to her dead brother, her eyes had perceived only flat blackness, as if she was blindfolded. In the tomb she'd had her vision back briefly, thanks to the drugs. *And thanks to blessed Pavmiraia, I got to see Michael's face.* Shalira treasured that one long moment almost as much as she was warmed by the memory of their single, never-to-be-repeated kiss. She was afraid to think about either too much. Those memories had to sustain her through the rest of her life, and she feared the years to come were going to be full of unhappiness and frustration, if her beginning with Bandarlok was any sign.

But now shapes occasionally moved through the darkness when she opened her eyes, and she saw flashes of white as if a door had been cracked open for a moment. She realized she'd seen Johnny full-on once during the long night when he'd checked on her so often. At the time she believed she'd been dreaming, perhaps suggested by his odd question during the initial examination. Later she realized she'd actually seen his face, only for a brief second, but undeniably genuine vision.

Will my sight keep getting better? Am I going to regain the use of my eyes? Even a slight degree of sight would be a blessing. Whether it was a lingering aftereffect of her nurse's medicine or had been caused by the blow to her head, or both, Shalira hoped for continued improvement. Ever cautious, she'd said nothing to anyone, not even Saium. *No use in raising anyone else's hopes until I know more.* She'd learned from living with the women in her father's harem that it was best to keep secret advantages to oneself. She would have liked to consult with Johnny since he was a medic, but Bandarlok had allowed no further contact between them after the first night, saying she was obviously on the mend and now the social conventions of his tribe must be respected.

She'd learned over the past few days that the tighter control she kept on her emotions, the more she had the encouraging glimpses of her surroundings, marred as they were by the flashes of squiggly lightning *Staying relaxed is easier said than done, in these circumstances.*

The wagon came to an abrupt halt, wheels locked, skidding sideways on the trail. Shalira braced herself, fearing the conveyance was going to roll over.

Hearing shouts, she was tempted to step outside, but the simple action would inevitably displease Bandarlok, so she folded her hands and waited. A few moments later, the heavy leather curtains were shoved aside. Bandarlok's sweaty scent announced his presence before he spoke.

"My permanent camp in the highlands lies around the next curve of the trail," he said.

Pasting a smile on her face, nervous and on edge, she responded. "Good news, indeed."

He grunted. "I've sent riders ahead to assemble the clans, so they may properly welcome you. This one time *only* I expect you to be on public view."

"It'll be a pleasure, my lord. I've missed riding my horse." Shalira extended her hand. "If you'd be so kind as to help me descend from this wagon."

Ignoring her hand, Bandarlok leaned into the wagon, locked his arms around her waist, and dragged her unceremoniously out, immediately picking her up and striding away.

"I can walk, if you escort me. Hold my hand, perhaps. Or have Saium lead me," she said, resisting a frantic urge to struggle. "Please, it would be more dignified."

"Dignified?" Bandarlok laughed. "What care I for that? Observing the customary proprieties for a woman's behavior is important but dignity is something else entirely."

She heard other men close by repeating his remark and guffawing.

"I hope to present the best first impression possible to your tribe," she said. "If we could take a few minutes and I could have some privacy, I have a dress and cloak the emperor had specially made for this occasion. They're in my trunks, on the pack animals."

He stopped walking. "You're going to present the impression I desire. My people will understand."

"But *I* don't understand— "

"My meaning will be clear, soon enough. For now, I desire to ride into my camp with you in front of me, sharing my horse."

Like a prisoner, a spoil of war? Is that what he intends? Shalira was trembling.

"Aww, pretty one, indulge me for a few minutes, then you never have to ride a horse again." He chucked her under the chin like she was a child, but he did set her on her own two feet. "Don't be frightened, I'll not drop you or let the horse throw you."

"I'm not afraid." She drew herself to her full height, blinking. Her vision right now was going black. The more upset she became, the more opaque the invisible film over her eyes became. The reassuring trickles of white light disappeared. Shalira turned her head toward Bandarlok. "Please, may Saium escort me to your horse?"

"Aye, fine. He can help my men hoist you to the saddle." Bandarlok strode away, leaving her stranded in the middle of the road she couldn't see.

Shalira had a moment to try to quell her panic before Saium took her elbow. Giving in to the temptation to cling to him, she didn't care who might be watching them. Head on his shoulder, she whispered, "What have we done?"

"We got out of the poisonous imperial court before your father died and Maralika was free to kill you," he said. "I don't think we had any choice."

Mike tried to offer me a choice, even if he didn't speak of love. What would he have said if I'd encouraged him?

Saium patted her back, allowing her a fleeting moment of weakness before raising her chin with one callused hand. "His men are gawking at you. And he's waiting." Tugging her into motion, her guardsman guided her along the rutted road with utmost care. "We'll not get another chance to talk, Your Highness. I wish you well."

"I love you," she said, finding it hard to speak with unshed tears clogging her eyes and making her throat ache. "I'll miss you."

"You know I feel the same. Take care of yourself, promise me." Saium's voice was fierce, though his words were rushed.

She had no time to answer as she was grabbed by Bandarlok's men and lifted into the air, boosted unceremoniously in front of him on the nervous horse. The chieftain's arms locked around her and the mount sprang forward, carrying her into her new life. Clenching her hands on the saddle, Shalira prayed to Pavmiraia she could find a way to make her new circumstances bearable, to create a place for herself in the tribe. Maybe her father's parting advice—to give Bandarlok a child as quickly as possible—wasn't so bad after all. But as the chief's arms squeezed around her, she shuddered, choking back tears.

As their party rode out from under the last trees at the edge of the vast clearing where Bandarlok had his seasonal headquarters, Mike found a huge crowd awaiting them. The massed nomadic clans, each standing clustered beside tall staffs bearing their particular insignia, made for an imposing display. There were several hundred men, women, and children gathered to welcome Shalira to her new home. As he rode closer to the assemblage, Mike assessed the mood of the crowd. *Something's seriously off for what's supposed to be a joyful occasion. This bunch is pretty reserved, watchful. I don't like it, but none of this is my business. All Command wants me to do is get on with my own assignment, stop taking unrelated detours.*

Mike watched as Bandarlok walked his horse along the entire line of his people, so they could all see Shalira. There was total silence, which Mike found puzzling, ominous. As if feeling distress or strong emotion, a few of the women in the crowd hid their faces as the chief and his bride-to-be rode by. Bandarlok drew his horse to a halt in front of a small wooden fence, behind which ornately patterned tents loomed. He handed Shalira down to two men who stepped forward to receive her.

Mike tried to edge his horse forward to see and hear more clearly, but the clan riders who'd been with Bandarlok on the trail closed in, blocking his access.

As the chief swung from his horse and took Shalira by the hand, a woman walked out of the gate to meet them. Tall, built as solidly as Bandarlok himself, she was dressed in blue robes accented with colorfully embroidered bartuks on the sleeves and at the hem. On her head she wore a filet of rose gold. Shalira looked like a child next to this newcomer.

Mike leaned close to the nearest rider. "Who's the lady?"

"Bandarlok's Chief Wife, Arananta," the man said before the warrior on the other side poked him in the ribs, hissing at him to shut up.

Chief wife? Mike and Johnny exchanged glances. Had Shalira known she wasn't coming here to be Bandarlok's only wife, or even first among the harem? He made a mental note to talk to Saium about the topic later, once the welcoming ceremonies were over.

He couldn't hear the words, but he knew Shalira well enough by now to tell she was stressed, even while her bearing remained regal. Arananta took Shalira by the hand and drew her inside the wooden fence, painted gates swinging shut behind them. Armed guards took up their posts and the next thing Mike knew, he and Johnny were being escorted across the open expanse of greenery, toward Bandarlok. The clanspeople were streaming in all directions, going about their business matter-of-factly, no one lingering to talk about the newly arrived princess.

Mike dismounted after he rode up to Bandarlok.

The chief gestured expansively as if the day's events had put him in a jovial mood. "You'll stay the night with us, Major Varone? I'm entertaining other guests as well—some chiefs from the east with whom I make an alliance. But we'll decree the feast to be in your honor as well. The least I can do, if I'm not supplying guides. Send you on your way to the Djeelaba with good food, soft women, and strong wine as your last memories, eh?"

"You're too kind, but we must be on the trail as soon as possible," Mike demurred. "We lost a lot of time escorting the princess."

"Nonsense, one more night won't hurt anything. The dead outworlder comrades you seek won't be any more deceased if you come upon them a day later, now will they? I insist." Bandarlok guffawed, slapping his thigh genially, but it was plain they weren't going to leave his camp this night. "My men will escort you to the tent we keep for visitors. Now I must go acquaint my new woman with her duties in my household." He stood grinning as a pair of warriors led Mike, Johnny and Saium off to another group of semi-permanent dwellings to the east.

Clearly searching for something he'd expected to find, Saium looked in all directions with a puzzled frown as they walked. The old man's increasing distress was obvious to Mike. *Another mystery to probe, as soon as we get somewhere private. Something's wrong in this camp, and we're stuck in the middle of it for at least one night.*

Technically a tent, their quarters had the most substantial construction Mike had ever seen in a temporary structure. Made of thick green fabric, sewn together in panels, and braced by a complex system of poles and thin struts, the tent culminated in a steeply pitched roof. The exterior had been treated with tree sap to make it water repellant. Inside, the space was large enough to house twice their number, with room left over. The entire encampment consisted of these tents, in varying sizes, laid out in concentric circles from the center. Completely encircled by the symbolic wooden fence, all the green-and-white-striped tents in the inner circle flew banners with the Bartuk Clan symbol. Mike's assigned shelter was outside the last of the circles and off to one side, near the edge of the forest.

Picking at his yellow, snaggled teeth with a small bone, one bored warrior said, "The feast begins at sundown. We eat in the large red tent there, across the camp. No weapons allowed."

Message delivered, he and his silent companion swaggered back to the main encampment.

A few minutes later, after taking care of their mounts first, Mike, Johnny and Saium stood staring at each other inside their large tent. Loosely hobbled, their saddle horses and pack animals waited outside the tent, grazing on the lush meadow grass.

After peering out the tent flap to make sure no one was within hearing distance, Mike confronted Saium. "What in the hell is going on here?"

"I don't know. I didn't see anyone I knew. I didn't even see our Windhunter Clan banner. My poor princess—the brute is no fit husband for her. What can the emperor have been thinking?" Face slack in a dazed expression, Saium sat heavily on one of the cots, hanging his head in his hands. "Things have changed so since I left as a young man, to accompany Shalira's mother to the emperor."

Stowing some gear under the bunk he was claiming for the night, Johnny said, "We going to the banquet?"

Mike nodded. "I think we'd better. We need to be congenial, unsuspicious guests, taking everything here at face value. Or so we let Bandarlok believe."

Testing the comfort of the thin mattress, Johnny asked, "What's your plan for tomorrow?"

"I don't have one, beyond you and me riding out of here, early in the morning, and getting on with our mission," Mike said, pushing his hand into the uninviting, hard pad covering what would be his bunk.

"I'd like to join you," Saium said. "You could use a guide in the mountains, no matter what maps you have."

Mike whistled in surprise. "You serious?"

"What about the princess?" Johnny asked, sitting up again. "Doesn't she need you?"

"Bandarlok made it clear to me I'll never see her again." The old man swallowed hard, blinking. "She and I said our good-byes. I only wish I felt I'd brought her to a safe place. I'll be powerless to help her."

"Did Shalira know Bandarlok had a wife already?" Mike asked.

"I don't know." Saium considered for a moment. "She might have. She didn't react as I would've expected when the woman came outside the compound. Don't judge my princess harshly," he said. "Her position at court was tenuous at best, and once the emperor dies, there'd have been *no* help, nothing to hold anyone back. People would have vied for the honor of ridding Maralika of her hated rival's daughter. The empress never forgave Kajastahn for the way he elevated Shalira's mother over her."

Johnny shook his head. "But what about Shalira?"

"It doesn't matter if she knew. This was her choice. She specifically asked me not to interfere or try to influence her." Mike looked his cousin squarely in the eye. "Shalira intends to carry out her duty to her father and marry this guy. End of discussion."

Johnny chewed his lip, obviously deciding to keep what he was thinking to himself. "Well then, guess we'd better get ready to attend the big feast," he said.

Saium shook his head. "I've no desire to eat and drink at Bandarlok's table. Perhaps I can nose around and find out more of what's going on here, where my clan is, while you're at the dinner."

"Be careful," Mike warned him. "For yourself and for her. Anything you do might reflect badly on her in Bandarlok's eyes. She has enough trouble right now."

"What about this no-weapons edict?" Johnny asked.

"I don't like it, but I don't see how we can refuse to comply. Lock our blasters with the other gear." Mike glanced at his cousin. "We'll keep our knives. From what I've seen on this planet, no adult male goes anywhere without some kind of knife in his belt."

"Better than nothing," Johnny agreed a bit more cheerfully as he took Mike's Mark 27 blaster, stacking it with his own in a black and gray military container, then thumbing the lock closed. "Sun's setting. Shall we go?"

"One more little thing," Mike said. "Where's the medkit?"

Shalira stumbled along after Arananta the Chief Wife, angry at being forced to move so quickly, but unwilling to make a fuss. "I apologize for my appearance. I'm sure I must look a mess but the chieftain was so—so anxious to arrive home, he wouldn't give me a moment to freshen up or change my dress. I blush to meet you in this state."

Her companion grunted, tightening her grip on Shalira's wrist.

Enough is enough. Pulling back a bit, she tried to dig in her heels, twisting her arm to no avail, but stopping short of clawing at the woman's fingers. "Please, may we stop for a moment? If we go more slowly I can begin learning my way around the compound. I count steps from point to point, you see. Then no one will have to lead me."

The woman laughed. "You don't have to learn the compound. Wasted effort."

"I'm sorry?" *Is she upset because Bandarlok has brought in another wife? Surely she can't feel threatened by me?*

"You'll find out soon enough." Shalira felt the surface change under her feet as she stumbled across a threshold. Arananta dropped her hand and it was all Shalira could do not to fall. Taking a deep breath to calm her racing pulse, she stood tall, wishing she wasn't so vulnerable and alone. She could hear other people in the room, breathing, clothes rustling, and a quickly stifled laugh.

"So, this is our high-and-mighty princess, girls, come to be a bride of the chief," Arananta said. "Not so grand now, is she?"

Extending one hand, catching the chief wife's sleeve, Shalira said, "Please, tell me who's here? Introduce us?"

The woman yanked the fabric out of her grasp with a sniff. "Your betters, that's all you need to know."

Shalira was at a loss. Behind her she heard the sound of men approaching, treading heavily as if carrying quite a burden. Arananta pulled her aside and whoever was coming into the room brushed past her, knocking her off-balance.

"Are those her trunks?" asked an excited, young, female voice. "Can we open them now?"

"If they've brought my things, of course you're welcome to see." Hoping to make a good first impression on her new companions, she added, "I also brought gifts from the capital."

A titter of laughter came from all around her. Shalira estimated there were at least ten women in the tent. The atmosphere was ugly. Something was going on she didn't understand. Even at its worst, Emperor Kajastahn's harem was more civil to newcomers.

"Get out," Arananta said, apparently speaking to the men.

As soon as the tent flaps fell behind the departing warriors, there was a rush of women to the area of the room where Shalira's trunks had been placed. She heard fingernails scrabbling at the locked clasps.

Arananta grabbed her shoulder. "Where are the keys?"

Jerking loose, upset, the princess said, "We should wait until the trunks are placed in my quarters. I need to be sure there's no confusion about what's mine and what's to be a gift. I can put things away as we're admiring them."

"Give me the cursed keys, girl. I'm in charge here, and I say we're opening the trunks now."

Fumbling in the pocket of her dress, she handed over the tiny ring of filigreed silver keys, which Arananta grabbed. The princess backed away as she heard the women screaming and exclaiming and fighting over her clothes and other possessions. Fabric tore as two girls both coveted one dress and then apparently fell to hair-pulling, accompanied by vulgar name-calling because the garment was ruined. Disgusted by their behavior, saddened by the loss of the few things in the trunks that had been precious to her, Shalira was tempted to flee, despite having no idea where to go. She thought she remembered how many steps it had been to the entrance and started sidling away, with no clear plan what she would do next, only desperate to be away from the melee.

Her sketchy plan was succeeding until she ran into Bandarlok as he strode through the entrance. He grabbed her shoulder in one hand, yelling at the top of his lungs, "What do you women think you're doing?"

Instant silence fell. Someone dropped a cosmetics box, sneezing as the expensively scented powder became a momentarily pervasive cloud.

"I'm perfectly happy to share, my lord," Shalira said. "Perhaps there's been a misunderstanding about what I brought with me."

"Arananta, has there been a misunderstanding?"

"No, my husband." The chief wife was clearly smiling as she spoke. "The other wives and daughters may have been a bit hasty in their excitement."

"And there's been no misunderstanding, because?" He drew out his last word.

Still held by Bandarlok in a too tight embrace, Shalira heard the woman tread heavily across the floor to stand in front of her.

"Because a slave *has* no possessions," Arananta said, taking her by the ear and yanking her forward.

Outraged, the princess instinctively slapped the woman's hand away. "How dare you touch me?"

A blow from Bandarlok across the face sent her tumbling to the floor, ears ringing, white flashes running across the black screen of her lost vision. Wind knocked out of her, she lay where she'd fallen for a moment, incredulous. Rubbing her stinging cheek, she fought back angry tears.

"Undress," he said, standing directly above her.

"What?" She was sure she must have misheard him.

Nudging her ribs with one booted foot, he repeated the command. "I said strip. I want to see what I've been paid to take into my bed. Hurry up, or I'll have some of my men in here to play lady's maid."

Awkwardly, Shalira peeled off her dress and then her shift, standing in her underthings. Arananta snatched the outer garments from her hands, tossing them aside, presumably to the waiting harem. Next she grabbed at the necklace and the princess clawed at her hands. "My mother gave me this. You can't have it!"

"Leave off. Let her keep the amulet of Pavmiraia," Bandarlok shouted, unexpectedly. "Have some sense, woman, the goddess still walks the forestlands. We've no need to anger a goddess unnecessarily."

Grumbling audibly, giving her rival a final push for good measure, Arananta stepped aside.

"Good enough for now. On your knees to me, girl," Bandarlok said.

Straightening her spine, heedless of her near nudity, Shalira shook her head. "I'm a princess of Mahjundar. I kneel to no man, not even my husband."

"You'd best learn to be more obedient, or your life is going to be even shorter and more unpleasant," Arananta said, grabbing her elbow, tugging at her, trying to kick her legs out from under her. Another woman came to join in the struggle and eventually the princess was forced to kneel.

"My father sent you my dowry in good faith," Shalira protested, shaking her hair out of her face, struggling against the hands holding her. "He expected you to treat me with dignity, not make me into a slave."

Bandarlok put his face next to hers and she recoiled from the smell of his breath. The wife wrapped a hunk of her hair around her fist, holding Shalira still while the chieftain answered, "My spies tell me your father's as good as dead. Once he's gone, I'll get the empress to pay me more gold to do her dirty deed for her. All Mahjundar knows she hates you. And my own vengeance will be complete."

"What wrong have I ever done to you?" Shalira was dizzy, her stomach in knots. Her head ached where the wife was threatening to tear her hair out by the roots. *This man is insane, his wife is just as bad, and I'm completely at their mercy.*

"Oh, not you personally, princess," he said, cupping her chin with one hand. "Your clan, now that's another story. I'll spare you the details, but I've dedicated my entire life to wiping out the Clan Windhunter for what they did to my people, to my father, to me. I swore on my mother's grave to have vengeance, spilling the Windhunters' poisonous blood down to the last man, woman and child." He laughed. "You and your worthless old guard will be the last members of your clan to die. When your father's emissary came, offering you in marriage, I felt the gods themselves must have arranged the final act of vengeance for me."

She heard someone walk into the tent.

"I've brought the items, sir."

Stepping away from her, Bandarlok rubbed his hands together, the sliding sound startling Shalira. "Good, good, let me have them."

He was opening the box in which they'd stored her mother's Clan insignia. Shalira could smell the faint tang of the wood the box was made from, which grew only in the lowlands. She flinched as the box was tossed to the ground, cracking to splinters by the sound of it. Bandarlok walked back to her. The strands of the golden necklace clinked together near her face, but still it was a shock when the cold metal encircled her neck. She tried to get a hand free as the chief fastened the necklace, but the women held her in a firm grasp, their hands like manacles around her slender wrists.

Laughing, he pulled the flat gold chains tighter and tighter, until she was choking, fighting to breathe, metal digging into her neck. "This is how you're going to die, when I decide the time has come." He bent over and spoke directly into her ear as she worked to inhale against the pressure of the necklace. "First, I'll let my personal guards have you for a few hours alone in their tent. When they're done with you, I'll strangle you in front of the entire camp, so all my people can see the final triumph of Clan Bartuk."

She was losing consciousness. He must have given some sign, because suddenly she was released by the women, falling forward onto her hands, frantically sucking air into her lungs. A coarse length of fabric was thrown at her head.

"Here, wear this," said the first wife. "It's good enough for a Windhunter slave. Get dressed. Be quick about it. You may be blind, but I've suitable chores to be done if you want to eat."

With as much dignity as she could muster, Shalira tried to still her shaking hands and figure out the unfamiliar garment, glad to have something to cover herself with. As she was led out of the room, she heard the women shrieking with laughter and arguing over her possessions again, while Bandarlok encouraged them to fight over the spoils he'd brought them.

The rest of the nightmare day passed in a blur of harsh words, slaps and pokes from the chief wife, and endless vegetables to wash and peel by touch alone. Shalira's hands were cut and bleeding by the time a guard took her to a small, unfurnished, unheated prison hut. After he'd locked her in, she crept into the farthest corner and wrapped herself in the thin blanket she found there. Only then did she dare give in to the weeping she'd held off all day, unwilling to allow her enemies to see her grief and terror.

After sundown, Mike and Johnny walked across the camp toward the designated red tent. Mike could hear raucous music, mostly drums and pipes. As he'd anticipated, no objections were raised to their retaining knives on their belts. Waved into the tent by two guards, he surveyed the smoky, noisy scene. Highland warriors were packed into the space, some already eating, others playing games of chance, and the rest ogling the nearly naked dancing girls in the center of the tent. It seemed there were different rules of conduct for a woman who danced for a living in the clan, versus Shalira and the other wives.

As he walked past the giant bonfire on the west side of the tent, a large branch broke with a crash, sending up a shower of sparks. Mike glanced at the blaze, and did a double take. Charred and glowing, the carved Windhunter insignia was lying on a pile of kindling at the edge of the pyre. As he watched, a man tending the fire shoved the wooden staff toward the heart of the flames, and the winged bird blazed fiercely as the inner core of dried wood caught. *What the hell? We go to all the trouble to retrieve the thing so Bandarlok can burn it like kindling?*

"What's the matter?" Johnny asked, retracing his steps.

"Nothing, tell you later." Mike shook his head, brushing ash from his shoulder. "Quite a bonfire they've got going. Perfect on a cold night."

The dancing troupe was two short, since Bandarlok had a buxom redhead by his side and a curvaceous blonde in his lap. The chief beckoned to Mike across the tent, his voice carrying easily above the pipes and drums.

"Come, outworlders! Sit by me, in the place of honor!"

Mike worked his way through the edge of the crowd, taking care not to step into the open space where the dancers gyrated and spun. As he walked up to the chief, trailed by Johnny, Bandarlok gave each woman in his lap a wet kiss on the lips and shooed them away. Pouting, the dancers stepped clumsily into the undulating rhythm of the dance troupe and whirled away to elsewhere in the tent.

"Wine! Bring wine!" Bandarlok took two bulging wineskins from a server. The food and drink were coming from an adjoining room, on an endless series of platters. "Sit! Meet my other honored guests, chiefs of the eastern tribes."

Performing introductions, their host was distracted from time to time by the gyrations of his favorite dancers.

Mike found it to be a long night. Bandarlok wasn't much for conversation, other than periodically urging the outworlders to eat and drink while they could, since they were surely fated to perish in the Djeelaba Mountains. He repeatedly offered them the company of his dancers, which Mike and Johnny graciously refused. The chieftains who'd come to make a treaty with Bandarlok didn't speak any dialect covered by Mike's hypnotraining. Eventually, Johnny accepted a stack of gaming tiles and dice, after which he and the chiefs had a fine time, making wagers and arguing unintelligibly about the results of each round of some incredibly complicated game of chance. A great deal of wine flowed. At one point, Johnny allowed himself to be drawn into the dancing by the well-endowed redhead whom Bandarlok had been nuzzling earlier. The sergeant's efforts to duplicate her swaying steps and alluring movements brought great gales of laughter from Bandarlok. Seeing his amusement, the clansmen felt free to laugh at the outworlder also.

Drinking deeply from the skin of potent black wine, Mike politely declined to try his luck at the gaming. Unbeknownst to his host, the headclear he'd taken prior to walking across to the feast neutralized the alcoholic content of the beverage as soon as it hit his bloodstream. Johnny was equally sober but they'd agreed it might defuse their host's suspicions if at least one of them played the drunkard.

Judging they'd done their social duty as honored guests long enough, Mike finally rescued his cousin from making a fool of himself with the over-attentive dancers. "Chief, I think I'd better get my man and myself back to our own tent before we overdo it and can't ride tomorrow morning," he said. "There's one remaining thing I have to do."

"And that is?" Bandarlok lifted his overflowing mug, sloshing wine on the cushions.

Shrugging apologetically, Mike said, "The emperor insisted I take formal leave of Princess Shalira, so I can report back to him before I leave the planet, and describe her state of happiness as your bride."

The chief paused in his drinking, eyeing Mike speculatively before finishing the mug's contents and wiping his lips on an already sopping sleeve. He picked up a roasted game bird, picking off the choicest bits to feed the giggling dancer in his lap. "There's no need. You can report the girl was safely delivered."

As if his request had no importance to him personally, Mike leaned closer, adopting a conspiratorial air. "And I will, rest assured. Damn nuisance when all I want is to hit the trail. But orders are orders. You know how it is. I need a moment in the morning. I know you're busy. You don't have to be there."

Bandarlok frowned. "Very well, you may take your formal leave of my newest wife *and me,* three hours after dawn tomorrow."

Mike nodded. "Fine. Suits me, see you then."

Fondling the dancer, Bandarlok waved him away.

Stepping out into the clear, fresh night air was a tremendous relief to Mike. He'd say goodbye to Shalira, assure himself she was fine, and he and Johnny would ride out, go on with their own mission before returning to their home in the stars. And he'd forget her.

Right.

The optimism lasted only until he reached their tent. "Saium?" Mike walked into their quarters, halting abruptly. It was late and there was no sign of the guardsman. Mike was expecting the Windhunter to have completed his private reconnaissance of the camp.

"Odd," Johnny said, crowding into the room behind his cousin. "His cot hasn't been disturbed."

"See if his horse is still here." Mike knelt to unlock the container holding their blasters.

Back in less than a minute, Johnny was frowning. "The horse is gone." He pointed at the stack of supplies. "But his stuff is mixed in with ours. Why would he leave without taking anything?"

Mike shook his head. "Something's not right about this. Saium would never leave without telling us."

Johnny squatted to peer at something, then came to his feet holding his left hand out to Mike. "Blood. He didn't go out of here under his own power."

CHAPTER SEVEN

The next morning, Shalira stood with as much dignity as she could muster when the door to the hut creaked open. A night of shivering in the unheated cell had left her weak and headachy, with stiff knees, but she was determined not to let the tribe break her will.

"You look more like a slave than a princess now," said the rough voice of the chief wife. "Come here, girl."

Clutching the scratchy blanket like a cloak, free hand extended in front of her, Shalira walked to the location of Arananta's voice. *I'll save my defiance for a moment when it might do some good.*

Grabbing her by the elbow, the wife gave her a shake. "Don't dawdle when I summon you. Fortunately for you, my husband needs you to be presentable this morning. But there'll be more work later, I promise."

Shalira said nothing as they hurried along, first outside in the bone-chilling cold, then entering the tent complex. Despite the anger burning hot inside her, she counted steps. The more she could picture the layout in her head, the greater her chance of escaping. Better to die of exposure in the forest than live as a slave. Having a plan helped keep the fear at bay, a little.

To her surprise, she smelled hot food as they entered whatever tent she'd been escorted to.

"Sit. There's breakfast on the plate in front of you. Don't tell me we have to feed you like a baby?" Arananta said with revulsion as she pushed her prisoner onto a bench.

Shalira felt carefully in front of her for the dish. Grasping the smooth edge, she brought the portion closer to her nose, sniffing for a hint of what they expected her to eat. Eggs, warm bread. Berries? No, fresh preserves. Setting the plate on the table and searching for a utensil, she said, "I'm perfectly capable of feeding myself." Finding a wooden fork, she lifted scrambled eggs to her mouth, alternating with bites of the bread, chewing the reviving, hot food appreciatively. *Who knows when they'll offer me food again? Certainly there wasn't any dinner.*

"Good. There's mare's milk in a mug to your right. Don't be too long about your meal. We have to get you dressed in your finery again, more's the pity." The wife sat beside her on the bench, which groaned and creaked under Arananta's weight. "The girl required to relinquish a new dress and shawl for the day wasn't happy. You'll suffer for her displeasure tomorrow, I assure you."

Concentrating on taking in as much of the food as she could before it was snatched away, Shalira didn't answer. Her curiosity was piqued. Bandarlok needed her to play the princess again today. She suppressed a tiny hope his need might present an opportunity for her. Arananta was drumming her fingers on the table beside Shalira and fidgeting, so she knew her time to eat was about over. Grabbing the mug and holding her breath, she managed to gag down half the warm, pungent contents.

"All right, enough. Time to get you dressed." The wife rose, and Shalira stood as well, hoping to avoid the indignity of being dragged about like an errant child. Grabbing her elbow in a viselike grip, Arananta led her out of the dining hall, through a confusing maze of open spaces and corridors, until they entered a warm, overly perfumed space. "My quarters." The Chief Wife released her with a shove. "The bed is right in front of you. Your dress and shawl are there. Hurry up, put them on. Your sandals will do. No one cares what you wear on your feet."

Dropping her makeshift blanket shawl, worrying if they'd give it back to her for the cold night, Shalira pulled the boxy slave's garment over her head and let it fall from her fingertips to the ground. *I hope I don't have an audience right now, other than Arananta.* She hadn't heard anyone else in the room. Locating her clothes, she dressed, trying to ignore the faintly sour smell of some other woman's scent overlying her own on the fabric. Clearly, bathing wasn't a high priority up here in the highlands.

"Is she ready yet?" Bandarlok strode into the room. "I want to get this over with, get these fucking outworlders off my lands."

Shalira's heart skipped a beat. Was he actually going to allow her to meet Michael? Her hands shook as she finished fastening her dress.

"Her hair's a mess," said Arananta, lifting a strand, tugging hard. "He'll question her unkempt appearance."

Bandarlok blew out an impatient breath. "Brush it then, but be quick."

Shalira stood still, biting her lip as the wife yanked a stiff, bristled brush through her tangled curls over and over. Finally, the woman tossed the brush on the bed. "I can't do any more with this."

Well, I'm certainly not going to offer to help. Shalira stood passively, waiting to see what they would do next.

"Fine," Bandarlok said. "This is only going to take a few minutes. He's a man, he won't notice anything amiss." Ponderously, he crossed the floor to Shalira. "The outworlder is leaving today. He says he was ordered by the emperor to take one last look at you, to report back." The chief snorted. "Sentimental waste of time, but since Kajastahn hasn't died yet, I can't afford to risk refusing this request, just in case."

Try as she might to contain the bubbling excitement, Shalira must have allowed something of her hope to show on her face.

"I warn you," Bandarlok said, gripping her arm tightly enough to leave more bruises, "I'll have warriors surrounding the tent. You say one wrong thing to this man and he'll die at your feet, understand? I don't care what weapons he has, he can't take on two dozen of my men in close combat and live. I want him gone, I don't want any trouble, but I'll kill him if he stays, or if you try to give him any hint of my intentions toward you." Laughing harshly, Bandarlok said, "I think his life means something in your heart. I'd have killed him for that insult alone but your father still lives, so my hand is stayed."

Shalira nodded, swallowing hard. The chieftain gave her a shake and pushed her forward, his hand at the small of her back, guiding her out of the wives' sleeping quarters and into the tent where he apparently conducted audiences.

I wish my vision would clear for even one minute so I could see Michael's face. But blank grayness interrupted by flashes of lightning was all she could see when she opened her eyes. She had to get control of her chaotic emotions if she wanted even a glimmer of sight in the next few minutes. Head spinning, she tried to slow her breathing.

"Your Highness, thank you for granting me a final audience," Mike said from ahead and to the left.

She stumbled over a wrinkle in the tent floor, half-dropping the shawl. Grabbing her in an iron grip, Bandarlok set her back on her feet.

Shalira pulled free of the chief's grasp, guessing he'd release her rather than have a scene. Taking advantage of the momentary freedom to move, she stepped quickly in the direction of Mike's voice. "I wish you well on your journey." Her mind was racing. *What can I say? How do I convey a sense of the danger I'm in? Plead for help without enraging Bandarlok—*

"I wanted to see for myself that you're fine and—and happy, a contented bride, before taking my leave." Mike's voice sounded strained to her ears. "To report to your father as ordered, of course."

An effective strategy to get Bandarlok to agree to the meeting. "I'm as happy as one can be in this new situation," she said. *Pavmiraia, please grant me sight for one second!* She blinked, squeezing her eyelids, took a deep breath, and raised one hand to rub her forehead. When she opened her eyes again, she was still beset by the flashes of light, but had a glimpse of Mike, his face tired and grim, his jaw set. She took a deep breath of his scent–man, leather, musk, some crisp spice unknown to her. Her heart beat painfully, realizing she might never be near him again. In a moment of inspiration, she grabbed her amulet and lifted the chain over her head, the enameled pendant swinging, tangling in the loops of the clan insignia. Frantically, she worked the disk free of the Windhunter necklace by touch alone. "A parting gift, Major, for luck."

The grayness closed in on her visual world again, no matter how hard she tried to channel power from the goddess, but she felt him accepting the necklace readily. He cupped her outstretched hand with both of his, pressing her fingers lightly for a heartbeat. Automatically, she curled her trembling fingers around his before forcing herself to lift her hand away. *I can't risk his life through any action of mine.*

Tears threatened to engulf her, but Shalira blinked hard to keep her composure a few moments longer. "May the pendant carry *your* deepest desire now," she said. "I—I'll have no further need of it."

"Enough." Bandarlok came to stand beside her, circling her waist with one beefy arm, hand casually cupping her butt, demonstrating her status as his possession. "You've satisfied your requirement to take official leave of my woman, outworlder. Time for you and your man to be on the trail."

Crushed against the chieftain's thigh, unable to see anything but the gray shadows, she heard a metallic clinking as Mike tucked her necklace away in a pocket. Would he remember what she'd told him, so long ago? That she'd never part with the thing until she died? Would he understand? He'd offered to help her before, back in the empty tomb. Did his offer still stand, now that they stood in Bandarlok's camp? *A pathetic straw to build hopes with. What can he and Johnny do for me anyway? Bandarlok has strength in numbers.*

Mike was speaking to her, she realized belatedly. "I wish you well, Your Highness."

"Good journey to you, Major."

She heard Mike walking away and took an involuntary step before Bandarlok's iron grip locked her in place. The tent flaps fell with a soft susurration as the outworlder left. A moment later she heard the sound of horses galloping away, and he was gone.

"I wish you well," she whispered, knees weak.

"Save your wishes for yourself, girl," Bandarlok said with a laugh. "I've had word from my spies in the capital. Your father slips in and out of a coma now and isn't expected to live beyond the new moon. You won't survive him long. At least now there'll be no more need for farces like this audience. Maralika certainly won't send for proof of how you're enjoying life as *my* wife." He spun her away. Off-balance, she fell into the waiting arms of the nearest guard. "Take her back to Arananta. Tell my wife I want this slave stripped of the needless finery and put to work scrubbing my sheets in the creek."

"Yes, sir." The warrior led Shalira out of the tent, his hand roaming a bit over her backside as they went.

At least Michael got away safely. I was foolish to hope he could do something to rescue me. Brushing away her tears, Shalira raised her chin, determined not to show her emotions to her lascivious guard or the chief wife. *I'll find some way to forestall their plans, even if I have to kill myself to deprive them of the pleasure.*

I'm going to kill them all if I have to, lay waste to this entire place if that's what's necessary to get her out of here. Seething with rage, hands fisted, Mike walked out of the tent, mentally counting the multitude of warriors Bandarlok had assigned to guard duty. Too many to take on, even if he and Johnny *were* now armed with their service blasters. No way to ensure Shalira's safety in a fight. Under the gaze of the silent, watchful clansmen, Mike took his horse's reins from his cousin and swung into the saddle. He shook his head ever so slightly, signaling Johnny that there'd be no conversation yet. Truth be told, he was so angry over what he'd just seen of how Shalira had been treated, if he said one word he'd be swearing for the next five minutes.

They trotted from the camp side by side, Johnny leading the pack horse, and rode for at least an hour, setting a path through the dense forest, heading to the mountains. Then Mike called a halt. "I don't think we're being followed."

"No, they appear to have accepted your assurances we just wanted to be on our way." Johnny eyed him. "Well? How was she?"

"She gave me this." Mike fished the necklace out of his pocket, dangling it from one hand.

Johnny touched the pendant with his index finger. "Pretty. I'm guessing there's more significance to this than a little parting gift?"

"Back in the city, Shalira told me the necklace had been her mother's, and she'd never take it off till the day she died." Mike stared at the bauble coiled in his hand. "Now today, she tells me she'll have no further need of it." Shoving the jewelry in his pocket, Mike shook his head as he sealed the flap. "They had her wrapped in a shawl, but when she was taking off the necklace, I saw her arms covered in bruises. Her hands were chapped and cut." He took a deep breath. "That's not the worst of it. She was wearing the Windhunter collar, but when she first walked into the tent I noticed deep red marks on her neck. I think the bastard tried to strangle her."

"You think Bandarlok is abusing her?"

"I think he's planning to kill her, or at least that's what she thinks."

Rubbing one hand along his jawline, Johnny tipped his head. "We never did get a straight answer about what happened to Saium. He vanished off the face of the planet, which seems ominous, given how you say the chief is treating Shalira."

"Did you see *any* signs of her clan in the camp? Any banners, anyone with a bird tattoo like Saium's?"

Dismounting to check his restless horse's rear hoof, Johnny shook his head. "No, and I didn't see any signs of preparation for a big wedding feast, either."

"I'm sure the wooden staff with the carved Windhunter bird totem we took from the tomb was burning in the fire pit last night," Mike said.

Johnny whistled as he dug a small pebble from the horse's hoof. "Not a good omen. What do you have in mind to do?"

"Go back in tonight, do some recon, extract the princess. Bandarlok is a dead man if he gets in my way." Mike eyed his cousin, waiting for Johnny to make some protest. "I'm taking her out of there and I'll kill anyone in the camp who interferes, including the chief. She's coming with me."

The sergeant merely rubbed his jaw and nodded slowly. "All the way to the Djeelaba Mountains? With Bandarlok and his highland warriors chasing us to add to the fun?" Johnny chuckled, tossing the pebble he'd removed from the horse's shoe as far away as he could. "Well, that'll reduce the boredom of the search and recovery job. And then what? Are we taking her into the Sectors?"

Mike nodded. "Home to Azrigone as my wife, if she'll have me. I won't be the first guy to return married to a local girl." He frowned. "You know the regs, I'm allowed to bring home a wife."

Johnny nodded. "Oh, I'm in. You know Command isn't going to like it, us complicating our mission with personal business. Bandarlok won't give her up without a fight."

"I don't care, this is my last job for them, we're basically doing Command a favor to take this mission on. They can court martial me if they want. Keep the veterans' acres."

"We have to accomplish our own mission objective," Johnny reminded him. "Only way to have what we want is to bring them what they want. Command made the parameters clear enough when they reassigned us to active duty." He spat.

Mike was undeterred. "We won't fail, my word on it."

"Just one thing, cousin. I hate to bring it up, but what if the lady insists on staying with Bandarlok, like she did back at the tombs? What if you're wrong and this necklace she gave you doesn't mean anything? If she still won't turn aside from doing what she sees as her duty to her father?" Johnny ran his reins through his gloved hands. "What's our play then?"

For a long minute Mike was silent. "Fair question. If I'm wrong, if she says no, then I ride away without a backward glance."

"Can you do that?" Johnny's eyebrows were raised to his hairline. "You seem pretty invested, old son. And if she's being abused—"

"I'll have to. But first she has to convince me. We're past the point where her loyalty to her father carries much weight with me. If the old bastard sent her to be abused and killed by this barbarian chief, there's no reason for her—or me—to go along with the plan. I screwed up the first time by not telling her straight out what she means to me. I should have told her I love her. I won't repeat the mistake. Now mount up."

"Maybe we can find out what happened to Saium while we're there tonight. Seems ominous to me the way he just disappeared." Johnny swung into the saddle.

Dinner had been a crust of bread and a half mug of the sour mare's milk. Shalira ate every crumb of the bread, even brushing the floor with the palm of her hand to be sure she'd gotten it all. It took her three tries, but eventually she forced herself to drink the milk. Foreign as it was to her, the fluid gave strength, and she couldn't afford to waste a single ounce. After the meal, she sat wrapped in the scratchy blanket with her back to the wall, concentrating. Although there wasn't much of the goddess's power available to be channeled in this place the more she controlled her breathing and stayed calm, the fewer flashes of white light strobed in her field of vision and the more distinct the gray shapes became.

She heard footsteps coming to the door of her hut. A moment later the door was unlocked.

"Bandarlok sends for you," a man said, his voice harsh.

Rising, Shalira smoothed her uncomfortable dress and walked to the guard as calmly as she could. She nurtured the cold ball of anger in her gut, trying not to give in to the fear pushing at her. Grabbing her arm hard enough to leave more bruises, the man hustled her along the complicated hallways and open spaces of the chief's family complex. She tried to count steps as best she could. If these barbarians kept her alive long enough, she'd figure out her way around and she *would* escape, even if only to drown herself in the river or die of exposure. *My death at least is going to belong to me, if I can manage it.*

She was in a new area of the camp, some place they'd never taken her before. The guard shoved her inside one of the tent dwellings. "I've brought the woman, sir."

Shalira smelled the chief before he spoke, his hot, sweaty body odor unmistakable in the room, mixed with the scent of potent black wine.

"Fine." A chair creaked as Bandarlok rose to approach her. Despite herself, Shalira tensed, startling reflexively as he took her hand, his touch less rough than usual. "Go," he said to the guard, his wine-sodden breath washing over her face as he spoke to the man behind her. "I'm not to be disturbed this night, understand? Leave orders for someone to fetch the slave at dawn."

So he doesn't mean to kill me tonight, then.

"As you command, sir." The warrior marched off.

Bandarlok led Shalira away from the entrance until her hip bumped a table. Releasing her, he hefted a wineskin, contents sloshing, and drank, sitting as he did so. The leather straps of his chair seat cracked, stretching under his weight.

"My wife thinks we should keep you alive, for a while at least," Bandarlok said. "She likes having a princess for a slave. It's amusing to watch you work, she says."

Shalira said nothing. *If he wants me to beg for my life, he's doomed to disappointment.*

"I haven't decided," he went on a moment later. "I like to keep my *wife* happy. She'll tire soon enough of having a clumsy, unskilled blind girl for a servant, royalty or not."

Standing still, Shalira blinked, trying to catch a glimpse of her surroundings. The gray mists were parting a little, but the view was hardly reassuring. Was there a massive bed across the room?

Clinking sounds were followed by scraping noises and the sudden odor of rubyfruit. *There must be a knife on the table if he's peeling fruit.* Her hand itched. Even a small knife would be enough to slit her wrists. *Or plunge into his eye, if I got the chance.* The idea was appealing.

"Have a little bite, princess?" He pushed a slice of the dripping substance at her lips, which she clamped shut, turning her head to the side. She might be half-starved, but she'd be damned if he was going to feed her like a pet. Rubbing the fruit slice over her lips enticingly, Bandarlok laughed. "It's quite a delicacy, rare here in the highlands. But suit yourself." Noisily, he sucked on his portion, spitting out seeds, chasing the snack with another long drink.

Licking her lips to remove the sweet, sticky juice, Shalira made a mental note of where he'd laid the knife. By the dull clunking sound, she'd wager it was on the wooden plate holding the fruit. Temptingly close to her.

"Take your wretched dress off," he ordered, leaning back in the chair if the creak of leather was any indication. "Slowly."

Realizing that if she refused, he'd tear the garment from her body and probably enjoy the violent act, Shalira efficiently stripped, ignoring his command to prolong the process. The room was warm, overheated, and she stood in her filmy underthings, the Windhunter collar heavy at her neck.

"Not enough meat on your bones," he said, critically, peeling another fruit by the sound. "I like my women substantial." After a moment of silence, he laughed. "Still nothing to say? Well, the emperor paid me a huge sum of money to fuck you, so tonight I'm going to carry out my half of the treaty. You might even like it." He drove the knife into the table and stood. "Get pregnant and I'll let you live till the baby's born, maybe even longer if it's a boy."

Moving like a striking snake, Shalira wrenched the knife out of the table, splintering the surface in her haste, and slashed out toward the sound of his breathing, hoping to catch some part of Bandarlok's body with the blade. He bellowed in pain and anger, grabbing her arm so hard she feared he might break the bone. Squeezing her wrist like an iron vise, he forced her to drop the weapon.

"Bitch, you cut me." He picked her up, Shalira kicked and punched fruitlessly as he carried her to the bed. Dumping her unceremoniously on the mattress, he held her down with one hand and slapped her across the face with the other. She lay stunned by the blow, while he undid his belt and bound her wrists together, pulling them over her head and looping them over part of the carved headboard. He grunted, climbing off the bed and standing for a moment, breathing hard. "Not so full of fight now, are you?" She aimed a kick where his voice was coming from, connecting with an unsatisfying, glancing blow. He laughed. "Well, maybe tonight will have its amusing moments after all. I didn't think you had any spirit."

Trying not to cry from the pain where he'd struck her, Shalira lay on the bed, tugging at her restrained wrists. Bandarlok walked away and she heard the sound of him bandaging the spot where she'd managed to wound him. Then he began peeling off his clothes, each garment falling on the floor as he discarded it. He fumbled with his pants, hopping on one foot, bumping into the table, swearing.

He's so drunk. If I could only get my hands free, maybe I could fight him off. She redoubled her efforts to get at least one hand loose. The leather was slippery, and the loops weren't as tight as she'd first thought.

"Oh, no you don't," he said, returning to the bed and kneeling with his bare, hairy legs on either side of her hips. "You're going to stay right where I want you until I decide to send you back to your kennel." As he ran one hand up her thigh he shifted on the bed, and she brought up her knee, hard. Howling, he fell away from her, only to come back a moment later. "Surprisingly rebellious. I think my wife is right—we should keep you around." He guffawed.

Terrified, Shalira said nothing, trying to calm her breathing. Her vision was completely black now and she was fighting to hang onto consciousness.

Bandarlok got off the bed, going to the table with wobbling steps. He guzzled more wine, burping loudly.

Shalira rolled herself over on the bed, one hand slipping free from the restraint. Since there was no reaction to this from Bandarlok, she hoped he was distracted, ignoring her. Frantic, she pulled the other hand free and slid to the floor, the bed between herself and the chieftain's voice.

Perhaps alerted by the sound of her body moving across the sheets, he cursed and came at her across the room, his footsteps heavy on the carpeted floor. Shalira pressed her spine against the tent wall, fists raised in self-defense.

"I'll put you in chains," he threatened. "Make sure you don't move from where I want you." He lunged across the bed and Shalira made a break for it, one hand on the bed frame as a guide, sprinting around the end and heading for where she remembered the small table being located. Tripping on the chair, which he'd moved at some point, she fell with a frustrated scream, grabbing at the table, which toppled over with her, spilling wine, food, dishes and utensils. Desperately scrabbling in the debris, hoping to find the knife by sheer luck, she was grabbed from behind by the hair and pulled to her knees.

"Enough games," Bandarlok said, breathing hard. "I like a bit of a tussle in bed as much as any man, but we're done with foreplay." He heaved her over his shoulder and carried her to the bed as she cursed and clawed at his back.

Throwing her on the mattress with a snarl of rage, he ruthlessly knotted a cord around her right ankle, securing her to the bed. Despite her strenuous resistance, pulling his hair, clawing at his face, he captured her other leg and prepared to restrain her further. "You'll pay for all this trouble," he said. "The harder you fight, the more I'm going to make you suffer."

Mike and Johnny watched the sentry patrols carefully from their place of concealment at the edge of the forest, figuring out the routes and timing. The guards were surprisingly lax, arrogant in their clan's superiority, perhaps. *Getting in is going to be a piece of cake. Nothing like infiltrating a Mawreg base.* Mike tapped Johnny on the shoulder, getting a nod in answer before the two Special Forces operators moved out in separate directions. Mike slipped through the loose perimeter and hid in the shadow of the central cooking hut. Working his way from the shelter of one structure to the next, he vaulted the low wooden fence and reached the back of the largest building in the camp—Bandarlok's private quarters. Guards stood sleepily at the front en-trance, leaving the sides and back of the massive, green and white striped tent unpatrolled.

Debating where Shalira might be held in the camp, Mike heard a scream from the closest tent, which was the chieftain's. Sure that the woman in jeopardy must be his princess, he crawled the final few yards.

Mike was thankful the full moons weren't due to rise till near dawn. Cutting a slit in the heavy fabric of the tent walls with his combat knife, he checked out the situation for a moment. Making no noise, he'd stepped inside the tent, finding himself in a small room full of boxes and baskets, when he heard crashing sounds and another scream that was definitely Shalira's. Taking a few steps forward, Mike was able to see into the main bedchamber, where candles blazed. Creeping to the doorway, he had a clear view of the large bed close to the far wall of the next room.

Bandarlok was struggling with an angry Shalira, trying to tie her up. As Mike watched, Bandarlok slapped her hard across the face before bending over her unrestrained ankle, rope in hand.

Moving like a panther, silently stalking his prey, Mike came up behind the distracted chief, jerked his head upright by his messy red braids, and slit his throat ear to ear in one smooth motion, his hunting knife an effective, noiseless weapon. Blood spewing, the chief fell from Mike's grasp onto the woven rugs without making a sound, dead before he hit the floor.

Shalira lay still on the bed for a second, breathing hard, hands clawed, ready to resume the fight. "Who's there?" Sitting up, still tethered by one ankle, she yanked the nearest fur to cover her half naked body.

"Sweetheart, it's me. I'm only sorry I couldn't get to you sooner." Mike said, taking a moment to wipe the knife on the sheet. "I'm going to cut you loose now so don't move."

"Michael." His name sounded like a prayer on her lips. "Thank the goddess." She swiped at tears on her cheeks with the back of her hand and took a long, shuddery breath. "Is he dead?"

"He'll never touch you or hurt you again. No one will, not while I'm alive to protect you, I swear." He severed the rope on her ankle.

Scooting closer to the end of the bed where he stood, Shalira opened one arm, still holding the fur against her body with the other, and Mike gave her a big hug, taking note of how she trembled. He wished he could transfer some of his strength to her. The sight of ugly bruises all over her body infuriated him. He kissed her cheek. "I'm sorry I had to leave you here, even for a day. Riding away was the hardest thing I ever did."

She leaned into his embrace, rolling her head against his chest, soft hair brushing his arm. "He would have killed you if you hadn't gone this morning."

Mike shoved the knife into its scabbard. "He could have tried."

"He was prepared—he warned me not to betray him. I prayed so hard you'd understand that giving you my amulet was a plea for help. Thank you for coming back."

"I never would have forgiven myself if I hadn't." He held her away from him, staring into her face. Her eyes were huge with shock, unseeing. *At least she'll never have to deal with the memory of seeing the chief's dead body.*

Keeping her voice low, she said, "What do we do now?"

"We escape." He paused, remembering how he hadn't said enough to her at the tombs. Frustrated, he knew now wasn't the time either. *She's traumatized. We've got to get out of here before we're discovered.* "We can't stop to talk now, but you need to know one thing—this rescue has no strings attached, okay? I want you safely away from this hellhole. We'll figure out the future, I swear."

"I know. You're a man of honor," she said, stroking his cheek with one hand.

Her simple faith in him touched his heart. "We need to get out of here, before someone comes in. Can you walk? Are those your clothes over there on the floor?"

Nodding, Shalira clutched the furs. "You mean the rags they gave me after stealing all my clothes?"

Scooping up the garments, appalled at the wretched dress and blanket shawl, he brought the items to her, along with the practical sandals. He placed them on her lap. "I won't peek, I promise. Unless you need help?"

Wrinkling her nose as she shook out the rough fabric of the dress, she shook her head. "I can manage. And you're right, we'll need to talk later. Although no one will come till dawn. He strictly forbade any interruptions in—in what he had planned."

"We need every moment to get as far away from here as we can." Hearing the rustling sounds as she dressed, Mike said, "I wish we had time to get you something better to wear, warmer. Mahjundan nights get cold. I promise, I'll outfit you with stuff from our gear, once we're safely away."

"I'm ready."

She was looping her unruly hair into a ponytail when he turned around. Grabbing the fur blanket from the bed, she stepped forward. He met her, taking her elbow in haste and steering her toward the exit, around Bandarlok's body and the debris from their earlier struggle. "I've cut a hole in the wall of the storeroom," he said as they crossed into the room. "From here we sneak across the rear of the compound. Stay low, try not to make a sound, and we'll take the same route out I used to come in. Bandarlok's guards are pretty lax."

"Where's Johnny?"

Bringing her to the slit he'd cut in the back wall, Mike said, "He's doing recon to see if he can find any trace of Saium."

She stopped walking, taking a sharply indrawn breath. "Saium's missing? I took comfort in believing he got away safely with you."

Cursing himself for not breaking the news more gently, Mike asked, "Bandarlok didn't say anything to you about him?"

"No. I do know he hated our entire clan, which he claims to have wiped out, leaving only Saium and myself." She touched the Windhunter necklace, tracing the design of the bird of prey picked out on the smooth gold of the collar in black pearls and diamonds. She was silent for a moment before raising her head defiantly. "A clan is more than a carved wooden totem and a golden collar. People are the heart of a clan, and as long as Saium and I both live, the Windhunters go on."

"That's the spirit, Your Highness," Mike said approvingly as he peered through the slit in the back wall of the tent. Still no sign of guards patrolling the encampment. "All clear. We need to go quickly and quietly. I'll guide you. We're going to meet up with Johnny outside the camp, find out what he's learned."

Drawing the fur cloak tighter around her shoulders, Shalira nodded, face set in determined lines. "I'm ready."

Mike patted her on the shoulder. "Quiet is essential now." Keeping to the shadows, he led her outside the boundaries of Bandarlok's large settlement. They had to lie low when a drunken warrior stumbled by on his way to the latrines, but in a few moments they were climbing the ridge to the rendezvous point.

Johnny was already there. He gave Shalira a hand up the last few feet, pulling her behind a tree on the ridge before accepting a hasty hug. "Your Highness, it's good to see you again."

"Any luck finding Saium?" Mike asked.

"Yeah. He's alive, but it ain't pretty." Johnny glanced at Shalira, eyebrow raised.

"Go ahead and tell us what you've found, Sergeant," she said, evidently hearing doubt in his voice. "Not knowing is worse than anything you can tell me."

"They're holding him in a tent off to the west, a few klicks from here. Not too far. Seems to be a makeshift prison. Two guards, both inside. They already beat the hell out of the poor guy, maybe tortured him. If we want to do something about it, we'll have to rush them through the front. No other way in. Can't cut through the back of the tent unobserved."

"But doable?" Mike asked.

Johnny nodded. "How much time do we have till Bandarlok raises the alarm?"

"He won't be raising any alarms. I killed him," Mike answered. "Shalira says he ordered the guards and his servants to leave the two of them alone till dawn, so it's a pretty safe bet we have a few hours. You'll have to go along with us," he said to the princess by his side.

"I don't want to slow you down or cause any problems. You must save Saium."

"She can wait with the horses while we go in and extract him," Johnny said. "We can ride to within one klick of where they've got him, but then we'll have to go in on foot."

It was a short distance from the camp to where Saium was being held. There wasn't anything resembling a trail, but Johnny found his way unerringly. Leaving the horses safely tethered in a grove, he led Mike and Shalira to the top of one last ridge overlooking a small tent set in a grove of trees. A fire was burning inside, flickering light visible through the open flap at the front.

As he drew his knife, Mike said, "Shalira, I want you to stay here, hidden among these trees. When the coast is clear, either Johnny or I will come fetch you."

"Wait, I need a weapon," she said, holding Mike by the elbow.

He exchanged puzzled glances with Johnny. "What for?" Guiding her to the closest sizable tree, he cleared some debris to make a spot for her to wait in a bank of fallen leaves.

"I won't be taken alive." She wrapped up in the fur as she sank to the ground, back against the huge tree trunk. "I know you think we're safe from pursuit for now, and I've every confidence in both of you but I'd feel better—more in control—having a weapon. And there's no time to teach me to shoot one of your blasters, even if I could see to aim it."

"No problem. Johnny, get the lady a combat knife, would you?" A moment later he gave her the blade his cousin took from a saddlebag. "Here's the signal for one of us coming to get you." Pursing his lips, Mike whistled a bird call from his home planet.

"Be careful." She clung to his hand for a moment.

"This is what we do for a living," Mike said, brushing a kiss on her palm as he gently disengaged from her grasp. "Knives only, Johnny. The sound of shots would carry back to the main camp in this still air, and then we'd have bigger problems." He didn't wait for Johnny's acknowledgment before descending the ridge to the tent, making use of all available cover. He and Johnny moved so quietly the guards in the tent had no warning of what was coming.

The clansmen's attention was on an unconscious Saium, strung up by the wrists on a framework of poles, his feet dragging on the hard-packed dirt floor. The guards had evidently been torturing him. A pattern of ugly, fresh burn marks trailed along his rib cage on the right side. Saium's head lolled to the side, a gag stuffed into his mouth to stifle any screams. Laughing and debating what to do to their victim next, the men were ready to revive him with a bucket of cold water.

Mike tackled the enemy on the left, Johnny taking the man to the right, achieving complete surprise. Both thugs fell dead in less than a minute. Johnny was already busy sawing at the rawhide thongs holding Saium to the poles, saying over his shoulder, "I took note of horses out back when I did my recon. Mounts for Shalira and Saium."

As if brought back to consciousness by the sound of his name, Saium groaned as they removed the gag and lowered him to the floor. Opening his eyes, he blinked slowly. "Major?"

Mike put a firm hand on the guardsman's shoulder. "Don't try to talk. You'll need your strength to sit on a horse. We're getting out of here in a minute."

The old warrior tried to sit up. "I owe you my life." He grabbed at Mike's arm. "You have to rescue the princess. Bandarlok's plans for her—"

Patting him reassuringly on the shoulder, Mike said, "I've already got her out of that snake pit. She's waiting for us on the ridge. Bandarlok's dead—there wasn't any choice if I was going to rescue Shalira."

"I only wish I could have done it," Saium agreed. "There's much evil he has to answer for in the afterlife. It would have been a pleasure to send him there."

Mike didn't disagree, but the point was moot. "Johnny, he needs a temporary patch job on these burns. Can you give him a shot of something so he can ride?"

"No problem." The always-prepared sergeant pulled a small medkit from one of the many pockets in his utilities. He pushed past Mike. "Give me some room."

"My entire clan has been slaughtered by Bandarlok and his people. I can't believe it, yet I must. The Bartuk Clan must pay for this treachery." Saium's voice shook with rage and suppressed grief. "And I'm just the Windhunter to take the blood price for my people."

"The best revenge is to go on living." Mike's voice was low and persuasive. "I'm going for Shalira, so she'll know we succeeded. She's probably worrying herself sick up there in the dark."

"She's used to the dark," Saium said.

"Not like this, she's not. She had a pretty rough time with Bandarlok before I got there."

As Mike climbed the ridge, whistling the little bird call periodically, he remembered when he'd gone to fetch Shalira after the battle in the Valley of Tombs. *Things between us are going to have a more favorable outcome this time.*

"Sweetheart?" he said in a low voice as he reached the tree line.

She stood up, back to the rough tree trunk, clutching the blanket in one hand and the big combat knife in the other. "Did you save Saium?"

"He's alive, pretty banged up." Mike reached her side. "Let me escort you to him. Johnny's pumping him full of drugs so he can ride."

He guided her down the hill, picking the easiest path for her.

Saium lay on the floor of the tent, eyes closed, jaw clenched as Johnny treated his wounds, but as soon as Mike brought Shalira in, the old man struggled to sit up. Tears in his eyes, he reached for her. Catching her hand, he said, "Can you ever forgive me for delivering you to that monster?"

She dropped to her knees, hugging him so tightly her knuckles went white in the firelight. "There's nothing to forgive. We both were doing our duty."

"And we've paid dearly for it," Saium said.

"I hate to interrupt the reunion, I know it's been a rough time for you both, but we'd better get going. If you'll allow me to finish sealing his burns, Your Highness, I'd appreciate it. Move a few steps to the left, please?" Johnny said.

"She might need some painkiller too, while you're at it," Mike said. "She got pretty badly manhandled back there at the camp."

Johnny nodded at the suggestion. "Sure, I got things that can dull the ache without putting you to sleep."

"I'd be forever grateful."

I'll go get the horses, bring them up so we can get the hell out of here." Mike squeezed Shalira's shoulder and ducked under the tent flaps.

A few minutes later, ready to make a getaway from the vicinity of the clans, Mike boosted Shalira into the saddle. "Let's ride before our luck runs out. We've got to get as far as we can under cover of darkness, while the camp sleeps."

"If we reach the banks of the Suaga River, I promise we'll go free," Saium assured them as they kicked their horses forward at a gallop. "This old Windhunter has some clan secrets those vermin can't dream of."

Mike kept the reins of Shalira's horse tightly wrapped around his right hand as they rode.

In the lead, he set a rapid pace, riding as fast as his horse could weave a safe trail through the forest. He kept them at this speed for a good three hours past dawn, stopping only for short breaks to rest the winded animals. As Saium had suggested, Mike was setting a course toward the Suaga River, which marked the official boundary between the foothills and the lower slopes of the Djeelaba Mountains proper.

During one of the breaks, Saium cocked his head, staring the way they'd come. "Hunting horns!" He swiveled in the saddle to stare at Mike.

Mike heard the horns sounding again. "Probably a couple of miles back. Sound carries a long way in the thinner air at this altitude. A race then, one we have to win. Shalira, are you ready?"

She was sitting straight in her saddle, chin up, composed. "Don't worry about me. I can hang on no matter how fast we go. This is a good little horse."

Mike shifted in his saddle, looking for Saium. "How much farther to the river?"

"Several hours of hard riding, at least." Saium frowned. "The trail gets easier in a few more miles, but it will be easier for those who follow, too."

The rest of the day was a blur forever after to Mike. He kept them galloping as much as possible to establish a greater margin of safety between them and those who hunted them, but always the horns would sound again.

Johnny rode rear guard. It took a shorter and shorter amount of time for him to double back to observe the pursuit and then rejoin the group.

Finally, in the late afternoon, Mike heard a roaring sound ahead.

"The Suaga!" Saium shouted, pointing ahead. "We must be close to the great falls, where the river drains into the low-lands. Not long now."

"Getting tight, Mike," Johnny warned. "They're going to be on us about the time we reach this river."

"Stop talking and ride, then." Mike touched his horse with his spurs.

Another short burst from the tiring animal and he came out on the banks of one of the most intimidating rivers he'd ever seen, on any planet. Wide, fast with wicked rapids, there was obviously a huge waterfall not too far from them.

Means a powerful current. Our horses are too tired to swim across. Mike pointed at the roiling waters, frowning at Saium. "You expect us to cross *this?*"

In the forest behind them the hunting horns blared again, much closer.

Saium was undaunted. "Trust me, there's a way across. One summer when I was a boy, drought left the river lower than any other time in memory, and I found a safe place to ford, even at full flood level."

Mike shaded his eyes with one hand and studied the desolate landscape awaiting them on the other side and the thickly forested foothills rising beyond. "We've got to get across this monster of a river now or the Bartuk Clan warriors are going to get their revenge for Bandarlok's death."

"Too close to the falls here," Johnny said, pointing at a tree trunk drifting past them at a rapid pace, "There's a strong current through this pass."

"Here would be suicide," Saium agreed. "We must find my boyhood landmarks. The way is more to the west."

Mike lifted the reins, urging the black stallion to proceed along the riverbank. "Lead on, then. We can't waste any more time or they'll be on top of us."

Following his lead, the others turned their horses, the tired animals picking their way carefully on the muddy surface.

Maybe half a mile farther on, Saium raised his hand for the group to halt. "We make the crossing here."

The first of their pursuers burst onto the riverbank back to the east, near the falls. Shouts and more horns broadcast their arrival and excitement at catching sight of their quarry.

Pointing to the opposite river-bank, Saium spared no attention for the rapidly oncoming warriors. "I recognize the rock formation directly across from us, the one shaped like a sleeping bartuk."

"This is a nightmare," Johnny shouted over the roar of the water. "We're never going to make it across."

"No choices left," Mike said simply. Pulling her horse closer, he leaned in to address Shalira, who had a death grip on her saddle and was pale and silent. "Hang on tight, no matter what happens. We're going to try fording the river now."

"I trust you, and I trust this horse." Her face calm, Shalira patted the little mare on the neck and sat straight in the saddle.

Saium forced his horse down the bank and into the narrow band of quiet water at the river's edge. Mike came directly behind him, tugging on the reins to ensure Shalira's mare followed. Johnny led the pack horse. Saium's mount lost its footing in the water and swam, fighting against the current. Suddenly the horse scrambled, finding something solid under the swirling water. Saium let the animal stand for a moment, man and horse gathering confidence before walking in madly swirling water up to the horse's knees, heading for the opposite bank. "The safe path is narrow," he yelled. "Follow my lead exactly."

Buzzing like an angry bee, a bullet whizzed past Mike's ear as he forced his reluctant horse deeper into the water, pulling Shalira's mare behind him. The horses started swimming for the point where Saium had found the narrow ridge that was his ford. Pausing to let loose a few rounds of sizzling blaster fire to set the trees ablaze, Johnny brought up the rear.

About the time Mike thought he'd have to allow the horse to attempt swimming across the river, the animal found the first rock under its hooves. Staring into the foamy, cold, greenish water, Mike could barely make out the black shadows of the stepping stones.

More shots rang out from the Bartuk Clan warriors on the bank. Risking a backward glance, Mike observed a large party of men milling at the water's edge, arguing amongst themselves. Some plainly wanted to abandon the chase, while others were gesticulating and pointing at the river, where their quarry was rapidly drawing farther away to the safety of the other bank.

Firing short bursts at the enemy from time to time, Johnny was bringing up the rear, shooting when he could spare attention from trying to navigate the hidden path. His aim was badly off under the stress of the river crossing, but accurate enough to cause the Bartuks to dodge into the cover of the trees.

Mike was on the other shore now, with Saium and Shalira, watching the last part of the drama play itself out. The faction among their pursuers who argued for following them into the river prevailed. Eight men urged their horses into the swirling water, swimming toward the point where they seemed to think better footing existed. Johnny shot one man, who toppled into the river with a startled yell and was swept away. The riderless horse clambered to safety on the opposite bank, but the other warriors kept coming.

As Shalira covered her ears and hunched low in her saddle, Mike and Saium unholstered their weapons and sent a barrage of covering bullet-and-blaster fire arcing over the river as Johnny and the pack horse finished crossing.

Mike took careful aim on the first warrior who reached the narrow band of shallower water. As soon as the man's horse found the welcome footing, Mike shot the rider, winging him. The Bartuk clansman fell partway from the saddle, but managed to grab his horse's mane, avoiding the water. As the next person in line tried to help him, their mounts got tangled up together on the rock. The third horse in the column made a plunging rush onto the stepping stone. In the blink of an eye, all three horses and riders had been swept away into the current. Misjudging where the stone was, the next man went rolling and bobbing downriver toward the roaring falls. The fifth man shouted and tried to redirect his horse toward shore. Confused and frightened, the animal collided with the horse swimming behind it and both were carried away.

By now, the remaining Bartuk Clan members had apparently decided they were in a no-win situation and retreated to safety. Clustered on the far bank, the enemy leaned around the trees sheltering them, waved their fists and cursed, firing wild shots at random.

Laughing, Mike snapped off a sardonic salute in the direction of their pursuers as he wheeled the black stallion to leave the riverbank. "Saium, my apologies for ever doubting you."

Well satisfied at having saved the situation, the old guardsman nodded, although visibly less jubilant over their escape than Mike was. "Not only are they afraid of your weapons and the river, they fear the natives who dwell on this side of the water. Venturing to this shore can lead to certain death. We'll have to keep a sharp watch."

"So how did you survive, coming into this territory when you were a boy?" Johnny asked as he checked his blaster charge and holstered the weapon.

"I was cautious and I didn't draw attention to myself." Saium nodded in self-satisfaction. "I remember my scout craft, never fear. We'll find your crashed ship and escape from these mountains unscathed, just as I did when I went treasure hunting many a time as a boy."

"Treasure hunting?" Shalira tilted her head in his direction as the group moved away from the river shore.

"The emperor's ancestors made many attempts to conquer the tribes who live here," Saium said. "Always they were driven back, sometimes slaughtered on the road as they fled. Finally the emperor himself—one of your ancestors—disappeared on a campaign into the Djeelaba. Legend has it he threw the Cherindor Scepter into the river with his dying breath, so the enemy couldn't possess its great powers. His heirs declared the crusades were over, honor and the gods satisfied. No more need to explore the area."

"And now here we are, hundreds of years later," Shalira said. "Traveling into the mountains again. I remember the stories."

Mike exchanged glances with Johnny as they rode. *Doesn't sound to me like her people actually won. I wonder if the tribes who did still roam here.*

Mike didn't waste time gloating over the escape, but led his party away from the river, deeper into the mountains. Not wanting to camp in the open, he was determined to reach the shelter Saium had promised before night fell. Sure enough, in another hour of riding, as the first spatters of what promised to be a hard rain began to fall, Saium led them to the huge cave he remembered using as his base camp many years ago. Mike and Johnny stabled the horses in a large room off to the side of the entrance, harvesting what fodder was available in the immediate area of the cave. Saium arranged accommodations in the other chambers and started a cooking fire and dinner, after which he joined Mike and Johnny as they stared out the mouth of the cave at the leaden sheets of rain.

Shalira laughingly refused to stir from the roaring fire, clutching her blanket closely. "There's no attraction to me in proximity to the downpour."

After making sure the fire was burning steadily, with a minimal amount of smoke, Mike clapped Saium on the shoulder. "Guess you were right about this cave having natural chimneys. I was dubious about making a fire in here, but I'm a believer now. You know these mountains like the back of your hand. We never would have made it without you today."

Standing a little taller, his eyes gleaming, Saium snorted. "I roamed all over the Djeelaba as a boy. I loathed being confined and following orders." Rubbing his chin, the guardsman said, "So then of course, I spent several decades cooped up in the city, constrained in every way on a daily basis by the palace protocols."

"Good thing the storm didn't hit earlier, while we were trying to ford the river." Mike pulled his collar tighter at his throat, glad the Sectors uniforms were water resistant.

"Mountain gales usually go on like this for a day and a night," Saium told them. "We rest here tomorrow. Her Highness is a strong-minded woman, but I think she'll benefit from the respite."

"She's been through a lot," Mike agreed. "Still, if we can ride tomorrow, I'd risk it. Finishing our mission and getting off the planet in one piece is the safest thing for all of us."

Saium watched the rain falling in sheets. "The day after will be clear, and we can travel onward. You'll need to explain to me more exactly where this crashed ship of your comrades' is."

"The fix isn't too clear," Mike admitted. "The beacon bounces off these mountains, making the signal erratic. Mineral deposits, no doubt. Which is why Command had to go to all the trouble of sending Johnny and me out here, rather than homing in on the distress beacon and doing a straightforward extraction.

Care to make a rough guess how many days' ride it'll be to the general area, based on what we told you before?"

Closing his eyes for a moment, Saium wrinkled his brow, lips moving soundlessly as he calculated. "Probably three or four at the most."

Mike nodded. "And you're sure we don't have to worry any more about pursuit?"

"Bandarlok's clan salved their pride by making the effort to capture or kill us. Having lost five or six warriors, they'll be more than satisfied about their honor." Saium laughed, the most carefree sound Mike had ever heard from him. "From this day on, they'll all be too busy fighting over the spoils of what Bandarlok held to care about us!" Cackling, he slapped his knee. "Maybe some other tribes will move against them, while there's a lack of strong leadership. I can only hope."

"What about the mountain people?" Mike asked, not sharing Saium's interest in the downfall of the Bartuk Clan. "How will they react to us riding through their territory?"

Saium sobered, straightening and peering into the rain as if he expected the enemy to be sneaking up on them. "It's true we must be careful. There are fierce warriors in the Djeelaba, with strange, cruel gods and bizarre customs. Luckily, when I was a boy, I always saw them before they sniffed out my presence, but now, thinking back, I marvel at the risks I ran. The overconfidence of youth. We can't take chances with the princess."

"Right, we'll have to be on guard and get our job done as fast as possible." The solid weight of the Mark 27 riding at his hip was reassuring. Mike didn't plan to be an easy target for anyone else on this planet.

"How about plotting a route through the mountains after dinner?" Johnny suggested. "I'm tired of stew, but this stuff Saium got started smells good enough to change my mind."

"You two go ahead and eat. I'll do guard duty," Mike said. "Save me a bowl if it's any good, will you?"

"Sure, but I'd be happy to take first watch." The sergeant raised his eyebrows. "I'm thinking Shalira might enjoy your company more than mine or Saium's."

"I do need to talk to her," Mike said. "But the conversation requires privacy, and a lot of time. So you two eat first, with her, and I'll come along later."

Saium caught some nearly invisible hand signal from Johnny and left them. As the old man sauntered away, whistling, Johnny gave Mike a measuring stare. "Want to talk about it?"

"I need to get my thoughts in order before I try talking to her. I blew it the first time she and I had this conversation, after the ambush at the tombs. I can't afford to get it wrong now."

Nodding, Johnny sat on a boulder across from Mike. "Hard to know sometimes what a woman wants to hear from a guy, what the magic words are."

Leaning over, Mike scooped up a handful of pebbles and started tossing them into the rain. "Yeah, so far my record on this job isn't too glowing. I've killed two men, neither one having a damn thing to do with our mission. I got drawn into local matters totally removed from what we came to accomplish. Hell, our involvement breaks a hundred regs on a closed world. Gonna be a hell of an after-action report." He gave his cousin a sideways glance.

"The emperor gave us no choice about traveling with Shalira. Would have taken a heart of stone to leave her with Bandarlok once we understood the truth of the situation." Johnny shrugged. "Last time I checked, neither one of us has gotten that jaded."

"I'd be the last person to disagree with your assessment, but the kind of mistakes and decisions I'm making would have gotten us killed on any other mission." Mike threw away the rest of the pebbles in disgust. "What's the matter with me?"

Tilting his head, Johnny winked. "Other than being in love?"

Mike gave him a half smile but said nothing.

Leaning against the rock, the sergeant pulled a new piece of wood from his pocket to carve, drawing his small knife and flicking it open with an efficient motion. He rotated the wood over and over in his long fingers, searching for the spot to make the first cut. "We've both lost our edge—I don't have to tell you that. The last deployment was one too many, now here we are again." Focusing on his carving, Johnny said, "We're Special Forces till we die, but we ain't in the mind-set any more. It was a mistake for Command to pull us out of the retirement queue and insist we take this job." The pile of wood shavings grew on the cave floor next to him.

Crossing his hands behind his head, Mike leaned back, trying to relax. "I'd say it was a mistake for us to agree, no matter how many extra allotments of veterans' acres they offered us. Or how much they talked about possible survivors trapped in the mountains. Of course, if we hadn't come, I'd never have met Shalira." He rubbed the back of his neck and sought a more comfortable position on the boulder. "Hard to imagine life without her now. I always wondered what it'd be like to fall in love, how I'd know I'd met the right woman." He rolled his shoulders.

"And?"

"You just know. She gets under your skin and becomes more important than your own life. I can't explain it any better." He stared into the rain. "Her time with Bandarlok would have been short and hellish, and I never would have known."

"Lords of Space move in mysterious ways, all right. She's tough." Johnny raised his eyebrows and nodded to himself. "I admire her. She was shook up by what Bandarlok did to her, but she rode like a trooper when we were escaping those revenge-happy thugs. She managed all those long hours in the saddle, then the river crossing. Drugs helped, but most of it was her stubbornness. Strong lady." Johnny held up the small carving, which Mike could already tell was going to be a rearing horse. "This is for her, a souvenir of today's wild ride. You planning to marry her?" His cousin bent over the tiny horse, shaping its mane.

Mike sat up straight and nodded emphatically. "As soon as we complete this mission, if she agrees. That's why it's so damn important I don't blow this conversation, now I have a second chance to make my case with her. Once Shalira's my wife, she's a Sectors citizen and no one can touch her, or send her back to Mahjundar against her will."

Johnny set the horse on the stone. "Yeah, I understand your plan."

Mike picked up the miniature equine, admiring the details in the fading gray light, which posed no barrier to his enhanced night vision. "I'm expecting you to be my best man, you know."

"Dress uniform, I suppose?" Grinning, Johnny brushed a hand over his less than inspection-state utilities, sending wood shavings flying. "For my wedding present, I'll help you pay her spacefare home. And Saium's. I think they're a package deal." He took the carving from Mike's hand. "But for now, I'll give her this."

Before Mike could say anything, his cousin strolled into the cave in search of dinner.

Happy to be alone for a while, Mike found it soothing to sit and watch the rain beat down on the forest outside the cave. Saium was probably correct——no one in their right mind would venture out in this torrential rain, but he had to maintain vigilance. An occasional bolt of lightning or rumble of thunder broke the endless hissing sound of the rain. He was glad the cave was situated so no runoff came inside.

When Johnny finally reported for duty four hours later, Mike was ready to eat, his stomach no longer tied up in knots.

"The others asleep?" He slid off the rock and stretched.

"Shalira's waiting for you with a bowl of stew. Quite domestic," Johnny teased, ducking the blow Mike feinted in his direction. He caught Mike's sleeve. "Listen, I don't know if it makes any difference but I've got a theory about her blindness, about how she got her sight back in the tomb and all."

"I snagged a few pieces of the medicine jar before we bugged out," Mike said. "Figured on having the substance analyzed once we got back to the Sectors."

"Waste of time." Johnny shook his head. "I'm no doctor but I do know whatever she drank didn't magically restore her vision. She did it herself."

"Wait a minute, she's not faking this disability, if that's what you mean." A spurt of anger shot through him.

But Johnny was holding up a hand. "No, I agree she's blind most of the time all right, but I believe it's not true blindness, not like your niece Cheryl. Saium told you Shalira was found unconscious at the scene of her brother's murder, right? Maybe was assaulted herself? Injured anyway."

Mike nodded, trying to curb his impatience, wondering where Johnny was going with this.

"And then woke up blind? Right, well there's a thing called conversion disorder, where a person has had something so awful happen to them, that their mind deliberately blanks out their sight, or maybe paralyzes them, or makes them mute. It's a form of escape from something too big to handle. I ain't criticizing. Hell, you know I have my own problems after that last mission, so I get it." Johnny rubbed his forehead. "I did some research for my own reasons then, fell over this conversion disorder thing. Stuck in my mind, probably because of Cheryl, although her case is different."

"Can this disorder be cured?" Mike's mind was racing with possibilities.

"Maybe. Better if it's treated right away and her highness has been told she's blind for what, fifteen years now? Don't go getting your hopes up and don't go talking to her about it, you gotta promise me. This is a delicate thing, gonna need experts, not just a field medic like me, who's guessing. But I do remember reading about some things that can be tried. The fact she had her vision back in the tomb, no matter how it happened, might be helpful when the time comes to open the subject."

"Thanks for telling me about this. I promise not to say anything to her until we're home and I can consult specialists." Even thinking about how to raise the subject with Shalira was daunting. Mike wasn't tempted at all to break his promise to Johnny. How do you tell a woman who's blind that maybe there isn't a physical reason for her condition? Now wasn't the time or place, especially with so little information to go on, only Johnny's half remembered research. No use to stir up her hopes until he knew more. "I guess I'll go have that dinner now. She and I have plenty of other things to discuss, trust me."

"Good luck." Johnny picked up a new stick and began peeling the bark off in long strips with his pocketknife.

Shalira sat cross-legged by the fire's embers, stirring the stew from time to time. At the sound of his footsteps, she glanced up, a huge smile on her face. "I'm so glad you're off duty now." She ladled out a big bowlful of dinner for him before rising gracefully to her feet. "Come into the side chamber Saium prepared for me. We can have some privacy."

Muttering in his sleep as if responding to his name, the old man stirred and rolled over in his blanket before resuming stentorian snoring which echoed in the cave.

Taking the bowl, Mike clasped the fingers of his free hand around hers. "Let me guide you."

Stepping carefully past Saium so as not to awaken him, he took her into the alcove set aside for them. He noted that a single sleeping place had been prepared, his Sectors bedroll under some blankets, topped with the fur Shalira had taken from the nomad camp. A small Sectors-issue lamp was set on low on the cavern floor beside the bed. "You should be getting some rest," he said as she made herself comfortable on the bedroll, wrapped in the fur, legs curled up under her.

She leaned back. "I'll be fine. Johnny gave me some more of those wonderful painkillers. I'm sure all three of you are just as tired and cold as I am. I wanted to wait up for you, because we've had no chance to be private today until now."

Seating himself cross-legged on the end of the makeshift bed, he sampled the stew. "You've had a grueling couple of days."

"No more than any of you." She took her hair down from its loose coils and spread the tendrils over her shoulders, combing out snarls with her fingers, as she'd done many times on the trail to the Valley of Tombs.

"Pretty busy, running from Bandarlok's warriors then searching for this cave in the downpour." Mike set the mug aside. The meal was lukewarm and too spicy for his taste. "Saium says it'll rain through tomorrow, so I've decided to spend the day here, rest the horses. We drove them pretty hard, especially the pack animals.

Then maybe four more days until we reach the wreck. Depending on the location and how badly smashed the ship is, maybe another day working onsite. Set the horses free, call for extraction and bug out."

"If you're not going to eat the stew I stirred so diligently," she said, "come and keep me warm, won't you?"

"Now, how do you know I'm not wolfing down the cooking?" he teased, reaching out to tug on a strand of her silky black hair.

"I heard you place the mug on the ground after only one or two swallows." She patted the blankets beside her. "Please?"

Scooting closer, he put an arm around her shoulders. "You're not getting chilled, are you?"

"No, I changed into dry clothes Johnny was kind enough to lend me from your gear, and I've been by the fire all this time. Surely you must have been admiring this outfit since you came inside?" Laughing at her own joke, she snuggled contentedly by his side, one arm draped around his waist. "And after you find this wreck you seek and we 'bug out' as you so elegantly express it, then what?"

"We go home. Eventually, we'll have to travel across the Sectors to my planet, Azrigone. Which reminds me, there's something I need to return to you." Unfastening his pocket, he brought out the enameled locket, which gleamed even in the scant light the lantern was throwing.

Tilting her head, she extended her hand, palm up, and he laid the necklace in the center. Drawing a deep breath, she closed her fingers over the precious possession, holding the pendant to her heart for a moment. "Will you put it on for me?"

Awkwardly, he reached to loop the chain around her neck.

Shalira adjusted the locket so it sat on top of the Windhunter collar. As she fiddled with the jewelry, she said, "What happens to you and me next?"

"Are you sure you want to have this conversation now?" he asked.

"We left words unspoken between us before." Her voice was low, almost a sigh. "It's only by the grace of the goddess we were given a second chance. We mustn't waste her gift. Tonight we're safe. Tomorrow?" Sketching a small sign in the air with her fingers, as if warding off possible bad fortune, she shrugged. "Who knows?"

He rolled his shoulders. "After what you endured at Bandarlok's hands, I was concerned you might not want to worry about these matters tonight. I don't have to sleep in here unless you want me to."

"Yes, you did say in Bandarlok's tent you were performing a rescue without strings." She smiled. "I'm more grateful for your help than I can ever express." She began braiding her hair. "There's no haven for me on Mahjundar any longer," she said. "Even if my father lives, he'd be the first to order my execution, for breaking the treaty with Bandarlok. He'd lose face if he didn't. And Maralika hates me."

Mike reached out, catching her hand. "Don't braid it tonight, okay? I like it down, around your shoulders." He let the silken strands flow through his fingers. "I've never seen such beautiful hair. Each filament practically glows in the firelight."

"Oh." Smiling, she folded her hands in her lap. "In that case—"

Taking a deep breath, Mike said, "Let's begin at the Valley of the Tombs, when I was completely out of line, what I said to you. I do understand your actions, going ahead with what you felt was your duty."

Shalira stared straight ahead. Twining her fingers through his and squeezing gently, she pressed a kiss on the back of his hand before rubbing her soft cheek against his palm. "You were so angry. And then we had no chance to talk. What were you offering me, there in the tomb?"

Lords of Space, why is talking about this stuff so hard? He'd rather charge into battle naked than talk about his emotions but this was his chance with her and he had to find the words. "Time to breathe, time to make another decision for yourself, time to fall in love with me maybe? Although, as it turned out, with Bandarlok arriving, it was a futile gesture on my part."

"I was already in love with you." Face set in serious lines, brows drawn together, she said, "I had to send for Bandarlok, or so I believed. I'd summoned him long before I met you."

Hugging her tight, he kissed her forehead. "I know. To be honest, I was probably buying time for myself, too, not laying it all on the line, what was in my heart. I wasn't sure myself. I said a lot of harsh things in the heat of the moment, there in the tomb. I apologize."

"No need. I understood your suspicions. And you were right in your accusations. Originally I was merely—what did you call it?— hedging my bets, by getting my father to assign you to escort me. I had little concern for you and Johnny, only that you were from the Sectors and Maralika and Vreely wouldn't want to have outworlder eyes on any of their black deeds. But the longer you and I were in each other's company on the road, the more I had to fight my heart when it came to you." She pulled the furs tighter.

Mike drew a deep breath. *Here we go, this is where I blew it in the tomb.* "You know I've got deep feelings for you?"

"But you don't want to rush me." Her voice held a hint of amusement again. A small dimple showed in her cheek.

"Right. What you said, about the goddess giving us a second chance? I don't want to miss the opportunity. I want everything to go right where you and I are concerned." He ran his free hand through his hair. "Riding away from that bastard's camp yesterday, leaving you behind, knowing you were being mistreated, in danger, was the hardest thing I've ever done. I wanted to take my blaster and level the place, grab you and get the hell off this planet. Anyone who knows me will tell you I never lose control on a mission, never get distracted from the job, but lady, you got through my shields without trying. I've never felt like this about a woman before."

Evidently pleased by his emotion, she tilted her head. "Should I apologize?"

"Don't you dare." Unable to resist temptation, he leaned over to kiss her, keeping the contact light.

Shalira seemed to have other ideas, grabbing him so hard she pulled him off balance and narrowly avoided falling on the bed. She kissed him with mounting passion, her tongue tracing the seam of his lips until he parted them with a groan and shifted to pull her into his lap, into a better position as their tongues tangled in an erotic dance. Her shapely bottom pressed against his raging hard-on and Mike broke off the caress, fighting to stay in control of the situation, remembering she'd recently been traumatized by Bandarlok. Ignoring her puzzled expression, he moved her off his lap, onto the blanket beside him.

Taking one soft hand in his, he said, "Back at the tombs, I was pretty mixed up, not sure of my emotions, afraid to trust myself, so I didn't speak plainly and I nearly lost you." He stopped, taking a deep breath against the pressure of emotion in his chest. His heart thumped so loud he was sure she could hear it. "I love you, and I don't ever want to be parted from you again. Will you—will you marry me? I'm sorry I don't have a ring to offer you, but I swear I'll have the *Andromeda's* captain marry us as soon as we arrive in orbit."

She rested her fingers on his lips in a gentle shushing motion. "Rings and ceremonies won't change what's already between us. The gods wouldn't have favored us this far if they didn't mean to see us through to the end. You answer my unspoken wishes, grant the dreams I'd locked in Pavmiraia's amulet. You give me the true love I never thought I'd find. I can't imagine any other future than being by your side."

"As my wife." Unwilling to accept anything less, determined to give her all the protection he could, in his world or hers, Mike pulled her close again and resumed the kiss. He slipped down on the sleeping pad until they lay wrapped around each other, his erection tenting his utility pants, pressing into the warm crevice of her equally clothed body.

Startling him a little with her boldness, Shalira yanked his shirt loose and ran her hands under the fabric, massaging his naked back in lazy circles as they continued to kiss.

Mike pulled away, rubbing noses with her for a moment before saying, "You'll be my one and only wife, by the way." He hoped she could hear the teasing tone in his voice. "In case you had any doubt."

Shalira laughed as she unfastened the unfamiliar tabs on her borrowed uniform shirt. "I'd better be! I'm convinced the Sectors model for marriage is far superior to the Mahjundan custom." She kissed his neck, nipping ever so slightly. "No concubines, either." She tossed the shirt aside.

"Not one, I swear." His eyes were drawn to her exposed breasts, covered now only by the filmy white bra she'd been allowed to keep by the nomad women. He cupped the soft mounds, one in each hand, and planted kisses on the pillowy tops, slipping one thumb under the edge of the fabric to tease at the left nipple, watching the sensitive flesh pebble under his attention. Shalira closed her eyes and arched into his touch, grinding her hips against his erection.

Mike swallowed hard, pulling his hands away from her delectable body. "Shalira."

Probably startled by the seriousness of his voice, her eyes flew open. Arms entwined around his neck to keep him close, she said, "What is it? What's the matter? Why are you stopping?"

"Are you sure you want to make love to me tonight?"

"Don't I look like a woman who wants to pleasure her man and be pleasured?" When he didn't immediately respond, she released her hold on him, rolling onto her side, propping her head on her hand. "I appreciate your restraint and I honor you for it, but I'm not as delicate as you believe. What Bandarlok tried to do was ugly and violent and full of hate. I'm leaving all of that on the other side of the river. We're here now. You're my future, the man I love, and I want to replace the bad memories with good ones. I need such peace. I need you." She reached out, touching his thigh and sliding her fingers until she found his cock, straining at the heavy fabric of the utilities. Her clever fingers undid the fastening and slipped inside his trousers. Wrapping her hand around as much of his erection as she could and stroking from root to tip, squeezing gently, she said, "And I don't want further delay in starting on those good memories. All right?"

"Anything you say, Your Highness." Capturing her lips, Mike went to work on disrobing both of them as rapidly as he could.

Glad she didn't have to spend any more time persuading Mike to proceed with making love to her, Shalira allowed him to remove her bra and slide the silky panties down her legs with aching slowness, before tossing them aside. He sat up for a moment to remove his boots and muttered something about turning down the light. She lay back against the fur, one arm pillowed under her head, while she heard him removing his trousers. Wishing she had her sight, so she could view her lover, she sighed.

Instantly Mike was next to her, his long, hard body pressed against hers, his cock jutting against her thigh insistently. "Are you all right?"

"Impatient." She trailed one hand along the hard sculpture of his chest, past his hip bone, and caged the impressive girth of his shaft with her nimble fingers. Rubbing her thumb across the head, then teasing the edges with a light caress before sliding her fingers to the velvet pouch below, she was pleased at his indrawn breath, the way he pressed closer to her as she stroked him.

With a shiver of delight, she felt his lips close over her nipple, licking and teasing the sensitive bud with just enough pressure. He pulled her gently into a better position and kneaded the other breast with his free hand, murmuring in apparent pleasure while he continued his attentions. She ran her fingers through his close-cropped hair, massaging the back of his neck as he traced a path over her belly, gently parting her thighs to explore the intimate area hidden there. Releasing her breast, he trailed kisses down her stomach, which tickled and made her squirm with pleasure. Raising his head for a moment, he said, "I've had all the injects for any disease known to humans."

"So practical. I wasn't worried," she said, pleased he cared to reassure her.

"But I don't have any protection with me. Johnny and I weren't expecting to be, uh, social on this trip."

"Protection?"

"Condom," he said, stroking her inner thigh, fingers coming achingly close to her already damp clit as he played with the curls at the vee of her legs.

"If we create a child together, I'll be happy, won't you?" She was puzzled and a bit hurt.

"A baby with you would be wonderful," he reassured her and Shalira heard nothing but the truth in his emphatic tone.

"Well then, now we've settled every possible issue—oh!" She gasped as he lowered his head and his tongue embarked on a series of skillful exploration of her most sensitive places. She squirmed in pleasure as Mike demonstrated his experience and talents as a lover. Delicious tremors ran through her, his attentions pushing her over the edge, into the throes of a glorious orgasm. Trying to be quiet and not awaken Saium in the outer chamber, she bit her lip and moaned with pleasure, arching in his hold and grinding her hips against him.

"Now then," Mike said after a few minutes, pleased satisfaction in his tone, "I think you're ready for me."

"You delight in understatement," Shalira answered. She grabbed at his shoulders, pulling him closer. His cock pressed against her and he reached to guide himself past her outer lips and deeper inside, thrusting carefully at first.

Locking her legs behind his back, Shalira pulsed her internal muscles, caressing his shaft and releasing as he pushed in and out of her body, moving faster and penetrating deeper with each movement of his hips, urged on by her reaction. Talk of how to best please a man was frank in the harem, and while she wasn't as experienced as many, she knew more than an emperor's daughter might ordinarily. People tended to forget she was present, so quiet she was, and she had excellent hearing.

Shalira blanked her mind, concentrating on the moment and Mike as the waves of pleasure coursed through her, every move of hers met by an answering one from him, heightening the sensations. His cock was buried deep within her and her orgasm was close. "Kiss me," she panted, "or they'll hear me scream your name."

He obliged, his tongue pushing to meet hers as they clung together, locked in the moment and the overwhelming sensations.

Mike held her close to his heart as the intensity of their mutual climax peaked and began to fade. "I love you," he said, smoothing her damp hair away from her face.

"I love you, too." Limp and sated, Shalira curled into his embrace as he pulled the fur over them. "I don't think I could be any happier than I am right this moment."

"A challenge if I ever heard one," he said, hugging her. "In the best possible sense."

True to Saium's prediction, the rain continued all the next day, but the skies were clear at dawn on the day after. Reenergized and optimistic about the success of his mission, Mike led the group away from the cave. After a few hours on the trail, a more gentle rain fell. They had to stop briefly to pull out rain gear before continuing into the foothills. His formerly ebullient mood fading, Mike's uneasiness grew. The thickly forested terrain seemed ripe for an ambush. He'd been briefed on the fierce, superstitious mountain tribes, who were sworn enemies of the lowlanders. Saium's earlier discussion about the people who lived on this side of the river rang true in accordance with the briefing they'd had. It was rumored an even more hostile tribe ruled in the heart of the Djeelaba but Sectors intelligence lacked any details on them.

Late in the afternoon, Johnny brought his horse even with Mike's. "We're being followed." He kept his voice low.

"Yeah, I've seen the signs. Small party of men, hunters maybe, flanking us for the past half hour." Mike glanced at Saium, confidently riding in the lead. Drawing his blaster, clicking the safety off, Mike raised his voice to ask, "How far to the next network of caves?"

Saium eyed the forest beside the trail and glanced at the mountains ahead. "Only a short distance."

"Which is what he said the last time you asked, too." Johnny spat. "I think our guide's forgotten a few things about the area since he was here as a boy. Want me to break off, go do some hunting of my own, find out what we're up against?"

"This terrain would be a bitch to fight in, too many trees to get a clear line of sight, us stuck on the trail, no cover." Mike glanced at Shalira behind him, hunched against the rain, clinging to the saddle on her horse. "I think you'd better go scouting. If they attack before we get to the cave, or somewhere else we can make a stand, I'll need you in reserve."

Johnny reined his horse in as Shalira's passed and a few moments later he vanished into the surrounding terrain, off to reconnoiter whoever was stalking them.

The attack, when it came, was silent and deadly. Multiple darts impacted Mike's body in a deadly rain. Unable to penetrate the tough Sectors material, the projectiles striking his utility uniform bounced off, but one lodged deep in his hand like a giant stinging insect, and another hit his neck. He yanked them out. A burning pain spread from the two spots immediately, and his hand went numb, the leading rein for Shalira's horse sliding from his fingers. His head swam as pain barreled through his veins. He tried to shout a warning to her but his tongue was thick and his jaw locked. Assaulted by double vision and weakness, he dropped his blaster. Dimly, he heard shouts and then he was toppling from his rearing horse, falling helplessly into the dense vegetation lining the trail.

Inwardly raging with anger, he landed face down, helpless to break his fall or turn himself over. Expecting to be trampled by the horses, or killed by the enemy troops, he fought against the pain and paralysis, to no avail. His mind was full of frantic worries over Shalira and what might be happening to her with him out of the way. Frustration burning like acid in his gut, he tried to at least move his head and check on her. Excited shouting and laughter from their jubilant attackers sounded from all directions.

Johnny, I hope you're seeing this and steering clear of the ambush until you can take action. As his consciousness flickered, he clung to the memory that his cousin was out there somewhere and would surely intervene at the first opportunity. *Lords of Space, let him rescue Shalira, get her to safety, no matter what happens to Saium and me.*

Defenseless, he couldn't avoid the violent kick in the ribs that rolled him halfway over in the clinging, wet vegetation. Another blow threw him onto his back, allowing him a hazy view of his enemy. Five or six heavily muscled warriors surrounded him in a loose circle, laughing, moving like a pack of feral dogs. One who seemed to be the leader poked at him with the finely chiseled stone tip of a spear, before raising the butt of the weapon. Mike saw the blow coming but was helpless to protect himself, the world blacking out as pain exploded in his temple.

Shalira felt the reins suddenly go slack in Mike's hands and her horse slowed, ambling to the left to nibble at something. "Michael?" Reaching one hand to where he ought to be, she found nothing.

In the next moment, a sharp pain arced through her arm and she recoiled, nearly slipping from the saddle, feeling as if she'd been bitten by an insect. A second sting as something lodged in her thigh. She yanked the projectile from her clinging skirts, which had blunted most of the impact. It felt like a heavy oblong wooden bead, feathered, with a sharp metal tip.

Throwing the dart to the ground, fear growing, she rose in her stirrups, listening intently, craning in all directions as she softly called his name. "Michael, what's happening? Saium?"

As the mare continued to move lazily from one browsing spot to the next, she heard strange men shouting in some unfamiliar dialect, voices rough with anger or excitement, but no sound from her own companions.

Panic swept over her like a cascade of ice water. Clenching her fists, she pressed them to her mouth in horror as memories of the terrible incident in childhood flooded through her mind. Unable for a moment to distinguish between the awful memories and the present, she slipped from the saddle, intent on hiding herself. Keeping hold on the stirrup as she landed, to prevent the horse from wandering off as much as to steady herself, she shook her head, trying to dispel the flashback. *I'm not a child any more, my brother's been dead for fifteen years, Vreely's dead, this isn't happening.*

A warm, burning sensation spread through her body from the two places where she'd been "stung". Dizzy, she clung to the reassuring bulk of her mare, fingers clenched on the edges of the saddle blanket. The horse swung its head for a moment to sniff at her before making a huffing sound and resuming its grazing.

I need to see, I need my eyes. She prayed desperately, but vision refused to come. *I should get back on the horse, attempt to flee.* But without someone to guide her, she wouldn't get far.

The sounds of assault were dying down, and a moment later Shalira sensed four or five people surrounding her. She heard their soft footsteps on the grassy woodland floor as they approached, smelled their sweat and some kind of paint. The newcomers stopped a few feet away from her.

Shaking with terror, fighting the memories of her childhood, Shalira called for Michael again, to no avail.

"Your men can't help you, pretty one," said a guttural voice directly in front of her.

Shalira recognized the dialect, a common trade talk used in the marketplaces all over Mahjundar. "Who are you?"

"You'll know us soon enough," said the man, an unpleasant glee underlying his words. At the same moment, two others grabbed her arms. Weakened from whatever drug had been on the tip of the darts, she struggled against their hold, trying to twist and kick her way free. "I demand you release me!"

Someone grabbed at the Windhunter collar, jerking the chain in an attempt to yank the jewelry from her neck.

"Don't touch her, you greedy fools!" yelled another warrior, much older from the timbre of the voice. "Can't you see she's blind? And wears the symbol of the Lady as well as the necklace you're trying to steal? You'd better heed her demands, and release her."

Apparently the newcomer had authority to back up his commands. The two men imprisoning her released their grip, and she staggered against her horse, then slowly fell, knees giving way from terror and the drugs.

A gnarled, callused hand smoothed her hair from her face, patted her cheek as she lay crumpled on the crushed grass. "I'm Bolomuzen, pretty one, high priest of this territory. What message have you brought us from the gods? Don't be afraid to speak."

"I—I don't know what you're talking about," she said, too lethargic to push his hand away. Her tongue was thick, causing her difficulty in swallowing.

He leaned closer, his reeking breath making her nauseated. "Then you must be here to *take* a message to the gods, a message of great importance."

"Maybe," said the person who'd grabbed her first. "Or perhaps you're not high enough ranking for her to speak words of the gods to you. Perhaps she can only share the message with the high priests at the sacred city of Chamacoyopa."

Wobbling somewhat, Shalira managed to sit up, one hand planted firmly on the wet ground. "Please, what have you done with my friends?"

The self-identified priest laughed. "They're safe enough for now." Callused hand under her elbow, he forced her to rise, the other man closing in to assist.

"Michael!" Frightened, she tried to resist, but heard her beloved's voice faintly from ahead on the trail. *At least he's alive.* She swayed.

"You must have been stung by a dart or two, although no one was supposed to be aiming in your direction," Bolomuzen said, tightening his grip. "We'll carry you to the village. Not to worry, the effects wear off soon enough." He fingered her amulet for a moment before gently letting the locket fall onto her chest, clinking on the Windhunter collar. "It's been many years since there were manifestations of the Lady's influence on our side of the Suaga River. You are most welcome, a good omen."

"We can't keep her," the first man said in a hard voice that invited no disagreement. "We don't dare keep her. It was one thing to hold on to the other captives until the spring ceremonies and make a gift of them, but the high priests will never forgive concealing a servant of the Lady for so long. I know your ambitions to rise in the priesthood, Bolomuzen, and I understand the desire, but it cannot be. We can't set up with our own oracle. Doing so means the risk of retaliation from Chamacoyopa, and then it would be our hearts on the altar. The best we can do is garner rewards for bringing the oracle to them."

Bolomuzen grumbled in his own language but offered no further argument in the strange debate.

The man in charge picked Shalira up as he finished speaking to his compatriot. "Can you sit on the horse if we boost you to the saddle?"

"Yes, I think so." Wild plans ran through her mind.

Her captor's next words dashed all her hopes. "One of my men will lead the beast, so have no thought of escape. The gods delivered you to us, and I've no intention of losing my prize."

But when the men tried to boost her into the saddle, Shalira was too dizzy, so eventually one of her captors climbed onto the patient mare and held her in front of him as the group moved out. She had no idea how long the ride lasted, drifting in and out of consciousness as the procession marched through the foothills.

The air held the damp coolness of night by the time she finally regained complete clearheadedness.

"We'll be at the village soon," said the man behind her, evidently realizing from her demeanor that she was conscious.

Breathing deeply of the fresh scent of night-blooming flowers and pine trees, she sat straighter and attempted to bring order to her hair and clothing, hoping to feel more in command of herself, look less like a prisoner. "Please, what's going to happen to us?"

"To you, Oracle, nothing." Her captor's voice was soft, reassuring. "Our chief has decreed you a welcome, honored guest. The warriors who accompanied you into our land will be held as prisoners taken in battle, destined for gifting to the Chamacoyopa. Don't worry, I'm sure your warriors will die with great honor."

Not a consoling idea, but at least Michael's still alive. And Saium and Johnny. "I don't understand. Who or what is Chamacoyopa?"

"Do you test me, Oracle?" The rider's voice squeaked with fear. "All men know Chamacoyopa, city of the Nathlemeru priests, rulers of the Djeelaba Mountains, the most beloved children of the gods because they are the fiercest warriors."

"Oh." Shalira had heard legends of the tribe her ancestors had battled time and again in their efforts to conquer the Djeelaba and acquire the rich gold mines of the area, before finally giving up after one final, disastrous attempt that claimed the life of the emperor himself, as he led the invading army. This must be the same tribe, or their descendants. She shivered, not just from the night air, but from fear.

Michael rescued me from Vreely and even from Bandarlok, but can he accomplish the impossible this time?

The horse's gait changed, and she heard shouts, excited greetings, noises of a crowd approaching. Soon she knew the horse was surrounded by people.

Smelling the smoke from cooking fires, redolent with the aroma of roasting meat, she realized they'd reached the village. The priest, Bolomuzen, came to hand her down from the horse. Keeping his grip uncomfortably tight on her fingers, he raised his voice. "I present the Oracle of the Lady, come to us from across the river."

There was a great oohing and aahing from the crowd, giving Shalira a good idea what a large settlement she'd been brought to. The knowledge was daunting. Mike, Johnny and Saium were fearsome warriors, but how could three men prevail against an entire village? While her mind was racing, Bolomuzen made her rotate in a slow circle with him. She felt hands brushing against her clothing and patting her sleeves and hair.

Are these people worshipping me? Appalled, she decided it was more likely they were showing respect to the goddess Pavmiraia, as embodied by her. *Curious such a fierce tribe would venerate my gentle woodland deity, but they do dwell in her forests. Can I use this to our advantage somehow?* "I wish to speak to my warriors," she said, summoning the imperious tone a princess should use.

"Not possible," said the chief from right next to her.

Startled, unaware of his arrival, she gasped but persevered. "What harm can it do for me to exchange words with them?"

"Not tonight. Being the defeated today, not the victors, they have no rights. Tonight they must rest in the hut of atonement, prepare themselves to face the trials and rituals of the Nathlemeru. Tomorrow you'll travel together to the ceremonial city. Talk to your men then, counsel them how best to die for your honor and the glory of the gods. Tonight, you belong to me and my village."

Thinking fast, not liking the sound of what the chief was telling her, Shalira said, "I warn you, the goddess will be angry if I'm not treated with respect."

Bolomuzen leaned in to whisper in her ear. "Have no fear, the womenfolk and girl children will take care of you and hear your prophecies. You and I'll meet at dawn and perform the greeting of the sun together. I'll guide you through the ritual."

Before she could ask any questions, the elderly priest had released his grip on her and moved away, lost in the crowd. The chief stepped into his spot, catching her hand. People pressed closer on all sides and despite herself, Shalira shrank against the stocky warrior, her heart beating faster. No matter how many times someone reassured her she'd come to no harm in this situation, distrust and panic threatened to overwhelm her.

"Don't crowd the oracle," said the chief to his people. "Take her to the hall of unmarried women and rejoice in her presence until dawn." To Shalira, he said, "My daughters have the honor of conveying you to the hall, but I know you're an unwilling guest. My best men will be stationed outside the building, so don't try to escape."

Shalira heard the sound of tiny bells and clinking beads as a group of women surrounded her. Sensuous perfume overlaid the smell of unwashed bodies, and she was drawn away from the chief, stumbling over the unfamiliar ground. She dug in her heels, pulling against the laughing girls who clung to her arms and waist. "I need one person to lead me by the hand, only one, please."

Someone gave an order, and the next moment Shalira was free, although she could tell she was completely encircled by villagers. Taking a deep breath, she made herself smile, turning her head from side to side. "Thank you. Now, who is to be the oracle's guide tonight?"

"As the chief's eldest unwed daughter, I take the honor," said a pleasant voice. "May I have your hand, Oracle?"

Shalira extended her hand and felt relieved at the touch of smooth, cool fingers a moment later.

"You seem overwhelmed," said her new guide as they strolled together, as close as sisters or best friends, still surrounded by the gaggle of other women, but at least now Shalira was able to keep from tripping over people trying to touch her or her locket. "Is it so hard, then, to come to this world from the home of the gods?"

Suppressing an urge to laugh hysterically, Shalira swallowed hard. "I—I wasn't aware I was coming here, exactly," she said, opting for a neutral reply.

Her hostess appeared to find the answer understandable. "The servants must bow to the whims of the gods, but they owe you no courtesy in return."

"I see you do understand. And I'm worried about my warriors," Shalira said, daring to hope this woman had at least some small sympathy.

But her guide's answer was matter-of-fact, almost callous. "Their fate is sealed now, having been taken in combat. I'm sure they'll die honorably for you."

What kind of poisonous society have we fallen into? As they continued to walk, Shalira racked her memory for any shreds of information about the Djeelaba Mountains and the tribes who lived here. Understandably, it wasn't a subject much discussed or taught where she grew up, since the peaks had been the site of her ancestors' most humiliating defeat.

"I watched both men carried in the nets to the hut of atonement," said a younger woman's voice close by. She giggled. "One is handsome, Oracle. Is he your lover? The other is old."

Only two? Did they kill Johnny? I know I heard Michael's voice after we were taken. Shalira was afraid to ask any further questions, in case Johnny had somehow gotten away. No need to reveal the presence of a third, deadly warrior if the villagers weren't aware of his existence. She felt a tiny flicker of hope. The sergeant would never abandon Michael, and Michael wouldn't leave her behind or leave Saium a prisoner.

"We're going up a set of stairs now," her escort said, taking a firmer grip on Shalira's elbow.

Allowing herself to be drawn into the building, Shalira was taken to a chair quite some distance from the door. She settled into the cushions, determined to be pleasant and try to learn as much as she could. "What now?"

"First we eat. My father the chief has provided special foods from the ceremonial stores for tonight. Then you can have a bath and we'll provide you with new clothing." The woman fingered the fabric of Shalira's borrowed Sectors utility pants. "These garments are hardly fitting for an emissary of the gods."

"Perhaps they were testing our charity," said someone close by.

"Very kind of you," Shalira said, accepting a cup of some hot beverage being pressed into her hands. She took a sip, enjoying the crisp taste, surprised to find tiny bits of some spice floating in the water. Swallowing, she asked, "What is this? I'm not familiar with this tea."

"It's made from the leaves of the sizquan flower. The dried petals are crumbled into the hot liquid. You like it?"

"Tasty, refreshing." Shalira nodded and took a big swallow. She did feel fresh energy flowing through her veins, whether from the spice or because the drug from the darts was wearing off, she couldn't tell.

"We use the sap as one ingredient to make the sleep darts for our hunters and warriors," her hostess said. "But the leaves and flowers give a person strength, and rest without sleep. You can chew the fresh leaves or let them sit in your cheek."

Someone took the mug from Shalira and she was handed a bowl of fragrant leaves with the admonition, "Try some."

Taking a tiny pinch of the velvety petals, she tucked them into her cheek. The taste was pleasant and she realized she felt more relaxed. *This stuff could be dangerous, better go easy.*

"The food is coming from the cook hall now," said the chief's daughter from somewhere close to Shalira's chair. "After we eat, after the bath and the new clothes, you'll spend the evening giving each of us our prophecy."

"Your prophecy? Like telling your fortune?" Shalira was puzzled. *Goddess, tell me what to say to each of these women. From the sound, there must be twenty or thirty of them packed in here with me.*

The chief's daughter laughed. "Yes, we're not going to waste this opportunity. Once you've been established in Chamacoyopa, the priests will charge many goats for a moment of your time, for one quick prophecy. And maybe refuse to grant access to you at all, if they themselves have need of your communication with the gods. You belong to us tonight."

So much for the thin pretense of my being an honored guest. Shalira groped for more of the energy-giving leaves and settled into the chair for what promised to be a long night. At least there was the promise of being with Michael in the morning.

CHAPTER EIGHT

Waking to the sound of Shalira screaming his name, Mike struggled to sit, finding he still had no control over his limbs. Two of his captors tied his wrists and ankles tightly with heavy, red-dyed vine while another man harangued him in an unknown dialect. As the warriors pulled him roughly upright like a rag doll, Mike saw the princess was unharmed, her borrowed Sectors utilities intact. Her horse stood placidly beside her, snatching mouthfuls of leaves from a flowering bush. Two men held her gingerly, as if afraid of bruising her.

He hoped the pins-and-needles sensation in his arms and legs meant whatever poison the enemy had used was temporary and wearing off. He'd had no chance to communicate with Shalira as the guards punched him in the stomach before throwing him onto the soggy ground, rolling him into a heavy vine net. Straining to move his head, he saw Saium, bound hand and foot as he was, loaded into a net. As he watched, the enemy warriors inserted thick poles through special loops on both sides of the mesh holding Saium. A team of burly men carried their burden into the surrounding forest.

A pair of dirty, sandaled feet stopped in front of Mike's face, splashing muddy water into his eyes. There was a scarlet-and-blue tattoo of a coiled snake on the man's ankle. Blinking hard, Mike squinted, trying to see his captor more clearly. This new player asked something in a demanding, angry tone, using a language Mike didn't know.

"I only speak the lowland dialect," he said. "Sorry."

Buffeted by another swift kick to the ribs, Mike was sure more than one was broken, or badly cracked, considering how much it hurt to breathe deeply.

Switching to the dialect Mike did understand, the tattooed newcomer's voice was contemptuous. "You and your companions will pay for venturing into our territory, foolish lowlanders." The man gestured to the nearest warriors. "Take him!"

The net was jerked off the ground, and Mike caught his breath at a stab of pain from his lower rib cage. As he was hauled away into the jungle, he silently cursed his own overconfidence. *I relied too much on Saium's knowledge and assessment of the danger. I hope Johnny laid low, avoided capture. We might have a chance, then.*

For more than two hours Mike was carried in the net, unable to see or hear his companions. The warriors gave no sign of tiring, ascending higher into the mountains. He had a raging headache and a pulled neck muscle from the awkward position they had trussed him up in. Lighting torches, his captors continued hiking after sunset, apparently determined to reach their destination, which appeared to be a sizable village perched on a series of terraces on the side of the mountain.

What he could see of the village as he was carried through it was on the primitive side, despite the plateau engineering feat. In the flickering torchlight he observed the huts had stone foundations but the walls and roofs appeared to be woven from plaits of brush. There were bonfires and women and children watched the procession go by. Some small children ran alongside, laughing and calling out to each other, throwing pebbles and sticks at the captives in the nets. Taken into a large hut at the top of a rise, hard against a sheer cliff face, Mike was unceremoniously dumped on the floor, trapped inside the heavy net. He heard the door slam shut behind him, cutting off what little torchlight there'd been.

Rolling onto his back with immense effort and considerable pain from his ribs, he peered into the blackness. "Saium?"

"Here, my lord, on the other side," came the older man's low-voiced answer. "For all the good it'll do."

Mike swallowed hard, licked his dry lips, tried to stretch against the ropes chafing his wrists and ankles. "Shalira?"

"They led her horse off to another part of the village as soon as we came through their first perimeter," Saium said. "They appeared to be treating her gently."

"Damn it all," Mike swore in Basic as he tried futilely to adjust his position.

"Outworlders? From the Sectors?" demanded a new voice in Basic from somewhere in the dark on the other side of the hut.

"Who's there?" Mike said sharply, peering into the gloom. As he activated the night vision implant to cope with total darkness, he made out a figure slumped to the floor.

"Captain Ted Everett, Sectors Special Forces. Who are you?" The man's voice was sharp and suspicious.

"Major James Michael Varone, Special Forces, sent to search for your party and your cargo. My companion is a local. What happened? How did you end up here if you survived the crash?"

"Ship was badly shot up by the Mawreg. We came out of hyperspace close to this system and the pilot was hoping to make it to the spaceport, but the engines flamed and we could only glide, into the damn mountains. Most of my team and the ship's crew died in the crash. A few of us got out."

"How did you get taken prisoner?"

The unseen Everett laughed, but with no humor. "Probably the same way I'm betting you did, ambushed, shot up with those damn poison darts. There were three of us who'd survived. One of my men had a broken arm and a fractured pelvis. After a lot of discussion, two of them tossed him off a cliff and walked away. Then they dragged Sullivan and me over here to their village in nets, like the rest of you poor fish."

"Can you speak Mahjundan?" Mike asked.

"Some," the other operator told him. "I wasn't anticipating landing here, as you know. No hypnobriefing for the local dialects. I've picked up a bit of the village's lingo from the women assigned to feed me. Wish I'd had gastro inoculations, considering the stuff they think a prisoner should eat." He spat. "Swill. I'd come over there and try to untie you, Major, but I'm chained to the wall myself."

"So where's the other survivor? Sullivan?" Mike had a sinking feeling he wasn't going to like the answer.

"After we'd been here about a month, they came in one night, stripped him buck naked, painted some kind of ceremonial target on his chest and dragged him out. I never saw him again. The screams lasted for hours."

Mike swallowed hard.

"What is he saying?" Saium hissed.

Mike gave an abbreviated translation. Tugging futilely at the strands of net entangling him, the grizzled warrior cursed. "These mountain people believe anyone injured or deformed is already not of this world and can act as a special messenger to the gods of death and war. Such captives are sacrificed immediately, before they can die on their own, without accepting the priests' message. The man with the broken bones had no chance."

Ice-cold terror washed through Mike's veins. "Lords of Space, what about Shalira?"

He sensed Saium shaking his head. "No. The mountain people believe a blind person is in a special state of blessedness. It is said they died as a sacrifice in a previous life and beheld the gods. So blessed, they were blinded for their next life and sent back to this world to relay messages from the gods."

"The priests will keep her healthy, then?" Mike wanted any crumb of reassurance he could glean.

"Ask your local guide what they've been saving me for, would you, Major?" Everett requested abruptly, breaking into the flow of Mahjundan from Saium. "I can't get a straight answer from the village girls. They giggle and talk about having a chance to die honorably, offer themselves to me on occasion, but won't help me escape."

Mike relayed Everett's request to Saium and translated the answer into Basic. "He says based on the season you crashed, Sullivan was likely sacrificed to the harvest god. There is evidently some more significant religious ceremony later in the year, at a main shrine even higher in the Djeelaba—my guide thinks we'll be sent as this village's special tribute. Sacrificing captives taken in battle brings high honors to the lucky village. Saium guesses the big event will be in a month or so, based on the configuration of the two moons." Taking into consideration this operator's grasp on sanity might be tenuous after a year of captivity, Mike tried to offer some hope. "We won't be here to participate, so rest easy."

"How can you be so sure, sir?" the other officer asked bitterly. "Reinforcements waiting at the bottom of the trail?"

"My sergeant was off scouting when we were ambushed. He escaped detection. He'll extract us somehow." Mike made his voice quiet but confident.

He heard the door opening again. Carrying smoky torches, a small group entered the hut. While a circle of women watched, holding the torches, Mike was surrounded by six mountain warriors and released from the nets. A particularly skinny and scarred warrior took a sharp stone knife and slashed the vines at his ankles and wrists. Mike bit his tongue until he tasted blood to keep from shouting at the pain of returning circulation in his hands and feet. Still too paralyzed to resist, he was dragged across the dirt floor and fastened to the wall with chains at the neck and wrists. It took every bit of strength Mike could muster not to show the agony his ribs gave him as he was roughly manhandled. The story of the unfortunate man with the broken bones who got tossed off the cliff was all the incentive Mike needed not to reveal his injuries.

The villagers filed out, the last man slamming the door, and the prisoners were left alone in the dark again.

"Any chance of pulling this chain out of the wall?" Mike asked.

"I've been working on mine every night for as long as I've been in this hellhole, with no results, but you're welcome to try, of course." Everett yawned. "Now the excitement of your arrival is over, I'm going to sleep."

Within five minutes, he was snoring. Mike shook his head and kept on rubbing his hands to ease the pain. Through the night he and Saium tried intermittently to work loose at least one of the plates holding their chains. It was no use; the plates had been set securely into the stone. Mike tried to get comfortable, but there was no position where his abused ribs didn't ache. Staring at the chimney hole in the roof, he watched the stars wheel overhead as the hours passed. *What are these bastards doing with Shalira? Where the hell is Johnny?*

"Surely the mountain people would have told us if they'd captured or killed Johnny, wouldn't they?" he asked Saium, sometime around dawn. "Gloating?"

"Most likely." Saium swallowed hard. "I want to apologize."

Mike considered for a minute. "Does it matter, Saium? We were ambushed. You'd warned us there were going to be hostiles, but I didn't keep a watchful enough eye."

"It matters to me. I failed in my duty to the princess and to you."

"Our job now is to find a way to escape and rescue her," Mike said. "Concentrate on the mission, not how we got here."

As soon as the sun rose, the guards came and released them from the wall shackles. Mike and the others were led at spear-point into the bright, cool mountain air. Shivering, he sat when the village soldiers pushed him, none too gently, with their spears. Laughing girls brought him a bowl of thick, tasteless stuff resembling oatmeal mixed with dried grass.

Blinking, Everett seemed to be having trouble handling the sunlight. "This is new," he said as the guards indicated for him to sit next to Mike. "They haven't let me outside in weeks. They were bringing me out for exercise until I broke one guy's neck and nearly escaped, before they shot me full of those damn darts again. Guess I scared them, because there weren't any more trips outside. The girls brought my meals in the hut, and I haven't been free of those chains for a minute."

"They order us to eat," Saium said, picking up his bowl and spooning the stuff out with curved fingers. "I advise compliance. Who knows when we may be offered food or drink again?"

The guards barely gave them time to choke down the unappetizing stuff before a large cart, drawn by two sets of yoked, shaggy beasts of burden, rolled up to the side of the prison hut. The cart was woven, like a giant basket, balanced on two massive wooden wheels with thin metal rims. The guards were pushing him into this vehicle when Mike heard a shout behind him. Turning, despite the point of the spear indenting his already suffering rib cage, he observed two men leading Shalira toward them, across the hard-packed square, detouring around the fire pits.

The princess appeared to be unharmed. Her long, curling black hair was loose, framing her face, floating down her back. She'd been given a native dress to wear, rust-colored with green embroidery at the hem and on the bell sleeves. The dress stopped above her ankles, as even petite Shalira was taller than most of the village women. The Windhunter collar adorned her neck and the Pavmiraia pendant glinted in the morning sun.

As she walked, village women pressed flowers into her hands and children clung to her skirts.

A more vigorous nudge from the spear forced Mike to clamber into the cart. He was led to the front, and his wrists were tied securely behind him to a rail on the inside at waist height. The other two men were placed on either side of the cart, almost close enough to touch.

Keeping an eye on Shalira's progress, holding his breath in hopes she was to ride in the cart with them, Mike asked Saium, "Now what?"

"I don't know."

Glancing over at his fellow Special Forces operator, Mike wasn't too surprised to see the man was a mess, pale, bruised, eyes red and staring. "Any ideas?"

"No, sir. They brought us from the wreck in the nets, like they did you. Never went on a field trip in a cart, so this is all new to me." Raising his face to the sun, Everett took a deep breath of the crisp air.

The men were now trying to boost Shalira into the vehicle. Resisting, the princess was pushing against their hands and struggling.

Mike raised his voice. "We're here, sweetheart. Let them help you into the cart with us."

"Michael! I was so afraid you were dead." She was lifted into the cart and stopped. "Where?"

"Take three steps forward. Be careful of Saium's big feet."

She took two steps, and her outstretched hand touched the fabric of his uniform. She came the rest of the way in a little rush and hugged him, followed by a long kiss.

"I don't care what happens to us now. At least we're together again." She laid her head on his chest for a moment, holding him tightly around the waist. Even though her embrace made his ribs ache, Mike welcomed the contact. After a moment, he said, "I think I've got some broken ribs, go easy."

Instantly her arms loosened, but she didn't move away from him. "My goddess granted me a blessing," she said, her voice low.

"We can use all the help we can get." He tried to sound cheerful, but wasn't placing any reliance on the generosity of a local deity.

"No, really, this may work to our advantage. I got my sight back."

Surprise kept him speechless for a moment, before fear for her washed over him in a cold sweat. "What are you talking about?"

"The women of the village chew these amazing leaves, and they gave me some because I was so scared." She yawned. "I had to stay up all night, telling fortunes for them, but somewhere after midnight I realized I was starting to see shapes. Then my vision kept improving until I could see their faces and the room we were in—all the details. Maybe my nurse used some of this herb in her potion. I know she came to the Djeelaba to collect a portion of her ingredients. I've been having tiny flashes of vision ever since the incident at the tomb."

He thought back to the moment when Shalira'd been brought to the wagon by the villagers. "But the effect faded?"

"Well, yes, eventually I had to spit the leaves out and gradually my vision dimmed. But I kept a handful of the herbs in my pocket."

She sounded so happy he hated to blight her hope. "Listen to me, being blind is your best protection right now. Saium said these people won't harm you because you're blind. Promise me you won't use the herb again. Or at least not unless you're absolutely sure it's necessary."

"Well, obviously not here and now, not while we're trapped in this cart," she said.

He lowered his head to nuzzle her hair. "The situation isn't too promising at the moment. As long as Johnny's still out there, we can hope. Hang on, they're trying to get this thing to move."

She'd discovered his wrists were bound to the cart behind his back. Evidently the mountain people had no intention of tying her up. Fingers probing the intricacies of the knot, she asked, "Do you want me to try to work the ropes loose?"

He stared over her head to meet the amused gaze of the burly guard sitting at the tail of their conveyance. Ten more men marched in a loose formation with them, spears and blowguns close at hand. "No, they're watching us too closely. You'd better sit, since we may be in for a long ride."

Nodding, she sat on the woven floor of the cart, leaning against his leg for a moment and then adjusting so her back was against the side. She reached with one hand to find his arm and curl her fingers around it. "Most of them don't speak Mahjundan, but one of them knows my mother's tongue. They wouldn't tell me anything about what had happened to you. I was going crazy."

"Are you all right?" He winced as he tried to see as much of her as he could.

Shalira leaned her head against the rough side of the cart. "They didn't know what to make of me exactly. Apparently they think I'm some sort of fortune teller or oracle, which gives me a certain status. They treated me well enough. I got a bath and clean clothes after dinner."

Further conversation was nearly impossible as the cart got up some momentum. The big wheels creaked and groaned, axle grease being an unknown concept in the Djeelaba, judging by the sounds. The noise grated on Mike's ears, aggravated his headache. The beasts huffed and wheezed, and occasionally let out long mournful whines as they plodded onward. Mike struggled to stay on his feet as the vehicle pitched and yawed over the rough surface of the mountain trail. The ropes dug cruelly into his wrists and after a while he lost all sensation in his hands.

The natives led the draft animals along a hard-packed dirt trail winding higher into the mountains. Mike kept a surreptitious but ultimately futile watch for any sign of Johnny. *Maybe he's dead and they didn't bother to tell me.* But he refused to accept the bleak thought. His cousin was wily and among the most skilled trackers in the Forces. He had to believe Johnny was trailing them, waiting for a chance to take some action on their behalf. Too much depended on that being true to allow himself to lose the hope.

By late afternoon the trail had widened into a road, which brought them onto the lip of a gigantic curving valley, deep in the heart of the mountain range. Craning to see what lay ahead, Mike made out the faint outline of a city in the distance at the far end of the valley, sitting on a terraced plateau.

"I didn't realize these mountain people were advanced enough to build anything but simple villages," he shouted across the cart to Saium.

"Not too much is known about them. I mentioned the legends of a higher class who live on the highest peaks and devote their time to religion and scientific pursuits, priestly nobles called the Nathlemeru. They impose taxes and tithes on the lower classes in exchange for intercession with the gods."

"I don't think the villagers are all that happy about the situation," Shalira said. "I overheard a lot of angry discussion last night about how much they had to pay to the rulers, and the fact they couldn't keep the spoils from our capture. Or at least not all the loot."

"But the Nathlemeru have the army to enforce their laws and taxes." Saium twisted his head to see their destination, but gave up after a minute. "We're in deep trouble."

Mike took another look at the faraway city. "Why?"

Heaving a deep sigh, Saium shook his head. "One of the things the lower classes provide to the priests who rule this land is living sacrifices for the altar."

Eyes wide, Shalira said, "I thought such things were only legends, stories to frighten children. What are we going to do?"

"I don't think they'll harm you, sweetheart." Mike tried to layer as much reassurance into his voice as he could.

"Because I'm blind," she answered bitterly. "I don't care about me. I can't bear for you to suffer such an awful fate."

"Remember Johnny," he reminded her softly.

Everett had been quiet all day but now, hearing Johnny's name in the flow of Mahjundan, he spoke up. "Somehow I can't be too confident about your sergeant getting us out of our next destination. The village maybe, but not a fortress like this." He nodded at the small city they were slowly approaching.

The road led straight across the valley to the plateau. It soon became apparent they were heading toward a single massive gate set into a wall of stacked boulders. Despite the lack of visible connecting material, the rocks appeared to be securely seated one on top of the other in an intricate pattern standing ten feet high, which must have taken thousands of hours to build. The gate itself was fashioned from huge tree trunks, bigger around than a man's arms would reach, lashed together lengthwise with tough leather strips. Mike couldn't begin to imagine the labor involved in bringing the old-growth wood here from the forest many miles below. As their cart approached the wall, curious guards, standing on an unseen walkway on the other side of the wall, pointed at them and shouted.

Dominating the city was a huge, pyramid-shaped, earthen mound several hundred feet high, built in five layers, top crowned by a temple. At one end of the building a curiously shaped stone tower reached into the mountain sky.

As the cart approached, the heavy gate was swung open by four men. Their captors had hasty, excited words with the leader of the city guards. The guards, dressed in maroon tunics and pants, equipped with leather helmets and crude shields, exhibited more organization and discipline than the motley crowd of villagers escorting the prisoners.

Mike checked with Saium. "Can you understand what they're saying?"

"Bits and pieces. The captain of the guard sent for an official to decide whether to accept the gift or not. Apparently it isn't the proper season for bringing tithes, but the villagers are arguing that since we were captured in combat, with an oracle, we must be given to the priests at once."

"Combat!" Mike snorted. "Nice way to characterize an ambush where we couldn't fight back. If it had been any kind of fair combat, I can guarantee you *we* would not be sitting here."

Sit they did, for more than an hour in the hot sun, waiting for the functionary who could make extraordinary decisions regarding offerings. The villagers left Mike and his companions tied to the cart, while they collapsed in the shade from the city walls. Mike watched their captors passing bulging water-skins to each other and tried not to think about how thirsty and dehydrated he was getting. Shalira was offered a drink by a city guard, who grabbed the container away from her when he realized her intent to share it with her friends. The water spilled onto the floor of the cart. No more was forthcoming.

Finally the priest arrived. Several inches taller than Mike, he wore sweeping robes of drab green, flecked with red. Heavy, elaborately worked gold earrings hung from his distended ear lobes, and more gold gleamed from his neck, wrists and hands. On his shaven head there was a single lock of curled black hair, clipped with three bold black-and-white feathers. He conversed with their captors from the village as he circled the cart, examining them cursorily from a safe distance before yelling something at the city guards.

Dropping their spears, two men jumped into the cart, causing it to lurch perilously. Cursing as men grabbed her arms, Shalira sought what little protection Mike could give from this new assault.

"Take your damn hands off her," he shouted. Reflexively, they stepped back, obeying the note of command in his voice. "Saium, tell the priest who she is, quickly."

Saium began talking in the lilting language of the hill people, which the priest gave evidence of understanding. Three Feathers, as Mike had labeled the man, inclined his head and answered Saium with a brief sentence. Then he shouted another command to the guards. They backed off and jumped from the cart. One extended his hands beckoningly to Shalira, looking beyond her to Mike, his meaning plain. *Tell her to cooperate or else.*

"They want you to get out of the cart," Mike told her. "I think you'd better do it."

She threw her arms around his neck, burying her face in his shoulder. "I have to stay with you."

He ached to be able to hold her. "Better do as they ask. Don't make them angry. The strategy here is to stay alive as long as possible, remember? Hope for Johnny to come through for us."

She was silent for a minute. Then her breath caught on a sob. She lifted her face for a kiss. "I love you."

"I love you, too," he said without hesitation or embarrassment, kissing her as long as he dared.

Turning carefully, Shalira walked over the rough wicker surface to the tail of the cart. The city guards lifted her to the ground. One of them kept his grip loosely on her wrist, drawing her aside.

Walking to her, Three Feathers put his hand under her chin and tilted her head left and right. He snapped his long fingers directly in front of her eyes. Evidently satisfied Shalira was indeed blind, he nodded and gestured impatiently for her to be taken farther out of his way. Then he gave his full attention to the matter of the cart and the remaining prisoners. The other guard moved smartly to assist the priest in climbing into the small space.

Muttering an incantation to himself, Three Feathers rolled the long fingers of his left hand in a black leather pouch at his belt as he stopped in front of Saium. When the priest withdrew his hand from the pouch his fingers were covered with a clinging reddish dust, glinting in the waning sunlight. As if admiring the effect for a moment, he spread his fingers wide. Then, with a serpentine suddenness, the official leaned forward and drew a strange symbol on the old man's forehead.

Apparently seeking to battle one magic with another, Saium shouted a defiant chant. Frowning, the priest cuffed the bound prisoner across the face with a beringed hand. The red powder clung to Saium's skin, continuing to glow. Reaching out with one obscenely long fingernail, the Nathlemeru forced Saium to meet his eyes. Satisfied, Three Feathers laughed derisively and moved away.

Now he stopped in front of Mike, who met the merciless stare measure for measure, straightening up as much as he was able against his bonds. This close, the stench from the priest was overpowering, a mixture of strange spices, blood and an underlying note of rotted flesh. Deliberately, slowly, like a caress, he drew the same intricate symbol on Mike's forehead, dipping back into the pouch for more powder while Mike swore at him. The priest only shook his head, unperturbed.

Everett too was quickly painted, and then Three Feathers stepped from the cart.

Coming out of the gate was an empty litter, carried by two more of the guards in maroon uniforms. The chair was an elegant affair of gaily painted wood, tiny enameled wind chimes suspended from the gilded handles. The cheerful music of the little chimes was an incongruous counterpoint to the deadly seriousness of the overall situation. The guards set the conveyance in front of Shalira. Striding to her, the Nathlemeru priest whispered something in her ear. She shifted away from him but the guard's grip on her arm forestalled any real attempt at escape. A moment later she'd been efficiently handed into the litter, which the waiting bearers lifted in a smooth motion, setting off through the city's entrance.

The cart lurched forward as the yoked beasts were driven through the city gate. Craning to look back, Mike took note of the priest chanting over the heads of the kneeling villagers while a guard paid them with small gold bars. One of the city men led two of the pack horses after the cart. Mike felt the first faint hope he'd had all day at the sight of their gear, lashed to the horses.

The priest shouted something at the cart, with a harsh laugh as punctuation. "What did he say, Saium?"

"He says Her Highness will make a fitting bride for Tlazomiccuhtli, their chief deity. There's no doubt the rest of us will be sacrificed, probably as soon as we reach the temple. Even in the lowlands we'd heard rumors of this insatiable god, who demands human flesh and beating hearts to feed upon."

Mike glanced at Everett, breaking into Basic. "We can make a fight of it, Agreed? I'm not going under the knife without trying to take a few of them down too."

The other murmured agreement.

He was given no chance to act on the brave resolve. For about ten minutes the cart lurched its way through nearly empty streets past houses firmly shut up, awaiting some future occupants. One cross street appeared to lead to a deserted open-air market place. Shortly thereafter, the cart came into a tremendous square where thousands of people could have stood. The five level pyramid and its crowning temple stood at the far end of this space.

"Why so few people here?" Mike stared at the vast courtyard in front of the pyramid.

"They have all the tribes gather for the great religious festivals, but only the priests, the soldiers and women dwell here. The priests do their work and studying free of less exalted influences." Saium shook his head. Continuing his analysis, "Doubtless they keep slaves as well, but we've already been marked for sacrifice, not for service."

The painted mark on Mike's forehead itched and burned slightly. Flexing his hands against the ropes, he was ready for any chance at resistance. Much better to die a clean death in an honest, if hopeless, fight than to be sacrificed like an animal to some alien god. Maybe Johnny could find a way to rescue Shalira, at least, if he found his way undetected to the city.

The sun was beginning to set below the peaks lining the valley. The remaining light was an ugly red tone, casting ominous shadows across the base of the temple. Once the cart stopped at the bottom of a set of broad stairs, the beasts of burden shuffled their feet nervously and blew, and, for the first time all day, demonstrated an independent desire to keep moving. The men carrying Shalira's litter hadn't paused, but proceeded up the several hundred stairs until disappearing from view into the gloom at the top.

Mike concentrated all his attention on waiting for their captors to make a mistake, however slight, giving him a chance to grab a weapon and make a fight of it.

The priests and their soldiers apparently were used to dealing with fiercely determined warrior prisoners. Two soldiers jumped into the cart and efficiently shackled each man's ankles with heavy chain. Then, one at a time, Mike and the others were released from the ropes binding them to the cart and their wrists quickly chained behind their backs. Finally the guards dragged each man to the ground, yoking them all together with a long neck chain and leather collars.

"Too good at what they do," snorted Saium. "Efficient killers. We've no chance at all, Major."

"I've been in worse spots and gotten out." Mike pointed with his chin. "There's a disagreement going on."

The three priests were arguing. Three Feathers pointed at the temple and made agitated gestures while the other two were plainly reluctant to do whatever it was he wanted. The senior official gained his way eventually through sheer force of will. Ascending the stairs, he didn't deign to see if anyone followed.

The guards chivvied the prisoners to follow him. Mike discovered the leg shackles allowed him exactly enough motion to handle the narrow steps and not an inch more. By the time he reached a small platform at the top of the first flight, his head was swimming, his leg muscles a solid mass of pain. Between the high altitude, his possibly-broken ribs and the exertion of climbing the deliberately difficult steps, his heart was pounding so loud he could hear it. Every time he inhaled his lungs pressed on the broken ribs with excruciating pain.

He was given no chance to stop and rest, however. The guards prodded them to continue up the next flight of the torturous steps. At one point, Saium stumbled, threatening to drag them all off their feet, but the nearest guard grabbed him, lifting him bodily to the next stair.

As he finally topped the fifth and last flight of steps, Mike reached a terrace in front of the temple, to find five bloodstained altars standing waist high in front of him. Breathing hard, Mike stared into the temple, hoping for a glimpse of Shalira.

There was no sign of the princess, but one swift glance revealed a mural composed of grisly scenes of some monster committing atrocities on men, women and children.

Raised voices brought his attention back to the priests who were arguing again, stating opposing views vehemently. Fidgeting, the guards stood, with the collective air of men wishing themselves elsewhere without delay.

A small flicker of hope kindled as Mike watched the priests debate. *Whatever the dispute is, it might work to our advantage somehow. I wish I knew what the discussion was about.* He glanced over at Saium, who was standing next to him, breathing in hoarse whoops. Mike raised a quizzical eyebrow. Saium shook his head.

"No idea, Major, can't speak the priests' dialect," he gasped out. "Sorry."

Fishing a carved ebony-and-maroon box out of his voluminous robes, one Nathlemeru went to his knees. Opening the container, he chanted fast, with anxious sideways glances at the deepening shadows. The man drew a set of small objects from the box and cast them onto the bloodstained surface of the terrace. Just as quickly, he scooped them up and tried the ritual once more. Leaning over his shoulder, the other two priests muttered, studying the patterns in the split second before their colleague destroyed them. This happened five times.

Three Feathers gave a curt order to the guards. Grabbing Mike, two men detached his section of the neck chain from the next, dragging him by the elbows to the nearest of the oddly humped red altar stones. Positioning him directly in front of the block, the men kicked at his ankles to spread his legs as far apart as the shackling chain would allow. Then they forced him back two more steps, until he bumped into the end of the altar.

Shaking his head vehemently, the priest who'd been casting the omens protested, pointing a trembling finger at the most recent pattern.

The high priest took his subordinate by the elbow and hauled him to his feet, barely allowing time for the man to retrieve his forecasting tools. The older Nathlemeru dragged the younger priest across the terrace to a spot right in front of Mike. He gestured at the nearest guard, who fumbled with the closures of Mike's uniform shirt, leaving his chest exposed. Gritting his teeth, Mike readied himself for whatever torture was to follow. Three Feathers produced a small black stone knife from his belt and drew it across Mike's skin above the heart with calculated, excruciating slowness, bringing the scarlet-stained weapon above his head for everyone to see. He bowed in the direction of the temple before shaking the drops of Mike's blood onto the other priest's cupped hands.

Imperiously the high priest uttered one word, pointing at the ground by Mike's feet.

Taking a deep breath, the lower-ranking priest surveyed Mike from head to toe. He squatted to throw the objects one last time, rolling them out of his red-stained hands so they clattered and bounced across the terrace directly at Mike's booted feet. He watched as the tiny bones of all shapes and sizes came to rest in a pattern surrounding him. Three of the smallest bones, those most freshly crimsoned with the drops of his blood, shifted yet again, as if they had been blown away from him. The bones settled in a new configuration, off to the side from the rest, like an arrow, pointing away from the altar.

Exclaiming in dismay, one guard dropped Mike's arm and stepped back, hand going to the knife at his belt.

As if waiting for the tiny bones to rearrange themselves into a pattern more to his liking, Three Feathers stared at the omens for a long time. Slowly, he lifted his eyes to meet Mike's. Refusing to give the enemy any satisfaction, Mike kept his face as blank as possible.

The priest moved so fast Mike wasn't prepared for the backhanded blow across his face that knocked him down, half-reeling across the surface of the stone altar.

Saium translated the next sarcastic words as Mike tried to regain his feet without any help from the guards.

"Tlazomiccuhtli is not pleased to accept you into his embrace this night, but wishes you to spend the hours until dawn contemplating the honor you await. I'll bring the living heart forth from you and feed it to the god still beating and raw for his breakfast. Perhaps we'll invite his newest bride to share the delicacy as well, hmm?"

Sneering, the Nahlemeru stepped effortlessly back as Mike lunged for him with a snarled curse.

The priest reverted to his own language to give curt orders to the guards. Mike had to wait a minute while the younger priest retrieved all his tools from the ground, but then he was pulled and tugged by the soldiers toward the steps leading into the temple foyer. Looking back over his shoulder as the gloom inside enclosed him, Mike watched the lesser priests making a hasty retreat down the pyramid's stairs. The one who'd been throwing the forecasting bones glanced back, and as their eyes met for a fraction of a second Mike read fear in the expression on the man's face. *Clearly the little ceremony with the bones didn't go the way the priesthood expected, or wanted. I'll take any good luck I can get tonight, if it bought a little more time for Johnny to attempt a rescue op.*

Flickering torches in the small entry chamber, cast light on more of the ghastly wall carvings. Mike was given no chance to study the surroundings, but was hurried into a wide hall, set with more torches and lined by heavy doors.

Then the prisoners were herded to a large, roofless chamber, open to the night air.

Dominating the room was a fifteen-foot-tall representation of the Nathlemeru's loathsome deity Tlazomiccuhtli. Mike was stunned by the sheer hideousness of the alien idol. He'd seen things repulsive to Outworlder eyes on a number of different worlds and been able to stay detached about them, but there was something so wrong and evil about this thing, he literally couldn't breathe for a minute. Horrified, he took in the clawed feet, each clutching a pair of writhing victims, distorted faces taking on a lifelike cast in the gloom. The multiple arms held more victims gathered to its chest. A necklace of real skulls, both large and small, ringed the thick neck. The flickering torchlight animated the face, made it appear alive and keenly avaricious, hungry. A crown of interlaced bleached human bones had been set on its head and scalps of all colors of hair dangled from the diadem. Hissing, snakes slithered in a cage on a small altar to the side of the statue.

A pounding in Mike's ears sounded like drums at first and then again like the low-toned growl of a hungry animal. He thought he heard several heartbeats in the room. The statue's exaggerated, empty eye sockets locked on his own in an hypnotic illusion.

Enjoying his prisoners' reaction, the priest laughed.

Mike tore his attention away from Tlazomiccuhtli. He shook his head, trying to clear the dizziness. *Maybe the torches are burning some hallucinogen. Not like me to imagine things.* As the guards poked him in the back with their spears he willingly kept walking. A shiver worked its way down his spine, and his nerve endings tingled. *Wish I could stop thinking those empty eyes are watching.*

Four guards who were laden with the prisoners' belongings stopped at an ordinary door in the next hallway and waited while Three Feathers unlocked it with a complex, heavy key.

Despite the agony in his rib cage, Mike paid close attention. *I need to remember the location of this storeroom, just in case.*

After the drama of the main chamber, it was a relief to Mike to be herded into a room with plain stone walls, save for one small frieze beside the door depicting Tlazomiccuhtli's horrific image for contemplation by his future victims. The guards motioned for them to sit against the far wall. Then the city dwellers fastened each man's manacles to chains hanging there. The neck chain and collars were removed and carried away. Favoring the prisoners with one last satisfied smirk, the Nathlemeru leader departed, taking the rest of the guards with him.

A single torch burned in a wall sconce.

Through the one small, barred window across from him, Mike could see the first stars coming out.

"I suppose we can forget about dinner." Everett's tone was conversational.

Resting his aching head against the rough stone wall, Mike wondered if Everett's attempt at a joke was a good sign of mental stability or an indicator of how far he'd come unmoored from reality during his captivity. "Probably a safe assumption."

"We're lucky we weren't Tlazomiccuhtli's evening meal," Saium said wearily, once Mike translated the remark. "Although I'm not sure what the ultimate difference will be. You heard the priest—first thing in the morning, you for certain, Major, and possibly all of us—goes to an awful death."

Mike's hands were beginning to regain some sensation since the manacles weren't as tight on his wrists as the ropes had been. Flexing his fingers, he tried to ignore the pain of returning circulation. He pulled against the circles of metal, but his hands couldn't even begin to squeeze through, no matter how hard he tried. Scrunching against the wall a little more comfortably, staring out the tiny window at the few stars, he refused to think about what was coming in the morning. As the night wore on, he replayed in his mind's eye all the moments he and Shalira had shared since crossing the Suaga. Sending a fervent prayer to the Lords of Space, he asked for her to be spared, rescued by Johnny perhaps and for them both to escape from this hellish place.

No matter what happens to me, I don't regret coming to Mahjundar and finding her. I just wish we could have had more time together.

After a terrifying ride in the chair, apparently straight up the side of a mountain, Shalira was relieved when they came to a halt and the conveyance was gently set down. She heard rustling sounds as the men who'd carried the chair left whatever chamber they'd come to.

"Lord Ishtananga will be here shortly to attend to you, Oracle," said the priest, standing off to the right, speaking the trade tongue.

Not waiting for permission, Shalira extricated herself from the chair and stood next to it, pivoting toward the man. "What have you done with my warriors?"

After an ominous pause, he said, "The omens weren't in harmony for a sacrifice tonight." He sounded troubled.

Thank the goddess. Releasing a breath she hadn't realized she'd been holding, she said, "But?"

"I believe Lord Ishtananga will offer the hearts of your warriors to the god at first sunlight. Normally we'd save them for the spring festivals, but he strongly believes their deaths are needed now."

"I want to speak to them tonight, with no further delay," she said. Remembering how the villagers had refused her request, she insisted. "The goddess will be highly displeased if my request is denied."

New footsteps on the stone floor, accompanied by the unmistakable odor she'd smelled when the high priest inspected her on the plateau below, let her know Ishtananga must have arrived. She heard the underpriest say something to his superior in their own language before leaving her alone with the high priest.

Determined to seize the initiative, she spoke. "I want—"

"Lovely one, what you want is of no importance to me. You need to forget the men you traveled with and focus on the future we're going to have." It sounded as if he was rubbing his hands together in anticipation. "After tomorrow morning their hearts will have been devoured by the god, and you'll become the bride of Tlazomiccuhtli, which makes you my consort here in Chamacoyopa. You'll be by my side as I rule."

"No!" She bit her lip. Angering the man wasn't going to help her outwit him tonight.

He came closer, the sound of his footsteps echoing in the chamber. She stood tall, waiting. *I don't care what he does, I'm going to find a way to save myself and Michael and the others. Johnny must be dead, so it's up to me.*

A small sizzling noise caught her attention right before she felt heat on her face. She shrank back against the chair, nearly falling as the wooden structure shifted sideways under her weight. "What are you doing?"

"Merely testing. You genuinely are completely blind, a true messenger of the gods." He pulled her hand down, tugging her forward. "You didn't flinch. You didn't even know I hold a candle, did you?"

Michael was right—blindness is my defense, up to a point. "I'd be wary of testing messengers sent by the gods," she said, drawing herself up.

He laughed. "You have spirit, which I appreciate. Come, we should dine. I'm sure you must be hungry. The villagers have only the most rudimentary fare to offer one such as you."

Taking her hand, the priest drew Shalira away from the chair. Their combined footsteps echoed from stone walls. "You and I will be married at the end of the ceremony tomorrow morning," he said. "It's my great fortune the villagers brought you directly to me, now, not at the time of the annual indrawing and festivals. I have rivals among the high priests, some of whom would have fought me over possession of an oracle such as you."

"The gods decree all things as they should be," she said, trying to be as mysterious and otherworldly as she could. If the situation hadn't been so serious, she might have laughed to hear herself speaking in such terms. He was clutching her left hand in his, so she slid her right hand into her pocket, seeking a few of the leaves.

In the next moment he grabbed her. "What do you have there?" He forcibly uncurled her fingers and she felt the tiny leaves drifting from her grasp. Ishtananga sniffed and sneezed, apparently testing some of the substance. "Where did you get this?"

"The village women gave it to me last night," she said. "It helped me relax so I could tell their fortunes in more detail."

"Humph. I should have known those greedy commoners would try to steal some of your magic for themselves. Do you have more of this?" Without waiting for her answer, he grabbed at her pocket, ripping the fabric of the dress. Edging away from him, Shalira felt the precious leaves falling, emptying her pocket.

"No, only those few," she said, resisting the urge to kneel and scrabble for the scraps.

"Not to worry, if you need some help to relax into giving the prophecies. I've much better herbs and potions, grown especially for our use in the temple. Not picked along the roadside." He sniffed.

As they began walking again, Shalira tried not to panic. *How am I going to see? I'm not taking anything he might want to give me, that's for sure.*

"I even have herbs and salves to enhance the physical interaction between us," he said.

Disgust at the idea of this man touching her made her nauseated. "The goddess insists I remain pure until married," she said.

Her declaration had the effect of amusing Ishtananga, who guffawed, running one hand along her chin. "You don't quite understand the relationship between your goddess and the gods I serve, do you? Pavmiraia was seduced by Tlazomiccuhtli in the earliest days of the world and has been forced by him to produce oracles ever since, when he dictates the need for one, lest he unleash the forces of hell across the mighty river and destroy the world of men there." He examined her necklace as she flinched. "It's my good fortune to be the priest who owns an oracle now."

He speaks no version of history I've ever heard. Pavmiraia could never have been involved with gods who demand human sacrifice. "You don't own me," she said.

"Yes, I do. And if you don't do exactly as I say, if your public prophecies don't indicate the results I want, your life will be forfeit." He leaned closer, threatening her in a near whisper, "The gods can recall you at any time, messenger."

Shalira shivered despite herself. This man sounded deranged as well as power hungry.

He held her chin with one hand, while his other drifted to brush against her breasts and then cupped her butt as he outlined his immediate plans. "Tomorrow your warriors die on the altar to carry the words I wish to send directly to Tlazomiccuhtli. Any day thereafter it could be your time to be sacrificed, if I will it so."

She shoved his hand away from her face and jerked from his loose embrace.

Chuckling, he took her hand, squeezed her fingers gently. "But why are we talking thus? I know you'll be a docile oracle, obedient to my will, following my lead. We should have many years ruling Chamacoyopa together."

Unable to break his clasp, unsure what to do, Shalira allowed him to draw her forward. She sensed they were in an enclosed space, a hallway perhaps. Instinctively, she counted her steps, both as a way to calm herself and also in case she got away and needed to find her path to the exit.

As they stepped into an area where their footsteps echoed, a wave of terror and revulsion swept over her. Shaking, stomach in knots, Shalira stopped, afraid she was going to faint, her skin crawling as if she'd been bathed in viscous, foul mud. The air seemed poisonous, burning her nostrils. Acid rose in her throat as her stomach revolted.

"Tlazomiccuhtli's inner sanctum, where his image resides, where I conduct many of the most secret rituals of the temple. His presence affects you, Oracle?"

"I—I can hardly breathe," she said, hearing herself wheeze. Something about the room, or the effigy of the mountain god, or both, was physically affecting her, even if she couldn't see the deity. Her chest was tight, as if bands of steel wrapped around her and her mouth was dry. Licking her lips, she took a step backward. The urge to flee was strong

"Excellent, I'm glad you're so sensitive to the god's emanations." Ishtananga sounded happy, adding a chuckle to underscore his pleasure.

She had the feeling he was studying her, noting all the symptoms of her physical distress. Willing to beg a little to escape the terror, she said, "Please, my head is reeling. Can we leave this room?"

"For now." He took her hand in a more normal grip and led her across the chamber. They went down another hall.

"Does no one else inhabit this place?" she asked. Odd to her she hadn't detected another living being since the litter bearers and the under priest left her alone with Ishtananga. If she managed to get away from him, how many people would be between her and freedom?

"Of course, you didn't see as you passed through the city. At this time of year, only the cadre of priests, our women, the servants and the main garrison of soldiers remain in the sacred city. Only the high priest of the season—me, at the moment—may dwell in the temple, closest to the god. We're going to my apartment. In fact, we've arrived."

He forced her to pause for a moment and she heard a door creak open directly in front of her. "We'll begin with dinner and expand our relationship from there." Escorting her into the room, arm around her waist, he let out an angry exclamation after the first few steps. "The fools haven't brought our food yet." Swearing, he dragged Shalira by the wrist across a stone floor, practically throwing her into a chair. "I'm going to find out what's happened to dinner. Begin obeying my orders now. Remain seated, understand?"

Rubbing her elbow where he'd shoved her against the wooden chair, she nodded.

He remained next to her for a long moment, tapping one toe. "I probably should tie you up."

Hearing the distaste in his voice, Shalira hoped she had an opening. "No, please, don't. I'll sit here, as you've commanded." She made her voice sound compliant and defeated. She ran her hands over the chair and arranged herself as if she was a student in a classroom, back straight, feet together.

Gripping her shoulder, Ishtananga lectured her. "There are guards in the other wing, watching over my prisoners. There are priests in the observatory tonight as well, so you won't get far if you wander off. And I'll punish you severely if you move from this seat, understand?"

Hanging her head, eyes downcast, hands folded in her lap, she said, "The gods sent me here to be your oracle, I understand now. I'll do as you say."

He walked away and a moment later she heard the door close with a slam.

Slumping against the hard wooden back of the chair, Shalira dropped her head into her hands. The leaves from the village had been her best hope. If she could have used them for the calming effect and regained even the slightest use of her eyes, she might have been able to help herself and figure out something to save Michael and Saium. There was no telling how long Ishtananga would be out of the room and he'd made his plans for the evening clear once he came back. Not a moment to waste, time for action. Shaking her head, Shalira sat upright, took a deep breath, and closed her eyes.

Calm. The calmer I am, the more chance of regaining my eyesight. Remembering the flashes of vision she'd had at Bandarlok's camp when she concentrated, she was encouraged. Breathing a prayer to Pavmiraia, although she had no idea if the gentle goddess had any influence on this side of the river, much less inside the blood-soaked temple of Tlazomiccuhtli, Shalira slowed her breathing, counting between inhalations, and tried not to think of anything. Michael kept coming into her mind's eye, as she'd seen him in her mother's tomb, high cheekbones, strong jaw, tall, broad-shouldered, concern for her in his expression. Trembling, she opened her eyes.

At first there were only the white flashes but then the room took on definition as if emerging from a fog bank—gray and white at first, color seeping into the furniture, the wall hangings, the vividly yellow-and-blue-striped blankets on the bed in an alcove beyond. Staying in the chair, she swiveled. A sturdy wooden table was behind her, pushed against the whitewashed stone wall. A second chair waited there. Along with the absence of food, there weren't any dishes or utensils.

Another alcove, opposite the bed, held embroidered robes hanging from hooks, feathered headdresses draped over pegs, sandals jumbled into a pile on the floor. Belts, undergarments and the like overflowed baskets.

Despairing, she swiveled in the opposite direction, to be greeted with the welcome sight of built-in shelves full of statues, ceremonial objects, and an array of gold-handled sacrificial knives. In a heartbeat, Shalira was out of the chair, dashing across the room to grab one of the smaller knives propped on a bottom shelf partially behind a golden bowl. Examining the translucent black stone blade, she realized the edge was honed razor sharp. Sounds outside the door sent her adrenaline pumping and she scrambled to the chair, hiding the knife under her thigh, spreading her skirt to conceal the hilt.

Realizing she'd never pretended to be blind before, Shalira closed her eyes and leaned back, as if exhausted. The door opened, and she heard Ishtananga stride in, already recognizing his aggressive footfalls. Two people came behind him, walking more slowly, steps heavy as if carrying quite a burden. The high priest was berating the newcomers in his own language so Shalira risked a glance, hoping he'd be too distracted to pay her any attention.

He was indeed facing away from her, giving orders to an elderly woman and a young boy as they laid heavy trays full of pottery dishes and platters and bowls of steaming food on the table and arranged things the way he wanted them. The woman kept her shoulders hunched as if afraid of physical abuse and unloaded her tray as fast as she could without spilling. The boy kept stealing glances at Shalira, who kept her head high, hoping her eyes appeared unfocused.

There was a heart-stopping second when, as she checked on the progress being made toward dinner, the serving boy's wide eyes met hers. He did a double take, stepping backward and tugging on his mother's or grandmother's dress, but she shook him off.

Greatly daring, Shalira frowned and put her finger to her lips for a second, praying the boy would think it was a game between them, or of no consequence. His eyes grew wide and he nodded once. Satisfied, she leaned back and closed her eyes to avoid further mishap. She heard the trays clanking together as the servant woman stacked them and then she and the boy left the room, drawing the door shut behind them.

Ishtananga walked toward her and she gripped the handle of the knife hidden under her skirt so tight her fingers ached, but he continued into the alcove where his clothing was stored.

Opening her eyes, she found his naked back was to her as he searched through his robes for a new garment. He must have stripped off his elaborately embroidered tunic at some point. Rising an inch at a time, grateful the chair didn't creak, she stepped as silently and as quickly as she dared toward him. Half-remembering some instructions from her father's bodyguards in a conversation years ago, she prepared to drive the knife into his side, up toward the heart.

The priest must have seen something out of the corner of his eye, because he turned to grab at her as she made the move to stab him. The razor-sharp knife left a deep wound in his arm. Yelling curses, he grabbed at the slash with his good hand and retreated into the alcove. Shalira, sick to her stomach and shaky from the adrenaline rush, but committed to the assault, advanced, trying to get in another blow.

"You she-devil," he said between clenched teeth. "Your goddess plays tricks on me with your blindness."

Shalira didn't waste breath talking. It was going to be his life or hers. She lunged forward as he lashed out with his fist, catching her on the jaw, knocking her off balance. Stung by the force of the blow, she tripped on the pile of loose sandals and fell, losing the knife, which skittered away on the floor. As she scrabbled backward on her elbows, trying desperately to retrieve her weapon, Ishtananga grabbed her by the hair, yanking her away from the blade.

He was in difficulties from the deep wound in his arm, but he took a hank of her hair with his fist. "I'll put out your treacherous eyes before sacrificing you on the altar, bitch."

"You can try." Gritting her teeth, she spun counterclockwise, ignoring the pain from his grip on her hair. Tackling him at the knees, she knocked his legs out from under him.

He released her hair as he fell. Rolling over, she grabbed the knife and stabbed wildly at him, landing at least one blow in the area of his lower ribs. The knife blade shattered against bone. Disgusted, she threw the useless hilt and its remaining stub at his face. Bent over from pain, he was attempting to reach the door, probably to call for help. Desperate to keep him from his goal, Shalira circled behind him, grabbing anything she could find on the table to hurl at him. She got him across the face with a heavy serving dish. A pitcher in her hand, she went on the attack, cracking the pottery against his head as he punched her again. The blow stunned her, and she fell, ears ringing, the room spinning.

Woozily, she attempted to stand, frantic to find something else to use as a weapon. Hand on the door, Ishtananga laughed at her efforts. "Although I'll probably bear the scars of your madness, your goddess should have selected a stronger champion than you, girl."

The door shifted under his hand and he moved aside. "Good, my guards have arrived."

He was turning to direct the men he expected when the panel flew open, knocking Ishtananga to the side. Johnny came in, crouched low, face painted with mud, hair hidden in a cap, blaster in his hand. Pressing the muzzle directly against Ishtananga's side, Johnny fired and the priest fell, his face frozen in an astonished grimace.

Wasting no time on the dead or dying adversary, Johnny came straight to Shalira. "Are you okay?" Helping her rise with one hand, he glanced over the chaos in the room. "By the evidence, you put up a pretty good fight, Your Highness." He held her awkwardly as she wept, overcome by what she'd done and relief the priest was dead. "We've got to get out of here," he said even as he gave her a hard hug. "You have any idea where Mike and Saium are being held in this place?"

Shalira took a deep breath, wiping her eyes. Tears wasted precious time. She nodded. "In the other wing. The priest said there were guards on duty."

"I hope to hell they didn't hear the shot or don't come investigate," Johnny said. "We need our luck to hold tonight, princess."

She broke away from his loose grip, off-balance from the blows she'd received, and hurried to the shelves to select another knife. Having a weapon was of the utmost importance to her right this moment and her heartbeat calmed a bit when she grabbed a larger, sharp-bladed dagger.

"Got your sight back? More magic potions?" Moving to assist her as she staggered, Johnny didn't sound surprised.

"It's complicated," she said.

"I look no gift horse in the mouth. Makes my job easier tonight." He held up a gloved hand as she was about to open the door. "Let me go first. Keep close behind me."

Blaster at the ready, he slid out the half-open door and along the corridor wall. Shalira did her best to manage his soundless, smooth glide, taking a second to pull the door closed behind her. Counting the steps in her head, she knew when they were approaching the large chamber where the effigy of the god sat. Surprised, she nearly bumped into Johnny as he slowed.

"In case you haven't already seen," he whispered, "I gotta warn you, there's some pretty awful stuff in this room we have to cross ahead. Try not to peek, okay? Put your hand on my back and follow me."

"I sensed the evil when the priest brought me though earlier," she said. "I didn't need to see it."

Despite the urgency of their situation, he didn't budge for a moment, swallowing hard. As if he was talking to himself, he said, "The worst part? That thing in there is carved a lot like a Mawreg would look. Not exactly, but close enough to make me think the sculptor had met one."

Surprised to realize he was fighting himself about entering the sanctuary, she squeezed his hand. "Mike spoke to me of these aliens. They menace the Sectors, yes? Are they so terrible?"

"We liberated an experimentation camp once. I've seen the Mawreg and lived. Most humans don't." He rolled his shoulders and stood taller. He got a better grip on the gun. As if giving orders to himself, he said, "All right. We're moving now."

Shalira got a grip on his shirt and copied his pace. The evil emanating from the room ahead was already taking her breath away. The sensations were much the same as when Ishtananga had led her past the statue, but now she was more nervous because she and Johnny were vulnerable, so much depending on their success in finding and rescuing Mike and Saium. She closed her eyes tight as they crossed the threshold, knowing she could make her way perfectly well without seeing the horror they were walking past.

She thought she heard a voice, whispering just below the threshold of her hearing, urging her to open her eyes and behold the glory of Tlazomiccuhtli. Horrified, she let out a little gasp and bit her lip, fighting the effects of the mental assault. The temptation to peek, a little bit, at the effigy they were passing became more than an irritation, then a compulsion she had to actively combat. She realized Johnny was barely walking.

"What's the matter?" she whispered.

There was no answer, and he stopped.

"Johnny." She shook his shoulder, horrified to find his hand was now at his side, blaster pointed at the floor. With her abnormally keen hearing, she was positive no one else had entered the room. Opening her eyes, she tried again to jar her companion into speech or movement. Following the direction of his gaze, she beheld Tlazomiccuhtli for herself and fell to her knees, retching at the sheer horror. Arms crossed over her gut, Shalira raised her head to take another cautious glance in the torchlight.

After a single, horrified glance, Shalira forced herself to look away from Tlazomiccuhtli, shaking her head, trying to clear the dizziness.

She stood, checking on Johnny who seemed locked into position, literally transfixed, either by the dark powers Tlazomiccuhtli wielded or his own memories, or both. Shalira glanced at her hands and realized she was projecting pale green light from every pore. Startled, she stepped back, losing contact with the sergeant. Instinctively she clutched her amulet and found it warm to her touch. *Pavmiraia must be protecting me, as much as she can in this horrible place.* Frantic with the need to move, Shalira tugged harder on the paralyzed Johnny but couldn't rouse him from the trance or traumatic state he was in. Unblinking, he stared straight at the effigy, his body rigid.

Dizziness was overtaking her senses, whether from the smoke or the influence of Tlazomiccuhtli she wasn't sure. Reaching a decision, she closed her eyes and took off her amulet, which she looped over Johnny's head. The end of the chain slipped from her fingers as if pulled and she heard the locket clatter onto the stone floor. Kneeling, Shalira swept the floor with her hands. Frustrated, she risked opening one eye and immediately felt the pull to turn toward Tlazomiccuhtli and worship him. Fortunately she caught a glimpse of her locket, shining with the pale green glow, half-hidden under a table supporting a cage of hissing snakes. Forcing herself to move away from the statue, praying the snakes couldn't escape the enclosure, she crawled to retrieve the locket and brought it back to Johnny. As soon as she fastened the chain around his neck, he jerked and blinked, rubbing his forehead.

"Can you walk now?" Shalira asked, closing her eyes against the hypnotic pull of the god, but not letting go of his sleeve. "Close your eyes and lean on me, soldier."

He mumbled something in Basic that she took for agreement.

She led him out of the chamber, counting the steps and listening to the echoes, although it was hard to hear over the voices in her head, calling her to return to Tlazomiccuhtli's embrace.

CHAPTER NINE

Once she knew she was out of the chamber, and the pull of the voices lessened, Shalira opened her eyes, and she and Johnny leaned side-by-side on the wall for a moment. Sweat was pouring off the sergeant and his hands were shaking.

"Are you all right?"

Cradling his blaster as if to anchor himself in reality, he nodded, swallowing hard. "Thanks. I owe you one."

"I owe you more than one," she answered. "Let there be no accounting between us."

"The Mawreg held me prisoner briefly, initiated their interrogation, not long enough to do real damage. Mike and a squad of operators rescued me, took down the base." He leaned his head back, closing his eyes. "It's a hard thing to get over. I've had all the standard military treatment, but I still have nightmares sometimes, which is the real reason Mike and I are retiring. I can't do the job any more. No one dreamed we'd come close to triggering a flashback on this backwater planet, begging your pardon."

"You appear to be doing all right to me," Shalira said, choosing to ignore the less than flattering reference to Mahjundar. "I know what it's like to have screaming nightmares, to not be able to remember what was done to you but knowing it was bad. You don't owe me any explanations, Sergeant. The important thing is to keep going, and I have a feeling we're both accomplished at that." She squeezed his arm.

"Speaking of which, we better locate Mike and Saium and get the hell out of here before someone finds the priest's body." Johnny straightened, face settling into the stern lines of a warrior. He brought the gun up. "You good to go?"

Shalira showed him her knife. Her hand was steady as a rock. "Ishtananga told me the guards took Mike and the others down this corridor."

Johnny set off in his smooth gliding walk again and Shalira followed. The corridor took a bend to the left, and he stopped her with an upraised hand. He risked a quick glance around the corner, eased back and whispered, "Two guards, bored as hell. Simple enough to kill, but this blaster is goddamn noisy in enclosed spaces. We're in trouble if reinforcements arrive. Can you distract them, so I can take them out from behind quietly?"

"No problem." Shalira handed him the knife as she had no place to conceal a weapon, ran one hand through her hair to restore some order, and sauntered into the hall.

The two men, who'd been playing a dice game, scrambled to their feet, staring at her with jaws agape.

"I've been given permission to talk to my warriors," she said imperiously, pulling on her memories of Empress Maralika's attitude. "I have messages from Ishtananga for my men to carry to the gods in the morning."

The man who was probably more senior checked the hallway beyond her. "How is it you've regained use of your eyes? Where's the high priest, Oracle? He gave strict orders no one was to see the prisoners tonight. They don't even receive the ritual dinner."

"Well, obviously he's changed his mind, because here I am." Shalira reached them and kept walking, stepping daintily over the dice and the coins, to stand at the other side of the door, fingering the handle. The younger warrior appeared to be in awe, staring at her. The older man was frowning, shifting his grip on his spear and shuffling his feet. She gave him her most beguiling expression, tilting her head and batting her eyelashes. "Use of my eyes comes and goes as the god wills it." Remembering how the village women had treated her, what they'd all

wanted, she tried another tack to disarm the suspicious guard. "I'm to tell your
fortunes while I'm here, in recognition of your service standing guard in the temple
at night. Do you want to know what your future holds before I speak to my men?"

They were staring at her, backs to the hall. Shalira kept herself from glancing
at Johnny as he slipped soundlessly toward them. She held out her hand to the
younger man, but the warrior yanked him away.

"Is that blood on your dress, Oracle?" he asked, pointing.

She grabbed at his spear, taking both guards by surprise, giving Johnny the
opportunity he needed to cover the final few feet, killing or knocking out the
younger man with a blow to the head and then wrestling the other to the floor,
locked in a chokehold. Too horrified to close her eyes, Shalira backed away, fighting
her emotions as the life-and-death struggle played out in front of her. She couldn't
see any way to help Johnny, who didn't require her assistance in any case. The
battle was short, and the guard fell limply to the side.

Rising like a lithe cat, Johnny took the key ring from the man's belt. "You
okay?" he asked, shooting her a sideways glance as he fumbled with the ornate
lock. "You did a terrific job."

"Are they dead?" she asked in a whisper.

Turning the key, he nodded. "We'll drag them into the cell as soon as I get
Mike free."

The sound of the heavy door creaking across the stone floor brought Mike
instantly awake, adrenaline jerking him up tight in the restraints. He hadn't realized
he'd drowsed off. A quick glance out the window reassured him it was not yet
dawn. The night sky was dark and quiet outside, with no sign of the rising sun. He
tensed, ready for anything. *Let them make one slip, give me any kind of opening—*

The sight of Johnny, blaster in one hand, dragging a dead guard behind him
over the threshold, was the best thing Mike had ever seen on any planet. He
gawked at Shalira hastening into the cell right behind his cousin, running to his
side. Her luminous eyes gleamed and he realized she'd fully regained her sight.

Relief flooded his heart at seeing the two people he cared most about standing free and whole in front of him. "How did you—?"

"Thought we'd never get here," Johnny said, hauling the guard's body another yard or two into the room before dropping it unceremoniously on the cold stone floor. Hands on his hips, face expressionless under the camouflage paint, he surveyed Mike. "You all right?"

"Basically." Mike closed his eyes for a second, thanking the Lords of Space he wasn't dreaming or hallucinating. Shalira threw herself at him, taking care not to jostle his ribs, but pressing herself to his good side, demanding a kiss which Mike was only too happy to supply. He broke the caress off after a minute, when a grinning Johnny unlocked the shackles. Rubbing his wrists before embracing Shalira, Mike said, "We've got to hurry, we only have till dawn and they'll be in here, wanting to make me the first sacrifice."

"Got one more guard to drag out of the hall." Johnny went to free Saium and Everett. "Can you take care of the chore?" he asked over his shoulder.

"Probably not." Mike leaned over, off-balance, hand pressed tight to his right side.

"What's the matter?" Johnny's eyes narrowed as he watched Mike favoring his ribs.

"I'm pretty sure I've got some busted ribs, not improved by being manhandled and chained to a wall. Don't worry. Nothing's going to stop me getting the hell out of here." Biting his lip till he tasted blood, Mike straightened gingerly, hand to his rib cage.

"How bad?" Johnny asked. "Do you think you punctured a lung?"

"No, I'll be okay till we reach the ship." As he watched Saium leave the cell to handle the question of retrieving the other guard, Mike said, "What about Three Feathers? How did you get away from him?"

"You mean Ishtananga, the high priest?" Shalira said, shuddering. She fingered her skirt, which still bore splashes of the man's blood. "He's dead."

"Her Highness was making a valiant effort to do him in with one of his own knives when I arrived. I kinda finished the deal for her," Johnny said as he dragged the other body into the cell.

"But you're all right?" Mike searched her face, noting how beautifully her eyes shone, now she was able to see.

Shalira nodded. "Your warning was accurate, I did need to be blind when we arrived here. He tested me with a candle flame, but then after his suspicions were allayed, I was able to summon my sight by the grace of my goddess. I grabbed a knife when he left the room. One of the servants realized I could see, but he was only a little boy. If he mentions anything to his mother we could be in trouble."

"I thought maybe you were dead," Mike said to Johnny over Shalira's head.

"They hunted me all right." He grinned but there was no mirth in his eyes. "I took care of the scouts on my tail and hid the bodies. But when I looped back again, there were too many of the enemy for me to take on, especially with you and Saium already incapacitated from those darts. I trailed you to the village. Even with a blaster I didn't think I could launch an assault and get you out without taking casualties. There were fifteen guards ringing the hut they kept you in. And they weren't anything like Bandarlok's lazy clansmen. These guys walked the perimeter and investigated the slightest noise, nervous as a bunch of cats. They kept the fires burning sky high all night, so it was nearly as bright as day. I had no idea where Shalira was, observed them leading her away, but couldn't see where. I was hoping for a break the next day, on the trail, but there isn't much cover along the road. Had to hang way back. No chance to stage a one-man ambush. Then I had to wait until dark to climb over the walls of this place." Johnny rubbed his jaw with one hand. "Strangest city I've ever been in. All those houses, no civilians. Big garrison of soldiers. I hoped this temple was where they'd taken you."

"Ishtananga said the city is for big religious festivals and in between only the priests, their women, staff and soldiers live here," Shalira said. "He told me normally that no one remains in the temple at night except the high priest, which was him. Oh, and priests observing the stars tonight."

"Astronomers? Could be the big tower at the other end is for star gazing," Johnny cracked his knuckles. "Couple of local scientists shouldn't be any problem. What's the plan?"

Mike rubbed his hands together and glanced over at the door. "See if we can get our hands on the rest of our gear and hightail it out of here."

"I'm good with that," Everett said. He held his hand out to Johnny, while nodding at Shalira. "Ma'am, Sergeant, I'm Captain Everett. Thanks for saving our bacon."

Johnny sketched a half salute and shook hands before giving his attention to Mike. "You know where the gear is?" he asked, left eyebrow quirked skeptically. "And is it worth our time to retrieve?"

Mike nodded. "Blasters, gear the villagers took from Everett, yeah I think we'd better have it. We have to call for extraction at some point and we can't do it without our equipment. There's sure no easy road to the capital to use the ambassador's private com."

"I can't go back there. It would be my death." Shalira shuddered and he hugged her closer.

"No worries, sweetheart. You're never setting foot there."

"Track back to the wreck maybe, use the coms in the ship he rode in on?" Johnny said, pointing at Everett with his chin.

The other operator laughed. "Sorry, no can do. We sustained heavy damage in the firefight with the Mawreg. Going into hyperdrive only made the problems worse, even if we did escape the enemy. The ship crashed here, cracked up on a cliff. The dying pilot's final act was to slag the engines without waiting to see if anyone on board had survived. I lost half my team in the explosion. My guess? He panicked, thought the Mawreg had followed us, which thankfully they hadn't. But all my guys and I made it out with was our blasters."

"So the information from your mission behind enemy lines was lost with the ship?" Mike asked. He understood where Johnny was coming from. The pressure of time ticking away was intense in the back of his mind too, but he had to know about Everett's data.

Everett tapped his forehead. "All here. Three of us on my team were enhanced with the extra memory lobe. We each uploaded the data, for what it's worth now, stuck on this crappy planet."

"Her home," Mike said, indicating Shalira.

Everett sniffed and dropped into pidgin Mahjundan. "Sorry, lady, but from my standpoint, this place is no picnic."

The princess didn't seem offended. "I understand."

"You must have passed the storeroom door on your way to us," Mike said. "The priests stashed our stuff in a room along the main corridor right outside the chamber with the big statue."

"Ugliest thing I ever saw in twenty years of service." Johnny actually shook himself, like a dog shedding water. "Creature from *someone's* worst nightmare. Thing's eyes follow you. Like—like a Mawreg." Johnny and Shalira exchanged an odd glance, piquing Mike's curiosity, but he decided now wasn't the time to ask questions.

"Exactly. I'm supposed to be its breakfast. Got any water?" Taking the canteen his cousin offered, Mike drank a few swallows to ease his parched throat. Then he poured some into his hand and swiped across his forehead, wiping the area dry with the tail end of his uniform shirt. In the process he was able to remove most of the symbol the late Three Feathers had marked him with.

Saium stuck his head in the half-open door. "Are we moving out soon?" Seeing what Mike was doing, Saium came inside, holding his hand out for the canteen. "Excellent idea, Major, remove the vestiges of the evil magic." He cleansed his own forehead of the red dust in two swipes. Then he offered the canteen to Everett.

"No more guards here in the temple at night, maybe a few scholarly priests. I like those odds," Mike said, rolling his shoulders, stopping halfway through the gesture as his range of motion was curtailed by the broken ribs. "Let's get our gear. Any other exits from this place?"

"I didn't see any, and believe me, I didn't miss anything. Walking straight up the damn pyramid in the moonlight wasn't my idea of a stealthy approach to a rescue operation." Johnny frowned. "Too much talk. We're tempting the Lords of Space by lingering here, let's move."

Moving Shalira behind him, Mike checked the hall. He indicated for Johnny to take point, since he had the only blaster. The sergeant led the others along the corridor in single file. Counting doors under his breath, Mike stopped at the one he'd marked in his mind's eye as the storeroom the high priest had opened earlier.

"No key," he said. "Nothing for it but to blast the mechanism." He stepped aside and gestured to Johnny.

The Mark 27's signature whine echoed loudly in the narrow confines of the stone corridor. The lock melted away in about thirty seconds and Mike was able to swing the door open. Shepherding his party into the room, he drew the door partially closed in the best attempt at concealment they could make under the circumstances.

Saium had brought the lit torches with him.

"Lords of Space, can you believe this?" Johnny took a torch from the old guardsman, raising it high to illuminate the storehouse. The room held tumbled piles of gold, jewelry, lengths of fine fabric, elaborately carved statues, bottles and containers of what could be wine or spices. Totally incongruous in this hoard, several black packs with the modest Sectors logo sat in a heap off to the side, close to the door. Johnny let out a long, low whistle. "These guys keep house like my mother! Major packrats."

Mike laughed as he moved forward to examine the pile of bags thrown on top of yet more treasures. "Well, at least your mom knows where to find her things." Squatting, he frowned, moving the kit bags aside. "These are ours, not Everett's, and one's missing."

"Maybe the villagers kept it, hoping for a little bit of treasure," Shalira said. "I heard them arguing about turning us and the entire set of spoils over to the priests. They wanted to keep some for themselves."

"As long as we have the uplink device to call for transport out of here, we'll be fine," Mike said. "If that's gone, the situation gets dicey. Let's see if the other blasters are in here, maybe the local guns. We need firepower."

The three Sectors operators knelt beside the black bags and began doling out blasters and other bits of equipment among themselves. Johnny switched on a powerful light and set it on the floor by his knee, casting the entire room into view.

"I don't think we want anything out of here other than our own stuff," Mike said, glancing around. "The Nathlemeru extorted all of this from people, tortured and killed innocent victims to acquire this treasure. It's tainted."

"Bad luck," agreed Johnny, tossing a blaster from the pack over to Mike.

"I for one don't want anything from this damn planet," Everett said. He kicked a small golden pot by his foot for emphasis. It rolled away from him, spilling some thick, highly scented oil over the floor. "Just to leave it behind in my rear vids as I head back to civilization." He checked the settings on the blaster handed to him and then headed for the door. "I'll keep watch while you finish up, but we need to move, sir."

"Saium, come get a blaster," Johnny said, pulling a spare from the bag. "Your Highness, you want my gun?"

"You can give me a weapon, but I'm not likely to be much of a shooter," she said. "No rush."

While the men divided the weapons, Shalira sank onto a nearby chest and leaned against the wall, wrapping her arms around herself. She tried to block the vision of Ishtananga dying at her feet. *Sometimes sight isn't such a blessing.* Now wasn't the time to break apart and give in to the emotions battering at her mind. They weren't safe yet.

Opening her eyes, she glanced at her companions in time to intercept a worried look from Mike. Straightening her back, unclasping her arms, she nodded and made herself smile. He had enough to deal with at the moment without adding her state of mind to his fears. She'd manage whatever was thrown at them next. Mike returned his attention to the matters under discussion and she rose to her feet. Suddenly she had the overwhelming need to be in motion, ready for action.

Shalira paced along the edge of the treasure hoard, somewhat impressed by the sheer volume, but not overly, considering the vaults of jewels and gold owned by her father. Shivering, she took a step away from the pile, overwhelmed again by the price paid in human lives to amass all this wealth for the uncaring god.

No, Mike was right. She wanted nothing from this place except to leave it as rapidly as possible. What was taking the men so long?

Turning to walk back to them, she paused, feeling as if someone or something had brushed her arm. Heart pounding, she stared around, but there was no one else in the room. *Foolish,* she chided herself. Everett, the new soldier, was rising to leave the room, a blaster clutched purposefully in his hand. Encouraged they'd be on their way soon, she took one step and froze. Something tugged at her, pulled on every fiber of her being. It was as if each cell in her body was inexorably drawn to a lodestone the way iron filings fly to a magnet.

Pivoting slowly on her heel, she ignored a remark directed to her by Mike. Facing into the depths of the chamber, she tried to figure out what had this hold on her. Almost unconsciously she was putting one foot in front of the other, walking into the mess, clambering heedlessly over treacherous piles of coins, gems, statues, slipping and sliding, but always moving forward in obedience to the force pulling her. With no thought of resisting now, Shalira gave in to the will ensnaring her, only raising one hand for a moment to caress the locket of Pavmiraia, silently breathing a prayer for protection.

Blinking, she focused on what had to be the object she sought and eagerly started forward again.

Mike was at her elbow, holding her in place. "Sweetheart, what is it? What are you looking for?" He gazed at the accumulated loot with a frown.

She balanced precariously on top of the loose pile of treasures. Annoyed, she yanked herself free, nearly toppling down the pile of loot. She crooked her finger at him even as the hoard under her feet threatened to collapse. "Come help me."

He hesitated. "We don't have time."

Driven by the need to possess the item calling to her, she stepped further into the room, and answered him over her shoulder. "I'm not leaving without this, so either help me yourself or send Saium to aid me."

Seeming curious to see what could have possibly skewed her priorities so badly all of the sudden, what could make her forget the need for immediate escape, Mike joined her, crushing small valuables under his space boots. She fell to her knees, tugging to free the object she sought from a tangle of other golden debris. He was just in time to catch her as the prize broke free and Shalira toppled over with a small scream.

For one precious moment, she cradled her find in her arms. Cold flooded her body as she touched the treasure. She closed her eyes, overwhelmed by a vision of warriors fighting, then the scene of a man dressed in an ancient version of the Mahjundan emperor's armor, on his knees, pleading for his life before knives plunged into him—

She recoiled, gasping, yet clung to the item she'd salvaged.

Mike grabbed her with one arm, blaster out and ready to cut down whoever or whatever had frightened her. Voice shaking, he said, "Sweetheart, what's the matter? I don't see anything here but loot. What's got you so upset? Talk to me."

Leaning into his reassuring warmth, she opened her eyes, finding the visions and the unbreakable pull were gone. "Do you know what this is?" she said, holding her treasure out to him.

He took an impatient glance at it as he steadied her on her feet, before executing a perfect double take. She was cradling a faceted purple stone as big as his fist, in a golden setting bracketed by two solid gold cherindors, wings spread. The gem was set into the top of a dark wooden staff, which ended in a jagged mass of splinters.

"Impressive. How the hell did you see this one object in the midst of all the loot, and what makes it such a big deal?"

"It's the most sought after item in all of Mahjundar, the Scepter of the Lost Emperor," Shalira said. "It called to me."

Eyes narrowed, Mike touched one wing with the tip of his finger. "So they killed your ancestor and tossed his scepter into this pile of loot?"

"Apparently." She gave a bitter laugh, remembering stories she'd been told as a child. "So much for all the gallant legends of how he threw it in the Suaga with his dying breath to keep the Nathlemeru from stealing it. Just now I was given a vision of him offering the scepter to the priests, in return for sparing his life, right before they cut his heart out."

Mike frowned, seeming troubled. He brushed her cheek with the back of his hand, as if to reassure himself she was all right. "Channeling the power again, sweetheart? I think this is a dangerous place to open yourself to unknown influences." Staring around the room, he said, "Probably a lot of tragedy and horror associated with all this loot."

Relieved that he didn't question her ability, she nevertheless corrected him on one detail. "The scepter called to *me*. I'm not sure why. It never would have occurred to me to search for it in this trove otherwise."

"I'm not sure I like that aspect of the recovery necessarily, but we can sort it out later, in a safer place. We've got to move. There's nothing else you need to find?"

Shaking her head, she got a better grip on the scepter.

"Good," Mike said, leading her from the stack of boxes and furniture.

Everett stuck his head in the door. "We're out of time, sir. Lot of yelling going on at the other end. We gotta find another way out."

Ignoring the surge of pain from his ribs, holding Shalira's hand, Mike was at the door in a few steps, joining Johnny and Saium. The sergeant edged out into the hall, blaster drawn. Mike followed, setting the princess on her feet in the corridor. Saium acted as rearguard. Mike could hear for himself the shouts Everett mentioned. Frustrated at the lost advantage, he said, "We're cut off. And as soon as someone takes charge over there in the other wing, they'll come running to check on us. Let's move, people." Mike gestured to Johnny. "Take point. We need to know what we're heading into."

"I'm on it." Johnny broke into a full run, disappearing around the curving corridor.

"Everett, back him up," Mike ordered. "Saium, you're the rear guard."

Renewed yelling broke out behind them and he tried to ignore his aching ribs, move faster. Saium half turned as he ran, firing the unfamiliar blaster over his shoulder at the newly arrived enemy. From behind, several poorly aimed arrows flickered past Mike, striking the stone walls and falling to the floor. Ahead there was the sudden buzz of blasters and a yell choked off in mid cry.

As Mike followed the curve of the featureless, white stone corridor, he found Johnny and Everett shoving a dead or dying local out of the way so they could pull a heavy pair of doors shut. Behind him, Saium fired his blaster on full power at whoever was coming to investigate. Making a mental note to instruct Saium later on saving blaster charges, Mike pushed the princess ahead of him and through the steadily closing gap between the thick, metal clad wooden doors. Saium squeaked through sideways at the last second and the two Sectors operators dropped a massive iron crossbar into place, sealing the opening as arrows bounced off the door.

CHAPTER TEN

Breathing hard, leaning on the wall because inhaling was like a knife in his rib cage, Mike assessed the room they were in, pleased to find it a good place to defend. There were no other entrances and no windows. The door was stout and made of some iron-hard wood, no metal cladding on this side. Still, with enough time, it could probably be burnt down or smashed through. *Hopefully we won't be here long enough.*

As if reading his mind, Johnny pounded one fist on the door. "This'll hold for a while. Guess the astronomers liked their privacy. But we gotta figure on the enemy breaking in sooner or later."

"Didn't Ishtananga say there were two priests on duty?" Mike asked Shalira.

Drawing in huge breaths, chest heaving, she nodded.

Mike issued crisp orders. "Johnny, see who or what's above us. We need the high ground. And find the other guy."

The sergeant nodded and cautiously ascended the stone steps, pressing himself against the wall as he climbed, weapon at the ready. A moment later he yelled, "Secure. Found our missing priest. He's no threat."

Mike looked at his newest recruit. "Everett, guard the door. Sing out if they make any progress on breaking through."

The other man nodded, flicking a casual salute. "Don't forget about me when the extraction ship arrives."

"No way, you're what this mission's all about." Clapping him on the shoulder, Mike moved to the stairs Johnny had recently climbed. Saium followed him, with Shalira on his heels, still clutching her ancestor's bejeweled scepter. Johnny tied the last knot on makeshift ropes restraining an unconscious man as Mike arrived on the second floor. Rising, retrieving his blaster, the sergeant said, "I barely tapped him. I think he fainted, to tell you the truth. Going to explore the next floor now."

"Yeah, make sure we don't have any other company in here." Scanning the chamber, Mike realized a feast had been laid out on a table close to the far wall, under a tapestry depicting men and women dancing while off to the side someone was stretched on an altar, about to die. Mike yanked the offending wall decoration down with a curse before perusing the crowded tabletop. "Guess they were planning an early morning feast after they took their star sightings." Glancing at Shalira, who had sunk on to a low couch close to the stairs, "Want something? You should eat while we have a lull. Keep your strength up."

"I'm a little hungry," Shalira admitted. Leaving the scepter on the couch, she joined him, filling a woven, leaf-shaped plate with fruit and a roll. "Saium?"

He shook his head, remaining at the top of the stairs, weapon at the ready.

Space boots clattering on the stone stairs, Johnny re-entered the room. "Two more levels, then the building's open to the sky. We're above the roof of the main temple complex. No other way in or out of this tower except for the big door below," he said. "Unless you want to take the scenic route straight down the sheer cliff face."

Mike shook his head. "Only as a last resort." His cousin nodded in mutual understanding of his unspoken vow not to allow the Nathlemeru a second chance at capturing them. "Any signs of activity on the temple roof?"

"No. It may take them some time to think of attacking us from there. Third level of this tower gets even smaller, with another trapdoor and a shielded balcony. There's a spiral staircase going from the balcony around the outside of the tower to the roof. Funny design."

Mike considered. "Sounds like a good place to survive a siege, although I'm not planning to linger. Any cover on the temple roof for them to attack from?"

"Nothing but red clay tiles. Hadn't we better get a move on, call for extraction? I'm not any too happy about only having one door between us and them." Johnny snagged a piece of fruit and took a big bite. "Nice of them to provide us with breakfast."

Mike rubbed his eyes for a minute. "You're right about calling for extraction. The gear's in our bags on the first level."

Johnny flung out a hand to stop Mike from moving toward the stairs. "You sit, rest those broken ribs. Enjoy the lull, like you told the princess a minute ago. I'll get the stuff and give Everett a quick sitrep."

When his cousin returned moments later, Mike left Saium with Shalira. Taking the curiously designed spiral staircase on the outside for the last section of the climb, the two operators ascended to the top of the tower. Johnny carried one of the black kit bags. Mike eyed the surroundings with satisfaction as they emerged into the pale dawn. "Signal ought to make it out of here clear. Nice of the Nathlemeru to build us a good platform. Things could get kinda dicey otherwise." Taking a second, he walked the perimeter, whistling at the sheer drop down the side of the mountain plateau the temple was sitting on. The ground far below was lost in mist. Exchanging glances with Johnny, he said, "Not a very appealing escape route."

"We could do it though," his cousin said. "Got an antigrav disk in the gear."

"Yeah, but only one. Spares must have been in the missing bags. One disk can't take five people."

"Come on, you and I both know the units are built to float two men our size in an emergency, so there's capacity to spare." Johnny joined him at the low wall. "You or I can ferry the others, one at a time."

Mike broke a tiny piece of rock from the crumbling wall and tossed it into the abyss below. He glanced at Johnny after watching the fragment disappear into the mists. "If our survival comes to descending this cliff while they're shooting at us from above, we won't be able to make more than one trip. Everett's the high value target of this mission, so we'd have to prioritize his survival. Send him with Shalira."

"He may have the memory enhancement, but he ain't got fastlink. I asked him. He needs you to call in the cavalry." Johnny's voice was matter-of-fact. "We can't send him off on his own, not even to save the lady."

Taking another look over the side, estimating how many thousands of feet it might be to the bottom of the cliff, Mike rejected the idea. "We've got no idea what's at the base. I think we're stuck here unless the situation deteriorates significantly. Then we'll see."

Leaving the question of the problematic descent, he walked to the uplink device, which Johnny had established in the exact center of the roof. He'd pushed aside a stack of crude Nathlemeru astronomical observation equipment and long rolls of paper-thin hides, covered in notations and charts.

Placing his blaster in its holster, Mike knelt next to the small black box. He punched in the sequence he'd memorized before the current mission—evac codes changed every time someone was sent out, to prevent the Mawreg from luring unwary military ships into an ambush.

A low-pitched hum purred across the roof, vibrating in the tiny bones in his ears. Barely visible, a violet beam pulsed skyward from the cone-shaped top of the device. "Now for the hard part, sending a detailed message in fast-link." Acknowledging Johnny's sympathetic grimace with a rueful smile, Mike sat cross-legged, next to the beacon. No Special Forces operator ever enjoyed hooking into fastlink. The technology took a toll on the operator, which made its use a last ditch choice. *I think Command likes it that way.* Mike flipped open a small compartment on the instrument's base, removing a black disk which he pressed to his skull behind the left ear. The violet glow spread to enclose him as well.

Concentrating to add his will power to the device's broadcast and send an intelligible request via the beam, Mike's muscles grew stiffer the longer he sat, which was his only clue how much time the process was taking. On the periphery of his awareness, Johnny was prowling, constantly checking the roof while keeping an eye on how Mike was doing.

Well, I've done all I can. Mike released his mental hold on the fastlink and let his hand fall away from his skull, the amplifier dropping to the roof from his nerveless fingers and bouncing across the floor. As suddenly as it had begun, the expanded violet glow contracted away from him, merging into the narrow beacon pulsing skyward, hum decreasing to its original, near subliminal frequency. With a shower of sparks and a whoosh, the beam cut off. The silence was startling.

Johnny moved fast to give Mike a steadying hand as he tried to rise. The sergeant restored the fallen fastlink enabler disk to its compartment and then the two men walked to the staircase, Mike leaning heavily on his cousin.

"Damn fastlink messes with my whole nervous system." His words were slurred. Annoyed at his weakness, blinking in an attempt to focus his eyes, he said, "Good thing this is our last mission. I'm getting too old for all this."

"You and me both." Worried frown lines bracketed Johnny's eyes as he studied Mike's face. Eyes narrowed, he paused at the top of the staircase. "Something you want to tell me?"

Knowing he was debilitated by the drain from using his body's resources to activate the fastlink, Mike opted to wait to share the result of his communication. "Help me get to the second level. It's not what we hoped, but I'll give everyone the bad news at the same time. I gotta sit before I fall."

Johnny assisted Mike to the couch on the second level of the tower, where he slumped onto the cushions next to Shalira. Everett came halfway up the stairs at Johnny's summons. Leaning against the cold stones to relieve the headache pounding behind his eyes, Mike took a deep breath. "Rush order on the adrenephix, cousin."

Raising one hand to acknowledge the request, the sergeant dug his medkit out of the other kit bag, spreading it open on the floor to search for the inject Mike needed to speed his recovery.

Shalira reached for Mike's hand with both of hers, leaning into his shoulder. There was no use in cushioning the bad news. "The *Andy* isn't on station, folks."

"What the hell!" Jaw dropping, Johnny sank back on his heels, abandoning his medical duty for the moment. "They promised us—"

"Nikolai told me he might have to pull out if there was a Mawreg incursion into the adjoining Sector while we were hiking down here," Mike answered, free hand over his aching eyes. Rubbing his forehead for a moment, he swallowed hard, throat parched. "He couldn't guarantee to sit parked in orbit and wait."

"You're calm about it," Everett said, eyes narrowed.

"I'm sorry, what does this mean?" Shalira glanced from one man to the other. "Who is Andy? And this Nikolai?"

"Not a who, a what. The *Andromeda*, or *Andy*, as we affectionately call her, is the battle cruiser that brought Johnny and me to Mahjundar. Nikolai Novikov, the captain of the ship, is an old friend of mine. He was supposed to stand by for my extraction signal. But now the ship isn't in orbit."

"Got a backup plan?" Everett asked.

"Working on it." Sitting straighter, Mike hugged Shalira, kissing the top of her head. "We're not completely abandoned. They left a small roboship on station in orbit around Mahjundar, set to send a drone to extract us on my command. Since they knew there was a remote chance we'd find survivors, the roboship and the drone are plenty big enough to take our party of five. *Andromeda* also left a message beacon in orbit to relay my transmission to Nikolai, wherever he is, but we have to get ourselves off the planet in the drone or wait maybe as long as thirty-six standard hours for the Space Marines to arrive."

Face contorted in a scowl, Everett hit the unoffending wall with the butt of his blaster, chipping the paint with the force of the blow. "We can't hold out in this place, and you know it. We don't have enough blaster charges to repel a concentrated attack. The door downstairs is thick and all, but it ain't gonna hold for a day and a half once those bastards start working on it."

"I'm guessing you didn't call in the drone, did you?" Johnny said, one eyebrow quirked. He stood, an inject in his hand.

Mike shook his head as his cousin walked to the couch and administered the adrenephix. Rubbing his bicep to ease the sting, he said, "Make the dose a double. We don't have time for me to sleep off the fastlink detox."

Johnny frowned, lips compressed into a thin line, but he complied, shooting a second dose of the meds into Mike's arm.

"Why not call the drone?" Shalira was surprised.

"I can't control its descent. All automated. It comes to where I am, homing in on the fastlink chip in my head and landing. Until I get inside to take command, that's all it does. The AI running it is a low budget kinda thing, not prepared to maneuver, no guns. No one anticipated a combat situation on Mahjundar." Mike continued with his list of the drone's disadvantages in the current situation. "It can't hover. I don't think we want to put our faith in the temple roof being constructed to hold the weight of a six person shuttle. I don't think we want to try fighting our way down the exposed side of the tower onto the roof to board, in any case."

"We're in a good position to wait it out," Saium said. "The only ways the enemy can get to us are through the door at the bottom of the stairs or they can come across the roof, through the window on the third level. When the guards try we'll pick them off."

"All right," Mike said. "Until they mount an attack, I need one man on the tower roof, one man on the third level balcony, where the stairs start, and a guard at the door on the first floor. I want to be notified the instant anyone pokes their head onto the roof, or starts an assault on the front door. The roof commands a view of the city all the way to the main gate, so keep an eye on what's going on, any unusual movement. We know the place is pretty deserted normally."

"I'll take the roof," Everett said. "I was locked in the damn hut for so long, I get the shakes being inside. Let me see the sky, and I'll be fine."

I understand where he's coming from. Mike nodded. "Roof's all yours. The Nathlemeru initiate any activity of any kind, call out the news." He surveyed his meager troops. "Who's taking the first watch on the third floor balcony?"

"Me for the balcony," Johnny volunteered.

"You relay any word from Everett to us here on the second level, which will be my command post for now." Mike gestured at the open kit bag. "Take our gear with you, while we've got some peace and quiet."

"Right." Johnny gave him a thumbs-up.

Mike looked at the last member of their small group. "Leaves the door for you, Saium."

"I can handle it. I don't mind being there by myself. There'll be plenty of warning if the Nathlemeru try an assault." The old man nodded. "I might be able to hear what they're planning, if they talk loud enough."

"I need to sleep off the effects of fastlink for an hour or two, if possible, even with a double dose of meds," Mike explained for Shalira's benefit as she continued to stare at him with concern. "Wake me if anything moves."

"They might decide to do nothing, starve us out," Saium suggested. "The delay could work in our favor while we wait for your Marines."

Mike shook his head. "The enemy's pride is going to force them to take direct action. After all, we've killed some of their people, including Three Feathers. They'll want vengeance. The Nathlemeru can't afford the tremendous loss of face if they fail to attack. From what Shalira told us during the cart ride, the villagers chafe at being subject to the Nathlemeru. If the ruling class doesn't end this standoff quickly and decisively, they might have more problems than the issue of our little band of escapees."

His troops dispersed, leaving Mike and Shalira alone on the second level. Closing his eyes, he leaned his head against the cold stones, trying to get comfortable. Adrenephix coursed through his veins, like a wave of icy water, leaving his muscles and nerves tingling as the damage from the fastlink was repaired at a molecular level. Throbbing dully, his headache receded, but not fast enough. Holding one shaking hand out for the princess to see, he said, "I hope I'm not going to be called on for any action soon, because I'm not going to be effective in a firefight. Reflexes shot to hell for a few hours." The trembling of his outstretched fingers emphasized the problem.

Shalira brushed his hair off his forehead and stroked his cheek. "I don't know what this—this fastlink is you spoke of, but I hear the exhaustion in your voice. We need you at your best when the Nathlemeru attack. I'd be happy to rub your shoulders, work out some of the tension? Let Johnny's medicine do its job." She scooted to the far end of the couch and patted the space beside her.

Worn out from two nights without sleep, not to mention the toll of the fastlink, Mike didn't argue. Putting his feet on the couch, he stretched out per her command, already drowsing as she massaged his tense neck and shoulder muscles, kneading them to undo the knots. Holding back the intense desire to sleep, he asked, "How are you doing? Vision still okay?"

"I'm fine, no need to worry about me right now," she said. "I seem to have fully regained my sight, although I can't help but worry a little that it may fade again with no warning. And I've no more herbs to take, if I even need them. I wonder about all of it but I'm trying not to question a gift from the goddess."

"We'll hope for the best," he agreed. "I think it's a good sign you've been able to see for so many hours now, despite the stress you've been under. But no matter what happens, we'll cope together, right?"

"Right." She leaned over to kiss his cheek. "Stop fighting now and get some sleep while you can."

Soon, the world faded away to blackness, and he slept.

As Mike began to snore ever so slightly, Shalira leaned her head against the wall and closed her watering eyes. As she told him, her vision remained fine, clear and in color, which was reassuring. She rubbed her hand across the large gemstone of the scepter, still marveling over the find. Amused at the irony, she wondered what Mike would think if she told him that with this in her hand she was Empress of Mahjundar. If she walked down the main street in the capital city holding this ancient symbol of authority, the people would proclaim her their ruler, such was the power of this emblem. Maralika would have to step aside. *The Princess of Shadows, vindicated indeed.* Shalira frowned, knowing even her father would have to vacate the throne, if he still lived. "But I've no desire to engage in bloody wars over the throne," she whispered, rotating the scepter so she could stare into the ruby eyes of acherindor. "If you asked me to rescue you for that reason, you're to be disappointed. I'm going off-planet to marry Michael. Have his children. Build a new life together, completely different from anything possible here."

The sentience or force within the stone stayed silent. Studying it, she thought maybe there was a faint glow, deep within the faceted depths, but she couldn't be sure. Apparently she was rescuing the scepter only to safeguard it for—what? Gooseflesh rising on her arms, Shalira set the emblem beside her. *Maybe I can donate it to a museum in the Sectors.* But she knew she'd never part with the symbol of the ruling dynasty.

"Better come to the door." Johnny's voice woke Mike from a pleasant dream of home, but he reoriented himself to the cold realities of Mahjundar in no time.

Drawing his blaster, he got to his feet, automatically checking to make sure Shalira was okay. "How long was I out?"

Johnny checked his wrist chrono with a sideways glance. "Three hours. They're trying to force the door. First attempt."

"All right, let's go survey the situation." Mike turned to the princess, curled on the couch, quietly listening to the exchange as she stifled a yawn. He laid his hand on her shoulder and squeezed gently, leaning over to brush a kiss on her cheek. "I'll be right back. Keep your gun close to hand."

Mike hastened to descend the stairs behind Johnny.

"Everett reported runners leaving the city gates and going in several directions," his cousin said as they descended the stone stairs. "Probably warning the villages to be on the watch for us. Didn't see any need to wake you for that piece of intel."

Mike laid a hand on the wooden door, calculating the sturdiness of their defense. The portal vibrated under repeated blows, but didn't budge.

"Fortunately the corridor outside is so narrow they won't be able to bring in a battering ram," Johnny said. "The nice decorative metal sheeting on the outside will keep them from burning us out easily."

"Saium, keep an eye on things. Let me know if there's anything new to report." The restorative effects of some sleep and the adrenephix were deceiving him into believing he was a new man, despite the nagging pain in his rib cage telling him otherwise. Mike ran up the stairs, taking them two at a time, Johnny on his heels. He walked to the couch, holding out his hand to Shalira and drawing her to her feet, hugging her for a moment.

"I want to move you to the third level now," he told her. "I refuse to trust our luck that the door will hold until we're rescued. I want you to be out of harm's way from the start, okay?"

"Since my only contribution to our defense is not adding to your worries and a dubious ability with the gun you gave me, I'll gladly go wherever you wish." Shalira scooped up the scepter.

Mike took her by the elbow, escorting her to the third level. Johnny followed, brushing past them to go onto the balcony.

Mike got her settled on the small couch which was the only furnishing in the third level, and then sat beside her, arm around her shoulders. They exchanged a quick kiss and she laid her head on his chest. Toying with one long curl, Mike said, "Things may get pretty tense as the day goes on. The Nathlemeru aren't dumb. They might figure out a way in here. Then we're in for a fight."

"A fight we may not win?" she prompted as he fell silent. "Even with your offworld weapons?"

"There's a definite chance, depending on how long it takes the rescue party to get here and how many men the Nathlemeru send against us. We don't have recharges for the blasters, which means only about fifty shots each, and we're short on clips for the guns. No more than a hundred extra rounds for the four Mahjundan weapons. Ultimately, we'll fall back to the tower roof for our last stand."

"And then?"

Mike was silent.

She waited patiently.

"We hope the Space Marines arrive in time." He tried a grin he knew wasn't doing the job of giving her reassurance. There was no denying they were in a tight corner. Swallowing hard, he kissed her. "I swear I won't let you fall into their bloodstained hands again. Johnny and I already agreed we aren't going to be taken alive."

She tapped the blaster. "I know you'd make my death quick, unlike the torture the Nathlemeru would deal out. At least we'd be together in the afterlife." Her voice faltered a little on the last word.

"The afterlife is *not* what I've been dreaming of us sharing." Framing her face with his hands, he kissed her lips gently. "I want us to live, get married, have kids, be together for a long time."

"So what do we do?" she asked.

"We might have a last ditch escape route, before we get to the point where we have to kill ourselves to foil the enemy."

She twined her arms around his neck, pulling him closer. Mike gave in to the emotions in his heart and tugged her into his lap. They kissed for a long moment, before he held her tight. "I've got to go to the roof and talk to Johnny."

"Go then." She gave him a tiny push. "When all this adventure is over, promise me we'll have time for ourselves with no interruptions."

"I promise," he said, squeezing her hand. "Once we hit the *Andromeda*, I plan to debrief Command about the operation and then retire on the spot. There'll be nothing but you on my scanners."

Full of adrenaline and unaccustomed emotions, unable to sit a moment longer, he hastened onto the balcony to confer with Johnny. Shoulder to shoulder, hidden behind the low wall, the two operators gazed across the slightly tilted temple roof. The sheer drop-off on the side adjoining the tower meant any attack would have to come from the other end, or the center. Mike couldn't see trapdoors or breaks in the roof itself, so the Nathlemeru would have to climb onto the surface to launch an attack, exposing the enemy to fire from the tower. The range was definitely close enough for accuracy, even with the Mahjundan guns.

"If they have bows and arrows, which they probably do, given the level of technology we've seen so far," Johnny said, gauging the distance, "we could be in trouble, even on the tower roof. Archers could get the angle and drop the fire right in on us. I doubt blowguns have the power, though."

They exchanged glances. Mike couldn't help chuckling, despite the gravity of the situation. "Never thought you'd be planning a defense against archaic weaponry, did you?"

"Yeah, this is a bad dream, but unfortunately I'm stuck in the middle of it with you, so if you could get back to being serious, I'd appreciate it." Brow furrowed, his cousin wasn't amused.

Mike rubbed the back of his neck. "Sorry, still a bit hyped from the adrenephix." He took a deep breath. "Okay, let's drag the tables out of level two and take them to the roof for some shelter. We need to get all our gear and packs to the third level now too, while there's a lull."

"And the food and water," Johnny said. "Have you eaten anything yet?"

Mike raised his eyebrows. "You know me, no appetite until the battle is over."

"Right, and then you eat everything in sight. I hope the cooks on the *Andy* will be ready for you. But do me a favor, follow your friendly medic's orders and eat something now. I don't want you keeling over midfight." Johnny grabbed Mike's sleeve as he was about to leave the tower's roof. "I'm serious. The meds burn through a lot of calories, mending the fastlink damage."

"Yes, Mom." Laughing, Mike headed back down the stairs.

Mike accomplished what limited preparation work could be done and then his meager forces settled into waiting and watching. Too restless to stay in one spot himself, he prowled from level to level, onto the balcony, up to the roof, and back again. He reminded Johnny and Everett to shoot to kill once the Nathlemeru did appear on the roof. "We can't allow anyone to get close to the tower."

At about midmorning, the Nathlemeru finally launched another attack on the first floor entrance. When Mike and Johnny joined Saium by the door, they could hear muffled shouts from men gathered in the narrow corridor, making a concerted effort to force the door open. The stout metal bar across the inside and the ornate iron hinges held fast, not even flexing under the assault.

"They won't succeed," Mike was saying with satisfaction when he heard the unmistakable whine of a blaster. "Stay here," Mike ordered Saium. Moving at double time, he rushed to the third level, his cousin at his heels.

Everett leaned his head in from the balcony. "Two hostiles tried coming onto the roof from the center of the temple. I killed one and may have wounded the other."

"Now they know for sure we're armed and dangerous," Johnny said. "Things could get interesting."

"Are you okay?" Concerned how she was reacting to being in a combat zone, Mike looked to where Shalira sat curled on the couch. The princess was white-faced, lips pressed together in a thin line, her fingers clasped tightly in her lap, but she smiled.

"I'll be fine. You do what needs to be done to protect us and don't worry about me."

"Your Highness, you're one tough lady in my book," Johnny said, admiration in his voice. "You're going to fit in fine on our home world."

"Go reinforce Everett. Keep an eye on him." Mike moved aside ever so slightly to allow the sergeant to squeeze past him, crossing the balcony in a few steps and working his way up the half-exposed stairway cautiously, so as not to present a target. Prowling onto the balcony, Mike crouched next to the low wall.

"Heads up, they're making another attempt," Johnny warned from above, as blaster fire arced out to meet the foolhardy temple guards reconnoitering the defensive situation on the tower.

"I wish we had an estimate of how many men the priests have to call on here in the city," Mike said, watching the squad scatter under fire. One man fell from the roof with a scream, apparently made clumsy by his desperation to escape the withering blaster barrage. Several soldiers lay unmoving as a result of Johnny's marksmanship. "Such a huge place, plenty of buildings, but so empty. Everyone keeps telling me the priests maintain a standing army to enforce their rule but does that mean a hundred men or a thousand? Or ten thousand?"

"I only passed a few occupied structures, mostly in the center, and some beside the temple," Johnny called in reply. "One building was definitely a barracks, big enough to house two hundred or more."

"Plus whatever priests and servants live here. So maybe two or three hundred at the most." Mike laughed. "Three hundred against five, not the best odds we've ever faced."

"Incoming!" yelled Johnny.

The temple guards had figured out a way to get more than two or three men on the roof at the same time. A force of thirty warriors was coming over the edge of the roof at the far end.

"Pick your targets and fire at will," Mike shouted, aiming at a man in the front of the attacking force.

This skirmish was short and decisively in the favor of those besieged in the tower. About half the attackers fell under the targeted blaster fire, dead or wounded, before the force had even had time to form a cohesive unit to advance closer to the tower. The rest abandoned their comrades and fled down unseen ladders, out of range.

"Not too bad," Mike said. "Now if we only had recharges for these babies, there'd be no problem." He checked the readout on the grip of his blaster, the low count giving him a sinking sensation in his gut.

He sprinted to the roof to confer in person with Johnny and Everett, relieved to find them in good shape on blaster charges.

"I'm going to check on Saium and tell him what's happening," Mike told Johnny. "And Shalira."

When Mike got back to the ground floor, there'd been no change, except those outside had apparently abandoned trying to force the door. "We can't expect our luck here to hold, though," he said to Saium. "The more effectively we discourage them from an assault across the roof, the more desperate they're going to get to breach our defenses here." He pounded his fist on the door to emphasize the point.

"Tell me the truth. Are we going to make it out of this situation?" Saium's face was calm, his voice level.

"I think the odds aren't in our favor, but we have a chance," Mike said. "If the Marines get here in time, there's no problem. We have to hold out."

"And what will happen to me once we reach your ship?" Saium's gaze was unblinking, his wrinkled face expressionless.

"Shalira wouldn't stand for leaving you behind on Mahjundar somewhere, even if I was so clueless. I know what she means to you," Mike told him. "I think you can be content on my world. Azrigone has unexplored wilderness where a man can carve out a good living for himself." Staring into Saium's eyes, Mike said, "I need you to be there, for Shalira's sake."

Eyes crinkling as he half-smiled, Saium nodded. "A new life will be hard on her in many ways, but she'll be free. And happy, which is all I ever wanted for her. I'll never forgive myself for helping betray her into Bandarlok's hands."

"You didn't know what the bastard had in mind for her. No one did, except possibly the empress." Mike squeezed the old man's shoulder. "You'll like Azrigone."

Saium had unshed tears in his eyes. "I never dreamed of such generosity, going to your home world with her."

"When we do get rescued, remember to swear you're Shalira's maternal uncle. I can insist on taking my wife's only surviving blood relative home, as long as I can pay the spacefare." Mike laughed. After all the ordeals he'd been through on Mahjundar, getting Saium a safe passage to Azrigone was a minor inconvenience. "My conscience can handle a small lie to make my lady happy. I'd better get back to the roof." *Good thing the Mahjundans have no idea what spacefare to cross ten sectors is going to cost.*

As the sun rose directly overhead, an incessant drumming began, reverberating from the front area of the temple. The beat was pounding, from more than one drum, continuing with no breaks. Mike finally had Saium question the remaining Nathlemeru astronomer as to the meaning of the drum code, but the man refused to talk.

Taking turns resting on the third level, the tower defenders ate sparingly of the astronomers' repast from the night before, washed down with sips of wine.

In mid-afternoon, Everett yelled from his post. "Major, I think you'd better come outside for a minute."

Going onto the balcony, Mike whistled in surprise. "They burning the temple?"

A huge plume of smoke was rising from the center front of the temple. The mountain winds snatched the grayish clouds away as soon as they spiraled above the roof, creating lazy patterns against the royal-blue sky.

"I thought I heard screams." Everett shaded his eyes with one hand.

"I can't imagine what they're doing now. Hold the fort while I go ask Saium what he makes of it."

Mike made his way to the first floor and questioned Saium, whose answer was chilling. "I imagine they're burning Ishtananga's body to send him to the gods. Many have probably been sacrificed this morning to accompany him. The Nathlemeru believe a funeral must occur before the next sunset, which has bought us some time. They've been distracted between trying to do him honor, picking his successor, and probing at our defenses."

Remembering how he'd been slated to die under the high priest's knife, Mike felt momentary nausea run through his gut. "At least Shalira and Johnny killed the man cleanly and quickly, unlike the way the Nathlemeru slaughter innocents for their hideous god."

When Mike arrived on the third floor to brief his companions, Everett said, "This planet is a cesspool, dregs of the universe." His face was drawn in lines of revulsion. "Sacrifice of sentient beings is barbarism." He retreated to his chosen post on the roof without another word.

"He was asking me why you couldn't go fastlink again and get status on the evac," Johnny said, voice low, back to the staircase. "I told him not only no but hell no, and don't you even think about it, you hear me? You aren't allowed to do it under field conditions more than once in forty eight hours, so don't try to get past me on this one."

Mike was touched by his cousin's vehemence. "I promise. I don't have any desire to scramble my central nervous system on our last mission."

"Yeah, well, good." The sergeant, red faced and apparently embarrassed to have shown so much concern, took his blaster and resumed his post on the balcony.

"Someday you must tell me more about what you and he did on other missions," Shalira told him from her perch on the couch.

"Remind me you want to hear more about my illustrious career once I've officially retired, okay?" She had no idea how much editing he'd have to do to render his past fit for civilian consumption. Even his unclassified missions had a high level of gore and unpleasantness. "Today's not the day."

"How are we going to stand watch tonight?" she asked. "I've only seen a few torches in the tower."

"We'll be better off with our night sight. Remember Johnny, Everett and I have enhanced vision." Contemplating the range of tactics the enemy might employ, Mike frowned. "I don't think they'll attack us tonight, though. Obviously we aren't going anywhere. And we've caused a high casualty rate whenever they did attack in the daylight. They don't have a clue how long we can keep using the blasters, or what else we may have."

"The Nathlemeru didn't seem to like the idea of being in the temple at night, anyway." Johnny's comment drifted in from his post out on the balcony. "Only old Three Feathers, and he's gone."

"Probably replaced by someone even uglier." Mike went to stare out the open doorway, across the roof. "We won't count on a quiet night, but it sure would be nice. I'm guessing the big assault will come tomorrow."

"I wish your Space Marines would arrive first," Shalira said. "It would make things so much easier."

"The only easy day was yesterday, ma'am," Johnny told her, leaning inside the room for a moment. "Old adage in our branch of the service. We'll be okay, you'll see."

The night passed uneventfully, if not quietly. Mike could see a huge glow from many torches out by the front of the temple, and the drumming persisted all night long, changing rhythm from time to time, but never stopping. Saium interrogated the priest again and was assured the sound was accompaniment for the burial ritual, not a summons for reinforcements. The defenders managed some restless sleep, in staggered shifts. Shalira slept the night through, assisted by an inject from Johnny's medkit, but had nightmares from which Mike would rouse her when she grew agitated. Not totally awake even then, she'd settle into his arms and sink into deeper sleep as if comforted by his presence.

He and Johnny had a whispered conversation about the advisability of using their one-man antigrav disk. Johnny volunteered to conduct a reconnaissance run to the bottom of the cliff under cover of darkness.

"I hear what you're saying," Mike told his cousin, "but I'm reluctant to split our forces. And I'm concerned about the charge in the disk, how may runs it can make. I'd rather keep it at full charge up here, in case we have to do a last minute evac. I'm counting on the extraction team showing up in the morning and saving our bacon. Nikolai *has* to be getting close to the planet by now."

"You're the boss." Johnny rubbed the back of his neck and stretched. "Those individual antigrav units have been known to short out just when a team needs them most, on more than one occasion. I heard scuttlebutt that Command was going to abandon the technology, cancel all future procurements unless fixes were made to improve the reliability."

"Right, I heard the same thing. The disks got rushed into the field without enough testing. I'm not taking the risk until I'm left with no other choices."

A little after dawn, the entire group congregated around the remaining food, except for Saium, who stayed at his post. Shalira carried a plate of fruit, rolls and a cup of the wine downstairs to him while the three Sectors operators conferred.

"All right, it's been more than twenty-four hours. So where the hell is the extraction team?" Everett was right in Mike's face, more belligerent than he'd been previously. "Don't you think maybe you ought to go on the roof and fastlink again? The situation is getting dicey. In case you hadn't noticed, we're low on ammo."

"You know damn well I can't fastlink again so soon." Unperturbed, Mike took a swallow of the wine, Johnny having given them headclear since the alcoholic beverage was the only liquid in the tower. "I'm sure the *Andy* got the message and is coming as fast as she can. I told them we'd found you and you had the intel Command is desperate for. Once he's in orbit, Nikolai won't waste a second getting us out of here."

"Major!" Saium's urgent shout carried all the way from the lower floor.

Shalira burst up the stairs, eyes wide with fright. "You need to see this."

"I'm coming!" Mike exchanged glances with Johnny. "Things heating up. You and Everett keep a sharp look-out. I don't think today is going to be as easy as yesterday was."

Johnny shook his head. "Me either. I suspect with the funeral niceties over, whoever is in charge is going to give his full attention to us. Hope our evac ship arrives soon."

What Mike found when he joined Saium was unnerving. As he came down the last few steps, he heard a sizzling noise. When he rounded the last curve of the staircase, he was greeted by the sight of wisps of oily black smoke seeping under the heavy door, coiling in proximity to the lower edges. As he watched, the lower metal hinge blackened as droplets of mist congealed on the surface. "What the hell?"

"Whatever it is, the smoke is eating through the door, there, and there." Saium pointed to two spots at the bottom where Mike definitely could see more light than there had been before.

Mike hooked a finger at Saium. "Get the astronomer priest so we can see what he knows about this."

The Nathlemeru's reaction was dramatic. He tried to climb the stairs against Saium's hold, shaking and gibbering in panic. Mike let him slink to the relative safety of the second level, before holding his hunting knife to the man's neck, nicking the artery to draw a trickle of blood. "Tell him I want answers now, or else he goes right next to the door, close to the stuff he's so afraid of. What is this?"

The priest was offering explanations even before Saium finished the translation in the trade talk, his words so frantic and rushed he had to repeat himself twice before Saium comprehended the full answer.

"He says it's a special mix—blood of sacrifices, blood of the priests, and poison milked from the snakes, with secret ingredients even he doesn't know. He says it takes a mighty ceremony and many sacrifices to create. Only the highest priests know the formula. The man babbles in fear." Saium snorted with contempt. "The key point is this stuff eats whatever it touches—metal, wood, flesh and bone."

"Some kind of acid. Chemical warfare on the most primitive level, but effective." Mike was silent for a minute, pondering his options. "All right. We abandon the first floor and the second floor. Leave the astronomer on the second floor, by the stairs. The poison gas seems too heavy to diffuse very far beyond the door down here. Knock him out, tie him up. Let's go, now!"

As soon as Saium had accomplished the task, he and Mike scrambled to the second level. Mike closed the trapdoor behind them, and shot the bolt of the lock, harboring no illusions about the barrier holding for long, but each minute was precious, now they were into the final twelve hours of the rescue window he'd been promised. *The Marines have to be on their way to us soon.*

There was nothing to further anchor the trapdoor, which was a pity. Sending Saium ahead, Mike did a three-sixty on the second floor one last time, making sure they hadn't forgotten anything. Then he headed to the third level, bolting the trapdoor behind him.

Above his head on the roof, Mike heard occasional blaster shots.

"Status?" he asked Shalira, who was huddled beside the couch, clutching her Mahjundan gun in one hand and cradling the gaudy scepter in the other.

"Johnny's on the roof. Everett is on the balcony with Saium. The guards keep poking their heads over the roof edge but haven't attacked again yet."

"Good report." He raised his voice, so Saium and Everett could hear him on the balcony. "Okay, people, we're abandoning this level and moving to the roof. We can't defend ourselves in here once they break through to the second floor, which they'll do once the acid eats enough of the door away at the entrance. Blasters don't do you any good in hand-to-hand combat, which is what we'll have if we stay here."

Johnny provided covering fire while Mike handed Shalira onto the roof and Saium guided her to the safest possible spot, next to Everett.

Working quickly, the men took the big table that they'd salvaged from level two during the night and placed it across the opening for the stairs. Mike placed the smaller table at the far wall of the tower, to provide some shelter for Shalira in case the enemy attacked with archers.

Johnny grabbed his arm and held up a hand for silence. "Listen!"

Mike heard the sound of axes hacking away at the trapdoor on level two.

"Only be a few minutes now," he said. "All right, let's move it!"

Five minutes later he'd done all he could to fortify their last stand. The table completely blocked the transition from the stairway to the roof itself. Mike and Johnny took their places behind it, somewhat sheltered by its width–six inches of hardwood. Saium and Everett took positions on the left side, commanding a field of fire on the staircase as it wound around the tower from the balcony they'd so recently been defending.

"I hope they can't bottle the acid stuff," Johnny said. "Someone might get the bright idea of throwing it up here."

Suddenly, two city guards in the maroon leather jerkins and helmets appeared on the balcony below. Saium and Everett fired within a breath of each other and both warriors fell. Unseen comrades hauled them back inside by the ankles.

"Testing us," Mike said.

"Invasion coming across the roof!" Johnny pointed toward the opposite edge.

"Do you see what I see?" Mike exclaimed, his worst nightmare confirmed. "Archers!" He called to the princess, "Get as far back under the table as you can. They're going to be shooting arrows at us in a minute."

"I'll be fine," she said, flashing him a smile as she obeyed the order.

"Count off your remaining charges," Mike said to his troops.

The result was disheartening. They were reduced to about a hundred shots each on the blasters, and then nothing was left but the projectile guns. Fifty men were massing across the roof, with more coming. A squad of ten archers was even now taking aim.

"Fire at will, gentlemen, but pick your targets. Try to disrupt the damn archers," Mike ordered, drawing a bead himself on the officer in charge, killing him as the first volley was loosed. The arrows landed short of the tower by a good thirty feet. The remaining archers were already taking aim again. The group of fifty soldiers advanced across the roof, holding small round leather shields protectively in front of their faces and upper torsos. This was no impediment to a blaster shot, and many fell, but still, the group kept marching. Reinforcements mounted the slippery roof.

"Damn, they're full of fight today," Johnny yelled. "Priests must have given them some heavy duty encouragement, what do you think?"

"Promises of some glorious afterlife," Mike shouted back, firing, selecting a new target and firing again in a deadly rhythm, thinning the ranks of city guards. Saium and Everett made their shots count, targeting the archers. None-theless, the next flight of arrows came clattering on the tower roof, sending the defenders ducking frantically in all directions. Mike spared a glance back at the table sheltering Shalira. Several arrows were lodged deep in the wood, but none had penetrated. Suddenly Saium crumbled, knocking Everett off-balance as he fell.

Mike grabbed the old warrior, dragging him toward the princess's makeshift refuge. "Cover my spot!"

A long maroon-shafted arrow had buried itself deep in the Mahjundan's right shoulder, and he convulsed, eyes rolled back into his head.

"What the hell?" Suspicions aroused, Mike grabbed an arrow embedded in the table and pulled it free. The arrowhead was a gleaming, sharpened piece of translucent stone smeared with thick, green, viscous liquid. He threw the wooden shaft over the side of the tower, wiping his hand on his pants. "Poison. Johnny, the arrows have poison tips. Anything in the medkit to use on it?"

The sergeant shook his head, continuing to fire a steady barrage of charges down the roof. "We've got antivenom for those snakes we were briefed about. Maybe this poison works on the nervous system the way venom does? Best I can do. Want me to give it a try?"

"Sure, better than nothing. Change places with me. Give me your blaster." Squeezing past Johnny, Mike took his place at the barricade.

Dragging his medkit out from the pile of their gear, Johnny searched through the contents, finally locating the set of injects he wanted. Hurriedly he shot the contents of the first directly into Saium's heart, speaking to Shalira, as he did so. "I can't sit here and wait. Can you take this—" He shoved the second sealed hypo into her hand. "Count to one hundred, set it on his chest here and push this." He demonstrated the necessary motions, placing her right hand where the drug needed to be injected, moving the thumb of her left hand over the tiny button.

Gun forgotten on the ground at her side, Shalira cradled her guardsman in her arms, tears coursing down her cheeks. She swiped one hand across her face and nodded. "Of course. Leave him to me." She started counting.

Johnny slithered back across the roof to the barricade.

"I think we've gotten all the archers out of the way," Mike said. "At least for now. Here's your blaster. The casualties got to be too much for whatever motivational technique the priests were using. Most of the survivors can't get to the ladders fast enough."

"The stairs!" Everett yelled. Johnny rose enough to see over the edge of the wall and knocked three more attackers off the narrow stairs with well-placed shots. Then his blaster flickered on the next shot and fell silent.

"Take Saium's," Mike said, handing it over. "I'm about out, too. Everett?"

"Same here."

The three men slumped behind the wall and the barricade, taking a welcome breather while the enemy regrouped. Johnny was checking his blaster. "If the priests can whip their rabble into one more mass attack—"

"Yeah, I know. I can do the math. Maybe we can repel one more attack, but certainly not two. I think we're about out of time and luck, gentlemen," Mike said calmly despite the cold knowledge in his bones that the end of the battle had come. He spared a moment to glance at Shalira, who'd given Saium his second injection and was whispering reassurances into his ear. She was trying to keep him from doing himself further injury as he twitched and convulsed. His eyes were screwed shut and his teeth were clamped into his lower lip so hard he was bleeding.

Even with the antivenom injects, the prognosis looked grim for Saium.

Mike met Johnny's steady gaze. "I think it's time to break out the antigrav disk."

"No other choices left." Johnny nodded. Tucking his blaster into his belt, he went to the pile of packs behind the table and rummaged for a moment before tossing Mike a black box.

"You realize this is a suicide run," Everett asked. "I'm on board with the idea, but even if one disk can somehow support all of us, once the enemy realizes we're not here anymore, they'll rush the place. We'll be pretty easy targets during the first part of the descent."

Mike slid to the relative protection of the table barricade, Everett right behind him. "Yeah, I know, but we're not going to be taken alive. We escape, or we die in the attempt."

"What's the plan?" Shalira asked, gazing from one man to the next.

Mike activated the antigrav mechanism with a flick of the wrist. Glowing as it took shape, a thin blue light flowed out until it was about the size of a small, two-inch-thick carpet. Strapping the controller to his palm, Mike directed the glowing blue sheet over the wall, leaving it floating next to the parapet. "We're going to lower ourselves to the bottom of the canyon. Try to find some flat place big enough to let the drone set down. Hope we don't run into any more locals."

"But we can't abandon Saium," she said, taking a stronger grip on her guardsman's shoulders as if Mike proposed to tear her away.

"Don't worry, I'm not leaving anyone behind. We'll carry him." Mike stowed his weapons to have his hands free.

"I assume you only have the one disk or we'd have bugged out of here the first night?" Everett said.

Mike nodded.

The other operator jerked a thumb at the antigrav. "It won't carry five people."

"Well, it'll have to," Mike said. "Better to trust the antigrav than stay here and die for sure. Now let's go. I'll carry Shalira. Johnny, you get Saium."

Obediently, the sergeant bent over Saium as Shalira rose and moved aside. Attempting to hook his hands under the old man's arms, Johnny met with resistance as Saium fended him off with a shaking hand.

Staring past him to Mike, Saium beckoned to him. "Major." Saium grabbed Mike's arm with surprising strength, yanking him closer. Features contorted in pain, a thin trickle of blood leaking from one nostril, the old man looked every one of his years and could hardly whisper. "I'm dying, we both know the poison is too strong for even your medicines. Save my princess, save yourself."

"We don't leave people behind," Mike said.

"We better get a move on," Johnny reported, voice calm. "They're regrouping for the next wave."

"We're out of time," Everett said. "Come on, what are we waiting for?"

"Fools." Saium's voice dripped scorn. It wasn't clear whether he meant the Outworlders or the Nathlemeru. He cleared his throat with visible effort and spoke louder. "Sergeant, do you have any more explosive? The stuff you used to seal the tombs?" Saium's voice was a hoarse whisper.

Back to them, keeping his attention locked on the far edge of the roof, where the next attack would come from, Johnny grunted. "Yeah, why?"

There was a moment of silence as tremors rocked the wounded man's body and he clearly struggled to breathe, much less speak. Blood leaked from the corner of one eye. Hand to her mouth in horror, Shalira stared at her guardsman and then at Mike. "I forbid this." Voice rising, Shalira fell to her knees beside Saium. "I'm not allowing you to sacrifice yourself for me. We're taking you with us. You heard Mike."

With an indrawn hiss of pain, he reached out to pat her arm. "Child, it's a sacrifice I make gladly."

Mike evaluated the old soldier for a moment, then nodded. "Johnny, activate the detonator and give it to Saium." He leaned closer to the trembling man, holding out his hand. "I appreciate your gallantry, sir. Proud to have served with you."

"Get my princess to safety," Saium answered, grasping Mike's hand feebly. "I'll set off the explosion when they breach the tower, fool the ignorant ones into believing we all died. You'll be able to escape to somewhere this ship of yours can land."

"Don't wait too long, sir," Johnny said. He placed a rectangular, gleaming package next to Saium and curled the old man's fingers around a small red ball. "You squeeze this, or you drop it. Either way, the stuff will explode. No more tower. Hell, the whole temple might go, if we're lucky."

Wheezing, each breath laborious, Saium nodded. "Good idea. Either way, I blow them to hell. Thank you."

Mike hunkered down next to the princess who had collapsed weeping, hugging Saium. Gently, Mike tried to loosen her grip, but she resisted him, shaking her head as she locked her fingers. Exerting more strength, he tugged her away from her guardsman. "Sweetheart, we have to go."

"Give me a smile to remember you by," Saium said, patting her back with his free hand. "Please, Your Highness. When I step into the afterlife, I want to tell your mother how brave you are, how proud I am."

Caught in Mike's arms, hiccupping, she swallowed. "Please, give me a moment." Mike released her. Placing her hand over Saium's heart, she said, "I love you. You are my father, if not by blood, then because of your love for me and my mother." Eyelashes starred with tears, she kissed him on the cheek, brushing his hair back from his brow. Saium held her close for a heartbeat before giving her a gentle push.

"There's no more time," he whispered. "If the gods be kind, I'll be watching over you always."

Mike pulled her to her feet. "Hang on to me," he said, picking her up. Tucking the scepter into her belt, she wrapped her legs around his waist, arms locked behind his neck, burying her face against his chest.

"We gotta go *now*," Johnny said, voice calm as ever. "They're taking formation."

"Good journey," Mike told Saium.

Coughing, he got a better grip on the detonator. "And to you."

Battle cries sounded on the temple roof. Hugging Shalira, Mike stepped over the crumbling wall onto the thin antigrav disk, allowing the device to latch onto his boots, ensuring he wouldn't fall off. Johnny and Everett stepped up, one on either side of him, locking their arms together in a tight grip with him and Shalira in the middle. The disk dipped alarmingly, moving sideways. Mike held his breath, but the unit stayed strong. Beginning the descent along the cliff upon which the temple had been built, he had difficulty keeping his balance. They were descending much too rapidly, their combined weight taxing the mechanism.

"Wish we could go faster," Johnny yelled. "If we're too close we're likely to get hit with debris or thrown off-balance by the shock wave. I set a fucking huge charge for Saium to blow."

Mike heard a spurt of gunfire from above as their dying companion apparently mounted as much resistance as he could, to buy them time. "I'm trying to vector sideways but she's overloaded, nonresponsive." With his fingertips, he guided the controller into taking them on a westerly course as they descended.

In the next moment there was a giant explosion from above. The observatory tower vanished in a fireball, flames shooting in all directions, shock waves spreading through the atmosphere. Mike tightened his grip on Shalira as they were buffeted, as if in a hurricane. The thin adhesion between the anti grav pad and the soldiers' boots was the only thing keeping all four of them from plunging to their deaths. Large chunks of the temple flew past, bouncing off the canyon walls, starting small landslides, shattering into dangerous shards ricocheting in all directions. Mike tried to put more distance between themselves and the striated rock walls, but the overstressed anti grav unit was balky. He figured they had several thousand feet to descend to the canyon floor.

Weeping, Shalira was clutching him. The damn scepter she insisted on keeping dug into his already painful ribs.

The rest of the trip to the bottom felt interminable. A small waterfall cascaded from the rocky ledges into the thin air at one point, rainbows shining in the mist as they floated past.

"I hope we're not going to land in a river," Johnny shouted.

"Not much I can do about it now." The controller was overheating against his palm. Mike glanced down, evaluating the canyon floor, and hoped the surface was on the sandy side in case the antigrav cut off prematurely.

The unit's humming sputtered and evened out again.

"I think she's about done," he yelled. "Brace yourselves for a fall."

They were maybe ten feet above the dry riverbed forming the canyon floor when the antigrav unit gave out. Falling with the others in a tangled heap on the loose soil, Mike cushioned the impact for Shalira. Pain from his already broken ribs was so intense he nearly blacked out. Vision narrowed, vertigo assaulting him, he was dimly aware as Johnny and Everett carried him from the landing spot, into the shelter of a nest of boulders. Behind them a cavern stretched deep into the cliff.

The pain made it difficult to focus. Any attempt to inhale was met with stabbing agony. "We've got no idea what the situation is down here," he said with as much strength as he could muster. "The Nathlemeru or their allies may patrol this area." He could hardly hear his own voice. Clearing his throat, he said, "Stay alert. Take shelter in the cavern."

Shalira sat cross-legged in the spot Johnny chose, next to Mike. Eyes misty, she stared at the canyon walls they'd descended, even though it was impossible to see to the top. Debris was still falling. "I hope it was quick. I hope he didn't suffer."

With difficulty, Mike looped his arm around her waist. "You allowed him to die the way he wanted, as a warrior in battle, saving all of us. Death by poison arrow would have been agonizing, drawn out." He struggled for air. "No dignity."

"Orders, sir?" Everett said, sliding the last few feet to take shelter behind the boulders with them.

"You can't travel, Mike." Johnny's voice was tight, betraying his worry. "We can't move you, likely you punctured a lung in the fall, given the symptoms. And I've got no meds."

Through a haze of pain, Mike glanced at the terrain beyond the jumbled boulders providing them temporary shelter. "Bring the drone in here, probably enough clearance. Keep a sharp watch. There could be roving patrols."

"Or more villagers," Johnny added. "Plenty of tracks in the loose soil along the stream, as if regular traffic goes through here."

"Just our luck on this damn mission," Mike said. His chest was tight. He couldn't draw in enough air no matter what he did, and the pain on each inhalation was crippling. Lack of oxygen in his bloodstream was making him lightheaded.

Everett was checking his blaster charge, lips compressed in a tight line. "Call the drone?"

"Right. Don't need fastlink, set it to respond to my com when I was in the flow two days ago." Mike tried to unfasten the small pocket on his lower pants leg where the com unit was, but couldn't make his hand stop trembling. Reaching over, Johnny fished the small device out, closing Mike's fingers around it.

Shutting his eyes, he concentrated on pushing the pain away so he could send the drone a clear signal. Activating the com, Mike let the unit carry his mental command through the atmosphere, to the waiting roboship. The first attempt failed. Opening his eyes, Mike licked his lips. "Give me a minute."

"How about a sip of water, from the stream?" Shalira asked.

Half-raising one hand, Johnny shook his head. "Bad idea. He's got serious internal injuries."

"Oh." She subsided, glancing at Mike with obvious concern.

He didn't have the energy to spare for reassuring her or telling her any lies about how great he felt. It was more important to call in the drone that would ultimately save her life. Allowing his head to fall back into her lap, he keyed the com one more time and sent the most basic signal he could, as hard as he could, against the blackness and the headache threatening to overwhelm him. The acknowledgment from the AI on the roboship reverberated in his head and he let the com fall to the ground. "The drone's coming."

"Well, all right, situation is improving," Johnny said with obviously forced good cheer. He retrieved the com unit and shoved it into his own pocket. "You rest till it gets here. Everett and I've got the guard duty."

"Yeah, good plan." Mike licked his dry lips and stopped trying to stay alert, now that his one vital task was accomplished. He stared at Shalira leaning over him until the blackness closed in and he passed out.

She choked back a cry of protest as Mike lost consciousness. Johnny did a rapid check as best he could without his medical supplies. Shalira could tell from the grim expression on the sergeant's face that the situation wasn't good despite his attempt to be positive. His frown told the tale.

"As long as we get him to the roboship pretty soon, he'll be okay. I can stabilize him in the sick bay and when we transfer to the *Andy*, the ship's doc will slide him into the rejuve regenerator. He'll be good as new."

"Really? I only want the truth," she warned.

"I wouldn't lie to you, princess." Johnny squeezed her shoulder. "It's not great, but it's not hopeless, either. We've both come back from worse injuries than this. Mike's tough. The Sectors rejuvenation technology works miracles."

"How long before this drone arrives?" She stared at the clear blue sky.

Checking his wrist chrono, Johnny gave her a crisp answer. "Twenty minutes."

"Is there anything we can do for him in the meantime?" Mike was pale and he was barely breathing. *There must be something.*

The sergeant shook his head. "Probably best he's unconscious right now. No matter how carefully we carry him to the drone it'll jostle his ribs."

Holding the major's limp hand in hers, Shalira nodded.

"We can't ever catch a break on this damn planet," Everett said. Crouching lower, he pointed with his blaster. "Here comes the canyon patrol."

"If we stay quiet, maybe they'll ride on by and never know we're here," Johnny whispered.

"Won't the drone landing scare them away?" Shalira asked, putting her lips next to his ear as a party of three riders and ten foot soldiers proceeded along the stream, a few yards from where they crouched.

He didn't take his attention off the enemy. "On any reasonable planet. The way our luck has been running on your world? Anyone's guess." He didn't sound hopeful. She sidled away, moving to the rear, to give Johnny and Everett room to fight.

Out in the canyon, the soldier in the lead came to a halt, squatting and examining the ground. The rest of the column stopped. Their discipline wasn't very good as the men milled around, disturbing the sandy soil until an officer shouted an order.

"Damn, we should have erased the tracks," Johnny said, as the point man gestured in their direction. "We're practically out of charges and ammo."

"Might have been more suspicious to have no tracks at all, as marked up as this area was. Don't second guess yourself, sergeant." Everett squared his shoulders. "We're not likely to prevail in hand-to-hand combat, not with these odds, but I'm not going out easy, not today."

"Your Highness, stay down," Johnny said over his shoulder. "If we can hold them off for twenty minutes we might make it."

The officer in charge of the patrol was staring in their direction, eyes narrowed. He said something to his companions, and a soldier took a large shell horn from his belt, blowing three blasts.

"Calling for help? From where?" Johnny reconnoitered.

"Maybe there's a secret path from the plateau," Everett said. "Or reinforcemnts farther down the canyon."

The soldiers were dispersing in an organized manner, apparently planning to outflank the hidden escapees. With a shudder, Shalira realized the strategy was probably going to work, since their only defense was the thin ring of boulders at the cavern's entrance.

The officer shouted in their direction, his gaze sweeping over the rocks, obviously searching for them.

Maintaining his unbroken surveillance, Johnny asked, "What did he say?"

"I've no idea," Shalira told Johnny. "I don't speak his language."

"Suggesting we give ourselves up," Everett said. "I have enough words to know that."

"Which we ain't doing." Johnny fired a targeted round, killing the enemy officer, who toppled from his horse. Shrugging, he said, "They know we're here, obviously, figured I might as well induce a bit of fear in the ranks over there."

Temporary chaos was taking hold, as the remaining soldiers scrambled for cover on the other side of the stream. "Bought us a few minutes, while they regroup," he said with satisfaction. His eyebrows drew together in a frown as he checked the remaining charge in the blaster. "They rush us, or get reinforcements before the drone arrives, we're not getting out of here."

"Yeah, we need some heavy duty firepower or more explosives," Everett agreed.

Shalira felt a cold breeze on the back of her neck. Next moment she had the sensation someone whispered her name. She glanced at Mike, but he remained unconscious. Half turning, she scanned the cave stretching behind her, wondering if there was an exit. Not that they could leave, with the drone on its way to them, but neither did she want to be surprised by an attack from the rear.

Blinking, she realized her eyes weren't playing tricks on her - there was a glow in the gloomy recesses of the cave. Rising to her feet, she crept cautiously toward the light. Behind her she heard Johnny say something but her ears were full of the whispering she'd heard before, in the chamber with the giant statue of

Tlazomiccuhtli. Goosebumps made her skin crawl as she came around the last rocky outcrop and confronted another effigy of the Nathlemeru deity. The voice in her head grew louder, and there was harsh, triumphant laughter.

Closing her eyes, the only defense she knew, she tried to back away but felt as if she was standing in glue. She caught her balance with an effort as she tripped over loose stones.

You are mine, little oracle. And I will have the heart of your warrior, as I was promised by Ishtananga before he died. And I'll loose the cherindors in your family's precious scepter on all who oppose me.

"No!" She screamed her protest out loud. Blinking, she stared at the statue, which was about eight feet tall, semidetached from the cave wall. The sculptor had made this representation of Tlazomiccuhtli somewhat less graphic than the one in the main temple in the plateau above but the effect remained horrific. She saw bleached human bones lying on the ground around the statue. Apparently the Nathlemeru conducted sacrifices here on occasion as well. Bad luck had drawn them into another place of its influence over humans. Voice trembling, she tried to deny the reality. "You have no power over us."

But I do. Your goddess owes me. And through his fears, one of your companions has given me mastery over him. Watch.

She heard Everett yelling and next moment Johnny came walking past her, blaster in his hand but aimed at the cave floor. His face was slack, as if he was asleep. He stumbled over the cave floor, dropping the outworld weapon. As he headed toward the statue, one hand fumbled with his belt knife. Horrified, unsure if Tlazomiccuhtli was going to try to make the soldier kill himself or her, or even Mike, helplessly comatose in the cave entry, Shalira grabbed the sergeant's arm as he shuffled past.

"Johnny, you have to fight this off," she hissed.

He stopped walking but the moment she moved her hand away, he lifted one foot to take the next step. Wondering where Everett was and why he didn't come to investigate, she snagged the back of Johnny's shirt and he paused again.

Red snakes of light had materialized from thin air and were writhing around the statue of Tlazomiccuhtli, becoming more and more solid, developing eyes and mouths. She wished she could close her eyes again rather than look at them but was afraid of what might happen if she cowered like a child.

"My goddess owes you nothing, and neither do I," she said. "You have no power over me."

Wait until you're in the grip of my servants, wait until I touch you myself and then tell me I have no power. Perhaps I'll make you sacrifice your warrior to me yourself. How much you humans have forgotten in the millennia since the world began. The cherindors were my dogs of war originally, until your ancestors won their loyalty with the help of ten treacherous gods. Pavrimaia was my lover in the days of chaos, before your puny race arose.

"I refuse to believe anything you claim." Shalira got a better grip on Johnny's shirt, trying to pull him back a few steps, away from the enemy.

Believe or not, it's true. We divided the world, she and I, blood and war versus peace and love, with the river as our boundary. But she promised me oracles who could speak to both of us, carry our commands and desires to those who worshipped us. And you are the most important one, the one of royal blood, the one the spirits of the last remaining cherindors reached out to. I must have you. I've waited a long time for you to come.

"If I surrender to you, will you let the soldiers go?"

"Shalira, no!" Mike was there, white faced, staggering, leaning on a stalagmite, blaster in hand. Clearly he'd expended every ounce of his remaining strength to come to her aid. "What the hell is going on here?"

"Stay back," she said, putting out her free hand as if to block him. "Tlazomiccuhtli's trying to ensnare us all to our doom."

"Fuck that." With a shaking hand he raised his blaster and shot the effigy in the middle of the forehead.

Even as the sizzling energy hit the stone, the swarming red snakes flew to absorb the fire, growing in size as they took in the offworld power.

Clutching his ribs, Mike sank to one knee.

Shalira pulled the scepter from her belt. Hadn't she boasted to Mike a few days ago how she could channel the old powers? Even the enemy admitted the scepter was a thing of power. She shook off the memory of what she'd been shown – the last emperor to venture into the Djeelaba taken prisoner carrying this very symbol, dying a terrible death on the Nathlemeru altar. The scepter hadn't helped him. Maybe the power of the old legends was exhausted? Cradling the scepter in her hands, she stared into the depths of the huge purple gem. Deep in the facets, tiny red and blue sparks whirled. She tried to summon the attention of the entity she believed dwelt within. "You need to help us if you don't want to return to Nathlemeru hands, owned by their god," she whispered.

The sparks twirled faster inside the stone but Shalira didn't detect any response.

Risking a quick glance at the idol in the grip of the red snakes, she saw the deity was still fighting to become a physical presence in the cavern. She didn't have much time before she'd be confronting Tlazomiccuhtli in all his might. Refusing to admit defeat, she tried channeling the cherindor power again. "Why are you hesitating?" she whispered. "We'll be dead and you'll be recaptured." In sheer frustration she gave the scepter a shake. "No one else of my bloodline will ever venture here. I'm your last chance."

A different voice resonated in her head now, rough, a growl. *Are you worthy?*

In her mind's eye, she saw the vision of her ancestor's last moments replaying, as he wept, on his knees, begging for his life, betraying his own men, giving up the scepter, all in a futile effort to avoid death on the Nathlemeru altar.

We refused to help him, said the cherindor's voice. *Greedy. Weak. Unfit to rule. Unfit to command powers like ours.*

"But then you were trapped here."

Silence from the cherindor scepter for a moment. *Are you worthy?* The question came reverberating through her head with weary doubt.

She wondered what answer the spirit of the scepter would accept, even as she could tell from the shouts of the enemy and the cursing from Everett at the entrance that a final assault on their inadequate defenses must have been launched. Trying to keep her voice from shaking, Shalira said, "I'm the Princess of Shadows in this time, the last person alive who can channel the powers you draw from."

Princess of Shadows? A strange title to claim, if what you wish is to wield my powers.

Anger burning in her veins at the entity's mocking tone and hesitation to help her, she said, "Very well then I'm the Empress of Mahjundar at this moment, with you in my hands and I *command* you to help me save my warriors."

The giant gemstone grew hot under her palms, but Shalira bit her lip and hung on. A wind rose inside the cave, swirling the dust, keening through the boulders. She concentrated on trying to harness the power, shape the energy into a weapon to launch at their enemy, hopefully with more effect than the Sectors' blasters.

There was the boom of a small explosion.

Shielding his eyes as if by reflex, Johnny cursed. "What the hell?"

A wall of translucent purple light now stood between her and Tlazomiccuhtli, stretching from wall to wall of the cavern. Like an uncanny spider web, strands composed of motes of light emanated from the stone in the scepter.

The spirit of your cherindors can't defeat me. The ancient god's voice in her head was derisive, amused. The red snakes began writhing their way down the statue's body. "You'll all die here. The power imbued with the stone can only delay me, never defeat me." The deity's voice had become audible, not just in her head. With horror, she saw a faint image of Tlazomiccuhtli standing in front of the stone statue, becoming more solid by the second. The snakes latched onto the shadowy version of the god as if feeding him their energy.

How am I going to do battle with a god? Shalira got a better grip on the remnant of the scepter's staff. She risked a quick glance at her two companions. Mike was slumped on the rocky ground, unconscious again and Johnny crouched beside him, seemingly dazed but at least not taking any action to harm either himself or his cousin. She heard the whine of a blaster from the entrance and knew Everett was keeping the human enemies at bay. The other fight, it seemed, was up to her.

Tlazomiccuhtli straightened, hands on hips, drawing in a gusty breath as the red snakes, now pale and thin, withered and fell away to writhe on the cavern floor. "Victory shall be mine, Oracle. First you feed me your life and power, then the warriors die, after which I'll direct my Nathlemeru to take up arms against the people on the other side of the river. Your goddess and her kin have withdrawn, no longer worshipped or even recognized. Which leaves a void for me to step into at long last."

Cracks began to form in the sheet of purple illumination between Shalira and the deity. Sections of the light sizzled and vanished. It wouldn't be more than a moment or two before Tlazomiccuhtli could touch her.

A fleeting thought crossed her mind. She wondered how well Empress Maralika's strange new pantheon of gods would fare against this monster from before time. Cupping her locket in her free hand, Shalira rolled her shoulders, attempting to channel whatever power the scepter could or would feed her. "You have to get past me first and in this moment, I'm the Empress *and* Defender of Mahjundar." Claiming the titles felt right but it was sheer bravado and she knew it. "I call on Pavmiraia to help me."

A cool breeze, smelling of the lowland flowers, blasted through the cavern.

"I stand at your side," said a new voice.

Nearly dropping the scepter, Shalira realized the goddess had joined them.

The newcomer put her hand over Shalira's on the half destroyed shaft of the royal insignia. The goddess's touch was cold but tingling energy flowed into the princess, making her giddy, making her feel as powerful as if she were ten feet tall, with strength to match.

"My time is done but so is yours," Pavmiraia said to Tlazomiccuhtli, her voice mocking. "I've waited these many centuries for you to step into the world, show yourself to me, not merely work through avatars and servants. I hoped the arrival of this girl, this last of my true believers, in your stronghold would be the tipping point."

"You knew I was going to end up here?" Shalira was dismayed, angry.

Pavmiraia shrugged. "There were multiple possibilities for your fate, paths to be taken. The coming of the offworlders tipped the odds in my favor and yours. You were the last hope I had. If you'd failed, or chosen otherwise, the world of humans on this planet would have suffered a dire fate and I would not have been able to intervene."

As the purple wall continued to crack and disappear into nothingness, Shalira felt a strong hand on her shoulder. Face drawn and grim, racked with pain, Mike stood on her other side, with Johnny flanking him. "I don't know what's going on and I don't know how to help," he said in her ear, "but we're guarding your six."

Tlazomiccuhtli grabbed one of his depleted serpents, which regenerated as he held it, becoming a massive spear in his hand, the tip a glowing ruby, its pointed end gleaming like the point of a dagger. "Much as I admire your foolish courage, outworld warrior, I'll start by taking your heart because I need it more than you do." He took aim.

As he hurled the uncanny weapon at Mike through the remnants of the scepter-generated purple shield, the goddess Pavmiraia stepped aside.

Furious, Shalira threw herself in front of her beloved, scepter raised above her head. Exerting all her willpower, the princess channeled the dregs of power she felt remaining in the gemstone, demanding that the cherindors help her.

Purple haze drifted from the surface of the gemstone, swirling around her, Mike and Johnny, coating them in reflected, glistening amethyst light, as if she were becoming a gemstone herself. Having difficulty keeping her eyes open against the glare, she hoped this was leading to something useful. In the next second growling laughter rang through her head and a wave of freezing cold shot through her like knives, gone between one breath and the next. The spear's flight was halted in midair and it fell harmlessly to the rocky ground, encased in glittering purple crystals that shattered, breaking Tlazomiccuhtli's weapon.

Pavmiraia strolled forward, a beautiful young woman, with lustrous black hair streaming down her back all the way to the ground. Her dress was shades of green, accented with precious gems and intricate designs in gold thread. She glanced back at Shalira and nodded and the princess was awestruck at how lovely and serene the face of the goddess was, even at this extreme moment. "No need for all this violence, Tlazomiccuhtli, my beloved. Take comfort in my arms as you used to do before the chaos was dispelled and the world of humans was created. Time enough to decide your next move after we've renewed our affair." Growing taller with each step, she held out her arms as she walked steadily toward the other god.

Tlazomiccuhtli's eyes narrowed and he retreated a step. Pavmiraia embraced the god and pulled his hideous head down for a kiss. As his multiple arms wrapped around her, there was an explosion, red, purple and green flares blending together, flying in a visible circle outward from the embracing lovers.

Mike yanked Shalira out of the path of the light, pulling her behind a stalagmite. Johnny came right behind them.

Folded in Mike's arms, Johnny trying to shield both of them, Shalira heard the three note song of the myrdima. She fought free of the men and stepped away from the stalagmite just in time to see thousands of the creatures fly from the spot where Tlazomiccuhtli and Pavmiraia had been standing. Of the two gods there was no sign. The stone idol at the rear of the cave was cracked into three pieces, crumbling into dust as she watched. The myrdima poured through the cavern, flashing past her, exiting in a solid wave of colors and shooting into the sky. The song was glorious, triumphant, deafening in the enclosed space.

One small green myrdima fluttered behind the masses of its fellows, landing on Shalira's shoulder for a moment. Its feathery antennae brushed her cheek and she heard the goddess's voice for the final time.

"Your dreams have been granted, my daughter, as have mine. I've rid Mahjundar of the ancient evil, with your help, and now I too am free." The crystalline three note song trilled as the creature lifted into the air and shot after the flock, wings blurring with the effort.

"Are you okay?" A visibly shaken Johnny was trying to get her to stand and Shalira realized she must have blacked out for a moment or two. "I don't know what magic you worked just then, but you sure saved our butts."

She stood and took two swift steps to where Mike had fallen, kneeling to check that he'd come through the event unscathed, even if he'd relapsed into an unconscious state.

"The scepter. Where is it?" Hand to her aching head, Shalira looked around for the stone and staff.

"I see it." Johnny picked it up for her before she could stop him or utter a warning. The great stone was cracked in half, clouded. The golden cherindors were melted, unrecognizable lumps of blackened metal. Speculating if the power had been depleted forever, if she'd ever be brave enough to try channeling the cherindor again, Shalira accepted the staff, tucking it in her belt.

"All dead out there," Everett reported, striding through the boulders. "I don't know what the hell that was but why didn't we pull that trick sooner?"

"I didn't know it was possible," Shalira said, glaring at Everett. "Don't you think I would have used it to save Saium's life, if I could have?"

Off in the distance, outside the cave, she heard the faint call of the shell horns. Exchanging glances with Johnny, heart sinking, she said, "And I can't repeat the miracle."

"You won't have to—I hear the drone," the sergeant said a moment later.

She could hear the noise herself now, a metallic whine, coming closer, growing to a deafening scream. "Thank the gods."

"Can you walk?" Johnny shouted in her ear.

"Yes, I'm fine. Please, take care of Mike."

The two soldiers lifted the unconscious major carefully, trying not to further jostle his injuries, and Shalira followed them from the shelter of the boulders as a trim silver and black ship settled onto the sandy soil, blocking the stream. Water diverted around the drone, forcing them to slosh through the redirected stream.

"How do we get inside?" she asked, glancing downriver as the horns sounded again.

Adjusting his hold on Mike, Johnny set his fingers in a shallow depression on the drone's hull she hadn't noticed. A virtual keypad revealed itself and he tapped something in. "Special Forces code," he said.

Silently a door slid open, and a short ramp extended to the ground. Needing no invitation, adrenaline high, Shalira scrambled into the drone, not knowing what to expect but desperate to be somewhere the Nathlemeru couldn't reach her ever again. The drone's plain interior was equipped with a set of thinly padded seats along both sides. Gleaming, complicated equipment occupied the stern, and this was where the soldiers carried Mike, placing him gently on a table bolted to the deck. Johnny immediately went to work, pulling medical supplies from drawers and hooking Mike to strange devices. "Stay in your seat till we're safely airborne," he called over his shoulder to Shalira.

Everett sprinted back past her and did something she couldn't see, causing the door to close. Sinking into the nearest uncomfortable seat, she realized she'd been holding her breath. The Special Forces soldier jogged forward, taking one of the empty chairs in the nose. Through the vidscreens above Everett's head and along the sides, she could tell the drone was already rising along the canyon wall without anyone taking any further action. As they cleared the top and the drone took a steep tangent into the sky, Everett raised his fists, threw back his head and yelled in triumph, a long whoop overriding even the sound of the engines.

Rising, keeping her balance with difficulty, Shalira joined Johnny in the back. "Is there anything I can do to help?"

"Keep me company," he said. "The drone got here in the nick of time all right. Mike's in a bad way, especially with the skirmish with your gods back in the cave, but I can keep him ticking till we reach the roboship."

"Hey, some good news for a change," Everett said from his position in the bow. "The *Andy's* going to be on station by the time we get there. They're ordering us to board directly."

Keeping his eyes on the readouts, Johnny said to Shalira, "You don't need to worry, I'll stay close. No one is going to send Mike's fiancée back to the surface, okay?"

"I didn't realize that was even a possibility," she said. "Is he going to be in trouble for rescuing me?"

Now Johnny did glance at her. "Well, the fact you helped us achieve our mission objective is a big point in your favor. And the *Andy's* captain is one of Mike's best friends in the service. So you coming home with us is unusual, but we'll get through it. He'd never forgive me if I let you get away now." Raising his voice, Johnny said, "Tell the *Andy* we need the med team to meet us on the deck."

"Roger."

CHAPTER ELEVEN

After the small ship floated to a landing inside the battleship's vast hangar space and the hatch opened, Everett bounded out, returning in a moment with a uniformed soldier who eyed Shalira in passing as he went to meet Johnny. Although she couldn't speak Basic very well, she inferred the sergeant was asking if the doctor was waiting for them.

The soldier's answer was affirmative. He activated an antigrav litter in some manner Shalira couldn't see and, working together, Johnny and the newcomer got Mike onto the stretcher. Johnny came to take her elbow.

"Lewis there will bring Mike, and I'm escorting you to the captain of the ship," he said in Mahjundan.

"I'd rather stay with Michael."

He shook his head. "Not going to be possible. He needs to go to sick bay pronto. I'll have to go in for a debrief on our mission, and I need to know I've left you in safe hands." Johnny steered her out of the drone and down the ramp.

Shalira gawked at her surroundings. The hangar was immense, crowded with sleek ships, some similar to the drone she'd ridden in but others clearly of a more lethal nature. Busy crew members shot her curious glances as they went about their duties. A white-clad man who must be the promised doctor waited to the side, clutching some sort of instrument set, tapping his toe with impatience. Everett was already gone.

"Dr. Tyree, let me introduce Her Highness, Princess Shalira," Johnny said in Mahjundan and then again in Basic.

Doing a double take, murmuring something, the doctor extended his hand.

Shaking hands, Shalira had the sinking realization Johnny and Mike were probably the only two people on board the ship who spoke her language. She knew a smattering of Basic from conversations with Mike on the trail, but not enough to get along on her own in this completely strange environment. She clutched at Johnny's sleeve in a moment of panic. *No wonder he swore not to leave me.*

"I told the doc you're going to need hypnotraining in Basic when he checks you out for injuries," Johnny said, moving her aside a few steps so the crewman could bring Mike to the deck.

"Thank you. This place is overwhelming."

Mike was conscious, agitated, swearing at the man directing his antigrav stretcher. He fought the restraining straps, glaring with a clenched jaw at the crew member trying to help him. Instinctively Shalira went to him, taking his hand and pushing him gently to lie back. "It's all right—I'm here."

Johnny joined her, as did the doctor. A furious conversation in Basic ensued. Shalira knew enough of the language to realize Mike was refusing medical treatment until he'd personally gotten the captain's word she was safe and protected on this ship. She clung to his hand, even as she remonstrated with him that Johnny would keep her safe and he had to go with the doctor for treatment. Mike wouldn't be budged. Johnny translated some of the doctor's increasingly insistent remarks for Shalira in an undertone.

"What is all this fuss on my hangar deck?" The new arrival's demeanor left the princess in no doubt he was Captain Nikolai Novikov. All the military personnel around her saluted and relieved expressions replaced the stress and concern.

The captain bent over Mike, eyebrows drawn together in a frown. "When I got the orders to check on a possible Mawreg incursion, I had to go investigate. I can see matters got dicey where you were." Novikov ran one his hand through his military crop of white-blond hair. "Problems with the roboship extraction?"

Face white and drawn, Mike lay back on the litter. "Orders are orders, Nik. I understood your situation. We're safe now so forget it. I brought back one survivor from the crash, and he's got the data the Sectors were so hot to retrieve." Switching to Mahjundan, he said, "Your Highness, may I present Captain Nikolai Novikov? This is his battleship we've come to stay on."

Shalira extended her hand gracefully. "I'm honored to meet any friend of Michael's."

"Nikolai, this is Her Highness Shalira, Imperial Princess of Mahjundar," Mike announced, switching back to Basic.

Clearly astounded, eyebows raised practically to his hairline, the captain bowed over her hand with as much grace and aplomb as he seemed able to muster. Shalira suppressed a smile.

Another shock was to follow for the poor man.

"I want you to marry us, as soon as possible. Today in fact. After I've been in rejuve and debriefed." Mike laughed at his friend's expression.

"What trouble have you been in?" Giving Mike no time to answer, Nikolai raised a hand. "Never mind, I won't believe it anyhow." Shaking his head in bemusement, he bowed to the princess. "Welcome to my ship, Your Highness."

"It is good to be somewhere I don't have to be afraid of being killed," Shalira said.

"I assure you, anyone who tries to kill you on my ship will be tossed off!" The captain guffawed as soon as Mike translated her remark.

The doctor was still trying to shepherd them toward the edge of the hangar.

Not releasing her hand, Mike persisted. "I'm not done yet, damn it." Grabbing the captain's arm, he said, "I want your personal word of honor that Shalira will remain on this ship until she and I get married, you'll issue her Sectors ID, and then you'll transport her with me to the nearest commercial spaceport."

Glancing at her, Nikolai nodded. "Of course. Don't upset yourself and don't delay treatment. She's my guest until she's your wife and a Sectors citizen. Someone on the planet wants her back, eh?"

"They would if they knew I was alive," she confirmed as soon as she heard Johnny's hasty translation.

"And you wish to marry this scoundrel and go off to live with him in the Sectors?" The captain's question was light hearted in tone, but his expression was stern.

"That's all I want," she said, squeezing Mike's hand. "But first I want him to have his injuries taken care of."

"Lords of Space, what an uproar this will cause!" The *Andromeda's* captain closed his eyes, small smile hovering on his lips, apparently savoring the mental picture. He rested one hand on Mike's shoulder. "You never could do anything routine, could you? Or by the book?"

"Having been through hell and back together, I can tell you she's a woman in a million. I love her, damn it, and I want you to marry us today."

"All right, my friend. Then I'll do it and to hell with what Command thinks. On my own ship, I don't have to ask anyone's permission. You can explain to the authorities later, and I don't envy you the job. Some regulations somewhere must have been bent a little, if not broken outright, for you to come back engaged to an imperial princess." Nikolai peered closely at him. "I imagine you'll be able to explain it. Now get yourself to sick bay and get cleaned up. That's an order. I'll personally escort Her Highness to suitable quarters and get my staff working on a wedding. See what Stores can create for a wedding dress."

Shalira bent over to kiss Mike and then stepped closer to the captain as the impatient doctor and his orderlies whisked her lover away for treatment.

The chapel on the *Andromeda* was nondenominational, per Fleet regulations, suitable for the basic rituals and observances of most of the thirty odd peoples found in the planetary systems making up the Sectors. As captain of the battleship, Nikolai was authorized to perform ceremonies from christenings to weddings to funerals.

Mike stood in his blue dress uniform, grinning from ear to ear, at the far bulkhead, beneath the stunning vista of the galactic star fields projected by the ship's AI.

Feeling a little foolish, as if he'd stepped from a recruiting holo since he was wearing a dress uniform, he was flanked by his best man, Johnny, who had never—to the best of Mike's recollection—worn a dress uniform before.

And we're both as nervous as we were on day one at the Academy and boot camp. Mike took a deep breath, hoping to calm the butterflies in his gut. *This is worse than any mission behind enemy lines.* At least he could breathe, thanks to the rejuve regenerator treatment. Not even bruises left. And he'd have the strength to give his princess a proper wedding night. A bed on the *Andromeda* would be much more conducive to what he had in mind than the mat and furs on the cave floor had been. He nudged his best man in the ribs. "You're sure you've got the ring?"

"For the tenth time, I've got the ring," Johnny whispered. He displayed the jewelry in question for a moment, before stowing it back in his pocket. "I won't drop it."

Ignoring the small group of wedding guests, Mike gazed at the empty doorway, impatience making his stomach churn. "What could be taking so long? You're sure she was all right?"

"When they threw me out this afternoon so she could try on dresses, she was fine," Johnny answered. "Calm down before you have an anxiety attack. Got no medkit on me right now."

The guests were mostly from Nikolai's command staff. Everett was in attendance, thin, pale, but looking like a different person in his dress uniform. Mike hadn't expected anything more than a bare bones civil ceremony, but a few minutes ago Nikolai confided that the *Andromeda's* Executive Officer's deepest secret was her love for steamy romance novels from the holo serial library. "Don't ask how I know," he said, throwing his hands in the air. "But when I told her there was to be a wedding between a princess and a Special Forces officer, with her challenge being to provide the dress, she went all-out. I promise your bride will have all the necessary details for her special day, my friend."

Now, the AI played a processional from the days of old Terra, which Mike's ancestors had carried with them to their new home world.

Shalira, walking alone, appeared in the doorway.

Her beauty took Mike's breath away.

She wore her silky black hair pinned on her head in a loose chignon, the hairstyle accenting her beautiful cheekbones and luminous eyes. The Windhunter collar lay clasped around her long, elegant neck, the locket of Pavmiraia resting on top. The white, sleeveless dress was floor-length, shimmering fabric, slit to the knee, with a short train. Shalira was barefoot, which she'd informed him previously was the custom on Mahjundar for a bride. Her toenails were painted pale silver to match the dress, but she wore no other makeup or enhancements.

Her huge cocoa-brown eyes were fixed directly on Mike's face. The ship's hydroponics section had donated a generous portion of real Terran roses and ferns, customarily never cut, and these had been fashioned into a bouquet with silver ribbons. Shalira carried this in the curve of her left arm.

The ceremony itself took only a few minutes. His bride's focus never left Mike's face as she recited her vows in response to his, and to Nikolai's prompts. Mike had asked his friend to omit the portion asking who gave the bride in marriage, not wanting to cause her pain by emphasizing the loss of her beloved Saium. She watched as Mike slid his Academy ring onto her left hand. It had been resized in the *Andromeda's* shop that afternoon to fit her slender finger. Sparkling in the overhead lights, the Terran diamond set in the center of the ring threw off rainbows. Surprising him, she had a ring for him as well, made from a sliver of the cherindor scepter's gold, worked by the clever techs onboard the ship on a rush basis at her request.

"I now pronounce you husband and wife," Nikolai intoned. "You may kiss the bride, Major!"

Folding Shalira in his arms, Mike kissed her long and hard, until the clapping and cheering of the audience reminded him where they were. Then the couple wheeled to face the gathering, Mike presenting her with a flourish.

"Ladies and gentlemen, I give you Mrs. James Michael Varone!" He could barely speak past the pride and overwhelming happiness in his heart.

"I've ordered a wedding dinner in honor of our newlyweds," Nikolai said. "The meal has been set out in the officers' mess, if you'll follow me."

The ship's cooks and the AI had outdone themselves in preparing a generous dinner. More of the precious hydroponic flowers decorated the table, and wine from the captain's private stock flowed freely. Countless toasts to the happy newlyweds were made along with calls for their long and prosperous future together. Johnny gave a short speech. Shalira ate and drank sparingly, as did Mike, but they managed to share a piece of the cake the head chef had personally baked, using an ancient recipe that had been in his family for generations. He'd never had the occasion to use it before and told Mike that he and the AI had puzzled over some of the ingredients, trying to find modern day substitutes the *Andromeda* actually stocked.

Finally Nikolai stood to make one last toast. "I've moved out of my quarters for tonight, in order to provide a suitable room for a honeymoon. As I recall, the bachelor officers' quarters weren't designed with newlyweds in mind. To Mr. and Mrs. Varone!"

Mike felt himself flushing beneath his space tan, but he thanked Nikolai for his kindness and consideration.

"I'll escort you to my private access gravlift and bid you good night, then," the captain said. "Please, I urge my other guests to remain here, finish your wine and cake."

As they stood to leave, Shalira lifted her bouquet and took a deep breath of the heady rose perfume before addressing the assembled guests. "I'm told on my new world it's customary for the bride to throw the bouquet amongst the unmarried women, for one lucky girl to catch and become next to wed. I choose instead to give these amazing flowers to the Executive Officer, who made so much happiness possible for me tonight, blending my customs and those of your Sectors." Looking down the table to where the woman sat, Shalira smiled. "My wedding was like a dream, so perfect—how can I ever thank you?"

The officer, visibly embarrassed, left her seat to take the bouquet. She mumbled a thank you, assuring Shalira the arrangements had been her pleasure to make, before stepping back. Nikolai took Shalira by one elbow, Mike at the other, and they left the officers mess.

Five minutes later the newlyweds were alone in the captain's quarters of the *Andromeda*. Nikolai had left another bottle of wine chilling on the table in the outer chamber, with two glasses ready. Mike felt drunk enough with the sheer joy of the occasion. *I don't need stimulants to enhance the evening. Nothing could be better than this.*

"Old tradition, my love, I have to carry you across the threshold. Actually, I should have carried you over the entry into this room, but I thought those crewmen in the corridor had seen enough for one night." Lifting her effortlessly, he carried her into the bedroom. She clung to him happily, seeming a little giddy, a bit nervous.

"Your friends gave us a beautiful wedding. So different from what we have on Mahjundar, but lovely. Everyone has been nice to me on this ship." There was a minor tremor in her voice. "The experience has been a good beginning for my new life in the Sectors."

"I'm about to be more than nice to you," he whispered in a teasing voice. She giggled—there was no other word for it—and nibbled at his ear. Placing her on the bed, he stood admiring her for a moment, not quite ready to believe she was his for the rest of their lives. As he undid the fastenings of his dress uniform tunic, he said, "I love you. All the trouble and close calls on this mission were worth it, to end up here, with you as my bride."

"I'm no longer the Princess of Shadows." Her smile was wide and the golden glints in her eyes fairly glowed with pleasure.

"Rescued by your true love?" Mike quoted the folktale even as he shook his head. "You had as much to do with rescuing yourself from the situation as I did. Rescuing both of us, to my great and everlasting good fortune."

"Perhaps the ending is better this way. Did you know my ancestors offered a fabulous reward for recovering the Cherindor Scepter from the Djeelaba?" she asked.

"I think someone mentioned it in the briefing, yes."

"The reward was the hand of a princess and a roomful of gold," she said. "I wish I had a dowry to bring to you. Even the scepter is worthless now, the stone cracked and dulled."

He settled onto the bed next to her, taking her hand and kissing it. "I only need you."

"And I love you." She reached to pull him onto the bed with her.

The beautiful gown and the dress uniform soon fell onto the deck in a tumbled heap. Mike and Shalira celebrated a proper wedding night in the privacy of Nikolai's quarters, undisturbed by any worries over what the future might hold, lost in happiness, being free to be together as the *Andromeda* sailed on through the galaxy, away from Mahjundar.

Thank you for reading *Mission to Mahjundar!* I hope you enjoyed it. If you did, please help other readers find this book:

1. This book is lendable, so send it to a friend who you think might like it so he or she can discover me, too.
2. Help other people find this book by writing a review.
3. Sign up for my new releases e-mail at *http://wordpress.us7.list-manage1. com/subscribe?u=2a337b96e2ee1ee1250004b9d&id=7462393c9e* so you can find out about the next book as soon as it's available.
4. Follow me on twitter *@vscotttheauthor*
5. Come like my Facebook page: *https://www.facebook.com/pages/ Veronica-Scott/177217415659637?ref=hl*

ABOUT THE AUTHOR

Best Selling Science Fiction & Paranormal Romance author and "SciFi Encounters" columnist for the USA Today Happily Ever After blog, Veronica Scott grew up in a house with a library as its heart. Dad loved science fiction, Mom loved ancient history and Veronica thought there needed to be more romance in everything. When she ran out of books to read, she started writing her own stories.

Married young to her high school sweetheart then widowed, Veronica has two grown daughters, one grandson and cats Keanu and Jake.

Veronica's life has taken many twists and turns, but she always makes time to keep reading and writing. Everything is good source material for the next novel or the one after that, right? She's been through earthquakes, tornadoes and near death experiences...Always more stories to tell, new adventures to experience—Veronica's personal motto is, "Never boring."

Veronica is a two time winner of the SFR Galaxy Award (for Escape From Zulaire and Wreck of the Nebula Dream.). She also received a National Excellence in Romance Fiction Award for Escape From Zulaire.

She's a proud recipient of a NASA Exceptional Service Medal but must hasten to add the honor was not for her romantic fiction!

Blog: *http://veronicascott.wordpress.com/*
Email: *veronica.scott.author@gmail.com*

For your enjoyment, here's an excerpt from the beginning of my best selling novel Escape From Zulaire, a standalone science fiction romance novel set in the world of the Sectors:

This is the most absurd thing I've ever done as assistant planetary agent for Loxton Galactic Trading—standing in as a bridesmaid in a borrowed puce dress because some other girl failed to show up. Andi Markriss sighed, feeling the garment binding too tight across her chest. *I didn't mind representing the company as a guest, but this is way outside the line of duty.*

Early afternoon on Zulaire was too warm for an outdoor ceremony, but the Planetary High Lord's spoiled daughter Lysanda didn't care to be ready any earlier in the day. Her guests' comfort wasn't a consideration.

An inch at a time, Andi shifted from her assigned spot into the shade cast by the towering stone pillars. *How did I get talked into this? Oh, yes, Lysanda wept, and her mother made vague threats about her husband reviewing our shipping contracts.* As the musicians played, Andi turned, watching Lysanda pace toward the dais in time to the music, smiling for her groom-to-be.

The local priest took a deep breath and launched into a lengthy blessing, invoking the deity and relating the history of the planet's three Clans—Obati, Shenti and Naranti. Andi chanted along with him under her breath. *Overlords, Second Class and Neutrals,* as her boss had told her when she'd arrived on Zulaire six years ago. Easy to keep them straight that way, he'd said, but don't ever slip and use the nicknames out loud.

"This young pair from two of the highest families will cement our peace," the priest proclaimed, lowering his arms and beaming at Princess Lysanda and her intended. "Their offspring will embody the union of Obati and Shenti blood."

Applause from the crowd, led by the bride's mother, made the officiant blush. As he bowed, Lysanda blew her mother a kiss.

That ovation will spur him to more oratory for sure. Andi smothered a sigh, wiggling her aching toes, held too tight in the borrowed silver sandals. *I thought the last three weeks of engagement parties, picnics and games out here in the summer compound were endless, but this ceremony tops them all.*

"The bride and groom will now light the symbolic candles." The priest led the pair to the side altar, where a trio of candles—blue, green and ivory—had been set into massive golden holders. Representing the three Clans, the candle ritual reinforced the political symbolism of this ceremony. Everything symbolic on Zulaire came in threes, Andi thought, watching the couple light each candle in turn.

Sneezing violently as the slight afternoon breeze carried colorful but pungent smoke from the burning tapers in her direction, she earned herself a glare and a hissed "Shh!" from the woman standing next to her. After taking a deep, cleansing breath of the fragrant bouquet she'd been clutching, Andi gave the other attendant a faint smile.

Lysanda had argued long and hard with her mother earlier about allowing Andi to substitute for the unaccountably missing handmaiden. Only the fact that without Andi to partner him, an important groomsman would be omitted from the ceremony swayed the decision. *Good for Loxton's business networking that I'm here. The Planetary Lord's family owes me personally now for preserving the precious symmetry of Lysanda's wedding party, at the cost of my aching feet.* With a flash of amusement at the ludicrous situation, Andi smiled. *Lucky for the princess, I accepted the invitation on behalf of Loxton, not my portly boss.*

Tuning out the priest's new recitation of more sacred writings, since the man had a nasal voice and a tendency to repeat himself, Andi studied the intricate carvings in the shiny black stone wall of the pavilion across from her, details brought to clarity by the slanting sun's rays.

The bas-relief depicted a stylized sun above a giant, multitrunked malagoy tree—each trunk symbolizing one of the three Zulairian tribes—Obati and Shenti locked in an eternal struggle to rule the planet, jockeying back and forth for thousands of years of bloody history. All the while the Naranti stayed neutral, filling a perpetual peacemakers' role, as their god, Sanenre, had legendarily decreed. Symbolic of their Clan's allotted role in the planet's history, the Naranti trunk was at the center of the tree, supporting the other two.

A skillfully carved herd of three-horned urabu grazed beneath the sheltering arms of the malagoy, the alpha buck depicted in a watchful stance, stone face staring at the occupants of the dais. The image of these legendary creatures, with their sweeping triple horns, was found everywhere on Zulaire, even on the Planetary Lord's seal. Beloved symbol of the god Sanenre, legendary bearers of good fortune and blessings, the gazellelike animals were extinct now, of course, hunted for the ivory of their sweeping horns.

Lysanda and her betrothed were repeating vows after the priest.

Apparently as bored as Andi was, the youngest attendant at the ceremony, just a toddler really, came across the platform with unsteady steps, reaching for Andi, her favorite playmate of the last few weeks. Missing her nieces and nephews, who lived far away in her own home Sector of the galaxy, Andi had been happy to skip a few adult entertainments to amuse the young ones of the house during her stay.

After a quick hug, the little girl plunked herself at Andi's feet, leaning against her legs. Pulling the flower garland from her glossy curls, she picked the petals off the blossoms while humming the processional tune off-key. The priest began to wrap up, raising his voice to override the toddler's song. Andi stared out over the crowd.

Quite a few empty chairs. A surprising number of high-ranking Obati guests had failed to arrive, which had driven the bride's mother into an angry tirade shortly before the ceremony. The failure of the missing bridesmaid and her family to show up had created another firestorm. Lady Tonkiln had a long memory for social slights.

It's been an odd summer, that's for sure. Andi would be glad to see fall arrive, when business always picked up and she could get back to the office, dive into the complexities of intergalactic trading and leave the socializing to others. *And decide if it's time to leave Zulaire for another assignment. Six years is too long to stay on one planet, if I want my next promotion. I wish I didn't love it here so much.*

Of course, no one had expected Planetary Lord Tonkiln to leave the important business of ruling Zulaire for his daughter's handfasting. He'd be at the formal wedding later in the year, held in the massive shrine at the capital, to accept the Shenti groom's petition for marriage to Lysanda. His oldest son, Gul, had been scheduled to stand in for the ruler today, but in typical Gul fashion, he hadn't shown up.

His careless attitude to responsibilities had been one of the reasons Andi had never let their casual, off-and-on-again affair become more serious. Charming as he was, Gul was unreliable.

Glancing along the fringes of the crowd where the invited Shenti guests were sitting, she saw everyone attentive, focusing on the glowing bride and handsome groom.

The Naranti servants clustered at the rear of the outdoor pavilion looked bored. *I suppose they just want to get this over with so they can clean up.*

Well, me, too. I want to get out of this dress. What a wretched color Lysanda picked! Andi sighed. *I'm glad I can wear my own clothing tonight at the reception, when I present the Loxton corporate bride gift.*

And still the ceremony continued. The bride gazed soulfully at her fiancé while he knelt, serenading her with a traditional Zulairian love song. *As if she hadn't been making fun of this very part of the ritual less than an hour ago. What a little actress.*

This was a coolly negotiated union of the ruling Obati family and an influential Shenti house to further cement everyone's power. *Lysanda and her groom are doing an excellent job of portraying lovebirds for the crowd. Both loving the spotlight.*

How fortunate he can sing—the family didn't have to hire someone to carry the tune for him. Andi blinked, turning her full attention back to the couple as her own most favorite moment of the handfasting ceremony arrived—the giving of the bridal shawl. In the old days, she knew, these shawls had been hand-woven, selected by the groom with much care to symbolically enfold his chosen one in his love. Lysanda's shawl followed current fashion in the capital – machine-made, trimmed with three kinds of lace, the two family crests outlined in semiprecious gems—all about the show, not the emotion. Two attendants carried the unfolded shawl to the groom, displaying the embroidery and jewels for the guests to admire.

Still, it *was* the most romantic aspect of this particular ceremony. Andi suppressed a somewhat wistful mental picture of an unknown man wrapping her in one of the traditional, simple shawls. She took another deep breath of the flowers' perfume. *What is with me today, all this nostalgia for the dreams I had as a kid? Romance, a husband, children… Traveling around the Sectors doing business for Loxton is the wrong career if I want to settle down. I already made that decision, no looking back, no regrets. Maybe after I make Sector vice president, I'll decide on a different course.* No telling how old she'd be by then.

After adjusting the shawl to her satisfaction, Lysanda leaned toward the groom for a brief kiss before the couple turned to face the applauding audience. Scooping the bored flower girl into her arms, Andi juggled her own flowers, plus the toddler and her tiny basket. Arm in arm with the prominent Shenti man she'd been rushed into the puce dress to accompany, Andi walked down the aisle behind the happy couple, in time to the music.

As soon as the ceremonial party had left the pavilion, Andi searched for a maid or family member to take charge of the toddler. Another of the bride's attendants, a haughty girl from the capital, brought her the Tonkilns' youngest son, Sadu, who'd been a restless member of the wedding party too. "Here, you may as well tend them both, outworlder," the other girl said. "How do boys get so messy?" She turned on her elegant heel and walked away before Andi could protest.

"Hungry," Sadu proclaimed loudly, tugging at her skirt with one grubby hand.

Lady Tonkiln hurried by. "Oh, good, you have the children, Andi. Thank you."

"But I should be getting out of this dress, getting ready for the evening's reception—"

"You know the nurse left suddenly for her village this morning. I've no idea why, and she needn't bother coming back, begging to be rehired." Lady Tonkiln reached to untangle an errant flower from the girl's curls. "Do take the children to the house for me, won't you? The maids can watch them. No one will care if you're late to the dance as long as you're in time for the presentation of the gifts."

And with that barbed insult, her hostess was off to greet more guests before Andi could protest. Shaking her head, she stared after the older woman. *Typical. The "overbearing Obati" clan indeed!*

Giving Sadu an awkward pat on the shoulder, she tugged him in the direction of the waiting Naranti servants. "All right, Sadu, walk with me and we'll find Cook. I know I saw her earlier —she can take you both back to the house, get you a snack before you and your cousin here take your naps."

After handing Sadu and the flower girl over to the family's genial cook, Andi decided to walk back to the Tonkiln mansion, rather than take the shuttle. She'd had enough of the family and their guests for right now. *I need some time by myself.* Taking off the too-tight sandals, Andi breathed a sigh of relief and strolled into the forest that surrounded the ceremonial glade. The path was clearly marked, and the hard-packed dirt felt soothing to her abused feet.

When she reached the halfway point, out of sight of both the glade and the house, Andi took a detour to the east to a meadow she'd discovered a few days ago. Heedless of the borrowed dress, which she knew would never be worn again by anyone, Andi hiked the skirt up enough so that she could sit comfortably on the moss under a big malagoy tree and relax for a few moments. Leaning her head against the rough trunk, she closed her eyes and listened to the soothing hum of the pollen-gathering insects and birdsongs overhead. *Just have to get through this one last reception tonight, and then I can return to the capital. I can do that.*

Close to drowsing off in this peaceful spot, Andi suddenly became aware that the meadow had grown quiet. Opening her eyes with a flash of alarm, she found herself staring at a myth come to life.

An entire family of majestic urabu stood in the center of the lush meadow. To Andi's knowledge, no one had seen a living urabu on Zulaire in hundreds of years.

Behind the proud alpha male were three females, a younger buck showing nubs for horns, and a baby. *As if they came just to find me.* Andi chuckled at the idea as the buck swung his head in her direction, nodding once. Standing guard, he watched the perimeter of the small meadow as his brood spread out to nibble the dense stand of grass and flowers. From time to time the buck lowered his head to snatch a few mouthfuls of fodder, before going back on the alert. A vivid green, his eyes were fringed by thick, black lashes.

She wasn't sorry to claim this incredible experience all for herself.

Trotting forward a few paces, the fawn stopped to check on its mother's whereabouts, then wobbled straight to Andi on spindly legs. Amazed, she held out her hand for it to sniff before stroking the little urabu's muzzle and playing with the soft, tufted ears. The fawn's golden-brown pelt was warm velvet under her fingers.

The buck made an impatient huffing sound. Startled, jerking her hand back, Andi watched as the fawn took three awkward jumps, to press against the biggest doe's flank. Leaving the clearing, the herd bounded off to the northeast in a flowing line, buck first, fawn struggling valiantly to keep up at the end of the procession.

A wave of longing engulfed Andi as they left her. *I wish they'd stayed longer.* Taking a few tentative steps away from the tree, she peered hopefully into the jungle, but the urabu family had gone on their way without a trace.

With a breathless little laugh, she pinched her forearm. "No, I'm awake all right." She studied the imprint of the hooves in the rich soil. Crushed, fragrant grass was already springing back to hide the evidence. "When I think how many times I was told the urabu didn't really exist, or had been hunted to extinction—"

Well, this experience certainly redeemed my day. Frowning at a grass stain as she dusted stray twigs and leaves from her skirt, she shook her head. *I'm not telling the Tonkilns about this magical encounter or they'll be out here hunting the poor things. My secret, my gift from Zulaire's god.*

Thinking of her imperious hosts reminded Andi to check the time. Whistling at how late in the afternoon it had become, she set out in a slow jog, skirt hiked above her knees. At the forest's edge, she stopped, planning to put her sandals on again. One of the gardener's legion of young helpers hailed her. Running along the center of the path, he made big summoning gestures. "Miss, miss, you're wanted at the house!"

"Why all the fuss? Were they afraid I'd gotten lost?" Andi said.

Coming to a halt in front of her, the boy tugged at her sleeve, trying to draw her along the path. "Men have come from the capital for you. Outworld soldiers."

"Soldiers?" Andi was startled, her heart beating faster. "What do I have to do with the military? There must be a mistake."

"We must *go*. The leader of these soldiers, he demands to speak to you." Lowering his voice, her companion intoned with relish, "At ONCE!" The skinny boy chortled at his imitation of the outworlder's less-than-exact accent. "He said it's important, a matter of utmost urgency."

Maybe something had happened at the office? Or to her boss? But why send the military out here with the message? The capital was hundreds of miles away, yes, but there were excellent comlinks between here and there. Breaking into a run, she covered the ground faster than the gardener's assistant's stubbier limbs could carry him.

Leaving the winded lad well behind, Andi sprinted the last few yards of the path, onto the main house's driveway. Skidding to a stop to catch her breath, she craned for a better look at a pair of military vehicles parked off to the side, between her and the mansion. One was a squat, two-passenger groundcar with an ominous-looking blast cannon mounted on the rear. Behind that was a much larger armored person¬nel carrier, also bristling with weapons, lights and scanners. Both vehicles were the gray, green and black camouflage design favored by Sectors troops on this planet.

Offworld troops seemed jarringly out of place in this idyllic playground of the Obati elite.